ETERNALLY YOURS

cate tiernan

poppy

LITTLE, BROWN AND COMPANY
New York   Boston

Also by Cate Tiernan:

Immortal Beloved
Darkness Falls

Poppy

Hachette Book Group
237 Park Avenue, New York, NY 10017
For more of your favorite series and novels, visit our website at www.pickapoppy.com

Poppy is an imprint of Little, Brown and Company.
The Poppy name and logo are trademarks of Hachette Book Group, Inc.

The publisher is not responsible for websites (or their content) that are not owned by the publisher.

First Edition: November 2012

Library of Congress Cataloging-in-Publication Data

Tiernan, Cate.
Eternally yours / Cate Tiernan. — 1st ed.
p. cm. — (An Immortal beloved novel ; bk. 3)
Summary: Ex-party-girl immortal Nastasya ends a 450-year-old feud and learns what "eternally yours" really means.
ISBN 978-0-316-03596-5
[1. Immortality—Fiction.   2. Conduct of life—Fiction.   3. Magic—
Fiction.   4. Good and evil—Fiction.]   I. Title.
PZ7.T437Et 2012
[Fic]—dc23
2012013844

10 9 8 7 6 5 4 3 2 1

RRD-C

Printed in the United States of America

Book design by Saho Fujii

With love to my readers—you guys keep me going.

CHAPTER 1

UPPSALA, SWEDEN, 1619

ali! Vali! Where *is* the girl?"

I heard my employer's voice and scrambled up from the storage cellar.

"Here!" I said breathlessly, setting the heavy box of gold thread on the counter. The wooden steps to the cellar below the shop were barely more than a ladder; I'd had to hold the box with one hand while the other kept me from pitching head over feet. In time I would become as nimble as a mountain goat, but I'd been here only a month and these stairs were, even by Scandinavian standards, steep and narrow. Factor in the long skirts and petticoats and you had potential disaster in the making.

My employer, Master Nils Svenson, gave his customer a smile. "Vali is new here; she's still learning the stock."

I made a little curtsey, keeping my eyes down.

"She's doing very well, though, aren't you, dear?" Master Svenson nodded at me approvingly, then turned his full attention to the man who was deep in the throes of deciding whether large ruffs were truly going out of fashion or not.

I took a feather duster from my apron pocket and began to dust the bolts of fabrics lining two walls. My master was one of the most sought-after tailors in Uppsala, known to have the finest fabrics: finely woven wools, smooth to my hand and dyed in deep jewel tones; plain and colored linen in various weights, from moth-wing gauzy to the heavy, sturdy cloth for breeches and bodices; unbelievably fine silk from the Far East in bright, parrot colors that were completely exotic and out of place in this country in November.

The silver bell over the shop door tinkled, and a very elegant woman came in, her hat trailing a turquoise ostrich plume that I knew cost as much as what I earned in six months.

"Hello, my dear," said the man, turning and lightly catching the woman's gloved hand to kiss. "I apologize for being late."

"I'm not inconvenienced in the least," she said graciously. "You finish your business." She seemed to glide across the shop on fine kid shoes that made barely a sound. Moments later she stood near me as I flicked the duster and tried not to stare at her beautiful storm-gray cloak, chain-stitched all over with black flowers.

"What exquisite fabric," she murmured, gently touching a peach-colored watered silk, its silver-thread embroidery making it heavy and stiff. She turned to her husband. "My dear? You really should have a waist—"

I don't know why she looked at me just then, but she did, her clear blue eyes skimming absently across me and then sharpening and locking on my face like a magnet. She stopped in midword, her eyes wide. Her hand gathered a bit of silk and held it, as if without it she would fall down.

"Yes, my dear?" her husband said.

She let go of the silk and gave a shaky smile. "One moment." She gracefully turned her back to the two men and looked at me again.

"You," she said in a voice too low for them to hear.

"Yes, mistress?" I asked, concerned. Then—I don't know how to describe it. I still can't. I don't know how we know or what it is. But I met her eyes, and there passed between us an instant of recognition. My mouth opened, and I almost gasped.

We had seen each other for what we were: immortal. I hadn't met another person like me in three countries, eight cities, and almost fifty years.

"Who are you?" she whispered.

"My name is Vali, mistress."

"Where are you from?"

The decades-old lie came easily to me. "Noregr, mistress," I murmured, hoping that there were in fact immortals in Norway. I hadn't met any when I lived there.

"My dear?" her husband called.

With a last penetrating look, the woman left me and joined her husband. Soon they went out into the dark, cold afternoon—it was only three thirty, but of course the sun had set already, this far north.

I stood still, my mind turning wheels, until I realized Master Svenson was looking at me. I started busily dusting again.

The next day my master called me over from the glass-fronted display of silk ribbons that I'd been arranging.

He was wrapping something in brown paper, folding it neatly and then tying it with waxed twine. "I need you to take this to Mistress Henstrom," he said. "She's requested several cloth samples." He took up his pen, dipped it in ink, and wrote her street and house number on the paper in his educated, slanty script. "Make haste, Vali. And here—buy yourself a bun on the way back." He handed me a few copper coins.

"Thank you, sir," I said. He was a genuinely kind man, and working for him hadn't been at all bad so far.

I retucked the scarf I wore always, pulled on my own loden-green rough-wool cloak, and hurried out. This Mistress Henstrom lived about a thirty-minute walk away. I dodged street filth, horses, and people crowding the high street's shops, and was glad again that I lived in a town and no longer in the countryside. Uppsala was by far the biggest town I had lived in since Reykjavík. In the countryside, night closed in on you like a bell placed over a light, silent and grim. Here even at midnight you could occasionally hear the clopping of horseshoes on the cobbles, a baby's wail, sometimes the off-tune and bawdy singing of men who'd drunk too much. And here, in this town, lived at least one other immortal.

The streets twisted and turned, and more than once I had to backtrack and take a different route. I walked as fast as I could, mostly to keep warm, but the damp, misty chill slipped under my cloak and through my ankle-high boots. By the time I found the correct house number, I was chilled down to my fingernails and shaking with cold.

The house was large and fine, made of brown brick with other colored bricks set into a pattern, and it had a false front with ziggurats. It was four stories high, with the entrance up a tall flight of stairs. I struck the lion's-head heavy brass knocker several times. The black enameled door was opened almost immediately by a big, round woman wearing a spotless white apron. She had the reddened, work-roughened hands of a servant but also an unmistakable sense of importance. So the head housekeeper, maybe.

"I'm from Master Svenson's shop?" I said. "With fabric samples for the mistress." I held out the package for her to take, but she opened the door wider.

"She's waitin' on you in the front drawing room."

"Me? I'm just the shopgirl."

"Go on then." The housekeeper nodded toward a double set of tall, paneled doors painted dove gray.

Inside, a woman sat before a white marble fireplace carved with fruit and garlands. Blue and white tiles with ships on them surrounded the firebox, and I wanted to kneel down and look at each tile, enjoying the fire's delicious warmth. Instead I stood uncertainly in the doorway, and then the woman moved and I saw her face. My heart sped up: It was the woman from the shop the afternoon before. The immortal.

"Oh, good—the samples from Master Svenson," said the woman, her voice smooth and modulated, the accent refined. "I need you to wait, girl, while I look at them. Then you can directly return my choice to your master."

"Yes, mistress," I said, bewildered.

"Thank you, Singe," she said to the housekeeper, and the woman reluctantly backed out, clearly curious and disapproving of a shopgirl in the fine drawing room.

When the door had quietly clicked shut, Mistress Henstrom beckoned me closer. "Forgive the deceit, but I couldn't call on a shopgirl," she said in a low voice, and I nodded. "You said you were from Noregr?"

I nodded again. "And you, mistress—where are you from?" I asked boldly.

"France," she said. I knew so little about immortals then

that I was shocked. Were there immortals all over? In every other country?

I'd been in my early twenties when I was first told what I was. I hadn't known it before then. After all, I'd seen my whole family slaughtered in front of me; they had died, and so, clearly, I could die also. But after the death of my non-immortal first husband when I was eighteen, I'd made my way to Reykjavík and become a house servant to a large, middle-class family. I learned that they too were immortal. The mistress there, Helgar Thorsdottir, had first instructed me about our kind. At the time I was actually young, so the concept of going on endlessly had no meaning for me.

That had been fifty years earlier. As time passed, first slowly and then more quickly, it started to become real for me: to look into a piece of shined metal or the occasional real looking glass or the still water of a pond or puddle, and see the same me. Decade after decade. My skin was unlined; my hair, though light enough to be almost whitish, had no gray of old age. I was the same, always.

"How old are you, my dear?" Mistress Henstrom asked. She neither asked me to sit down nor offered me refreshment; I was just a shopgirl.

"Sixty-eight," I said faintly. And still looked barely sixteen.

"I'm two hundred and twenty-nine," she said, and my eyes widened. She laughed. "Surely you've met people older than I."

I didn't know how old my parents had been. I wasn't sure how old Helgar or her husband had been, though from things she'd said she seemed about eighty. Back then. So she would be about 130 now.

"I don't think so. I haven't met many others like us." .

"But my dear, we're everywhere!" She laughed again, and a small spaniel I hadn't seen before came out from under her chair and jumped on her lap. She stroked its silky head and preposterous butterfly ears. "France and England. Spain. Italy. Here in Swerighe," she said, gesturing out the window.

I waited for her to say "Iceland," because that was where I'd been born, but she didn't. I hadn't been to any of those other countries, but that one instant, that moment, stood out so sharply against countless moments, because right then I knew that someday I would. The thought caught my breath, opening up a future I had never contemplated. In fifty years, the idea of being something more than a servant or shopgirl or wife, the thought of living somewhere besides these northern countries, had been a dream so without form that I had never grasped it.

Likewise, questions I hadn't asked Helgar, things I'd wondered about, uncertainties that had simmered in my brain for years now boiled to the surface, and I could hardly get the words out fast enough.

"Do you know many other—people like us?"

Mistress Henstrom smiled. "Yes, of course. Quite a few. Certainly the ones who live in Uppsala—which was why I was so surprised to come across one I'd never seen."

"Your husband?"

"A mortal, I'm afraid. A dear man." Sadness swept over her lovely, porcelain face, and I understood immediately that one day he would die, and she wouldn't.

"Are all the ones you know like you?" I waved my hand at the damask wallpaper, the furniture, the house. I meant rich, fancy.

She tilted her head to one side, looking at me. "No. We're at all classes of society, at each level of birth, education, breeding."

I'd been born to wealthy, powerful parents. We'd had the biggest, most luxurious castle in that part of Iceland—made of huge blocks of stone with real glass in the windows; at least fourteen rooms; walls hung with tapestries; servants, tutors, musical instruments; even books. When I lost my childhood, I'd lost everything about it.

"The nature of the thing is," Mistress Henstrom said, "that when one lives quite a long time, one has quite a lot of time to fill. With educating oneself, in whatever way you can. With meeting people—influential people. With taking a small occupation and being around long enough for it to grow. Money grows over time. Or it does, at least, if you're not silly about it."

"I don't have any money." I hadn't meant to say that, but I had absently given voice to my thoughts. I blushed because it must have been glaringly clear that I didn't have money.

Mistress Henstrom nodded kindly. "Have you never been married?"

"Twice. But they had no money, either." I didn't want to think about them, not the sweet, uneducated Àsmundur I was married off to when I was sixteen, or the awful man I'd thought I could make a life with, some forty years later. They were both dead, anyway.

"Perhaps you married the wrong men." Mistress Henstrom wasn't being sarcastic—it was more like a suggestion. She waved her hand toward the room, much as I had done. "I have money of my own, but I also take care to marry wealthy men. And when they die, their money becomes mine alone, do you see?"

I gaped at her. "Do you mean...I should try to marry a wealthy man?"

"I think marrying poor ones did nothing to advance your position," she said, stroking her little dog. "You have a lovely face, my dear. With different clothes, a hairstyle au courant—you could catch the eye of many a man."

"I have no family, no connections," I sputtered. "I'm an orphan, with nothing. Who would want to marry me?" Not to mention I never wanted to get married again.

Again Mistress Henstrom tilted her head to one side. "My dear—if I told you I was the fifth daughter of a wealthy English landowner, how would you determine it was true? The world is so big—there are so many people. No one knows them *all*. Letters, inquiries, take months and months. Create a family for yourself, a history, the next time you're scrubbing a floor...or dusting bolts of fabric. Then *be* that person. Introduce yourself that way. Become a new person, as you've no doubt done before—don't just be the same person with a new name."

Her words tore through my brain like a comet, leaving room for new ideas, new concepts. Then my limited reality set in again. My hands plucked at my rough cloak, my plain skirt with its muddy hems. It was all too much. I didn't know where to start. It was frightening. "I don't—" I began.

Mistress Henstrom held up her hand. "My dear—it's November. Stay at Master Svenson's while you think of who you want to be, if you could be anyone—anyone at all. I'll send for you in March."

"Yes, mistress," I said, overwhelmed and scared and… exhilarated.

And in March Mistress Henstrom did indeed send for me. I left Master Svenson and took the money I had scrimped and saved in the last six months and went to the Henstroms' country house, a good ten miles out of the city. Her personal seamstress was there, and under the lady's direction, three new dresses were made for me, indulging my particular whim of keeping my neck covered. They were much fancier and grander than anything I'd had before, but not so fancy as to arouse curiosity.

As I looked at myself in the mirror, my sunlit hair coiled in complicated braids, my blue dress so much nicer than anything I had owned since I was a child, I met Mistress Henstrom's—Eva's—eyes as she smiled with approval.

"May I ask..." I began hesitantly.

"Yes?"

"May I ask why you're doing this for me? It will likely be years before I can pay you back."

A thoughtful look came over Eva's face. "Because...more than a hundred years ago, I was very like you. Twice the age you are now but no further advanced. I was ignorant, with no dreams for the future. And then I met someone. And she—took pity on me. She simply wanted to help me. She was the oldest person I had met—well over six hundred then." Mistress Henstrom smiled, somewhat wistfully. "Anyway. She did for me much the same thing that I'm doing for you. I've always wanted to help someone myself, as a way of paying her back." Another gracious smile. "This is my good deed. Take it and enjoy it, my dear."

A lot happened after that, up and down, but a mere twenty-eight years later I was Elena Natoli, middle-class owner of a lace shop in Naples, Italy. I could have been much richer, with a much more leisurely lifestyle, but I just couldn't bring myself to marry again.

I've never again seen the woman who called herself Eva Henstrom back in the early sixteen hundreds. If I did, I would thank her. She changed the course of my life, the way a storm can make a river jump its banks and surge ahead.

CHAPTER 2

WEST LOWING, MASSACHUSETTS, USA, PRESENT

kay, raise your hand if you've ever (1) dropped food or ice cream or a drink in front of (or on) someone; (2) realized you had a big stain on your clothes and it has apparently been there all day and people must have seen it but no one said anything (extra points if it's related to a female cyclic event); (3) realized after an important dinner with someone that you had a big crumb on your lip and that's what they kept trying to subtly signal you about but you didn't pick up on it; (4) mispronounced an obvious word in front of a bunch of people.

I could go on. The point is, those kinds of things happen to everyone. I bet you're still upset or embarrassed about it, right?

Well, you can *freaking get over your lame-ass, sissy-pants, drama-queen self.*

When *you've* run away from people who were only trying to help you; taken up with a former friend who everyone (including yourself) knew was bad news; hung out with him even as he showed signs of being certifiable; and then witnessed his complete meltdown, which, unlike some meltdowns, did not simply involve quaintly taking off his clothes and dancing in a public fountain, but instead featured huge, dark, horrifying magick, kidnapping, dismemberment, and death—well, when you've done that and then *gone back* to the people who were only trying to help you...you call me, and we'll talk. But until you're there, I can't deal with whatever pebbles you've got in your shoe today.

"Nas? Nastasya?"

I blinked, focusing quickly on the face of one of my teachers, Anne. Her round blue eyes were expectant, her mink-brown hair in a shiny bob above her shoulders.

"Um..." I fiddled with the scarf around my neck. What was her question again? Oh. Right. "Marigold," I said, naming the familiar orange flower on the card Anne was holding up. Flash cards, designed to help us students learn the endless facts about Every. Single. Thing. in the physical, metaphysical, and spiritual world. For starters.

Next to me, Brynne uncrossed her long legs under our table and recrossed them. I could feel her vibrating with the urge to jump in—she knew way more than I; everyone here did—but she managed to keep her mouth shut.

"Properties?" Anne was not as patient as River, and we were both starting to chafe at spending so many hours together, trying to funnel knowledge into my brain as fast as possible. I hadn't been doing too badly—I was willing to learn—but today, focusing seemed out of reach. My cheeks started to heat as the silence swelled to fill the room. I was skin-tinglingly aware of Reyn, sitting silently next to Brynne, and Daisuke, who was studying by himself in the corner. Defeat was imminent: Searching my brain for facts about marigolds was like running around trying to catch lightning bugs. Turbo-charged lightning bugs. On coke.

"They're used extensively in . . . Thailand and India, for religious purposes," I said, trying to save face. I hated looking stupid, though by now it should feel as natural as breathing. But Reyn was here, and I hated, hated, hated looking stupid in front of him, of all people.

"Yes?" Anne said, prompting me.

Images flashed through my mind—wheeled wooden carts piled with musky-smelling bright flowers lining street markets in Nepal. No doubt they still did that today, but the memory I had was from the late eighteen hundreds. Going through Nepal on my way to Bombay to catch a merchant ship to England. And right now, let's all give props to the

Suez Canal for chopping a good four, five months off that whole journey. Who's with me?

"Nastasya." Anne sighed and brushed her hair off her forehead. "It would help you to know things like this."

"I know," I said, trying not to cringe as I heard Reyn shift in his seat. "I want to. I know I need to. It's just—my head is really full of stuff already."

I mean, *obviously*, right? Four hundred and fifty-nine years' worth of stuff. Identities, adventures, lifetimes and lifetimes lived, each one as full as the last. Part 'n' parcel of the whole immortal gig.

Brynne was now wiggling like a greyhound that had spotted a rabbit.

"Okay," I said briskly, sitting up straighter. I knew this. I'd learned it a million times. "Okay, mainly used for . . . protection. And strength. Like to strengthen your heart or protect you from evil. Oh."

The point of learning about the marigold sank in, and I realized that it, along with a daunting number of other things (like frankincense, fleabane, vervain, nettle, iron, and onyx, to name *just a few*), was intended to help me protect myself from evil. Some people try not to catch colds. I try not to attract ancient evil to me. It's all relative.

Ancient evil. How odd that it actually exists. But it does. And my most recent brush with it, the whole horror show in Boston with my ex-bestie, Incy, had demonstrated with searing clarity how inadequate my mastery of magick was. If I'd known more that night, I might have been able to save Katy and Boz. Might not have had to witness their nightmarish deaths. I might have been able to save myself sooner, and without almost causing my head to explode.

I'd been back here at River's Edge for a month now. I could have, probably should have, run off to a distant corner of the world, hidden in a cave, and licked my wounds for, like, an *eternity*. But I was far gone enough to admit that yes, I really did need help. I needed help more than I needed to be proud, or brave, or cool, or even just not gut-wrenchingly humiliated.

So far everyone here had been awesome about what had happened. No one rubbed it in, no one *tsk*ed, no one even looked at me funny. Because they're all so much cooler than I am, right? So much more experienced, both in the ways of the world and the ways of redemption. By not giving me a hard time, they were advancing on their own karmic joyride. So, actually, they should thank me. For giving them so many opportunities to shine.

But it was clear that my centuries-old pattern of not learning anything was not, in fact, working well for me. So I'd sat pinned, a fish on a hook, and had lesson after lesson thrown at me: spellcrafting; the uses of stars in magick; magickal properties of plants, stones, crystals, oils, herbs, earth, sky, water—everything everywhere is connected, and everything around me can be used for good or for evil. My head felt crammed full of facts and lore, history and tradition, forms and patterns and sigils and meanings—if I barfed right now, actual words would spill out onto the floor in a spiky, tangled heap.

"Nas?"

I blinked and tried to look alert, but Anne sat back and put the flash cards down. "Let's all take a break," she said. She looked tired—teaching me wasn't anyone's idea of a good day at the fair. Doing most things with me wasn't a rockin' good time; I know this, and traditionally I haven't given a flying fig. Lately, with my gradual uphill meandering toward maturity, I'd started to feel guilty and a twinge embarrassed. But so far I've been able to shake that off.

"Okay," I said, trying not to sound elated. I glanced toward the window; the early February sunlight was trying to be brave but not quite succeeding. I judged it to be around ten in the morning and couldn't help flashing to just a couple weeks ago, when at ten in the morning I would have been tidying the shelves at MacIntyre's Drugs. If I still worked there. If I hadn't been fired twice.

"I hope there's coffee left in the kitchen." Brynne unfolded her long, lean self and stretched, the tightly wound coils of her caramel-colored hair bouncing slightly. She was the closest thing I had to a friend here, even though we couldn't be more different: tall and black versus short and snow-white; American versus Icelandic; 230 years old versus 459; cheerful, friendly, confident, and competent versus . . . not. With a large, loving family versus having no one.

"Maybe I'll go check the chore chart," I said. "Do something mindless for a while."

"Good idea," said Anne, smiling gently at me. She came over and rubbed my back for a moment—Anne was real touchy-feely, in the literal sense of the words. I'd been practicing my not-flinching, and I barely hunched my shoulders before making myself relax. "Sometimes doing something boring or repetitive is a good way to have knowledge sink in."

I nodded and picked up my puffy coat. If doing something boring or repetitive was the path to knowledge, then I was on the fast track. Daisuke stayed behind in the classroom as Brynne, Reyn, and I filed out. Of all the students, Daisuke was the furthest along, in my opinion. He was the closest to peace, the one who had the fewest large, visible flaws. But no one ended up at River's Edge just for kicks. I didn't know what kinds of things Daisuke had done to make spending years in rehab seem like a good plan, but there had to be something. I'd learned that much in my four months here.

Brynne slanted me a tiny smirk, then strode quickly out the door ahead of me and Reyn, oh-so-obviously giving us space.

I glanced at him, but his face was—and I know you'll be surprised by this—impassive. As usual, being close to him made my heart carom from skipping a beat to racing, feeling like hard rain hitting a metal roof. I was about to say something that had a 99 percent certainty of being inane when I heard a skittering sound in the wet leaves behind us. We turned to see a small white object catapulting our way: Dúfa, Reyn's runt puppy. She must have been watching, waiting for him.

Reyn stopped and knelt, the easy smile that crossed his face making my chest feel tight. Dúfa galloped clumsily toward us with a puppy's single-minded intent, giving a couple of high-pitched yips in case we hadn't noticed her. She flung herself at Reyn, rising up on her hind paws to lick his face, and I have to say, I knew where she was coming from.

"Okay," he said softly and held up his hand. *"Sitta."* Instantly Dúfa's small hindquarters dropped to the cold ground, her odd hazel eyes focused on Reyn's face. He kept his hand up as he stood, six feet of overwhelming attractiveness and danger, and Dúfa's eyes didn't leave his face, though she allowed her overlong, skinny white tail to give a small swish. "Okay," he said, and released her. She sprang up, leaping into the air and yipping.

"She knows *sit* already," I said, with my gift for stating the obvious. "In Swedish." How could I put my next plan into action? *I want to lure you someplace. Jump on you. Not think about whether our "relationship" makes "sense."*

"*She's* smart," he said, scooping the puppy up and tucking her into his corduroy barn coat. Her white face and long, floppy ears poked out below his chin, and she looked both adoring and self-important.

A small *ding* sounded inside my head. "Like, she's smart, but I'm not?" As soon as the words left my mouth, they sounded ludicrous—I mean, how paranoid am I, to assume a simple statement about his dog was somehow aimed as a dig against me?

"Exactly," he said coldly, and my eyebrows shot up.

"What?"

He stopped abruptly on the path and turned to me, his face angry. "You almost died in Boston!" he snapped. "You're a thousand times more powerful than that pathetic waste, but he had the upper hand. You were *this close* to getting your power ripped from you like ore from a rock!" He held out two long fingers very close together in case I needed visual representation.

"I know!" I said defensively. "I was there! I remember. *Muy* bad. So?" I crossed my arms and tried not to notice when Dúfa gave Reyn a lick on his neck.

"So why aren't you studying your ass off?" he exclaimed. "Why are you not taking this seriously? You saw two of your friends die horrible deaths. You should be scared, doing everything you can, reading, studying, practicing." Narrowing his eyes, he jabbed me in the chest with a strong forefinger, which actually hurt. "Next time you might not be able to pull your magick off," he said. "Next time you might get killed. You might be dead *forever* because you were too much of a *lame-ass* to get your shit together and learn how to *protect* yourself!"

How *dare* he? My own eyes narrowed and I started to jab *him* in the chest, except Dúfa was in the way and I couldn't tell where she began and ended. So I scowled and gave him the old threatening schoolmarm finger-shaking—so much less satisfying. Between that and the fact that he was almost ten inches taller than me, I might not have presented as fierce a picture as I hoped.

"You—" I started furiously, but I really had no follow-up to that. "I—" As I began to vigorously defend myself, it dawned on me with crushing humility that he was right.

He waited, his breath making little puffs in the air.

"I *am* trying," I said stiffly.

"You're full of crap," he retorted, completely unappeased. "You're here to begin taking things—like life, and yourself— more seriously. Let me know when you start." Before I could even pretend to come up with a snappy response, he pushed past me and strode to the house, his long legs covering ground fast. I hesitated for a few moments, unsure of what to do.

After I'd gotten back from Boston, Reyn and I had almost come to theoretical terms with how we may or may not feel about each other. Okay, maybe not exactly how we feel about each other, but more like we agreed that we would attempt to stand each other. Like, enemies with benefits. *Enemies* is too strong a word. Maybe *benefits* is too strong a word.

But right now he was really furious with me. Why did he even like me, anyway? Why did he keep grabbing me and groping me and kissing me with that hot, hot mou—

Okay, this was bad. Nastasya? Get it together, I told myself sternly. Yeah, that should have some effect. Very, very slowly, I started toward the house, giving myself some time to think.

Finally I went up the steps and opened the kitchen door, to be greeted by the scent of baking bread and Reyn still in the kitchen.

At the worktable, Rachel nodded at me, her tan arms strongly kneading a smooth, elastic lump of dough as big as a melon. She was wearing a dark green sweatshirt, her shaggy black hair held back by a bandanna. I knew she was originally from Mexico, and was about 315, younger than me by more than a century. She looked like a college student.

"Hey," I said, striving for normalcy. "That smells great."

She nodded again—Rachel wasn't a smiley person, but her face did soften when she glanced over at the gorgeous man holding the small, ugly puppy under his coat. I mean, could you come up with a more estrogen-spurring picture? Scowling again, I went past him to the dining room just as the swinging door opened and Charles came in. His face brightened when he saw Reyn, and he came over to scritch Dúfa under her chin, which she relished.

"Glad I ran into you," Charles said to him. "Can you come help shift the big hall wardrobe upstairs?"

"Sure." Reyn gave me a look that made me shiver, and followed Charles out.

I tore my eyes away from his back to see Rachel watching me.

"Uh-huh," she said, and pushed her glasses up on her nose, leaving a floury white streak.

"Uh-huh what?" I said coolly.

She just nodded, looking amused, and I rolled my eyes at her and headed into the large, plain dining room where we ate. Right now there were thirteen of us—four teachers: River, Asher (who was River's partner), Solis, and Anne; and eight of us students: me, Brynne, Rachel, Daisuke, Charles, Lorenz, Jess, and the forbidding Reyn. Plus Anne's sister Amy, who was visiting.

I hung up my coat and actually checked the chore chart in the hall, and the mere fact that I did this and did not, say, quietly slip upstairs to my room for a little naparoonie was testament to the strength of my commitment to taking *life* and *myself* seriously. Said commitment was stronger some days than others, and there were days when I had to force myself to recommit, like, fifty times.

Damn Reyn. Who did he think he was?

All of a sudden the hairs on the back of my neck stood up. Footsteps vibrated on the wooden front porch, and a tall shadow appeared across the frosted glass of the front door. The paranoia I'd felt since I got back from Boston kicked in instantly as the doorknob turned.

The door opened. And if you were going to cast someone in the role of "Devil" in an old Hollywood movie, this would be your guy. He was tall, dark, and handsome in a severe, possibly soul-snatching way. Gull-wing brows arched over eyes as black as mine—no, blacker, deeper, with no light shining from them at all. Shark eyes. He focused on me instantly, then set a suitcase down on the floor and put his head back. I watched tensely, expecting a wolf howl.

"River!" he bellowed, filling the hallway with reverberating sound. I shrank against the steps, planning to edge backward a bit to disappear into the back parlor.

Almost instantly the door at the end of the hall opened and River came out of the small room she used as her office. I glanced at her; if she showed anything but delighted good cheer, I was going to snatch up the brick holding the parlor door open and brain this guy.

It was delighted good cheer, mingled with astonishment around the edges.

"Ottavio!" River exclaimed, and then I remembered him, vaguely, from when River led me on a guided memory from her life. (One of those immortal magicky things.)

This fierce-looking guy was River's big brother. She had three younger brothers as well.

Holy moly, I thought, the weight of it hitting me. This is River's *brother*. He was even older than River, and she was one of the oldest people I'd ever met. She'd been born in Genoa in 718, and at one time had been very, very dark (magickally). Today River was just about the best person I'd ever met. Here's hoping her brother had also made a few strides forward.

"Dearest!" said River as they hugged and then kissed each other's cheeks—both sides, the European way. "Why on earth—why didn't you let me know you were coming?" She drew back, searching his face. "Is everything okay?"

Ottavio nodded, and I again noticed his severe handsomeness, the perfection of his Roman-statue features, the faint lines around his eyes.

"I'm fine," he said, then pointed to me. "I'm here because of her. She shouldn't be here."

My eyes widened. Very nice. So much for the Italian charm.

River blinked, surprised, then glanced at me. "Maybe just give us a minute," she murmured.

I managed a tight smile and nipped sideways into the dining room, then escaped outside, wondering what the hell Ottavio had meant.

Now what? It was cold out here, and of course I had no

coat. My eyes fell on the big barn, straight ahead across the yard. I headed for it.

Inside I heard Anne humming in her classroom, probably still enjoying the Nastasya-free space. I put my shoulders back and knocked.

"Hi." Anne looked surprised to see me.

"Hi," I said awkwardly. "I thought...if you had time, or wanted to...maybe we could go over herbs again?" Please don't say no. Don't be too fed up with me already.

Anne looked at me, as if weighing her options. "I would like that. Sit down."

"I know I need to get better. And...I'm avoiding the house," I admitted. And admitting this instead of making up a white lie to make myself look better was *more* progress, visible to the naked eye. "River's brother Ottavio is there."

Anne's surprise changed to astonishment. "Ottavio! Here?"

I nodded. "He already hates me. And he just got here. Usually I have to, you know, talk or something."

"Hmm," Anne said thoughtfully. "Curiouser and curiouser."

Yeah. What*evs*.

CHAPTER 3

n my life, I have had to: hide from blood-thirsty raiders; pick my way through piles of pox-laden corpses just to get out of town; barely escape from a flood on a stolen horse; pull guns on men who tried to rob me during the gold rush; kill a wild boar that was charging (I had, like, a freaking *spear* and some *rocks*); talk my way out of any number of harrowing situations with any number of forged papers and identities; and come back to River's Edge after running away and almost getting killed by Innocencio.

So why was facing Ottavio at dinner causing my stomach to knot up?

Maybe because I was so *known* here. After four months, these were no longer strangers and I couldn't talk my way out of anything. You can get out your handkerchiefs if you want, but I cared about these people now. I...didn't want them to think badly of me.

So to have Ottavio show up, all dark and stern and righteous, and immediately want to boot me out of here, this place I was finally starting to sort of settle into—it sucked.

By the time I was halfway down the stairs, I could smell Rachel's bread and some kind of chickeny situation. We often had vegetarian meals, so the thought of actual chicken made me speed up.

I paused in the doorway, then very quietly slipped into the last free place at one end of a long bench. (Yes. We use benches here. Too quaint for words. At least words I can say here.)

"Hey, girl." Anne's younger sister, Amy, was next to me. Despite her crush on Reyn, I couldn't help liking her. She seemed to have cottoned on to the fact that Reyn and I were (usually, not right this minute) making eyes at each other, and she had graciously stepped back. Which was thoughtful and mature of her. Unlike Nell, a former fan of Reyn's and a past student at River's Edge, who had tried to kill me. True story.

"Hi," I said. "What did you do today?"

"Ahem." Amy patted the loopy glob of yarn around her neck. "I'm learning how to knit. After resisting the process for two centuries, I'm giving in. This is my first effort." She made a smug face and unwrapped the scarf to show me.

"Uh . . ." I said. It was a disaster—a garbled throng of yarn and knots and gaping holes and, here and there, bits of recognizable knitting. I glanced at Amy, racking my mind for something diplomatic to say, and then I saw her face, the suppressed humor, the glint in her eyes as she tried not to laugh. She knew it was awful.

"Wow!" I said with overdone enthusiasm. "Gosh, that is *something*, Amy! You're a *natural!*"

She laughed and passed me a bowl of sliced chicken and the platter of bread. "Tell me your favorite color. I'll make one for you."

"Periwinkle," I said, unconsciously tucking my current scarf a little tighter around my neck.

"You got it. Want some mustard?"

It was sandwich night here at hacienda River, and I took the mustard. So far, I was successfully ignoring Ottavio, sitting next to River on the other side of the table.

But not for long.

"Everyone?" River tapped her water glass with her knife. "Many of you know my brother Ottavio. For those who don't, this is my brother Ottavio."

Smiles and nods of welcome. What she didn't say was

that he was the king of their house in Genoa—one of the eight main houses of immortals, worldwide. A few houses, the one in Russia and the one on the border between Egypt and Libya, had been destroyed and had no living survivors. The others—in Australia, Brazil, Africa, Italy, and here in America (Hi, Salem, Massachusetts!)—still maintained their ancestral sources of immortal power and inheritance. Ottavio was the oldest member of the Genoa house. The last house, in Iceland, had been completely destroyed by raiders back in 1561. Not many people knew this, but that house had one survivor who recently surfaced. That would be *moi*.

"He's come for a surprise visit, and I'm thrilled to see him," River went on. A glance passed between brother and sister, but I couldn't read it. I began to hope that maybe he'd just been cranky or jet-lagged or something and hadn't really meant what he said before. I'm highly skilled at deceiving myself like that. How else could I have remained friends with Incy for a hundred years?

"Lovely to see you again, Ottavio," said Anne, putting some winter lettuce on her sandwich.

I kept my eyes on my plate, working busily with the mustard and mayo.

"And you, Anne." Ottavio's voice was deep and grumbly, like a bear woken too soon from hibernation. He seemed so different from River, though his hair was gray, as hers was. When I'd first met River, I'd been struck by her unusual looks—the smooth, light olive skin; the wise face that still looked barely thirty; and the not-often-seen-in-immortals silver hair that came a bit past her shoulders. Obviously she was the *nice* one of the family.

"What brings you to town?" Charles asked politely, just a bit of his Irish accent detectable. Usually by the time an immortal is more than a hundred years old, they tend to lose their original accent and become more neutral, in every language they learn. Like being newscasters. For eternity.

Wait for it. . . . I took a bite of my sandwich.

Ol' Ottavio didn't pull punches. He pointed his knife at me (way to go with the symbolism) and said, "I'm here because of her. Because of the danger she represents. She shouldn't be here; my sister shouldn't be harboring her. And I've come to find out what else she knows."

I tried to swallow quickly so I wouldn't spew crumbs across the table. It felt like a marble going down my esophagus, slowly and painfully.

Forcing myself to look up instead of crawling under the table, which was my first instinct, I saw irritation on River's face and saw her try to temper it. Others looked surprised, even shocked. I focused on trying to breathe normally and glanced at Reyn. His obvious anger, the tautness of his shoulders, at first cheered me up because I thought it was aimed at Ottavio for attacking me; then I had the icky thought that he might still be mad at me from this morning.

On top of that, a fast scan of the rest of the table revealed a couple of people *actually nodding in agreement*—Jess, Charles, and even Solis, who had taught me so much.

Blood rushed to my cheeks, and I wanted to sink through the floor.

"I was home, in Italy," Ottavio went on. His black eyes seemed to bore through my skull as his long fingers ripped apart a piece of bread. "News came to me of big, dangerous magick—Terävä magick—being worked in America. In Boston. Because of its proximity to my sister, I tried to gather more information."

I nodded. Yep. Big, dark magick. It sure was. Actually it had truly been so bad that I couldn't even joke about it. Not after a month. Not after a hundred years. "I didn't work any dark magick," I said.

"No. But you were involved with the person who did." Ottavio dropped the bread onto his plate, as if he hadn't realized what he was doing.

"I'm not anymore," I said, aware of how incredibly limp that sounded.

Ottavio made a derisive sound.

Yes, I had screwed up—not just once but over and over. That's usually how rehab goes, people. Being involved with Incy when he'd wrought such destructive magick, when he'd killed two of our friends right in front of me—that had been a tragedy. But I hadn't made him do it. I hadn't had any part of his madness. It had been the last thing on a very long list of Things Beyond My Control. Like being born into my family. Like being the only survivor the night everyone—my parents, my sisters, my brothers—had been killed by northern raiders, trying to usurp our house's magickal power.

Ottavio's black eyes were hard. "Why are you here? What are you trying to pull my sister into? Who—if anyone—sent you here, and for what dark purpose?"

I stared at him, so appalled that he was doing this in front of everyone. I tried to think of how to explain Incy and our century-long friendship. How could I describe how lost I'd felt, how inadequate, the night I'd run away? Did he know that Incy had been working magick on me for a month, so I would crack and leave River's Edge? I felt panicky: Everyone was watching this. Was River going to ask me to leave? Did any progress I made no longer count? Maybe I could talk to her, alone—

Wait a second. Wait. A. Second. I wasn't ten years old. He wasn't my father. He wasn't my teacher or my uncle. He wasn't the Tähti police. What was he going to do? Ground me?

Hold on, Nastasya, my brain cautioned. Think this through, don't do anything rash. This is River's brot—

"Who the hell do you think you are?" I said, smacking my palm flat on the table. Ottavio's eyes flared, and Charles actually jumped. I stood up, pushing my plate back. "I'm not answerable to you. This is River's place. She apparently still wants me here." I frowned. "Are you saying you don't trust her judgment?"

River blinked at that, and Ottavio started to open his mouth.

"If River asks me to answer your buttinsky inquisition, I will. But until she does, Ott—can I call you Ott? Until then, *Ott*, you can *bite* me." I stepped over the stupid bench and got ready to stalk out the dining room door.

Lorenz's eyebrows arched. Ottavio went pale and stood, towering over my five-foot-three. Reyn pushed back on the bench, as if getting ready for action. River was solemn but biting her lip, and I would have sworn she was trying not to laugh. And it was right about this time that I remembered that I was still pretty fresh off my latest personal disaster, and that maybe I shouldn't be so self-righteous. Oops. Well, too late now!

"And you guys, sitting there like bobbleheads?" I looked at Charles, Jess, and Solis. "Are you *blanking* on your own pasts? Do you *really* think you're in a position to *judge* me?" Jess and Charles looked down at their plates, like they were remembering, *Oh, yeah, I'm a total screwup waste myself. That slipped my mind for a sec.* Solis met my gaze, looking thoughtful.

A smart person would have turned then and left the room with dignity. But we're talking about me here, so that was out.

"Do you know who I am?" Ottavio thundered. His depthless eyes were practically aflame, and two spots of anger appeared on his aristocratic cheekbones.

Reyn stood up, maybe an inch shorter than Ottavio, but with a look of deadly calm on his face that would have stopped a lion in midleap.

"Yes," I said to Ottavio. "You're River's *brother*."

At the other end of the table, River gave a muffled cough behind her hand.

Ottavio stood up even straighter.

"I am Ottavio di Luchese della Sovrano," he boomed. "King of the sixth house, Genoa!" He was tall and imposing, seeming to take up that whole end of the room with his dark suit and pristine white shirt. Extremely kinglike. The combination of thick, wavy silver hair and a relatively unlined face that put him in his early thirties did nothing to soften his imposing effect.

The hoodie I was wearing had been an innocent bystander in an unfortunate laundry incident, and my jeans were, I noticed just now, streaked with dirt and something—perhaps strawberry jam. Not so kinglike.

"That's very special, Ott," I said.

Everyone in the room was watching with round eyes, holding their breath: Here was more Nastasya-provided drama, for their benefit. Dinner and a show.

"Yes, it is," he ground out. "And you're a dangerous stray dog my sister found! A piece of Terävä flotsam!"

I can never remember the difference between flotsam and jetsam.

River reached up and tugged on his sleeve. He ignored her.

"Not *exactly*," I said. Everyone here knew about my past, the unexpected legacy that I'd denied and avoided for 449 years. Apparently River hadn't mentioned it to ol' Ott here. He probably hadn't let her get a word in edgewise, the windbag.

My fingers were tingling, and I felt kind of otherworldly and weird. I'd spent a long, long time not thinking about my heritage, suppressing all memories of my childhood, my parents, my siblings. I think I would have been able to truly block it completely out of my mind if it weren't for the permanent, irrevocable reminder I carry with me always: the scar on the back of my neck. It's round, almost two inches across, and is the exact image of one side of the amulet that my mother had worn every day. It had been burned into my skin the night my parents died. Every day for the last 449 years, I've worn a scarf or a high collar or both, and in all that time, only three people had ever seen it, that I know of: Incy, River, and Reyn.

The point is, I'd invested huge amounts of effort into forgetting my identity. But I was suddenly itching to drop a bomb on Ott.

"Yes, *exactly*!" His voice was loud in this plain room. "And whatever plan you have here, whatever goal you have in mind, you will fail. I'll see to it."

"Now that's seriously bad news, Ott," I said. "Since my only goal is to learn and become all Tähti-tastic."

My parents had been Terävä—practicers of the "dark"

kind of magick, where you take power from things around yourself, stealing their energy to increase your own power. This process tended to kill things. Tähti magick was a relatively newish form where one channeled the earth's innate power through oneself, thus not killing anything around you. Most immortals are still Terävä—it's much easier than being Tähti. Incy was Terävä. I was choosing not to be.

"Ottavio," River murmured, and again her brother ignored her.

"You may have fooled my sister," Ottavio said.

River sat up. "Hey."

"But *I* see you clearly: an opportunist, here to weaken our house, to learn our secrets, to plant evil here. The events that took place in Boston—they were unforgivable."

"I totally agree with you," I said seriously, and I meant it. "But I didn't set those events in motion."

"You deny that you took part in that desecration?"

"I deny that I caused it or helped it," I said, losing whatever passed for patience in my life. "I mean, please. I can barely match my socks in the morning, much less cook up some big plot. Long-term siege? I can't commit to a cellphone plan. I need to be here—I need to become better. But I have *no* need to weaken your house. I have no need for anyone's power but my own." I stood there and crossed my arms over my chest, trying to look serious and determined. Eleven sets of eyeballs followed us left to right, like a Ping-Pong game.

When I had acknowledged myself as my mother's daughter, my father's heir, I'd chosen to claim my ancestral power and my position as the sole heir of the House of Úlfur. It was like an effete hamster choosing to become Mr. Universe. I had a long way to go, to use understatement of galactic proportions. But that didn't mean I was going to take this crap from Ott lying down.

Ottavio gave a derisive laugh. "Your power is laughable. Of course you would want ours."

"Not *that* laughable," I said. I was getting more and more wound up, more anxious to have this be over.

"Ottavio," River said firmly.

But he was on a tear now and drew himself up, ready to launch into me again.

"My name is Lilja af Úlfur," I said quickly, almost quaking with nerves. Across the table, Reyn's eyes were riveted on me. "Daughter of Úlfur the Wolf, king of the Iceland house."

River sat back, giving a slight nod, and seemed proud of me. The knot in my stomach relaxed.

The *best* part was Ott's face—the slack jaw, the pop-eyed stare, the draining of blood. "That's impossible." He glared at me coldly. "That house was destroyed in 1559. The family was killed; the tarak-sin was lost. How dare you try to usurp a noble lineage!"

"Oh, Ottavio," River murmured, dropping her head into her hands. Asher reached out and patted her arm.

"It was 1561," I said quietly. "And not everyone died. Not me."

Ottavio said, "I don't believe it!"

I started to think that River should have killed all her brothers after all. Or at least this one. Long story. But here was a man more than thirteen hundred years old who was, like, still bullheaded. Still full of himself. Running on ego. I mean, you'd think that he'd have had enough life experience to have that beaten out of him.

"It's true," River said in the silence.

Ottavio gaped openly at his sister. She gave him a rueful smile. "I tried to tell you," she said.

"Yes!" said Brynne, smiling. "Fiver on being the Iceland *heir*." She held up her hand, and her silly, friendly gesture made me smile. I leaned over and smacked a high five.

The whole room was silent as Ottavio processed this unappetizing information. My fellow students, reminded of my past, were clearly trying to mush together what they knew about me: Immature Embarrassing Failure + Tragic Family History + Potentially Big Power = Nastasya. Well, I do like to keep people on their toes.

A lot of Ott's bluster was gone. He sat down somewhat heavily, his eyes never leaving me, and said, "Heir to the Iceland house. Úlfur's daughter."

"Yep," I said, suddenly feeling both more cheerful and starving. I sat down, too, and picked up my sandwich. My father's name, Úlfur, meant "wolf." So I had basically called him "Wolf the Wolf." But it had sounded awesome.

"Well," said Lorenz, placing both his hands on the table.

Lorenz was Italian, and only about 120 years old. He was one of the most perfectly handsome men I'd ever seen, with crisp, straight black hair and bright blue eyes, yet he'd always left my heartbeat completely unaffected. "I will go ahead and say it, since no one else appears brave enough to."

I looked up, taken aback.

"We know that you are the heir to an ancient throne," he said, enunciating carefully. "The daughter of a king."

"Looks that way," I said cautiously, chewing.

"I will say it." He gave me a serious, accusing look. "Your fashion sense is all the more incomprehensible."

Several people gave muffled snorts, then quickly focused on their food.

I smiled, then started chuckling and couldn't stop, feeling curiously lighthearted. As others started laughing, too, I felt a delicious sense of relief, of—I daresay—belonging.

Take that, Ott.

CHAPTER 4

s it turns out, Ott wasn't about to take that or anything else I hurled his way. The next morning as I came downstairs, I heard River and her brother arguing in her office. Naturally, I made my way quietly to the door and stood there, listening. I mean, just how good do you want me to be?

At first it was garbled and hard to make out—it was possibly really old Italian. Maybe. It switched around as they bickered—I picked up some form of German, then something that sounded of the Hispanic persuasion, but nothing I could instantly translate in my head. Which was a little weird, because I'm good with languages, picking them up easily, jumping back in when I need to. But River and Ottavio seemed to be drawing on older dialects. I can go back to the mid–fifteen hundreds in the Nordic tongues, and then the early sixteen hundreds with most of the Romance languages. And later for the others: the Slavic dialects, Russian, Japanese, a bit of Mandarin, English.

"You're so pigheaded!" I heard River snap. That, I understood.

"You're naive!" said Ottavio harshly. "Gullible! How do you know this girl is Úlfur's heir?"

"Once more. I will tell you one more time. I've been inside her head. I've shared images of her past with her. Her story rings true. She has the tarak-sin."

"She could have stolen it!"

This was hurting my tender, delicate sensibilities, and I wished they would switch back to old German or something.

"*Où est-il maintenant?*" Ottavio demanded.

"*Avec Asher,*" River answered wearily. "*Il est cassé. Asher le répare.*"

Yay, I thought, Asher is mending my tarak-sin. I decided to leave River and Ott to their argument. Because eavesdropping is *wrong*.

I was on milking duty that morning, so I trudged across the yard to the cow barn, which also housed a couple of sheep and a few goats. Jess was mucking out their pens and Daisuke was mixing up the feed, supplementing their hay with goat chow, sheep chow, and cow chow. He nodded and smiled at me as I came in with the sterilized buckets.

I'd felt weird after dinner the night before and had escaped to my room as soon as I could. Revisiting the tragedy of my childhood always made me feel like there was barbed wire inside my chest. Part of me wished I hadn't shot off my mouth like that. And isn't *that* a familiar feeling? Which was one reason I'd been self-medicating so determinedly over the centuries. Just to feel... less. Less pain, less anxiety, less self-loathing.

Since I'd come here, I was in fact feeling less of all of those things. Another decade or two and I'd be as good as new!

I grabbed the little three-cornered milking stool that looked like it had come original to the house, and set it down on the left of, yes, Buttercup. I think it's some sort of farm law that if you have more than one cow, one of them must be named Buttercup. Anyway, the Cupster gave me a disinterested glance and swished her tail, but I was ready for that and leaned back quickly so it didn't flick my face. Then I dove in practically under her side, set the pail in place, and began milking.

My tarak-sin. My amulet. It was heavy and solid gold. My mother had worn it almost all the time, and when I was little I'd loved looking at it, feeling the thick links of its gold chain. It was carved all over with runes, magickal symbols, sigils, and things I didn't recognize. I had no idea how old it was—very? Like, really, really very? Back then I'd thought it was just a favorite piece of jewelry, but now I knew my mother had worn it to keep it safe, to not let it out of her sight. Now I knew that it channeled and amplified the ancient source of my family's power, the power of the immortal house of Iceland.

I pulled at Buttercup's udder with gentle firmness, hearing the warm milk hissing against the side of the metal bucket. As always some of the barn cats gathered around, watching intently, their tails whipping back and forth on the straw.

I sighed and pressed my head against Buttercup's solid flank, and everything about my tarak-sin, my family, and Reyn came back to me in a rush. Because Reyn was inextricably tangled up in my whole family tragedy, with my tarak-sin, and with me—my family's appalling end mirrored his own.

When I was ten years old, a horde of northern raiders broke through our city walls, then the bailey gate that surrounded my father's hrókur—like a small castle. The chieftain of that horde was the aptly named Erik the Bloodletter, and he was Reyn's father. Erik and one of Reyn's brothers had smashed through the thick library door where my mother, my siblings, and I were barricaded in, weapons in our hands, even in my little brother's. Háakon had been seven years old.

Reyn's father and brother killed my sisters, Tinna and Eydís, slicing ferociously through their necks with curved, wide-bladed swords. My older brother, Sigmundur, had charged manfully, swinging the heavy blade my father had given him when he turned fifteen.

My mother, holding her amulet, worked dark and terrible magick and flayed Reyn's brother, causing his flesh to fly off his body, right through his chain mail. The man had stood there, sluicing blood, a surprised look on his skinless face, his lidless eyes popping from their sockets. Sigmundur cut off his head, because flaying wasn't enough to kill an immortal.

Then Sigmundur made a deep slice in Reyn's father's arm, forcing him to switch sword hands. But it hadn't been enough, and Sigmundur's head fell to the floor moments before his body collapsed like a Jacob's ladder.

Terrified, I'd dropped my dagger and leaped behind my mother as the marauders burst through the door. And when her head with its long blond braids had tumbled to the floor, her body had fallen on top of me, hiding me in her wool skirts. I'll spare you the long story of my escape, of finding out that my father and every other person in our castle had been slain.

But as it turned out, my family had their revenge: Erik, Reyn, Reyn's two remaining brothers, and seven of Erik's men had gone a mile or so down the road, where they could still enjoy watching my father's castle burn. Then they'd tried to use my mother's amulet, our house's tarak-sin, weighty with centuries upon centuries of immortal power and magick. But they didn't realize the amulet was broken—

one half was with me, back in the burning castle—and their stolen magick backfired. Every man standing in that circle had been incinerated, literally turned to ash. Except for Reyn, who had fallen backward.

Their half of my mother's amulet had burned itself into the skin on Reyn's chest, giving him a permanent scar that matched mine but wasn't identical. After I'd gotten back from Boston, Reyn had stunned me by giving me the piece that had marked him four centuries earlier. He'd kept it all that time, though it was useless to him. He'd told me that he kept it as a reminder not to want too much.

In a twist that had made Irony wait four hundred years for its completion, Reyn and I...had a thing. I didn't know what it was yet, but we were caught up in each other and it was clear it had a long way to go to run its course. It left us both bemused, upset, torn by memories, conflicting feelings, longing, desire—you name it.

"I think that cow's empty."

I broke out of my sad memories to see Daisuke leaning against the slats of the pen. He pointed downward; my hands were moving but nothing was coming out. The cow had turned her head and was looking at me curiously, like, *Um, excuse me?* I'd been so lost in events that happened more than four centuries ago that I hadn't even noticed the opportunistic cats that had crept beneath Buttercup and now had their triangular heads muzzle-deep in the milk bucket.

"Oh, shoo, guys!" I said, brushing them away. I pulled the bucket up and grimaced when I saw the few stray cat hairs floating on the surface. Well, those would strain out.

"Still only two gallons or so, I see," Daisuke said. His voice was always calm and even—I don't think I'd ever heard him raise it in either excitement or anger. "She'll give more later in spring, after she calves."

This was not my first time at the cow rodeo, so I said, "Yep," and stood up. I realized that last night I hadn't seen any kind of reaction from Daisuke about Ottavio's accusation, and with typical, not-recommended Nastasya impulsiveness, I said, "Daisuke?"

"Yes?"

"What do you think about what Ottavio said about me?"

His dark brown, almond-shaped eyes looked into mine, as if he could see right through my head. And who knows, maybe he could. I have no idea of what a really learned immortal can do. I waited, my throat feeling tight as the uncomfortable idea filtered in that I did actually care about what he thought. I hadn't known that until just now.

"I think Ottavio is trying to protect his family," Daisuke said carefully. "And really, all Tähti immortals."

I slowly let out a breath. "Do you think I'm actually a threat to all this?" I held the heavy pail with one hand and gestured with the other, to encompass River's Edge and all it stood for.

There was a long pause, and my cheeks started to heat as

I began compiling smart-ass responses to whatever hurtful thing he was about to say.

"No," he said at last. "I think you have a lot of baggage, and some of it may be dangerous. The people who come to River's Edge tend to be weighed down heavily with it." He gave a slight smile, looking down, rubbing his chin with one hand.

"I can't imagine you with baggage," I said frankly. Yes, I'm discreet. I don't pry. I always think through what I say to make sure it doesn't hur—

Daisuke gave a sad smile. "Appearances are superficial, as we all know."

I wasn't sure I myself knew that, but he seemed quite certain, so—

"I was born in the 1760s," he said, "in Nippon. For some reason that I'll probably never know, I was left on the stone steps of the local Buddhist monastery, still wet from being born." Daisuke reached up to touch his hair, as if he could still remember the sensation. "The monks took me in, and I grew up there among them, not knowing I was immortal. First I was a ward, then a student, then an apprentice monk." He gave another rueful smile, focusing his gaze in the distance, looking past me into his history.

"I was...not of a suitable temperament to be a monk. Over and over I was punished for fighting, for showing anger. I now understand that the monks thought my soul was in danger—so they did everything they could think of to set me on the right path. But at the time I saw only their oppression and what I felt was their cruelty."

I'd wondered about Daisuke—his past was more convoluted than I'd been able to imagine.

"When I was eighteen, I ran away. I wandered, lost in both body and spirit, until I came upon a training house, a place to learn the art of bushido." Laughing, Daisuke rolled his eyes. "If I thought the monks were tough, the master of the training house was fifty times worse. We were beaten, starved; we trained at all hours. I was there for eight years before I was given the honor of the title samurai. I was chosen to serve the most important shogunate in our district— the House of Five Peonies."

Even now, when he had clearly renounced violence and pride and every other fun thing, Daisuke's eyes gleamed as he recalled being first in his class, being chosen for the best shogun. I tried to picture him young and hard and tough, with a belligerent chin and fire in his eyes, and it wasn't easy. Today he was so refined, as smooth as a stone worn down by the ocean for millennia. Can people really change that much, over hundreds of years? It was something I wondered about myself. And about Reyn.

"At the shogun's house I became a bully over the younger samurai, the servants." Daisuke swallowed, ashamed of his younger self. "I made their existence one of pain and dread and humiliation. It appeased something in me, something dark and ugly. Finally I left the house and became *rōnin*—a warrior for hire."

I looked at him, unable to reconcile this with the Daisuke of today.

"I worked for anyone," Daisuke continued. "Traveling from town to town. I became morally weak, almost unable to tell right from wrong. It would have been far better for me to commit seppuku and spare the world my worthless existence, but that would have required me to recognize what I had become, and I...couldn't. And of course, it wouldn't have worked anyway. Just made a horrible mess."

I looked down. I too had tried to kill myself before I knew I was immortal. My husband had died; my family had been destroyed; I lost the baby I was carrying. There had seemed no point in going on. But an immortal is forced to go on. And on.

"I didn't age, didn't die." His voice was a monotone. "I believed I was too evil to be granted another life in which to live more usefully. I lost count of how many murders I committed, how many treacherous acts I visited on strangers. The years blurred together; each life I took less important than the one before."

My throat got the familiar tightness I felt when emotions hit too close to my heart. I swallowed and focused on a wisp of hay that stuck out from a crack in the pen's boards.

"Then one night I was approached by a messenger. He

wanted to hire me to kill the local lord's two nephews, who were due to inherit their father's land. If they were dead and the brother had no more children, then the lord would one day own the combined estates and become very powerful. The two sons were five and seven years old."

Oh no, I thought, feeling his anguish. This was the person who I thought was the most advanced of all the students, the one who seemed the closest to achieving peace.

Kneeling, Daisuke picked up one of the barn cats and cradled it, stroking it softly. "That commission changed something in me," he said. "I couldn't do it, and it shocked me out of my miserable complacency. That day I gave away everything except the robe I was wearing and became a beggar, making myself the lowest of the low, the most humble of the unfortunates."

I nodded sympathetically.

"One day, a monk in saffron robes came up to me. It was one of the monks who had taken me in, more than a hundred years before. An immortal himself, he had seen me as one when I was very small. I said, 'Why did you never tell me?' He said, 'Because you never deserved to know.' And he was right. But he took me in once more, and I began the long, painful path toward redemption. Eventually I met River. This is my fourth time here and the longest I've ever stayed—five years so far."

"Holy moly," I couldn't help saying. Five years was a long freaking time in rehab.

"But you worry about your baggage—" Daisuke said, his face solemn. "Four years ago, a man came here to kill me."

"Here to River's Edge?" I asked.

"Yes," Daisuke said. "He had suffered at my hands—one of the younger samurai I had bullied and tortured, almost a century before—and he came for retribution. He was immortal, obviously, and he'd spent a lot of his life looking for me, increasing his power for when he found me." Daisuke's voice trailed off.

"What happened?" I asked.

A thin, bitter smile surprised me. "He was still pissed. But he chose not to fight me one-on-one. Instead he bided his time and waited until I was in the hex barn—the one that was painted with a Pennsylvania Dutch hex pattern."

I frowned. "There is no barn painted with a hex pattern."

"Hiroshi locked me in the barn and set it on fire," said Daisuke, ignoring me. "He set spells on the doors so they couldn't be opened from the inside, even if we broke through the locks. He had planned it well—most of the household was at a local farmers' market.

"Unfortunately others were in the barn with me. Asher, Jess, and two other students at that time, Ivan and Solidad. Soli raced up the ladder to the hayloft and jumped out the little window at one end. It was about twenty-five feet from the ground, and she broke a leg. Jess wouldn't jump, and Asher wouldn't leave Jess. So after Soli, I jumped, then Ivan, and we managed to finally put out enough of the fire so we could axe our way through the doors. The rest of the building was completely aflame.

"We flung open the doors. Thick, choking smoke poured out. Inside, both Jess and Asher were unconscious from smoke inhalation. Three horses were already dead, and one's lungs were so badly damaged by heat and smoke that he had to be put down. Soli's leg was broken. Ivan's hands were badly burned. Ivan and I were covered with burns. Hiroshi had disappeared."

His face showed a wealth of regret and guilt and sorrow and horror, a mirror of how I had felt after following Incy to Boston.

"And that's why there is no barn with a Pennsylvania Dutch hex symbol painted on the side," he said. "And why we have only six horses in a ten-stall barn." He straightened and put the cat down, then rolled his shoulders as though to roll away those years of torment. "So you see, Nastasya, you are not the only one who has drawn darkness to this place. And after you are gone, another person will come here. And he or she will be guilty. And have baggage."

I was processing the tragedy of what he had described, but I looked up as he took a deep breath.

"And I think we're late for breakfast," he said, sounding more like himself. "And no doubt they're waiting on that milk." He held out his hand to me and I took it. I picked up the milk pail and we walked back to the house.

CHAPTER 5

e had missed breakfast entirely, so I grabbed some bread and wrapped it around some bacon. I was shaken by Daisuke's story—the parallels to my own life were unnerving, though I hadn't gone around killing people. At least not on purpose. That set me to wondering if all—or maybe just most—immortals shared similar traits in the patterns of their lives. Was anyone born good and just stayed good, all along? Had anyone lived who hadn't needed saving, eventually?

I was pondering this train of thought and heading back into the kitchen for more bacon when Asher came down the stairs.

"Oh, there you are. Thought you were hiding in your room." He grinned, and I gave him a smarmy smile in return.

"I'm telling you!" Ottavio's voice rang out from the library, and Asher and I both turned to look at the doors as if he might burst through them. We heard River's much quieter murmurs, and then, "Always were you *insensible gibberish I couldn't understand, old Italian, likely, words words* and you see where it has gotten you!"

Asher smiled at the doors, then turned back to me. "Anyway, lick the bacon grease off your fingers, grab your coat, and come with me. Time for a lesson."

I raised my eyebrows. "Are you sure you want to teach the devil spawn any more magick? Aren't you afraid I'll turn you into a jackass? You can see what I've already done with *him.*" I motioned my head toward the parlor.

"You know there isn't any devil, much less spawn of one," Asher remonstrated. He pulled me toward the front door and handed me my coat. "Besides, I'm afraid Ottavio was like that long before you came on the scene."

I knew I shouldn't ask, but when has that ever stopped me? "How long have you and River been together?"

He held the front door open and we went out into a morning that had turned not mild but definitely less frigid.

"I've known River for about two hundred years," he said, surprising me by answering. "And was in love with her since the first day. But she saw me as more of a brother type."

I wrinkled my nose.

"Exactly," Asher said, leading me toward the side yard. "We lost touch off and on, especially during World War Two. But right after the war, I found her in Italy. And we've been together since then." He looked thoughtful. "Sixty-six years. It's the longest I've ever gone steady with anyone."

I laughed, then remembered hearing that Asher had been in Poland during the war and that he was Jewish. What had happened to him?

"Okay now," he said, all business. "Today we're going to practice spellcrafting. As you, I hope, know by now, focus and concentration are a crucial part of making successful magick. The quicker you can achieve a pure, focused state, the quicker you can craft magick—until it's all second nature for you."

"Okay."

"Now, find something around here—anything—and use that to focus on," he directed.

I looked around and saw piles of mushy leaves. And... okay, a twig. I bent over to get it and saw a chicken feather next to it. Focusing on a feather seemed all cool and Native American, so I picked it up and showed Asher.

"Fine," he said. "Use the feather as a focal point, and sink into concentration the way we've been teaching you."

"Then what?"

"Then craft a spell to make this walnut husk split open." He held out his hand to reveal one of the katrillion walnuts we'd harvested last fall. My hands had been stained brown for weeks. We'd hammered most of them out of their husks and shells, but not all.

"Split the husk open?" It was a round, dark thing, dry and wrinkled. Last autumn it had been green and slightly patterned like an orange.

"Yes."

I opened my palm, and Asher placed the walnut in it. A spell to split a walnut husk. At first my mind went blank, and I tried to keep the panic off my face.

"Use the feather," Asher said softly.

Oh, right. It was small, fluffy, speckled brown and white. Not as impressive as, say, a falcon's feather. But I concentrated on it, praying for a spell to pop into my brain, fully formed and walnut-appropriate. Obviously it would be much easier to use a hammer here, but it seemed bad form to point that out.

Was I taking too long? Should I already have the spell together?

Come on, feather, speak to me. Suddenly I wished I were holding my mother's amulet, and I wanted to ask Asher if he'd fixed it yet. I bet I could split this shell wide open with *that*.

Concentrate. Breathe. Release all thought. Open yourself to the universe. Anne's quiet words came back to me.

And... the more I calmed down, the more I was able to push other thoughts out of my head, and the more my spell-crafting lessons came back to me. Without deciding to, I began to hum my mother's song, the ancient tune of unrecognizable words that she had used to call magick to her. But unlike her, I made pathways to channel magick *through* me, not *to* me, protecting the feather and everything around me so I wouldn't take their magick from them.

The walnut grew heavy in my hand. It was the only thing I could see. My surroundings faded but also sort of melded with me so that the lines between us blurred. The feeling of power, of magick, rose up inside me, the familiar chrysanthemum of light and joy. I felt part of everything, and everything felt part of me. Including this walnut. I smiled. After that, all I had to do was think, *Split open, reveal yourself*. And the hard brown husk bloomed in my hand, peeling back like a fruit rind. I gasped in delight and saw the walnut shell break in two, showing the tan, convoluted nut inside.

I breathed in, and the crisp sounds of nature came back to me. I blinked, and Asher's face was near, his brown eyes solemn.

Excited, proud, and way impressed with my newbie self, I held out the walnut. "It's beautiful," I said. "That was a beautiful spell. It felt so easy, once I got out of my head." I beamed at him, waiting for him to clap me on the back and tell me how awesomesauce I was, how brilliant and advanced.

Instead, Asher coughed slightly and pointed off to the left.

My eyes widened as I saw a young maple sapling maybe ten feet away—that had been completely stripped of bark. Its bare, pale wood gleamed in the sunlight.

"Did I do that?" I squeaked. "I didn't mean to. I made all its bark fly off?"

Asher nodded. "Did you remember to set up limitations?"

"Jeez, I guess not enough. I'm sorry." And then I saw the chicken. River's chickens ran loose through the yards during the day, being all free-range, and this chicken...had apparently wandered too close, during the spell? "Um... that chicken," I said faintly. "It's...naked."

Asher nodded again, then captured the featherless, very indignant chicken and tucked it under his arm. "I'll take it into the barn," he said. "It can't be outside till its feathers grow back."

"Will they grow back?"

"I hope so," said Asher.

"What about the tree's bark?"

"I don't know," he said. "I hope that comes back, too—if it doesn't regrow soon, the tree will die."

Well, now I felt like crap, my proud victory turned into an embarrassment. "I need more practice," I said glumly. I know, right?

"You did very well, my dear." I could hardly hear him over the squawking of the angry chicken. "You need practice, and you need to set up all boundaries of limitations, not just some of them. But you still did very well. We'll practice again tomorrow, or this afternoon."

I rubbed my forehead.

Asher and I were headed for the barn when we heard the

big-throated growl of a powerful engine coming up the driveway. This was something new and different, and we stopped to watch.

Sure enough, a neon-yellow, low-slung sports car pulled too fast into the unpaved parking area, sliding to one side and spewing gravel as it stopped a mere six inches from the red farm truck. The top-hinged door rose, and a dark-haired man unfolded himself from the car. He looked around with interest and with one hand removed his sunglasses.

"Daniel," said Asher.

"Have you seen him yet?" Brynne practically hissed in my ear as we headed down to dinner.

"Only from a distance," I said.

"Well, *mreow*," she said, wiggling her eyebrows.

So another of River's four brothers had decided to vacay here in rural Massachusetts. Excellent.

I'd slithered away while Asher and the naked chicken waited to welcome Daniel, and once inside I'd gone up to my room wishing I'd never have to leave it again. Just how dangerous was I? Could I be this bad without knowing it? What were these guys doing here?

When the dinner gong had sounded, Brynne had stopped by my room, and then I was on my way to what was no doubt going to be another intensely unpleasant dinner with the Two Horsebutts of the Apocalypse.

"He seems younger and less stuffy than the king," Brynne

whispered at the bottom of the stairs. Abandoning me, she entered the dining room, bright and pretty, calling cheerful hellos to all.

I hesitated at the doorway. When my skin tingled, I whipped around to see Reyn, who had come up behind me silently.

"Could you not sneak around?" I said irritably. "I'm going to put a little bell on you."

Reyn glanced at me, then looked into the dining room.

"Would you like to go out to dinner?" he asked a trifle stiffly, and my jaw dropped. Last time he'd spoken to me, it had been an angry bellow. He was...unpredictable. Being out alone with him seemed...deliciously risky.

But he was the devil I knew. As opposed to the ones I didn't.

"Oh *God*, yes," I said, lunging for my coat.

This was like a date. It was probably a date. Our first date. Mostly we'd been making smoochy-face in weird, out-of-the-way places, when we weren't arguing. But this seemed like an open proclamation somehow.

I was tense and quivery, sitting in the middle of the truck's bench seat. I hoped he wouldn't seize this opportunity to lecture me some more while I was stuck inside this moving vehicle.

"This was a good idea," I said, trying not to seem as thrilled as I felt.

"I figured dinner was going to be a little rough," he said. "Probably."

"Yeah, you think? That's all I need, another disapproving man glaring at me squinty-eyed."

He snorted.

I glanced up at him, his hard-boned face outlined in the moonlight. Once again I was slammed by a rising tide of attraction, which was always followed by wonder and confusion. As in, I wonder why I'm so attracted to him? He was my family's enemy. Confusion.

But right now he had gotten me out of Inquisition Thursday, so it was cool.

"Where are we going?" I didn't care.

"Halfway to Turner's Falls," he said. "There's a Mexican place."

"Great." As long as he wasn't carping at me, I was content to sit there beside him. We drove through the night, and for a few minutes it was oddly reminiscent of crossing the prairie in a covered wagon. The darkness; the quiet; the always looking forward, unsure of what lay ahead.

Except I knew what lay ahead. Mexican food.

As we walked into the restaurant I wished I didn't have eau de barn all over me and that I'd remembered to brush my hair. Like, in the last few days. Reyn was used to seeing me like this, and so far he hadn't seemed put off by it (or by anything, really). But being out in public with a bunch of people around reminded me of all the dinners I'd had with

Incy over the last century. I remembered him looking at my clothes, up and down, and saying, "Are you planning on wearing that?" Sometimes I would say haughtily, "That is my intention, yes." Other times I let him cajole me into changing into something more Incy-approved. It had seemed funny at the time—kind of flattering that he cared what I wore, that he thought I should make the best of myself.

What was worrisome about Reyn was that he'd seen me at my worst, taken every barb I'd thrown at him, watched me be an ungrateful failure, and yet still…seemed to care about me. I mean, what was I supposed to do with that?

We both got carded when we ordered drinks: me a girly margarita and Reyn a beer with lime and a tequila chaser. It was strange seeing him against the backdrop of a restaurant instead of in the barn, in the yard.

Reyn squeezed the lime into the beer bottle and took a sip. He was just so freaking manly, I couldn't stand it. I drank my margarita in small, icy tastes, remembering getting plastered in Boston, how awful it had been. What would happen if Reyn got tipsy? Would he loosen up, get funnier or sweeter or—

Raging, furious, violent. I'd known some mean drunks in my day—perfectly nice guys who turned into nightmarish alter egos when they got soused. Surely Reyn wasn't like that. I'd never seen any inkling of it. Now I watched him toss back a shot of tequila without wincing and wondered if this was possibly the start of finding out Reyn hadn't changed much in the last three hundred years.

"What's wrong?" he said. His eyes hadn't left my face.

I sat up straighter and tried to look casual. Saying "nothing" would be such a sissy cop-out.

"Did you ever go to school? Like college?" Avoidance, something I'm much more comfortable with.

"College?" Reyn looked bemused, then drank more of his beer. "Yes. Have you?"

"I started a couple times. I didn't last very long." And that had never, ever bothered me until now. Thanks, self-awareness. You're a peach.

"How come?"

"It seemed so...slow. It seemed to take so long." I shrugged. "Can an immortal have ADD? 'Cause that would be bad."

Reyn smiled, which for him was not as wide and toothy as it might have been on someone else. "That *would* be bad."

"What did you study?" This was probably the most we had ever talked that didn't involve sniping at each other or raking over the past.

"Different things." He was distracted by our food arriving, and I tried to suppress whimpers of happiness as I dug into the hot, cheesy, fat-filled, totally-not-River's-Edge food. Without being asked, the waitress brought me another margarita and Reyn another beer, lime, and shot of tequila, smiling deeply at him and leaning over as she placed them on the table.

I gave her a look, like, *Really?* and she bustled off. I picked up my margarita, instinctively planning to subdue my anxiety, and then realized what I was doing. Slowly I pushed it back and looked up to see his golden eyes on me.

I managed a little smile. "Things like what?"

"What's wrong?" As oblivious as he had seemed to the whole Nell thing—her undying love for him—he sure did seem all over the subtle-face-change thing with me.

"Nothing." *Coward.* "So—what did you study?"

Reyn looked at me as if deciding whether to pursue it or let me drop it. "Um, history."

"So you wouldn't be doomed to repeat it," I said, nodding. "Good plan."

"Economics—tracking money all over the world. That was interesting. Medicine—once in the 1870s and once right before the First World War. Tech stuff that they teach you in the army—the Canadian army, Russian army. The SEALs."

"The what?"

"SEALs. Part of the navy. In America."

"Oh." Of course he had been in the military. A bunch of militaries. "So you've been to school a lot."

He shrugged and finished his second tequila. My eyes followed it like a laser pointer.

"Are you worried about something?"

I don't care what anyone says—my face is not that freaking expressive. "Just wondering if you brought your sword," I mumbled.

"What?"

Jumping right into it, I shrugged and said airily, "One shouldn't drink and raid."

His eyebrows came down, questioning if I was serious. "I don't raid," he said mildly. "I don't pick fights in bars. I don't mouth off to tough strangers. Is that what you're talking about?"

By this point I had no idea what I was talking about. All these thoughts in my head, past and present, and someday I really needed to sit down and sort them all out. I scooped up some beans and rice on a tortilla chip and shrugged again. He was probably regretting asking me out.

Reyn took the last of the guacamole. "My sword's in the truck."

My head jerked up. His face was totally serious, but his eyes were...softer. Not so lasery. I laughed nervously, and he smiled.

"So...how does it feel being back?"

His question stopped me, instantly bringing Boston to mind again.

"Um...good, in that I know I should be here, and because everyone—mostly—has been really great about it. Some people have told me why *they're* here, and that helps. 'Cause I'm not the only disaster."

"No," he said. "You're not the only disaster." I heard the deep thread of regret in his voice, and for a couple minutes we sat there and looked at each other like a couple of dorks.

"It was awful, in Boston," I said slowly. "So awful. I was so glad to come back here to normalcy—even normalcy with chores and lessons and a shared bathroom. I've always been able to just...leave awful behind, you know? Just move on."

"New town, new name," Reyn said.

"Exactly. Once I became someone different, it meant that I hadn't even done that stuff, made those mistakes, hurt those people. Or whatever."

Reyn nodded slowly, his long fingers smoothing the napkin under his beer bottle. "At River's Edge, all the other names and pasts and excuses and lies get pared away." He finished his second beer and waved Miss Thing away when she swept toward us all alert with a third round of drinks. Looking back at me, he went on, "Like, here you can be only the one you. Only the core you. Most of us have no idea who that person is. Or...we're afraid of who that person might be."

"Yeah, exactly," I said again, wanting to fall against him. He knew just what I meant. Incy had never wanted to talk about this stuff, covering his ears and saying *nyah nyah nyah* on the very few occasions I tried to be profound and self-reflecting. Usually I wouldn't, couldn't admit these feelings to anyone. But without a doubt, Reyn of all people might be afraid of who he really was, underneath it all.

"Let's get out of here," he said, and put some money on the bill tray.

"Okay," I breathed, scooching out of the bench.

The ride home was darker and quieter than the ride out—Reyn took small back roads, and there were no street-lights, few houses. What would it be like to travel across the country with him? One thing's for sure—I wouldn't have to worry about robbers or carjackers or anything.

Reyn turned the truck unexpectedly, and we bumped over a dirt road in the middle of what looked like old corn-stalks. The moonlight tipped them with white and if I looked far enough away, they resembled whitecaps being kicked up on the ocean.

"What are we doing?" I asked.

Reyn looked at me as he shut off the engine. "Parking."

My heart thudded to a slow stop inside my chest. We were miles away from River's Edge, completely away from every-one and everything. True, we were in a truck and it was going to get cold, but I didn't care. I got light-headed and realized I'd forgotten to breathe.

"Oh," I said faintly, almost incandescent with anticipation.

Slowly, deliberately, Reyn put his arm over my shoulders against the back of the seat. He brushed a quick kiss against my lips, almost absently, and right as I was gearing up to glom on to him like a piranha, he reached down behind the car seat and pulled out . . . *a long sword.* From behind the car seat. I swear to God. *An effing sword.*

I was wordless, my mouth gaping, as Reyn tested the edge of the blade against his thumb. He hadn't been *joking* in the restaurant. He really had a *literal sword* in the truck. A *sword*. He looked at me calmly as he fit his hand around the grip, testing the weight of the pommel.

I just could not believe this. After everything, after all I thought might be happening between us, how much I wanted to trust him, he'd gotten me to the middle of dark nowhere and pulled out a motherlovin' sword.

I slammed my open palm down on the dashboard. "Fine, goddamnit! Kill me! I don't care! I'm sick of learning all that crap anyway!"

Reyn looked at me calmly, now balancing the flat of the blade on one finger.

"Go on," I dared him. "Do it! Get it over with. Go ahead and kill me!"

Reyn sighed and rolled his eyes. "Before I even get in your pants? I don't think so." He popped the door and swung to the ground as I blinked, trying to regroup. "But I'm pretty sure your sword skills suck. I bet you couldn't have cut off Incy's head if you tried. Come on, get out."

I felt like I was going to throw up my actual heart, and took several small, wheezing breaths. "You silver-tongued devil, you," I said finally, but every bit of punch was gone. My *sword skills*? I had a horribly clear memory of Incy slicing off Katy's head with a powerful downward stroke. Actually, you know, sword skills might not be a bad thing. I got out of the truck.

An hour later my nose was running from the cold, my arms felt like overcooked fusilli, and I couldn't catch my breath. I'd never been good with a sword, though I'd held one before. You know, *centuries ago.* This one was too long and too heavy for me, but too small for Reyn. He'd no doubt used weighty, two-handed great swords, back in the day. The bad days.

"Okay, clearly you need to practice," he said, leaning against the truck.

"It *has* been four hundred years. Or so."

His sudden grin disarmed me, so to speak, and I let the sword dangle to the ground.

"You have a ruthless bloodthirstiness about you, so that helps," he offered.

"Oh, good."

He opened the passenger-side door and gestured me in, taking the sword from me and tucking it behind the seat again. I hoped he got stopped by a cop and got searched, I really did. I climbed wearily up onto the seat, but Reyn pulled me around to face him.

"Now what?" I asked. "Jumping jacks?"

"This," he said, standing against my knees. He put one hand on the back of my neck and kept his eyes open as we slowly, finally, met in a kiss.

Oh, yes, yes, at last, I thought, putting my arms around him. He leaned into me, pushing my knees apart, one hand holding my face gently. I heard a muffled moan and hoped it wasn't me but couldn't be sure. I do know it was me who pulled him into the truck, sliding backward on the bench seat. He climbed in and managed to shut the door, and then we were awkwardly tangled together on our sides. I'd been wanting to kiss him, really kiss him, for days.

He stroked my hair away from my face, being slow and thoughtful when I was trying to keep myself from ripping off his clothes. He seemed, in general, to be holding himself back. Which I was not into. So I wiggled even closer and tilted my face up so I could reach his mouth.

He kissed me but was clearly using restraint.

I drew away, not knowing what to think. "So . . . are we not doing the ravishing thing, then?" That's me: cool and disinterested.

"No, we are," he said, sounding unsure. "We definitely are." Okay, that sounded certain.

"Front seat of a cold truck not working for you?"

He looked down at me, and suddenly I saw a deep amber glint in his eyes, a glittering intent that made me shiver. "It will work for a bit," he said. "Not for everything."

How easily he took my breath away as my fevered brain instantly came up with several scenarios, none of them in a truck.

"It's just—this feels so different." His voice was quiet and rough in the stillness.

"What do you mean?"

He shrugged lopsidedly, since one shoulder was pinned to

the seat. "I'm old. We're old. We've been with lots of people. Way too many to remember."

Great.

"This isn't what I expected," he went on, frowning at me as if it was my fault. "At first I thought it was just physical, that it had been too long since I—was with anyone, and so I focused on you. But it isn't." He sounded mystified.

"I know what you mean," I said, feeling his chest rising and falling under my hand. "I didn't think I'd ever want to be with anyone again. And I was fine with that." I let out a breath as messy breakups and slinking escapes formed choppy images in my head. "And, really, *you*. Who woulda thunk, you know?"

One side of his mouth rose. "Yeah. But…I want to know why."

"Because I am freaking *adorable*, that's why."

"Nope. That's not it." Leaning closer, he kissed me, his mouth strong and sure on mine. I pressed myself against him, loving his warmth, curling one leg over his hips and holding him in place. Minutes passed, our kisses growing harder, our breaths quicker. I felt his hands all over me, holding me to him, smoothing over my hips, my legs, my arm. Then I was pulling his shirt out from his jeans, and he was sliding his hand under my sweater. My fingers found the scar on his chest easily, and I traced it as our mouths grew rougher and more insistent.

His hand on my breast was shocking, and I gasped and

pulled back for a second. He didn't stop but kept his eyes on mine, tracing the slope as if he were memorizing it.

"Beautiful," he whispered.

I couldn't breathe.

"Beautiful." We kissed again, losing ourselves in frustrating sensations, swearing and laughing when his head hit the door handle or I jammed my funny bone on the stick shift.

Quite a bit later, when we returned to River's Edge, we snuck inside like teenagers because the windows were dark and everyone was asleep. We crept up the stairs in our stocking feet, holding our shoes, and kissed one last time, very, very quietly, in front of my door.

I closed the door behind me, amazed, breathless, and exhilarated, and a little scared, and unable to wait to see what happened next.

It was only when I was tucked into my narrow little bed, reliving the whole evening, still all aglow, that I remembered I'd had this excellent first date, had made out once again, had made myself vulnerable to...Eileif, son of Erik the Bloodletter, murderer of my family.

That truth caught in my throat like a chicken bone, leaving me bereft and even more confused than I'd been before all the hot, breathless making out in the truck.

I curled into a little ball. My past would never let me go.

CHAPTER 6

eing on breakfast duty was better than milking or gathering eggs. Especially since I got to decide what to make. So this morning ground flaxseed was nowhere in sight as I stood at the big stove, pouring pancakes onto a griddle. Not buckwheat; not whole wheat with extra wheat germ. Plain old pancakes.

Anne was cutting up oranges. Solis, the third member of our team, was manning the eggs and bacon. I hadn't forgotten that he had seemed to agree with Ottavio about the danger I presented, so I was a little stiff with him this morning. Okay, actually I was refusing to acknowledge his existence. There are so many forgiving and mature people here that I have to provide some kind of balance.

Anne put the sliced oranges into a bowl, glanced at the clock, then perched on a stool and took out a fuzzy little something she was knitting.

"Is that a hat?" I asked, pouring eight rounds of batter onto the griddle.

She grinned at me. "A sweater." She held it up—it was triangular, made of speckled brown and white mohair.

"For...a Muppet?" I asked.

"For the naked chicken," she said, and snickered.

I flipped the eight rounds and gave her a look, and she started chuckling outright. Yes, word had gotten around about my amusing little defeathering trick. Apparently we couldn't just eat the poor thing and be done with it. Apparently we had to knit cunning lil' sweaters for it so it could squawk around the yard, feeling fancy.

"Nastasya?" Solis was right next to me at the stove, so it was extra work to ignore him, but I managed.

"Nastasya, you know I care about you," he went on. I quickly flipped the done pancakes onto a platter and covered them with a clean dish towel. As Solis waited, I poured eight more rounds of batter, then gave him a bland look.

"Did you say something?"

"Nastasya." He looked at me patiently, which is something many people around me have to learn to do. "I care about you, and I find your power, the possibilities you represent, to be very exciting. But you're not just another immortal with a hard past."

Anne was watching us, her face now solemn.

"You're the sole heir of one of the eight houses. That will make you a target for the rest of—forever."

"How do other people handle it?" I asked, piling more onto the platter. I decided to get artistic and made the next ones in the shapes of crescent moons and amoebic blobs that were supposed to be stars.

"They have a lot of power. They've created safe networks around themselves. They know how to work powerful spells of protection."

I drizzled batter, giving myself time to think. I made a bunny head and a tulip shape and a bunch of squiggles, but I felt myself getting angrier.

"I can't help who I am," I pointed out. "I mean, do you think I should just hide?" I tapped one finger against my chin. "Gee, if only there was *some place*, some *safe* place, like in the middle of freaking *nowhere*, where I could surround myself with strong immortals and maybe learn how to protect myself and . . . oh, wait!" I looked at Solis, my eyes wide with excitement. "Oh my God—that sounds like *here*! It sounds like I'm *already* actually doing *exactly* what *you* think I should be doing! Awesome!"

A muscle in Solis's jaw twitched as he regarded me, embarrassment and anger on his face. Obviously I was totally right. It was a relative rarity, so I savored it. Solis dumped the scrambled eggs into a serving bowl, grabbed the platter of bacon, and headed into the dining room. River and Ottavio came in on the next door swing, and I gritted my teeth. It was barely seven in the morning, and already my stomach was in knots. Thank God I had the hot memories of being with Reyn last night, or this morning would be sucking.

"Hey," I said.

"Morning, sweetie," River said easily, opening the fridge and taking out bottles of juice and milk.

I poured more batter and glanced at Ottavio to see him looking at me with narrowed eyes, like he was trying to read me. River's back was to me, so I stuck out my tongue at him. His dark eyes flared in outrage and he immediately hissed something at River in Italian. I won't bore you with what he said, but let's just all agree he's a butthead, okay?

River straightened and looked at him.

"*Se seduto qui*," I said irritably. "Pick a language I don't know."

Ottavio's jaw tightened—a handsome, angry killjoy, fulfilling his mission of going around, sucking the fun out of everything.

Shrugging, he said openly, "She's dangerous. You don't know her. She could be here as a spy."

A look passed between them, and I thought I saw warning on River's face.

"A spy!" I said, interested. "That is just fascinating." I

raised my eyebrows at Anne, who sighed and applied herself to the chicken sweater. "A spy," I repeated, pleased. "That sounds kind of chic and exciting, you know? My name is Crowe—Nastasya Crowe. Jeez." I poured the last few dollops of pancake batter. "Unfortunately it's not true," I said regretfully. It occurred to me that I knew some pretty unsavory things about ol' Ott here—things I had learned when River shared her memories with me. Things she had told me about when she and her brothers had been very, very dark and power hungry. But did you see me throwing them in his face? No. For one thing, River had shared that stuff in private. She trusted me, rightly or wrongly. But I sure wished I could toss out one or two snide comments about fratricide. See who's all high-and-mighty then.

I turned off the griddle and shoved the heavy platter at Ottavio. "Carry these in for me, willya, Ott? And the ones on top are for you."

I swept past him into the dining room, where almost everyone had gathered. As the swinging door opened again, I heard River laughing and smirked to myself. The pancakes on top had been shaped like a certain part of the male anatomy that seemed synonymous with Ottavio, to my way of thinking.

I grabbed a plate and got in line. Ottavio pushed the platter onto the sideboard, anger wafting off him like heat.

"Whoa!" said Brynne. "These are my kind of pancakes!"

"Oh, Nas," said Lorenz, smiling as he helped himself.

"And you must be the notorious Nastasya."

Daniel was behind me, and he did indeed seem younger and less forbidding than Ottavio. His brown hair was not yet streaked with gray, or maybe he dyed it. It was perfectly cut and every strand in place. In comparison, I thought of Reyn's usual disheveled appearance. Now, *he* was heart-melting.

I looked back into Daniel's coffee-colored eyes, a bit warmer than Ottavio's. His face was attractive, slightly more rounded and not harsh, but there was something about him that gave me pause. Maybe it was his too-groomed, country-club air.

I nodded and filled my plate.

"I hear you're evil," he said conversationally.

My head whipped around. "Am *not*."

"I hear there was a girl here, and you made her go crazy and had her shipped off."

My mouth opened. "Oh my God! I didn't have anything to do with Nell." Peering around his shoulder, I looked for River. She rolled her eyes and mouthed, *I'm sorry*. I faced Daniel again, my jaw tight, but then I heard River murmur to Ottavio, "Weeniecake?" and I almost snorted.

"And then you killed some of your friends." Daniel's quiet words made my stomach drop. Shocked, I stared at him, my breath seeming like a hard piece of ice in my lungs.

"Did not." The words were thin. I tried to swallow but couldn't. Appalled, I felt the heat of tears forming behind my eyes and turned away, moving numbly to sit between Rachel and Daisuke. Uncharacteristically, Daisuke reached out and patted my back.

After that I couldn't eat but had to pretend to so Daniel and Ottavio wouldn't know how upset I was. Daniel sat down opposite me, and I faced him stonily. He looked thoughtful, not hateful, but I was glad when River smacked the back of his head as she walked by.

"Don't be such a putz," she said.

Reyn came in and sat down. I felt his eyes on me but didn't trust myself to look at him when I was still hovering at the corner of Tears and Humiliation. And of course Daniel's words reminded me of the thoughts I'd had last night when I was trying to fall asleep, how I couldn't escape my past. This was only more proof of it.

I had managed to gag down part of a pancake and a piece of bacon when Anne stood and said, "Nastasya, let's go to work. Does anyone want to join us for a meditation session this morning?"

Perfect. Meditation on top of everything else. I pushed my plate away.

"Let me change first," I muttered, and went upstairs.

Upstairs, I dawdled as long as I could, hoping everyone would have cleared out of the dining room before I resurfaced. I hadn't even had a chance to undress Reyn with my eyes. I hadn't come to terms with our situation and how I could integrate my past and my future, but I was comfortable with objectifying him while I worked things out.

Finally I dragged myself downstairs. As I grabbed my coat off the peg, Daniel appeared.

I gave him a sour look.

"My brother is right about you," Daniel said quietly. "You're dangerous, and you're causing River to be in danger."

I kept a tight grip on my anger. "It's been pointed out to me that I'm not the only one here who might possibly attract bad things."

Daniel's eyes were intent. "You're the only one here with as big a bait. If someone killed you, they could inherit the power of the Iceland house."

An involuntary shiver went down my spine. "Good thing you're here to protect me, prince of the Genoa house." I tried to push past him, but he took my arm.

"I'm not here to protect you. I'm here to protect my sister, *from* you if necessary. And I can make it worth your while to leave here."

Now, this was interesting. "How?" Like, could he arrange for me to meet the guy who played Wolverine? 'Cause that might be worth my while.

Daniel shrugged. "I can offer you money. So much money that you could go anywhere in the world for years and years without having to work."

Well, that was a disappointment. I mean, jeez. Did he think I'd gotten to be 459 without managing to sock away a few coins for a rainy day? "Daniel. Come on. Money? Really?"

He looked affronted. "A significant amount of money."

"A hundred million dollars?"

"No. Of course not."

"Then I guess we don't have a deal." I yanked my arm from his grasp and stomped through the dining room and kitchen and out the back door. God, River's brothers were such fatheads.

There was a small, person-size door in the wall of the big barn, and I pushed through to find Jess, Charles, and Solis talking together in the hallway. They stopped when I came in, and it couldn't have been more obvious that *moi* was the subject of their conversation. My cheeks heated, but I ignored them and went past them to Anne's classroom.

"Hi—I'm glad you came," Anne said.

"Oh, wait, was this *optional*?" I asked.

She smiled at me. "No."

The others shuffled in after me, and Anne said, "Thank you all for coming. I'd like you to help me with this morning's session. I think a good group meditation will be very useful."

Various murmurs and lame excuses, but Anne was pretty firm, and in the end, the five of us sat in a circle with a lit candle in the middle. Without looking at anyone, I picked up on their feelings of resentment and discomfort. I felt like the unpopular kid in the schoolyard.

Still, I focused on the candle, trying to rid my mind of the forty-seven unrelated thoughts that were crowding into my brain.

I was almost startled when Anne began to hum, then sing softly under her breath. One by one, we joined in, our voices and songs blending. The barn walls faded away, and I forgot about my cold butt and my embarrassment. Anne added words to her song, words in English, saying, *Show us what we need to see.* I felt her crafting a spell all around us, weaving it together out of our voices.

Spells have forms and structures; some of them are bottom heavy; some are elegant, like cages, ethereal, made of gossamer. Some are solid and sturdy, built to hold weight and intent and power. This spell felt like a basket, like thin reeds and split canes woven in and out and around one another. Then I was conscious of Jess's mind touching mine tentatively, and within another minute, the five of us were sharing one vision.

Ħ Ħ Ħ Ħ Ħ Ħ Ħ Ħ Ħ Ħ Ħ Ħ Ħ

It was a farm. Fields of shrubs studded with white lumps stretched away into the distance. Cotton; they were cotton fields. The vision shimmered and expanded to show a large, white, columned house in the distance, raised up on pilings, with long French windows everywhere.

I heard a *boom!* The ground trembled. In the distance the horizon was lit by a burst of light, and even this far away, the smells of sulfur and gunpowder reached my nose. Another *boom!* made us jump. This place was on the edge of a war, and the war was coming this way.

People ran across my field of vision. A small boy in a sailor suit collapsed, crying, beneath a huge tree, and a woman in long skirts swept him up in her arms, looking around wildly.

We were suddenly behind the house, by the fields. To the left was row after row of shacks, with glassless windows, holes in the walls, and crumbling chimneys, some of which had smoke curling away into the sky.

Fear splintered in my chest as more screams filled the air. Dogs barked, a horse broke free of its tether and galloped off beneath the trees, and still, the heavy *booms* of cannons shook the ground, and the smaller popping sounds of guns began to fill in between them.

A man on a horse rode up to the shacks, shouting harshly and cracking a whip. The horse's eyes rolled in fear and its sides were lathered in sweat. Hesitantly people began emerging from the shacks, their dark skin shining in the dim light. The man shouted at them, pointing with one hand toward the big house. The people cowered, even the men, and none of them seemed surprised when he snapped the whip so it caught one of the men on the shoulder, slicing his raggedy shirt. Soon its edges were red with blood.

The man slid down from his horse. The sound of guns and cannons was louder. A woman cried: "They're coming! Dear God!"

Rows of heavy chains hung from the horse's saddle. The man grabbed them and headed toward the slaves, even as another *boom!* sounded so close by that it seemed like the barn itself should shake. The slaves saw the man coming at them with the chains, and one of them shouted something. They began to scatter, racing away into the chaos, leaving the man enraged, purple-faced, and chasing them with his whip.

Off in the distance an army began to swarm over a low hill, carrying an old-fashioned American flag.

The angry man, Jess, had sandy hair and rough features.

I was glad when the awful sounds and smells of the war faded and we were transported to ... what was this—England? Ireland? Stucco walls fourteen inches thick, open windows letting in raucous laughter from outside. It was an inn. The moon shone into the room like a searchlight, framing the red-haired man sliding silently out of a metal-framed double bed. A man with old-fashioned whiskers lay next to him, still wearing his undershirt, his mouth open and snoring.

The red-haired man looked like a farm boy, with fresh pale skin and clear eyes. He wore nothing but old-fashioned drawers, and he tightened the tapes around his waist so they wouldn't fall down. Slowly he crept to the big, plain dresser, glancing back at the man to make sure he was still sawing logs. Voyeuristically we watched as he drew a wallet out of the man's pants pocket, opened it, and removed most of the bills. Then he glided like a shadow over to the potted plant on a wooden stand. Grasping the plant carefully at its base, he pulled it up, dropped the money into the hole, and pushed the plant down firmly on top of it. He was smiling as he lightly slid back into bed.

That was Charles, being a male prostitute in Ireland, who knows how long ago.

A shift, and then we saw a burning building. A city street stretched away, fire dotting many houses in a random pattern. Was it London? Boston? I couldn't tell.

This house was going up in flames quickly. A second-story shutter crashed open, and a man wearing street clothes climbed up on the ledge. Behind him a woman cried, "Don't go! Don't leave me!"

"I'm going to get a ladder!" the man said, shaking her hand off his shoulder. "Let me go!"

Crying, she stepped back. The man launched himself out of the window, landing hard on the sidewalk below. He shook his head, looking stunned, then got himself together and stood up. Our last sight of Solis was him racing away, as far from the burning house as possible. The blaze crept up the side of the house to the window frame, as if it were peering inside. We could still hear the woman crying, but couldn't see her through the flames. Soon the entire house was burning, and her cries stopped.

In the next scene, Anne was very heavy. Her clothes looked like...the mid–eighteen hundreds? We were in a general-type store that carried everything from pieces of farm equipment to bolts of cloth to pocketknives, though the shelves seemed picked bare. Through the glass window we saw a crowd of people knocking anxiously at the door. Anne bustled over to it and flipped the sign over; the word *geschlossen* was on the back. People poured in, waving money. They started grabbing everything in sight, hardly caring what it was. With arms laden, they staggered to the counter. Anne began quickly writing up sales lists, totaling the sums on a piece of brown paper.

That's when people began to notice the price cards. The original price was crossed out, and a new price was written in. In moments we saw that the prices on every single thing had been marked up at least four times as much as they had been, and some things, like tools, were ten times as much. The customers started yelling and waving their arms, but Anne remained calm.

"You don't have to shop here," she said in German. "No one is making you."

"You're the only shop that didn't flood!" people shouted. "Now you're gouging us on prices! This is thievery!"

"I can set my prices however I want," Anne said firmly. She was bulky behind the counter, almost round, with dark hair in braids pinned on top of her head.

"How can you sleep at night?" a man cried. "We're your neighbors! You're a thief!"

The crowd took it up as a chant: "Thief! Thief!" Anne stood there stoically, not budging.

Then a woman pushed through the men surrounding the counter. "She might be a thief, but my man needs nails!" She started counting out money on the counter, carefully, coin by coin, out of a threadbare purse.

Anne looked triumphant.

All these hard memories were exhausting me. The weight of concentrating was fraying the edges of my magick. Plus the other thoughts—the things I was picking up from the four people with me. Shame, defensiveness, even nostalgia— it was pretty crowded inside my head.

But we weren't done yet.

The light changed to that peculiar haunting quality you find only in the far north, in the countries I grew up in. We saw a room with furniture from the sixteen hundreds. Frowning, I examined the wall hangings, the Dutch kast against one wall, the wide, dark planks of the floor. Though it was reminiscent of rooms I'd seen, I didn't think I'd ever actually been in it.

Then I came through the door, in servant clothes. The rough linen overdress, petticoats, apron, and the white kerchief covering my hair placed this around four hundred years ago. With effort, I lugged a heavy copper coal scuttle to the room's large stone fireplace. The northern countries had little to no coal deposits themselves; this must have been imported at an exorbitant price. I set the scuttle down and knelt to clean the old ashes out of the fireplace, but a sound outside caught my attention. The windows had wavy glass and opened lengthwise on hinges. Pushing one open, I leaned out to look down to the street below. A procession filled the narrow street: nobles on horses, two men at the front carrying color guards, other well-dressed men behind the nobles. I stepped back as I realized that the flags were my father's coat of arms—five black bears on a red background. Scanning the crowd, I recognized no one.

"Ragnhild! What is it?" The mistress of the house hurried to the window. From four hundred years away, I recognized her as a real person I had known.

"A procession, my lady," I said. "I don't know why."

The lady also leaned out the window to look.

The two men carrying the color guards stopped their horses and stood to the sides of the narrow street. People craned their necks to see who was coming, who the trumpets were announcing. But then someone shouted: "He will kill everyone! Hide your gold! Hide your silver! He is coming!"

Gradually I became aware that Anne was guiding us out of the meditation, and the vision was fading like smoke. It took us a while to come down—it had been the most ambitious meditation circle I'd ever been in, and I got the feeling that it had strained the others, too.

I took a couple of deep breaths, trying to process everything I had seen. Anne leaned over and blew out the center candle. I wondered what the rest of them were thinking—we'd seen each of them at real low points in their lives, and we'd had a weird vision about me. I thought about how everyone here except for Anne had nodded when Ottavio had been ranting about how dark I was.

Well, to hell with them.

"What was the purpose of this?" Charles's voice sounded thin.

Looking weary, Anne brushed her dark bangs off her forehead. "My only guideline was that we see what we needed to see." Her chin came up. "I think we can all agree that we've had dark pasts and, as such, can't be in a position to judge others." The *like Nastasya* went unsaid.

"It isn't that," said Solis, his voice strained. "It's like I said—Nastasya is more than just an immortal with a hard past. Who she is, what she represents, will draw others here; others who want her power, possibly want her dead, like her friend in Boston. That will affect all of us."

"If a battle comes to us," said Anne, "we will be ready for it. And we will all stand together to protect our own. There are precious few Tähti in the world—we cannot lose another." There was a fine thread of steel in her voice, and Solis looked at her without saying anything.

"What was all that stuff at the end?" Charles asked. His fair skin was still pink with embarrassment over his memory.

"I don't know," I said, my heart aching. "Those banners— those were the flags of my family, our color guards. But I don't think that was my father—he never led his army to big towns like that. I never saw any procession of his, ever. I don't know what it was about." But I'd found it painful, all the same.

My parents had been Terävä, but I'd been happy, as a child. For the first ten years of my life, I'd felt loved, happy, and secure. I'd had no idea that my parents were murderers, that my father had sought to increase his power by any means necessary. My whole picture of them was changing, and it was so sad. I hated the truth of it.

"What was with the bears?" Jess's voice sounded scraped raw. Now we would always know who he had been. We would never unknow it. His face looked bleak, shuttered.

"That was my father's crest," I said. "Five black bears on a red background. Sometimes the bears wore crowns." I let out a breath. "My sister and I used to tell stories about the bears, giving them names, making up their adventures." My sister. Oh, Eydís. I still miss you, after all this time.

I needed to lie down, or maybe go cry in the shower. Abruptly I stood, muttered "Thanks," and headed out.

Maybe Anne's exercise had been useful. I didn't know.

But, oh yeah, now I remember: I hate meditation.

sually after dinner, if I don't have classes, I escape upstairs to my room. I have a big, ancient book about immortals' magick in the Middle Ages, and behind that I keep the paperback romance I'm actually reading.

But now I felt that maybe I should join the others, who were probably in the double parlors. Of course I would no doubt run into Ottavio and Daniel, both of whom I now loathed almost as much as they loathed me.

But I was getting to be a big girl, so let's see just how far we've come, shall we?

In the parlor Brynne was curled up on a loveseat, reading, her shoeless feet draped over the back. When she saw me, she swung her feet down and patted the space next to her.

"Hi," I said. "I'm here to mingle and strengthen my social skills." I sat with my back against one arm, she sat against the other, and our legs overlapped in the middle.

Brynne laughed softly, then inclined her head toward the other side of the room. All of the teachers were gathered there, along with Daniel and Ottavio.

"Ooh, serious faces," I said under my breath. "Have you heard any of it?"

"Nope," said Brynne. "Not for lack of trying. But River hasn't smacked either brother yet, so it might not be about you."

"Ugh. You know they're here because I'm a dangerous, uncontrollable menace, right?"

"Are we talking about your clothes again?" she asked innocently, and I kicked her with one foot. She snickered, then became more serious. "I believe that has been mentioned, yes." Leaning back again, she whispered, "What do you think of Daniel? Hot, no?"

I glanced across the room, where Daniel's face was outlined in red by the fire. "I guess," I said. "He's kind of ruined for me, with all the judging and attempted bribery and whatnot."

Brynne's even, white teeth shone against her caramel-colored skin. "He tried to bribe you? To what? To leave?"

I nodded, and Brynne snickered. "Did you go for it?"

"He was offering less than a hundred million dollars."

"Oh, well, to hell with him, then. Anyway—I have taken it on as my personal mission, you know. I must somehow convince him how wrong he is about you." Her eyes followed Daniel's every move, and I was forcibly reminded of, like, a snake watching a rat. "No matter what it takes," she added dreamily. "It will be my sacrifice, my gift to you."

Stifling my laughter, I kicked her again, and she covered her mouth, her eyes crinkling until they were just slits.

"Seriously," I said finally. "They think I'm bad news. You're not worried?" Please don't be worried.

"Oh, right," Brynne scoffed, arranging a pillow behind her. "They just don't know you, is all."

A warm glow of gratitude surrounded my heart, but I pressed, "*You* don't really know me, either."

That got her attention, and she stopped fussing with the pillow and looked at me. "I do," she said slowly. "I do know you. I've been living and eating and working and studying with you for four months. You're a lot of things, and God knows you need work, but one thing you're not is evil." She shrugged. "I *know* that."

My breath was caught somewhere around my solar plexus as I carefully let myself feel the comfort of friendship. "Thanks," I croaked, and rubbed my nose against the sleeve of my sweatshirt.

Tearing her eyes away from Daniel again, Brynne gave me a knowing look. "Speaking of hotness, is there anything you want to share about our dear, monosyllabic Reyn?"

Oh, he's so hot, I want him so bad, I don't understand it, I'm scared....

"He's not monosyllabic," I said. "*Idiot* has three syllables, and I hear that a lot from him."

Brynne wasn't going to be put off. "Are you guys *an item?*"

I dropped my head into my hands. "I don't know! I just don't know. We constantly piss each other off, but we also—"

"Mmyes?" Brynne purred.

"It's not that simple." Brynne didn't know about the part Reyn's family had played in the destruction of my life, and I didn't want to enlighten her.

"It *is* that simple," she urged, nudging me. "You guys seem like a pair. Get out of your own way and give in to it!"

I wish. I said nothing but nodded. Brynne looked like she wanted to say more but was deciding not to push me.

"Nastasya." River's voice was quiet, but it carried through the room. "We've been talking."

"Okay," I said, already not liking where this was going.

But River's eyes, the color of wet stones in a stream, were kind.

"How do you explain the death of a hundred songbirds in Boston?" Ottavio burst out. The look of pained irritation River gave him was classic, but I almost fell off the loveseat. How in the world did he know about that?

"I didn't do that," I said, a pinball of alarm pinging in my head.

"And the crippled London cabbie?"

This time, River actually punched his shoulder. He ignored her.

"I didn't do that," I said more strongly.

"The train wreck in India? That killed almost a hundred people?"

I stared at him. That had been at least eighty years ago. "Again, something awful I did not do."

Just then, the door behind them opened and Anne's sister Amy walked in with a tray. "Pot brownies?" she asked cheerfully, looking around.

We were nonplussed.

"No, really?" Brynne was the first to find her voice.

Amy sighed regretfully. "No, not really. Just regular. Anyone still want one?" Then she seemed to pick up on the room's tension, the expression on my face, and her brow furrowed. "I think everyone needs to take a brownie." Her tone implied this was an offer we couldn't refuse, and she took the tray around, staring us down until we caved.

But it would take more than a brownie to stop Ott, now that he was on a roll.

"The things that took place at a club called Miss Edna's?" His face was dark and angry.

Amy stood right in front of him. "Take. A. Brownie."

"Is she sure these aren't loaded?" I whispered to Brynne. Brynne shook her head.

Not answering her, Ottavio tried to nudge her out of the

way. Amy planted her feet, refusing to budge, and he finally looked up at her. "Move, please!" he snapped.

"You're a guest in this house," Amy said in a low tone, and I swallowed a crumb wrong and coughed. I'd never heard her sound like that, and apparently no one else had, either. Brynne and I made *huh?* faces at each other.

It took a moment, but Ottavio became still, glaring at her.

"What are you doing?" Her voice was still soft but inescapable. I glanced at River to see her watching Amy with a look of surprised speculation.

"I want the truth!" Ottavio sat back, his black shark eyes shooting sparks.

"Then let the truth come to you!" Amy said, sounding more normal. "Quit trying to bludgeon it out of everything, you pompous jackass!"

Mouths dropped open like frogs at a fly convention. Amy balanced the tray on her hip and swung out the door, perhaps leaving before she said anything worse.

River looked astonished. Okay, pretty much everyone looked astonished. Except Anne.

"She's a little scary sometimes," she said conversationally, and took a bite of brownie.

Ottavio seemed completely undone, absolutely speechless. It was great.

But during the stunned silence, I was thinking.

"Who told you all this stuff, Ott?" I asked. "Where did it

all come from?" I couldn't think of any one person who had been at every instance he mentioned. "I mean, the train wreck was just a train wreck—it happens all the time in India. Especially back then."

"The train wreck was caused by someone working Terävä magick," Daniel said.

"What? Why do you think that?" I shook my head and stood up. "I mean—what is all this about? I didn't do any of these things! I just happened to be there." Wow, that sounded so . . . lame.

"Yes," said Daniel, his voice still calm. "You just happened to be there."

I crossed my arms, trying not to throw something at his head. "People all over the world make Terävä magick every day," I said tightly. "And have been for thousands of years. Even before I was born." Like you, for example. "I was not nearby or the cause of every bit of dark magick that has been worked in this world. So what, *exactly*, are you getting at, Ott?"

Ottavio opened his mouth, but River leaned forward and literally clapped her hand over it, shutting him up.

"Both Ottavio and Daniel have been hearing rumors of very dangerous magick being worked here," River said. "Or, at least, close to here. I've heard from some other friends as well—one in England, one in Russia. I don't know what's going on, but stories have been flying." She frowned and took her hand away from Ottavio's cold, furious face.

"We believe that what happened with Innocencio—as well as the things you witnessed at that club in Boston—are part of something larger, something truly dark and truly dangerous," River went on.

I nodded slowly, thinking. "But why is it about me? Why are you questioning everything that's happened in *my* life?"

"We don't think it's a coincidence that Innocencio came for *you*," River said. "We assume that he knows who you are, your heritage, and that he wants to take your power. He's safely at Louisette's right now, but it seems clear that though he worked the magick he used on you, he didn't instigate this whole thing. So who did?"

"Okay." I felt shivery and cold and went to stand with my back to the fire. "But I still want to know: Who told you all these things? Where are these rumors coming from? Why would someone want to discredit *me*, in front of *you*?"

Daniel and Ottavio looked thoughtful.

"I think it was...my secretary who told me," Ottavio said, frowning. "I'm not sure. Or maybe I heard it at a circle? I'm trying to remember. Someone told me..." His voice trailed off.

"It was my friend Didi," Daniel said, but he didn't sound rock solid, either. "I think. I was in Canada, researching old spells, and maybe Didi mentioned it? Said something about my sister—and then the story of what happened with Innocencio and Nastasya seemed to be common knowledge."

I stared at him. "The only people there that night were

me, Incy, Katy, and Stratton," I said. "And I guess everyone here learned about it. So *who* is talking?"

"Could it have been the mirror?" Brynne suggested.

Shortly after I'd gotten back from Boston, I'd repeated what Incy had told me—that he had caused a bunch of bad things to happen to me here, to make me run away. Asher had searched the place and found that the large dining room mirror was overlaid with dark spells—it was how Incy had been affecting me. They'd destroyed it.

"We burned it—what, several days after you were back?" Asher asked. "Three days? Could someone—not Innocencio—still have been in contact with it?" He shook his head. "Either that, or there was someone else at the warehouse that night. Someone none of us knew about."

"Oh God," I said. "I've never considered that. That place was huge, dark as the belly of a ship—you could have hidden a hundred people in there, and I never would have seen them." It was a new and horrible thought that made me feel creeped out down to my bones.

"And you were under a holding spell," River added. "Your vision, your awareness, would have been compromised anyway."

"I will conduct a complete sweep of this property," said Ottavio. "Sometimes a fresh pair of eyes sees what others can't."

"I'll help." Anne looked concerned, as if already thinking of places something could be hidden, something that could affect any of us or spy on us. On me.

Solis was remaining silent, and I hated that he still wanted me gone. Then River nodded at Asher, as if in reply to a question, and Asher picked up a small wooden box from the end table next to the couch.

Solis looked up. "You know I disagree with this."

River nodded gently. "I know. But I believe it's for the best. Nastasya, come here, please."

Asher held the box out to me, and I took it cautiously.

"This is yours," he said. "We were waiting for the right time."

I pressed the release of the lid. Inside, nestled on a bed of coarse salt, was...my mother's amulet, repaired and whole and on a chain, exactly as it had been the night she died.

In wonder, I lost myself in it, the room around me fading as my fingers traced every detail. The half I'd always had was as familiar to me as a blade of grass; the half Reyn had given me was both new and dearly remembered. And in the middle, glowing and milky and translucent, was my moonstone, the moonstone I'd chosen blindly from a velvet bag last fall. The moonstone that had helped save my life that night in the warehouse.

The amulet was not as heavy as I remembered, but the last time I'd held it whole, I'd been ten years old. The ancient gold gleamed with fresh polishing, the runes and sigils still distinct. It was a living thing in my hand, warm and full of energy, like a bird.

With difficulty I looked away from it to search River's

face. She was both watchful and loving, but I picked up on tension among the others. "It's mine?" My voice was thin, almost childish.

"Of course," River said. "It always has been."

"Are you out of your mind?" Ottavio said, looking horrified.

I gave him a big grin, but inside I felt awash in emotion. This was the only thing I had from my original life, my family. I'd gotten used to having just the broken half. It had never occurred to me that someday it could be made whole again. Now I examined it, holding the chain, seeing the pendant twist slowly. In my head I heard my mother's voice singing her song of power and magick-conjuring.

Would it work as well for me?

"What if—" I began, looking at River. "I mean—my parents were Terävä. The magick they made was Terävä. And this—"

"Will help you channel *your* magick," River answered, "light or dark. We've worked powerful spells of cleansing and purifying on it, and tomorrow we'll show you how to bind it more completely to yourself. It, in itself, will not make Terävä magick. Unless you want it to."

More solemn faces. You could practically hear everyone thinking, *Let's hope this isn't a huge mistake, to give it back to her.*

I nodded. It was so much to take in—my mother's amulet, whole again! I knew Asher had been repairing it, but at this moment I realized that I hadn't actually believed it could be repaired, that I truly would have my family's taraksin, perfect and complete.

My eyes began to sting, and I knew that I was about to cry. Which I absolutely could not do in front of Ottavio.

"Thanks," I managed to whisper, and then I ran out of the parlor and up the steps to my room, clutching my amulet to my chest.

CHAPTER 8

ou'd better move," I snarled quietly, engaged in a fierce stare-down with a chicken. This one chicken, the devil-chicken, was hell-bent on hatching her clutch of eggs. Usually I didn't even bother with her, not wanting to get my eyes pecked out. But today I was Lilja af Úlfur, possessor of the Iceland tarak-sin, and I was going to get these freaking eggs.

Or...um, maybe not. The cold, glittering stare in her beady eyes made me think that perhaps I needed to be Lilja, possessor of asbestos fireplace gloves that went up to my elbows, before I could really tackle this situation. Giving her one last dirty look, I grabbed my basket and ducked out of the short door of the chicken coop.

"So, you have it."

I stopped just short of running into Reyn, lurking right outside the coop. No human being should look that good this early in the morning. I myself was sporting my traditional cat-dragged-in look, but Reyn was beautifully rumpled, with a sheen of beard stubble that begged to be touched.

"What?" I wanted to climb him like a tree.

"Your amulet," he said, falling into step as I headed toward the kitchen.

"Yes. It's so...beautiful," I said, still in awe. "I never thought I'd have it. I can't believe—" *Oh, I can't believe I'm gushing about it when it killed everyone in your family.*

"I'm glad you have it," Reyn said as he opened the kitchen door for me. "I'm glad it could be repaired."

I stopped and looked up at him, reading the honesty in his strong, chiseled face. There passed between us an understanding: Reyn did not kill my family, though he was connected to it, and I did not kill his family, though I was connected to it. But neither he nor I had *caused* those tragedies. He and I were guilty merely of surviving.

What were we, to each other? What could we become? Maybe it was my hormones talking, but I thought I saw the same questions, the same wondering, in his eyes.

"Thank you," I said inadequately.

"You're letting in the cold air." Daisuke stood in the doorway, looking at us. "And we need the eggs."

"Sorry," I mumbled, handing him the basket. How could I be alone with Reyn again? When? I wanted it as much as I was scared of it.

Everyone seemed subdued at breakfast, lost in their own thoughts. There were so many weighty matters going on: River's brothers and their suspicions; wondering about the larger picture; wondering about me and my tarak-sin; our general safety...

"Hey!" I said, breaking the silence. "Did y'all know I can summon dead spirits with my amulet? It's *awesome!*"

Sometimes one has to shake things up a bit.

"Here." River pushed a shopping list at me. "Lorenz has to go to town to see the dentist, so you might as well join him and get these things for us."

I nodded and took the list. "How's Ott?"

"He's lying down," River said pointedly. "Having to be Heimliched upset him."

"That bit of sausage was bad timing," I agreed.

"Please don't forget the whole-wheat pastry flour," she said.

West Lowing, Massachusetts, is a small town with one main street, imaginatively called Main Street. Five weeks ago I'd gone there every day to work at MacIntyre's Drugs.

Then I'd gotten fired, twice. I hadn't been there since I got back from Boston.

"Okay," said Lorenz as I parked the car. "I'll be back in about half an hour. I hope." His long-fingered, elegant hand rubbed his cheek as if it ached.

"Let's hear it for modern dentistry, eh?" I said, and he grimaced. Actually, as much as people dislike going to the dentist now, try doing it two hundred years ago, when having a cavity meant some quack knocking it out with a chisel and hammer in the market square. With no anesthetic.

That's the kind of thing that makes me crazy when immortals (or even regular people) gripe about missing the good old days and how much more civilized things used to be. I'm like, civilized? Like before indoor plumbing? Before novocaine? Before bug spray? Please.

The one grocery store, Pitson's, was actually pretty well stocked. We grew most of our own food at River's Edge, but we hadn't gotten around to grinding our own flour yet or making our own baggies. I guess River was just slacking off.

My basket had four smooth wheels and didn't list severely to either side, so, score. Up and down the aisles I went, crossing things off my list, feeling productive. In one corner of the cart I stacked an assortment of contraband items to squirrel away in my room: Pop-Tarts, Twizzlers, some Fudge Grahams, a six-pack of Coke for medicinal purposes. Sighing,

I thought longingly back to Coke's early years, when it had trace amounts of cocaine in it. Talk about a pick-me-up.

After checking out, I put the groceries in the car, then leaned against it to wait for Lorenz. It wasn't too bad today, weatherwise, and with the sun shining brightly, I could pretend that spring was on its way.

What this town needed was a cute coffee shop. One girl's opinion. I had no idea when Lorenz would be done, and I would have killed for a nice, hot latte right then. The only time I'd had coffee with Dray, we'd had to go to a garishly lit diner way down the street.

Dray. One of the two nonimmortals I'd become acquaintances with here. She and my other sort-of friend, Meriwether MacIntyre, were high schoolers and about 180 degrees from each other. But something had drawn me to each of them—and then I'd ruined both friendships, of course. Because that's what I do.

Come on, Lorenz, I thought, starting to feel chilly. I didn't want to just sit in the car. Maybe I should go check out Early's, the general store next to Pitson's. I could stock up on some Now and Laters. Then I happened to glance across the street, at the row of run-down, empty buildings there.

West Lowing had once been four times as large and much more bustling. When the local mill had shut down in the late seventies, the town had lost more than ten thousand jobs. It wasn't exactly a ghost town yet, but apparently it was too small to support, say, one freaking coffee shop.

Nowadays Main Street looked like a ratty patchwork quilt, with the few remaining businesses popping up between abandoned buildings and empty lots.

Abandoned buildings like these, right here. Crossing the street, I saw that what looked like four separate shops were really part of one larger structure. They looked individual on the first floor, but the second floor was more unified in design. A weather-beaten sign hanging by one nail said APTS. FOR RENT with a phone number.

The shops had wide bay windows in the front and inset doors—a style popular back in the thirties. Small, hexagonal blue tiles spelled out SCHWALBACH'S in one entryway. Pressing my face to the glass, I saw a large empty room with the same kind of pressed-tin ceiling as in MacIntyre's Drugs, and tall, round columns supporting the roof. Chunks of the walls had fallen in, and there was water damage beneath one broken window. Someone had tagged one of the walls with graffiti.

"What are you doing?" Lorenz's voice startled me, and he smiled lopsidedly when I wheeled to face him.

"Waiting for you," I said. "How was the dentist?"

He made a so-so gesture with one hand and cupped the other around his swollen cheek. "I need to get a prescription."

"Okay. I'll wait at the car."

Lorenz grinned at my too casual tone. *"Bawk, bawk, bawk."*

I narrowed my eyes. "Fine. I'll go with, shall I?"

Bigger grin, on only one side, because the novocaine hadn't worn off yet.

So my pride—and it's always good to be bullied into something by one's pride, isn't it?—made me march across the street and push open the door to MacIntyre's. The last time I'd been in there, Old Mac, the owner, had fired me for the second time. The time before that, I'd been shouting awful, hurtful things at him, with Meriwether standing there looking like I'd punched her in the stomach. That was when I'd been fired the first time. And I'm not saying I was jonesing to have my promising and glamorous career as a stock girl back, but it had been humiliating, and I'd felt like a failure.

Inside, Lorenz headed toward the back, where Old Mac filled prescriptions. No one was minding the front counter. All the cute posters Meriwether and I had made had been taken down. I wanted to stay put and be able to leap through the door should Old Mac come near me, but disgust at my total weenieness reared its judgmental head, and I forced myself at imaginary gunpoint to actually look for Meriwether, see if she hated my guts.

I found her a couple aisles over, unpacking one of the large blue plastic bins that stock came in. She sat on the small stool I used to sit on, seeming in her own world as she took boxes of nasal spray from the bin and pushed them into place on the shelf.

For a moment I stood and watched her as she moved

methodically but without thought. Her hair was a pale ash-brown color, and again I was struck by how her hair, her skin, and her eyes all seemed so much the same tone as to make her virtually colorless. At first glance, one might not even notice her. But now that I knew her, she seemed lovely, in a quiet, old-fashioned way.

Something made her look up, perhaps just me being all creeper at the end of the aisle. When she saw me, her eyes widened and her mouth opened, but no words came out.

What should I say? One gets so tired of apologizing for being an insensitive ass, doesn't one?

"Hey," she said, and stood up.

"Hey" was my witty riposte.

"I haven't seen you in ages." She gave a slight smile. "Thought you'd started shopping in Walgreens or something."

"Heaven forbid," I said, and she smiled wider. "No—I was... sick for a while, and then I just didn't need to come to town."

"I'm glad to see you." Her simple statement undid me, and with huge relief I hurried to her, surprising both of us with a hug.

"I'm glad to see you, too," I said. During that awful night with Incy, I'd thought of Meriwether and Dray and realized I would never know what happened to them, wouldn't see how they turned out, because Incy was going to kill me. Seeing Meriwether today made me extra glad he hadn't. "Anyway. How have things been?" I tilted my head toward the back of the store.

After a fast, instinctive glance to see if her dad was nearby, Meriwether said, "Well, since that day—he seems like he's trying to be . . . less hard, you know? Like he's trying to mellow out a little. I mean, he's been sadder but hasn't been yelling as much."

"I'm so sorry for the stuff I said," I told her. "My mouth never waits for my brain to catch up."

She nodded. "We were both—shocked. But I think what you said—about my mom—maybe made us both think a bit. Like, after my mom and my brother died, Dad had gotten rid of every single picture of them that we had around the house. Like if we couldn't see them, they hadn't died or something. But after that day, a couple days later, I saw that he had put one of the pictures back on the wall in the kitchen. One of the four of us."

"Wow," I said quietly. "But I'm still sorry. Really."

"Okay." Meriwether nodded and glanced around again, then leaned closer to me. "You know, I think Mrs. Philpott has been coming in extra often. Like to talk to Dad."

"Reeeaallly?" I said. Mrs. Philpott was a local widow who had gone to high school with Old Mac.

Meriwether pressed her lips together, her eyes alight. "I think she comes in *just* to talk to him."

"Whoa." We looked at each other for a few moments, sharing our fascination at this new wrinkle in Old Mac's life. I really wished I still worked there, and then Meriwether and I could gossip about everything that was happening, like we used to. Instead I'd run off at the mouth and gotten fired. I'm sure there's a lesson in there somewhere. For someone.

"Ah, there you are, Nas." Lorenz flipped his Italian wool scarf artfully over his shoulder. "And you, miss—could you please tell me where you keep your aspirin? I have a tooth-ache." He unleashed a smile on Meriwether, and even though it was lopsided, she still blinked like a stunned rabbit under the force of his charm.

After a second she snapped out of it and started to lead him to the other aisle. "If it's just for a toothache, you should take ibuprofen or Tylenol," she murmured. "Aspirin thins your blood. People take it to help heart attacks."

"Oh, thank you," said Lorenz. "How helpful you are." Again the smile, the deep gaze of his Mediterranean blue eyes. Coupled with his beautiful light olive skin and black hair, he was stunning, and he knew it. It was actually a source of real pain in his life, and I planned to remind him of that.

"I'll come back soon," I said, wishing again that we could just run across the street to a, what? Yes. A cute coffee shop.

"I'd like that," she said, then blinked at Lorenz's smile as he said good-bye.

I wanted to skip back to the car. Meriwether didn't hate me. We might possibly still be friends. She had been glad to see me. I was so, so happy about that.

"Your friend, little... Meriwether, is it?" Lorenz said. "Do you know if she's eighteen yet? She's a senior in high school, did I hear you mention that?" He spoke casually as we approached the car, but his words hit me like cold water: Lorenz was barely more than a hundred years old but had already fathered 235 children. Two hundred. And thirty-five. Children. None of whom he was being a father to. Part of why he was at River's Edge was to figure out (and then, one hopes, end) such criminal irresponsibility.

I stopped in my tracks and after a few steps he turned to me, his smile faltering when he saw my face.

"Lorenz, if you seriously pursue Meriwether, I will cut you off at the knees."

He started to laugh, thinking I was joking, but I stared lasers at him.

"What? Oh, no. Don't be silly, Nasya." He tugged on the car door, but I hadn't unlocked it yet.

I faced him across the hood of the car. "Lorenz. Listen to me carefully. We all need to deal with our own mistakes. God knows I have a lot on my plate, dealing with mine. But Meriwether is my friend, and if you pursue her, I will make you regret it." My voice was quiet and serious, all grown-up sounding. It was very unlike me, to speak this way—I usually don't take care of myself, much less a friend. But Meriwether was different—truly a nice person, with hopes and dreams. She'd been through a lot, and there was no way I was going to let Lorenz make her life harder.

"Please, Nastasya," he said a little stiffly. "You mistake me."

I clicked the car doors open, and we got in. He looked huffy and embarrassed and of course guilty, because he was realizing that was exactly what he'd been planning, without even meaning to.

"I do not mistake you, Lorenz." Starting the engine, I checked behind me and put the car into reverse. I met his eyes again—his were frosty. Mine probably looked like black holes. "I do not mistake you. Are we clear about this? You will not go near Meriwether. Are we absolutely clear?"

He snorted, looking out the window, the image of offended sensibilities.

"I'll take that as an 'eff yeah,'" I said, and peeled out toward home.

As soon as I walked into the house at River's Edge, I felt waves of quivering, powerful magick sweeping over me. I looked at Lorenz. "What's that?"

"What's what?" He was distant, still pissed about what I'd said.

"You don't feel anything?"

He stopped, a bag of groceries in his hands. After a moment he shook his head. "No, not really. I have a headache. I'm going upstairs." He set the groceries on the kitchen island and left, while I stood there trying to figure out what I was feeling. Magick reverberated through my chest like heavy music. The only other time I'd felt something like this was that night with Incy, as he wrought huge, dark spells to rip my power from me. But this—today—didn't exactly feel bad or scary. It didn't make my stomach roil with nausea. It just felt big.

And I so did not want to be here to find out what it was. I quickly stored the fridge stuff and set out again through the kitchen door. A small white figure sitting in the doorway of the horse barn caught my eye, and I headed toward Dúfa as she stood, her whiplike tail wagging. These days, Dúfa = Reyn.

"Hey, pup," I said, walking into the dim, horse-smelling warmth. I tried not to glance up at the hayloft, where Reyn and I had fallen prey to our first soul-searing kisses.

The man himself was standing in the middle of the aisle currying Titus, one of the big workhorses. He hadn't seen me, and I was able to pause and appreciate the smooth move of flannel-covered muscle, the warrior grace that informed everything he did. He's been currying horses for more than four hundred years, but each sweep of the brush looked deliberate and full of thought.

When he finally looked up and our eyes met, it was like someone flicked my chest, giving me a small jolt of tingling awareness.

He cocked one eyebrow. "Stalker."

I was surprised into smiling, and Dúfa trotted around my feet, giving a little *yip*. "You wish."

"How was town?"

"Towny. Meriwether doesn't hate me, so bonus there."

"Good. Things with her father okay?"

You know, it struck me right then that all those years with Incy, he never asked about anything in my personal life. He was eager to hear all the latest gossip, to know what everyone wore and if any drama had happened. But asking about more serious stuff? Not so much. It was nice that Reyn did. He had actually listened when I'd talked about Meriwether. Add several points to the Sensitivity column.

"She said they're better. I don't know. Hey, when I went into the house, a big whoosh of hoodoo practically knocked me down. Where is everyone? What are they doing?"

Reyn frowned at me as he unclipped Titus and led him to his large stall. Titus huffed at Reyn's head and was given one of the small windfall apples kept in barrels around the barn.

"What do you mean you felt it?" Reyn asked finally.

"The house. It's full of..." I didn't know how to describe it. "It feels like people are doing big spells there. I didn't see anyone. Do you know if something's going on?"

"This morning River mentioned that she and the teachers, and I guess her brothers, were going to do some scrying," Reyn said. He went to another stall and led one of the riding horses out into the aisle. "But I'm surprised you felt something. You know Sorrel," he told me, handing me the horse's lead.

"Hi, Sorrel," I said, uncomfortable about being this close to a horse. "Scrying spells for what?"

"I don't know. Hang on." He went to the tack room and

returned with a small, light saddle, the kind used for jumping. "Hold her."

He knew I didn't like being around horses, so he was losing whatever points he had gained in the Sensitivity column.

"Scrying spells for what?" I repeated.

"I really don't know," said Reyn, cinching the saddle. "Maybe to see if they can figure out the bigger picture, with Incy and 'the master' and all. Okay, here." He gestured to Sorrel and then interlocked his hands as if to give me a leg up.

I stared at him. "What are you doing?"

"It's a nice day. Let's go for a ride. You can have Sorrel."

"No. Way."

The look of calm patience that came over his face made me wary, as if I were a village about to be under siege. "I know you know how to ride."

I rode very well, and used to do it a lot. But having or even riding horses was one of those things that I'd let fall by the wayside over the years, as I (unsuccessfully, of course) tried to limit how many different ways I could get hurt by losing things. It was why I didn't have pets and why my closest friends had been people who could come and go without either of us feeling pain. Except for Incy.

These days I was uncomfortably aware of the tendrils of caring that were gradually ensnaring me: River and the other people here, Meriwether and Dray, the place itself, Reyn. My amulet. The more things I had to lose, the less safe I was. So far I'd been able to mostly quell the white-knuckled terror I felt at forming these connections, but every once in a while it smacked me upside the head again, full force—like when Reyn offered to let me share Dúfa or now, when he was pushing me to ride.

"I know you know how to break rocks with a hammer, but that doesn't mean I expect you to do it," I said.

Anyone, not just me, would have felt uneasy at the calculating glint in his amber eyes. Without a word he turned and got another horse from a stall. This one was almost solid black and larger than Sorrel, but its fine bones announced that it too was for riding and not for pulling a plow.

"I want to go riding with you." He quickly cinched a bigger, Reyn-size saddle on the black horse.

"I want world peace," I retorted.

Holding the black horse's lead, Reyn came to stand close enough to me that I could see the pulse beating at the base of his throat. Moving slowly, as if to give me time to run away like the coward I am, he lifted one hand and cupped my chin gently. My breathing sped up. Tracing one finger down my cheekbone was his next insidious move, and I pressed my lips together so I didn't humiliate myself with a little whimper. He leaned his head down, and I felt my stone wall of reserve start to wobble.

But he didn't kiss me. "Let's go riding, you and me," he said in a low voice. "Let's get away from here for a little while."

The heartless bastard. My worthless, tissue-paper resolve.

Ten minutes later we could no longer see River's Edge. The brisk air had whipped roses into my cheeks and burned in my lungs, and my legs were already feeling the ache of years spent doing nothing more than walking, shopping, and occasionally dancing.

Sorrel's tall, alert ears framed my view, and from the top of this low hill I saw splashes of brilliant yellow here and there, as far as I could see.

"Forsythia," I said, pointing.

"Spring." Reyn, of course, looked amazing on the back of that beautiful horse, riding effortlessly and with perfect form, reins held loosely in one hand. He'd probably learned to ride as I did, bareback and holding on to nothing more than a mane.

"I didn't know all these trails were here." Winding paths that Reyn clearly knew by heart led through acres of trees, gradually taking us uphill until we reached the top and could see for miles around us.

"They've been here for ages," Reyn said, brushing wind-blown hair out of his face. "They're pretty, but I wish there were some flat land where we could just tear across, going fast."

In my mind I saw him bent low over a horse's outstretched neck as it galloped across the northern steppes. He'd grown up like that, moving with his clan over thousands of miles of flat, treeless plain, shifting their herds from water to grass as the years spun out their cycles.

"It was a freer life." I didn't realize I'd spoken out loud until he turned and looked at me.

"There's a small clearing down this way." He kneed his horse forward, and I followed him, ducking under branches. Here and there I saw the first, tiniest buds of new growth on trees.

For several minutes we rode along a line of fencing, curving back toward River's Edge, and with a start I suddenly recognized the place where Incy had found me the night I'd run out, run away. Listening, I heard the faint sound of traffic—Incy had parked his car on the road and then searched for me. I'd been huddled, almost frozen, on the ground right by that fence post. It was a painful memory—how broken I'd felt, how without hope. I'd lain there and cried in the winter night until I'd practically made myself sick.

Then Innocencio had found me and plucked me up like a ripe cherry.

"How many times have you been married?" Reyn's quiet voice carried clearly above the sounds of hooves on leaves.

I blinked in surprise, my mind shying away from the memories of my marriages. But this was Reyn, and it would be more trouble to evade the question than to stumble down bad-memory lane. "Twenty-seven," I said primly.

"What?" His eyes were wide and startled as he half turned to face me.

"No. Two, actually. Both disasters, in different ways." Ugh. "How about you?" I asked, just as I realized that I really didn't want to hear about Reyn being married.

"Three." He shrugged. "To form alliances among the different tribes on the taiga. I either had to marry them or kill them."

I started to laugh and then swallowed it as I grasped that he meant it: He really would have had to kill them. Jeez. No pressure.

"The last one was in 1630 or so," he said. "Somewhere around there." He rubbed his chin, looking pensive. "Modern women…don't seem to think of me as marriage material." He looked at me and gave a short laugh, as if surprised to say something so personal. "More like a one-night stand. Or one crazy summer. More like that."

I could understand that. "Taciturn" and "dangerous" were probably not qualities one looked for in a life partner, but I'm just guessing here. Reyn seemed self-conscious, his back straight, and I wondered what had made him reveal so much.

"Well, you can imagine how wifey I come across as," I said, and checked off flaws on my fingers. "Not domestic, not affectionate, not nurturing, not patient. I could go on all day."

He gave me such an odd, speculative look that I pretended to suddenly be fascinated with a squirrel that was leaping from branch to branch overhead.

"Through here," he said. Another minute more and we passed between two large trees, like a gate, and were in the clearing. It was about thirty feet across, vaguely oval; scattered, rotting stumps told me it had once been tree-filled but then cleared for some purpose. To build a log cabin or something.

Reyn swung down smoothly and led his horse to a low-hanging branch. "Good boy, Geoffrey," he murmured, and smoothed his hand down the horse's velvety muzzle.

There was a strong possibility that my legs would just buckle under me if I tried to get down, but Reyn came over and took my hand.

"Come on," he said, with no-nonsense written all over his face.

I got down and stifled a shriek as my muscles straightened out again. "Why did I do this? Tomorrow I won't be able to walk."

"It always hurts at first, but then you get used to it." He shot me a laughing glance, and I rolled my eyes. "Let me know if you need me to rub you down." His voice was light, but the look in his deep golden eyes was hot and full of thrilling promise. I quickly turned away, double-checking my stirrup strap so I wouldn't drop to the ground and beg him to take me. That kind of thing makes a girl seem easy. Especially the begging part.

When I could finally control my face, Reyn was pulling a sword from a sheath.

"Again with the sword," I groaned.

"Yes," he said. "Again with the sword. And look what I brought, just for you." Reaching into his saddle pack, he pulled out a finer, thinner sword, maybe half the weight of the one I'd used last time. A girl sword. He presented it to me with a pleased look.

I took it. It was an épée, beautiful, inlaid with gold filigree. It looked quite old but had been so finely made that age hadn't touched it. Much like myself. It fit my hand as if I'd commissioned it, instantly becoming a seamless extension of my arm. I gave it an experimental swish.

"Some guys just give flowers," I pointed out.

"Yeah, and when whapping your bouquet against some enemy's head doesn't strike him down, don't come running to me," Reyn said. He swung his own sword into position. "En garde."

After an hour, I was practically weak with hunger—it was well past lunch—my arms were floppy foam approximations of their former selves, and my legs would never forgive me. The next day was going to be such a bummer. The palms of my hands were already blistered, I was tired and dirty, and my lungs burned from exercise. I felt so...alive. For the first time in—I couldn't remember when. I thought of my amulet, whole and complete, in my hidey-hole in my room, and thought, My life is not too bad right now.

And that unfamiliar feeling lasted several more minutes, until we arrived back at River's Edge and found total pandemonium: All the windows on the first floor had been blown out.

CHAPTER 9

t was one of those situations where you're glad you weren't on the *Titanic*, because look what happened. I was glad I'd been far away in the woods, so there was no way this could be pinned on me. Unless it had been aimed at me. In which case that was bad.

Reyn took the horses while I rushed to the house. Every single window on the first floor was shattered, their tall frames gaping. Glass and wood shards littered the yard. Rachel and Daisuke were wrapping large pieces in newspaper; Charles and Anne were raking up everything around the house, the four inches of leaves making that chore so much worse. After thinking a second, I ran and got our big rolly garbage bin. It was almost as big as me, but the wheels made it easier to push across the yard. My palms still burned from sword practice—as soon as I had a minute I would go in and slap Band-Aids all over them.

"Thanks—good thinking," Rachel said, and started filling it.

"What in the world happened?" I asked.

"It was during the circle," Anne said tensely, dumping a cardboard box of leaves and glass into the trash bin. She took the empty box and began to refill it. At this rate, we should have the area around the house spick and span by, like, August.

River came around the corner of the house. She looked harried and concerned but seemed relieved to see me.

"Nastasya!" She gave me a hug. "Are you all right? This whole thing happened, and no one could find you. I was worried this was part of something worse, and that you'd been hurt."

"Oh no, I'm fine," I stammered.

"Then we realized Reyn was gone, too," Brynne said, trying not to smirk. She wiped sweat off her forehead with one gloved hand. I shot her a look behind River's back, and she stifled a hint of a smile behind her worried expression.

"Reyn made me go for a ride," I said, throwing him under the bus.

"I'm glad you're both all right," said River. "Get yourself a pair of the leather work gloves so you don't cut yourself. God's wounds, what a mess." She hurried off toward Reyn, who had reappeared with a snow shovel and a tarp to pile leaves on.

"God's what?" Brynne asked.

I remembered that Brynne was only around 230 years old. "God's wounds," I said. "I haven't heard that in centuries. People said it in the fifteen hundreds. All the swears were God's teeth, God's wounds, God's eyes, God's blood. *God's wounds* became *zounds*. You've heard that one, right?"

"Yeah." Brynne straightened and looked around the yard. "This is going to take forever."

"Yeah," I echoed. "Maybe someone could put a spell on the glass pieces and, like, make them levitate or something?"

Brynne rolled her eyes. "You're an idiot."

"There's that word again," I muttered, and she laughed.

The trash bin was almost full now. Charles came and took it, saying, "I'll dump this down the well and bring it back." River had an old well that had gone dry. We often dumped trash down it, then set the trash on fire. It was about half-filled.

River came back toward us, looking pretty dispirited. "We've got some plywood in the barn to board up some of the windows, but Daniel and Reyn are going to the hardware store to get more. I guess I need to call a window company to get all of these replaced. How am I going to explain it?" She brushed a lock of silver hair off her forehead, leaving a faint streak of dirt.

"Science experiment gone wrong?" Brynne suggested. "Or frat party?"

"Seriously, though, what happened?" I asked.

River sighed. "We were having a circle in the front parlor. We wanted to try to find some bigger picture, see some sort of pattern of magick out in the world. It was all going fine—we were very strong, very powerful. And just as something was starting to take shape"—she frowned, as if trying to remember—"it all suddenly went weirdly, awfully awry. I couldn't even say what it was, but we looked at one another, each of us filled with dread and confusion. I was about to suggest dismantling the circle—and then all the windows blew out, not just the parlor ones. But everything inside is fine."

"That's really weird." I felt self-conscious, still feeling like I'd brought all this here.

"To put it mildly," River said.

"Okay, do you need anything besides a ton of plywood?" Daniel asked, walking up and jingling the truck keys. Reyn was with him—he looked serious and distant, a big contrast to how he'd been on our ride and during my sword lesson.

"Who's that?" Brynne shaded her eyes and gazed toward the driveway leading to the gravel parking area.

I looked where she pointed and saw a tall, raggedy-looking

character heading toward the house, a bag slung over his shoulder, like an old-fashioned hobo.

"Why..." River's voice trailed off. Astonishment widened her eyes, and her mouth dropped open.

"Whoa," said Daniel.

The tall man saw us in the side yard and headed toward us. River murmured, "What's his name now?"

Daniel shook his head. "Don't know," he said quietly. "It's been fifteen years or more since I saw him."

Behind me, I heard Reyn's quickly indrawn breath. His face was set in stone, his eyes narrowed. His chest rose and fell quickly as he stared at the stranger. What was that about?

River shoved her gloves at me and rushed at the man. "*Tesoro!*" she said, throwing her arms around him.

Darling? Okay, so maybe he was another one of her lost souls, come back for a refresher. This close I could see he appeared in sore need of rehab: His clothes were tattered; he looked hungry and in need of a shower. His face was hard and tough, his eyes bleak, as if he'd seen awful things and hadn't gotten over them. Had maybe been the cause of them. I shivered, glad that I was standing in a group of people and not meeting this guy in a dark alley at night.

The man returned her hug, but tentatively, as if his ribs hurt. Pulling back, he gave her a crooked grin, but even from twenty feet away I saw that it didn't reach his eyes.

He held River away from him, looking at her as if to memorize her face.

"Joshua," he told her.

"Joshua," River repeated. "My dear. I'm so glad to see you." She hugged him again and he put up with it, biding his time until she stopped.

"Come, *caro*," River said, leading him toward us. He followed slowly, his eyes running over us, but then he stopped so suddenly that River jolted, his hand clasped in hers.

I followed his gaze; it ran straight to Reyn. Glancing at them, I saw they looked eerily similar, with anger flushing their cheeks, their eyes narrowed and mean, hands clenched into fists at their sides.

"So," River said, letting out her breath in a sigh, "I take it you two know each other?"

As it turned out, Joshua was the third grumpy bear in the River's Brothers Collection. Was she the only one who had inherited a pleasant disposition?

Our dinner table was filling up with people and yet not exactly a gathering of light and lively conversation. Talk so far had been quiet and brief: *pass the salt, how's your cut?*, and so on. At this time of year, dinnertime was always dark, but today it seemed claustrophobic because the windows were boarded up; the large, ugly plywood panels screwed into place, chill wind seeping around their edges. Solis had lit fires in all the fireplaces downstairs because the radiators couldn't keep up.

River, Daniel, and Ott were happy to see Joshua but also

clearly shocked. Whether it was his appearance or just the fact that he was here, I didn't know. Also, they seemed to treat him tenderly, as if he were damaged in some way. Joshua himself looked tense and uncomfortable. He reminded me a lot of Reyn; a wild thing at heart, better suited to being outside and unconfined in any way. Sounds like a recipe for the perfect boyfriend, right? Someone who can't settle down? God help me.

Speaking of Reyn, he and Josh hadn't looked at each other since that first furious glance outside. They sat as far away from each other at the table as possible, and acted as if the other didn't exist. Veerrrry interesting.

Also very interesting was watching how Brynne watched Joshua, speculation in her brown eyes. Had Daniel fallen from favor so quickly? Was Brynne that self-destructive? Even clueless me could see that Joshua was an even worse romantic prospect than Reyn was.

Halfway through the meal, River sat up straighter and said: "Reyn, you and Joshua obviously recognized each other outside. What's the past history between you two?"

There was a tightening awareness all along the table as eyes focused on them and people quit chewing to pay attention.

Joshua said nothing, just looked at his plate and cut his meat into ever smaller pieces, like it was the liver of his enemy.

Reyn shot him a quick glance, and that alone was enough to make his face darken ominously. But all he did was shrug, mumbling something that no one could understand. He wasn't going to tell us anything. Gosh, guys are so fascinating and mysterious! It was *such fun.* I made a note to myself not to stand in between them—it seemed likely that they would suddenly try to kill each other for no reason. Or no reason that we knew, anyway.

"Joshua, what brings you to River's Edge?" Brynne's voice was calm and clear, her eyes expectant.

Joshua, startled, actually glanced at her. Of the four siblings, he looked the most different: His hair was medium brown and streaked by the sun, his face tanned and a bit weathered, where Daniel and Ottavio were both more groomed. Ottavio's eyes were black. Daniel's and River's were a lighter, clear brown, like tobacco juice, but Joshua's were tortoiseshell, marbled brown and green and blue.

Brynne waited, her gaze fixed on him.

Joshua looked around the table until he saw me. He nodded in my direction, then returned to his meal, eating deliberately as if forcing himself not to wolf it down.

Me again. "Oh, Jesus Christ," I muttered, putting my fork down.

"Not really, no," Reyn said with a cold cynicism. "Not quite."

Joshua's eyes lit with quick fury, and I held my breath because it seemed like something awful was about to happen.

River put her wineglass down hard. "There's dried-apple pie for dessert," she said, but she made it sound like a threat.

"I'll help you," said Daisuke, starting to gather plates. The weird mood was broken, or at least tamped down. But we were all left wondering what the hell was going on.

"Nastasya, wait." I paused at the top of the stairs as River caught up with me. Her face was drawn, and she looked tired. Tired of having grouchy siblings, I bet. "Slipping upstairs? What, you don't feel like having a fireside chat with my family?" she asked, humor lightening her lines of tension.

"Gosh, no thank you," I said. She chuckled, then grew more serious as she reached out and smoothed my hair off my shoulder, touching the fine wool scarf looped around my neck. She nodded down the hall. "Let's go to your room."

In my room I sat on my bed, but it was difficult—I itched to circle restlessly, trying to outpace the jumble of thoughts careening inside my head. The arrival of yet another brother, here because of how deeply dangerous I supposedly was, had shaken me. Ottavio was bad enough, then Daniel, now Joshua.

River hadn't said anything, and I looked up. She sat next to me, wearing her patient face.

"What?" I said.

"I don't want you to go," she said.

Until that moment, I hadn't realized that the idea had continued to slowly build inside me, even before Daniel offered to pay me to leave. But yes, in one bright insight I saw that it would be far better for me to leave here, to quit drawing negative attention to this place of healing and respite. I should leave; I should take my amulet and—

Then I realized what she had done: read my face. This time before the thought was even *on* my face.

"God*damn* it," I said, and she laughed. "You're just *creepy* now."

"I keep telling you: Your face is a map," she said, holding up her hands. "Ooh, we should have poker night, and with high stakes."

"Oh, ha ha," I said. I leaned over and turned the knob on my radiator to take the chill off the room. I did want to leave and knew she would talk me out of it. Time to change the subject. "So. You have to have all the windows replaced."

River nodded, looking serious again. "It was truly strange. It was...scary. We had raised so much good power, and I'd really hoped to get some answers. I want to know who the master is that Innocencio mentioned. I want to know who was controlling him."

I fiddled with the ends of my scarf. "It's because of me. If I weren't here, this wouldn't be happening."

"I don't know that," River insisted. "I have no idea why our circle went wrong—we have to figure that out. But one thing I do know is that...you're not really strong enough to be out in the world on your own." Her voice was gentle.

I wanted to disagree with her, so wanted to be a strong, together person who wouldn't be a liability, who could be trusted to set off into the world with only good things ahead. But with humbling honesty I had to admit that River was right—I wasn't strong enough to be out in the world by myself. I wasn't solid enough to be able to fight darkness and resist temptation.

"Whatever," I muttered, and she patted my knee, satisfied.

"I do have a suggestion," she said.

If it was another meditation circle, I was going to scream.

"I suggest that you find a larger project to occupy yourself with," she said. "I know you're studying, and that's good. But I've found it's also good to have a larger focus, to work toward something outside yourself."

I frowned. "Like what? Macramé?"

"No. Bigger. Something like..." River looked thoughtful. "Training a new horse? We could get one that's just for you. Or...the horse barn needs painting. We have ladders and everything. You'd need to scrape it first. Or we could give you your own plot of land, for whatever kind of garden you wanted." She seemed to warm up to this idea. "Like an old-fashioned herb garden, with knots made of boxwood! We could put a fountain in the middle. By the time it's ready for planting, it'll be warm enough. That could be really fun."

I was trying not to stick my fingers down my throat at these suggestions. River was only trying to help.

"Okay, well, think about it," she said, standing up. "But in summary: leaving, no; project, yes. Right?"

"Could you write that down for me?"

Smiling, she leaned over and kissed my cheek. "I'll tattoo it on your butt while you sleep."

"I wouldn't be able to see that!" I called as she slipped out my door. I heard one final chuckle as the door closed, and then I was left alone with my thoughts.

And I'd forgotten to get her to speculate about what was going on between Reyn and Joshua.

here are books written about the known history of immortals. Every once in a while one makes it into some rare book auction, where it's treated as a fascinating work of fiction. It's common knowledge that quite a few books are in hidden libraries in some of the oldest monasteries around the world. The scuttlebutt is that the monks know it's all true, but are keeping mum until they figure out how we fit in with God and the hereafter and salvation and whatnot. We're, like, keep us posted.

Over the centuries, I'd seen books written by immortals. I mean, of course, there are many immortals who are writing current bestsellers and cookbooks and children's books, etc. (No, I'm not giving up names.) (Though you would no doubt recognize them.) But I mean books *about* immortals. I myself have never actually read one written by an immortal. Part of the whole keep-my-head-in-the-sand plan that I've clung to for so long.

But no more! New Alert Nastasya was hunkered down in the workroom this morning, poring over a weighty tome called *The House of Morcroft*. It was from 1679, badly typeset, and beautifully bound in embossed leather once accented with gold leaf. I'd been wading through the text, wishing that the quaint custom of standardized spelling had caught on hundreds of years before it did.

After I'd skimmed the boring and obsessive history of the illustrious Morcrofts (one of whom I'd actually met in the late seventeen hundreds—total yawner), the book got more interesting and branched into a more general history of immortals. This guy, Sir Thomas Morcroft, claimed to trace his family back almost two thousand years, but of course the earliest records were oral histories handed down for centuries. If you've ever played a game of telephone, you'll understand my skepticism at believing that these tales even remotely resembled the truth. But Thomas included many of his dealings with other immortals and recounted what he knew of certain families or individuals. He'd tried to be a true historian, and it was interesting. If dense.

I wondered how far back my own history had gone, how

much my parents had known about their pasts. My father had had a library—a rarity at the time but appropriate for the local king. All the books had been burned to ashes, of course, in the fire set by Erik the Bloodletter. Had any of the books been our family's saga? Or my father's own diary? If only there were some way, some other source to find out where my family had come from, what they had done.

When my head started aching (so far, seven different spellings for the word *chronicle*), I put a candy wrapper in place as a bookmark and turned my attention to a book about crystals.

Though my interest in crystals and gems is most heightened when they're set into gold and worn on my person as decoration, they *are* intriguing in and of themselves. I mean, this planet is basically made of dirt and water. Yet all over the world, physical events have changed some of the dirt into stunning crystalline formations in every possible color. Very early on, humankind attached special importance and value to these unusual rocks. And now, knowledge and interest in them can easily fill years or decades of study.

Which I, you know, was not willing to sign up for. But I was perfectly happy to flip through some books, look at the pretty pictures, and brush up on the most pertinent info.

Take salt, for example. From the earliest of times, salt has been considered sacred for a multitude of—

The workroom door opened, but I was busily making notes and wanted to keep going long enough for whoever it was to see me busily making notes. Then I looked up, ready to enjoy the virtuous feeling of being found studying *on my own*, only to see...Joshua. He seemed more rested and was wearing clean clothes, his hair still wet from a shower. He still didn't look civilized. Like someone else I know.

He left the door open behind him, his marbled hazel eyes taking in me, the room, the boarded-up windows. Reyn always did that, too—scoped any room he was in. It had taken me a while to realize why: He was unable to *not* plan escape routes. In case a rival horde sprang on him with no warning. Here in modern-day western Massachusetts.

"What do you want?" I said, launching the first sally.

"Asher said I could look through some of his books." Joshua's voice was low and even, not as raspy and ruined as Jess's, but not even close to the modulated, sophisticated tones of his brothers.

I waved a hand at the low bookcases framing the window seats. "Wear yourself out."

He moved the way Reyn did, with controlled animal grace and implied power. I had personally seen Reyn in action as a marauder, hundreds of years ago—he'd been terrifying, bloodthirsty, violent. He and his clan had been the scourge of the northern countries for several of my lifetimes, until I finally moved far enough south, out of their range. It was still odd for me to see him as the Reyn of today, the puppy-totin', cow-milkin', um, sword instructor, kissing master, and heart-stealer that I'd gotten to know a bit.

Now here was Joshua, clearly not a northern raider, not a Viking, but with all the Viking berserker qualities I recognized. Here because of me.

"I meant, what do you want with *me*?" I spoke to his broad back, the maroon henley sweater stretching over his shoulders as he knelt to see a lower shelf. He pulled a thick book out of the shelves, flipped through a few pages, and then came to sit at my table in a chair opposite me.

"Really?" I said. "You're going to sit there and pretend to read, right across from me, and I'm not going to suspect a thing, right? Are you serious?"

His quiet gaze would have gotten to me if my skin wasn't as thick as a rhino's. "River said you bluffed a lot."

"What? No, she didn't! I'm not—I don't bluff!" Of course, I bluffed all the time, but I couldn't believe River was telling everyone.

"Ottavio said you were yappy and annoying, like a Chihuahua."

I saw red. For one thing, Chihuahuas are awfully cute, and have been totally maligned in modern culture, in my opinion. "Well, Ottavio's a pompous windbag, so there you go. And don't even start with Daniel's pearls of wisdom."

Joshua opened Asher's book on herbal spells and began to read. I didn't for one second think he was truly here to read, but I took a deep breath and focused on the page about rubies while I regrouped. We both looked up when Brynne passed the doorway lugging a vacuum cleaner, but only I saw her lean back in the doorway and make an OMG face, shaking one hand as if Joshua was *too* hot. Then she pressed her hand to her forehead and pretended to swoon out of my sight. Daniel was definitely a thing of the past, but I had no idea what she saw in Joshua. His major qualities were the ones I found the least attractive in Reyn.

Speaking of which. "So how do you know Reyn?" I asked.

The colors of his eyes were like...oil on water, shifting and unfixed, green and brown and a deep shade of gray blue. Unnerving and not nearly as compelling as, say, eyes that were a deep golden color, the gold of buried treasure, of my amulet itself.

"How do *you* know him?" he countered, like a second grader.

"His father killed my family and burned our castle down," I said evenly. "My mother killed his brother and then caused the death of his father, a couple brothers, and seven of their men. Your turn."

Surprise flickered in his eyes, and he looked at me more deeply. I gazed steadily back at him. Inside, my breathing had quickened and my heart had sped up, as it always did when I even got close to the memories of my family. But I'd wanted to shock Joshua; I'd wanted to strip this situation down to the bone and put it into perspective.

"Reyn and I have been on...opposite sides of quite a few battles," Joshua said slowly. "I was a mercenary, and so was he."

Oh, a mercenary. A soldier for hire. There's a surprise.

"Wait—hold the phone. Let me get this straight," I said.

"You guys were fighting for *money*, fighting battles *not even your own*, and you were on opposite sides, so now, *however much later* this is, you're going to be assholes to each other? These weren't even your wars, defending your own families or whatever. You were there for *money*. But you're right, and he's totally wrong? And vice versa?"

Joshua regarded me stonily.

"Oh my God, you're such morons." I rubbed my eyes and pushed my growing-out bangs off my face. "Such freaking idiots. Just quit talking to me. My God." I shook my head and focused on my book again, the words swimming across the page as I blinked angrily.

Joshua shifted in his chair, got another book, and spent minutes watching me, which I could feel like a caterpillar on my skin, but I spared him not a glance. Instead I wrote down some spells of protection that used crystals and made a list of crystals that I hoped we had in the storeroom.

I found a long section about moonstone, which I regarded as "my" stone. It had been my mother's stone, too—perhaps our family's stone for centuries. Another thing I would never know. As I read about different rituals using moonstones, River's words about having a larger project came back to me. I hadn't come up with anything. I could barely clothe and feed myself, much less take on anything bigger. In the old days, I'd been all about getting ahead, piling up the coinage. Most enterprises I'd attempted had been successful: my lace shop, in Napoli. My decades as a thief. My oil-baron shenanigans in Texas. But the last real "project" I'd had was a hundred and fifty years ago, in California, during the gold rush.

If you weren't alive during the gold rush, I don't think you could really understand what it was like. It truly was a fever, sweeping around the world. I was in France when the newspapers started to be full of stories about the rivers of gold in California. Followed quickly by reports about California becoming part of the United States. Coincidentally.

Well, I was up for an adventure, so I took a ship to New York, then a train as far west as I could go, then joined one of those picturesque wagon trains you've heard about, and headed to California.

Once we left from Ohio, the journey took four months. Out of fifty-two wagons, there were three women, and I was the only unmarried one. But I'd had money enough to buy some sturdy horses, a well-made wagon with a canvas roof, and a bunch of practical supplies. Such as a large German shepherd and a whole bunch of guns.

By the end of the trip, there were fifteen wagons left. More than thirty people had died. We'd passed uncountable numbers of discarded belongings; dead horses, oxen, and cows; broken wagons; human remains that there was no time to bury. When we reached Sacramento, I weighed about ninety pounds, had long since given up bathing, and my three dresses were essentially rags. But my cargo was intact, my horses were alive, and my dog, Heinz, had proven his weight in—ha ha—gold.

I settled north of Sacramento in a shantytown called Hastings Bar. When I first got there, Hastings Bar consisted of ten canvas tents, four men to a tent. Within three months, it was a town of almost twelve thousand people, with hundreds more coming every day. I say "people," but really, they were almost all men. There was no police force, no court, no law except what the locals organized themselves. Of the twelve thousand people, all but about five hundred lived in tents, winter and summer. The houses and buildings that were there had been thrown together in a hurry by men who thought only of gold with every board they sawed and every nail they sank. But my establishment was sturdy enough.

My name had been Charity Temple, and I told everyone I was a widow. I ran a combination hotel/brothel, and in eighteen months I made close to a million dollars. In 1850s currency.

That had been a successful project, larger than myself.

I was grinning a little, remembering how I'd pulled a rifle on a would-be thief—the look on his face had been priceless—when I realized that Joshua was still sitting across from me, his eyes boring holes in my forehead.

"What do you *want?*" I asked, irritated.

"I want you to leave my sister alone." Heat and danger seemed to shimmer off him.

I frowned. "How about we all agree that River is a big girl and can decide for herself?"

"How about you leave here and never come back? How about you run back to your master and tell him he's got a bigger fight on his hands than he could possibly imagine?"

If I were a regular person, I would probably find his threatening scowl and implied threat intimidating. But you go through enough wars, famines, attacks, etc., and it takes more than a mean look to make you quake in your boots.

"You know, one day your face will freeze like that," I said, sounding bored and standing up. "Then, my friend, your career as a gigolo will be *over*." I swept out of the room as he was still trying to find words.

I needed to move. The sun outside was trying to shine a little more brightly, but here at River's Edge there was a frowny face wherever I turned. Without asking anyone, I grabbed the keys to one of the farm cars (the little car I'd bought had been totaled), and drove off toward town.

Like, our big, exciting town, right? The one street. The bright lights and madcap excitement. I parked in front of Early's and rested my head in my hands on the steering wheel, trying hard not to feel pathetic, and failing. I mean, even failing at *this*. Just too sad.

Time for some candy.

Early's was a big, old-fashioned general store, with the same wide plate-glass windows as Pitson's on one side and then the smaller shops like MacIntyre's Drugs on the other side. Early's stocked clothes (not cute clothes—practical clothes), animal feed, books, magazines (but no comfy place to sit and read them), candy, kayaks, shoes (not cute shoes), seeds, garden tools—most anything that anyone around here might need or want. Unless you were me.

I came in here regularly either on errands or for myself, to stock up on cheap tabloid magazines and candy.

As I perused Ye Olde Candy Aisle, I noticed all the hearts and cupids littering the place. What day was this? I wandered over to the newspaper stand and glanced at a date. February 7. So Valentine's Day was rocketing toward us. But you know, all this stuff was really...cheap and typical. There was nothing interesting or crafty or homemade. Surely some people here would want something like that? There needed to be a little shop with craft supplies for ambitious knitters or scrapbookers or whatever things people did to keep themselves off the street.

As I checked out, I thought about Dray. I hadn't seen her since before I'd gone to Boston. She'd been pissed at me. I'd been pissed at her, having seen her jacking stuff at Early's when I'd been convinced that Saint Nastasya was helping her turn over a new leaf.

Anyway, I wondered if she was okay—if she was still living with her loser family, or if she'd managed to get out of this town like I'd told her to do.

And since I was down here, and Meriwether, at least, didn't hate me, I decided to pop in and see her. I checked my watch—it was after five; she should be at work. The bell over the door at MacIntyre's jingled as I went in. I heard Old Mac talking in the back, but I walked quietly along the aisles until I saw Meriwether—who was talking to a boy. The boy's back was to me, but from Meriwether's face I could tell that he wasn't asking her where the jock powder was. She was smiling and blushing, keeping her voice down.

When I caught her eye, I gave her a silent thumbs-up. Just then the boy looked down, and Meriwether quickly mouthed *Lowell* at me. Lowell was the boy she'd had a crush on, who had taken her to the Christmas Dance that Dray and her friends had crashed and ruined.

I gave a big smile back and silently edged away and left the store. My heart was lightened by Meriwether's budding romance. I was such a softy. Not really. But this was still fun. I was opening the car door when my eyes fell once again on the abandoned shops. I dropped the candy bag on the front seat and headed across the street.

CHAPTER 11

ou...what?" River's eyes were wide with surprise.

I slid into a place at the dining table—dinner was almost over, since I'd gotten held up in town. Rachel passed me the bread, and Asher ladled some soup into a bowl.

"I bought those abandoned shops on Main Street," I repeated, gulping down some tea. My nose was still cold, and the warm mug felt good in my chilled fingers.

"What do you mean, bought?" Brynne asked.

"I mean I called the agent and bought the shops," I said,

dunking the bread into the chicken matzo-ball soup. Oh, God, it was so good. Hot, chickeny—yum.

"You couldn't have gotten a mortgage so quickly." Ottavio's eyes were—wait for it—suspicious. About my dangerous, property-buying ways.

"I don't need a mortgage. I wrote them a check. I have lots of money." I gave Daniel a meaningful look, like, keep your stinking hundred million dollars.

"Lots of money?" Ottavio seized that information. "And where did you get this money?"

Even I was startled when Amy pelted Ott with a piece of bread. Don't get me wrong, I was loving the hard time she was giving him, but it was like throwing rocks at a land mine. Sooner or later there would be an ugly explosion.

Ott's face turned purple, and he opened his mouth, but River sighed. "Please, Ottavio."

I cut up my matzo ball with my spoon. "Weirdest thing. Some guy named the master transferred millions into my account." I stopped cutting and looked up. "Wait—is that bad?"

"What are you planning to do with the shops?" Charles asked before Ottavio could reply.

"I confess I was thinking more along the lines of you taking up watercolors," said River.

Watercolors. Because I'm so good at sitting still, right?

"I was thinking that I would throw money at the shops

until they become cute, and then open this town's sorely needed cozy coffee emporium," I said, and poured myself more tea from the insulated pitcher. "There will be three shops left. I can't help but notice—and don't take this the wrong way, I know you love it here—but West Lowing desperately needs a source of fashionable footwear. And where is the local craft nook, with Tuesday night Stitch 'n' Bitch sessions? Again, a distinct lack thereof."

I inhaled more soup and took another piece of bread. All of this real-estate mogulry had made me starving. "And a good consignment shop, or perhaps an ice-cream parlor, would not come awry." I tilted my head and assumed a dreamy expression. "That's my big project: to save West Lowing. As I myself am being saved."

Reyn swallowed something wrong and coughed.

I shot River a glance. "I'm still being saved, right?"

"Still giving it the old Girl Scout try," she said wryly.

"I think it sounds superfun," said Brynne. "And of course you would do anything to get out of painting the barn." She grinned at me, and I shrugged cheerfully.

"I'd like to point out that this is a totally nonevil thing for me to do," I told the brothers with sickening earnestness. "It's creating something, making jobs for people, helping the town's economy." I batted my eyes innocently.

Ottavio looked like he'd swallowed a frog, but he didn't need Heimliching this time, so that was good. Daniel's face was a mask of irritation, probably from finding out that I didn't need his money. Joshua's weary, cynical eyes looked at me with steady speculation.

"It's a great idea," said Anne. "I've often wished someone would do something with those shops. River, remember when we would always go to Schwalbach's for their lunch special? And the watch-repair shop was right next door. Who was it who kept breaking all his watches?"

River thought. "Ted."

"Oh, right, Ted. The man with the cursed wrist." Anne shook her head. "Anyway, Nastasya, it's a very ambitious project. Good for you."

"Thank you. Is there dessert?"

"Pear cobbler," said Asher. "And then you, Reyn, and Anne are on cleanup duty."

Someday, grasshopper, *someday*, you too may experience the heart-pounding, burning frustration and excitement that arises from washing dishes with your crush. Maybe it's the soapy, sudsy warmth, or the splishy-splashiness of the— okay, I'm making even myself ill. What I mean to say is Reyn up to his elbows in suds, doing dishes, was a huge turn-on. Of course, Reyn walking around covered in muck was a huge turn-on, too.

Anne had slithered out of cleanup duty by offering to make cookies. True, they were healthy cookies made with tofu and sesame seeds and whole-wheat flour, but they were still good enough to bribe me with.

"The more magick I do, the more I crave sugar," Anne said, scraping dough off a spoon with her finger. "I noticed that maybe a hundred years ago. I wonder why that is?"

"I read that in a fantasy book," I said, wiping a plate dry. I'd casually mentioned the efficiency of a commercial dishwasher several times to River, who had pretended not to hear me each time. "They kept eating muffins and honey."

"I haven't noticed it," said Reyn, and Anne and I made faces at each other behind his back.

Anne slid one cookie sheet into the oven and started filling another. The kitchen windows were still boarded up, and thin streams of late-winter air whispered in around their edges. But with the oven going and all this hard physical labor I was doing, the kitchen was warm and cozy. This place, River's Edge, seemed warm and cozy to me. (Okay, except for the three ancient Italians muttering grumpily in the dining room.)

I stopped drying for a second when I realized how much it felt like home, a real home. My home. Would I still be here three years from now? Would I be here long enough to see what happened with my shops? Buying them had been a commitment.

Not that I haven't walked away from a thousand commitments, big and small, all over the place for hundreds of years. But time had yet to reveal whether I would walk away from this one. It would be interesting if I didn't.

"So," I said to Reyn, "are you up for helping me with the

shops?" He'd been stiff and distant, or, I should say, stiffer and more distant ever since Joshua had arrived. During dinner he'd said not a word, and even here in this sudsy wonderland, he wasn't getting into all the comforting domesticity of the scene.

"Why?" Reyn's voice was, yes, stiff and distant. "You want me to be a creator, instead of a destroyer? Is that it?"

Anne and I exchanged a quick glance, and she raised her brows.

I rolled my eyes and took a plate from him. "Yes. Because helping me with these shops will make up for everything else you've ever done." The plate joined its friends on the table, and I flicked Reyn's arm with my dish towel. "What's wrong with you?"

In that endearing way he had, he didn't answer me, just washed plates and glasses with a bit more force than necessary. I let out a deep breath, kept drying, and directed all of my conversation to Anne. Gosh, he was a heartthrob.

I stood at my bedroom door, listening. I'd left it cracked just a bit and so far had heard Lorenz, then Rachel and Amy, then Solis, then Charles come up the stairs and pass my door. Finally I heard it. Or rather, I almost didn't hear it: the faintest of footsteps. I got ready to put my plan into action, and then prayed this was Reyn, because I'm guessing Joshua would sound exactly the same.

I closed my eyes and held my breath for just a few

moments, opening up my senses. Yep, it was Reyn. And...

Dúfa. Every person (and apparently every dog) has a unique energy pattern, and when I concentrated, I could feel it.

Just as they were passing my door, I opened it, lunged, and grabbed Reyn's arm. Of course he reacted instinctively, already snaring my wrist to break my hold even as I tried to drag him inside my room. Dúfa yipped and jumped around my feet as we fell clumsily through the doorway. I kicked the door shut behind us.

"What are you doing?" He sounded angry. "I could have killed you!" Dúfa gave a couple more yips, like, *Yeah! We could have* killed *you!*

Keep in mind this was a very young puppy that was probably still nursing.

"I know, you big bad warrior you. But I thought if I just asked you in, you might ignore me and stalk past."

Golden eyes narrowed.

Now that I had him here, I had no idea what I'd been thinking when I concocted this stupid plan. I hadn't really thought it through—just, oh, get Reyn somewhere private so you can talk. Now I was faced with actually having him in my room, and all coherent thoughts were running for cover. He made my room seem so much smaller.

Plus, you know, we were alone and there was a bed, right there. I'm just saying.

Long-legged, skinny Dúfa started sniffing around my room, and I cleared my throat. Time to pull out the gentle, caring sensitivity I'm not widely known for. "You seem even more uptight and angry than usual. What the hell is wrong with you?"

Muscles tightened in his jaw, and perhaps this was a bit late, but I quickly reviewed my most recent actions, weighing them for rage-worthiness.

Bluffing, I widened my eyes and raised my eyebrows in a *Well?* gesture, and when he continued to be all seethy, I picked up Dúfa and sat down on my bed so he wouldn't see how unnerved he made me. Dúfa sniffed me and licked my chin.

"Good dog," I muttered awkwardly, giving her narrow back a little pat.

Reyn stood very still, various unpleasant emotions crossing the rough, lovely, angular landscape of his face.

"Are you having trouble narrowing it down?" Oh, yes, there will be snideness.

His chin lifted. "Maybe this is a bad idea," he said, his voice so low, I leaned forward to hear better. "You and me."

My heart dropped down into my stomach and curled up into a cold little ball. I had not seen that coming. He'd been pursuing me with winter-raider tenacity for months, and for all my complaining and pushing away, I'd gotten used to him coming back, again and again.

"What?" I managed. Then I went from zero to pissed in a millisecond. "Oh, no, you don't! You don't get to wear me down for months and then suddenly back out."

"I hadn't really thought it through." He was practically twitching with discomfort.

I stared at him, then pushed Dúfa off my lap, went to my wardrobe door, and yanked out my sword. "Do not make me use this," I threatened. "You're not weaseling out of this!" I pointed the sword at him, aware, of course, that he could snap the fine blade in two with his little finger.

His chin came up and the sudden crafty look in his eyes made me wary. "Weasel out of what?"

And that's why he'd been able to have a long, successful career as an alpha male: He could think on his feet, effortlessly forcing me to define what he was trying to weasel out of. Which meant I had to give it a name. Which I'd refused to do, even to myself. The closest I'd gotten was "this thing between us."

"This thing between us," I said haughtily.

"Our *relationship?*" he pressed, and I almost gagged. The whole thing between us was so inexplicable. My psychological comfort insisted that it be kept as nebulous as possible. Something in me needed to be able to pretend this didn't exist, partly because I still couldn't understand it or justify it, and partly so I wouldn't be hurt when it went wrong. Except now he was trying to get out of it, and I was mad and upset, so clearly I was already emotionally invested. Sparks of panic flickered around my brain, and I wanted to throw up.

"Ew," I said, and sat down on my bed, the sword dangling from one hand. I hate emotional insights. Can't we just keep the closet of my psyche firmly locked? Perhaps boarded up? I really think that would be better for everyone.

Reyn looked less bleak. "So you don't want me to go?" "Less bleak" turned to "cautiously pleased," and I began to realize how much I'd given away. Because I had pulled a sword on someone trying to break up with me. Crap.

"Of course I want you to go," I said, unbearably vulnerable. "Just . . . when *I* say so. Not you."

"Uh-huh." Reyn pushed a hand through his hair and sat down on the end of my bed. Dúfa ecstatically climbed onto his lap to lick his chin. She sure was a licky little dog. "Okay, well, I don't want to devastate you."

Oh my God. Such a jerk. And I had brought this on myself. Goddamn sword.

"It's just . . . sometimes I forget who I am," he said. "And sometimes I remember who I am." We were back to bleakness, and it came to me: Joshua's arrival, even more than mine, had brought back memories, things he regretted, aspects of himself that he was trying to leave behind.

"That was who you were," I said. "Not who you are today." See how easy it is for me to tell other people the exact same things that I can't hear myself?

"You don't understand."

"I know. *I've* never done *anything* I regret."

That earned me a searing, golden-eyed look.

"Then help me understand," I said. "Also, don't let your dog chew on my sock."

"How?" Frustration underlined his voice.

"Take it away from her."

"No." I heard the implied *You idiot*. "I meant, there's no way to make you understand."

Outside, the night wind was blowing against the windowpanes, but my radiator hissed with warmth. The clean-laundry scent of Reyn's plaid shirt floated around me and obviously contained pheromones designed to make me want to knock him down and—

I got an idea. "There might be a way...."

iver and I had done this twice, so that I could see parts of River's past that were intended to make me feel a weensy bit better about my own. And they had, because River had been—extremely ambitious. Ambitious and conscienceless. A bad combination.

This was almost certainly not a good idea. I was positive we weren't ready to share anything but the most superficial of emotions. But maybe it would help him, the way seeing River's past had helped me.

I got off the bed and slid beneath it, aware that I would now have to find a new hiding place. With my fingernails I pried off the piece of loose molding that hid the hole chipped out of the wall plaster, and the space behind it. My fingers tingled as I reached for the knotted handkerchief, and my breath felt shallower as I pulled it out and sat on my bed again.

Reyn was very still as I undid the knots with trembling fingers.

"I don't think—" he said, his voice quiet but with a harsh edge.

"So many men don't," I muttered, and pulled out my amulet.

We stared at it as it dangled from its heavy gold chain, twisting slowly between us, this thing that had marked us both forever.

"Have you seen it repaired?" I asked.

He shook his head silently and didn't reach out to touch it. It was so alive in my hand, vibrating with energy. Now I was going to make magick with it. Like a teenager with a learner's permit deciding it was a great idea to borrow her dad's Porsche.

I put the amulet around my neck, the first person to do so in 449 years. Even Dúfa seemed affected by the solemnity of the event, and sat on the end of my bed with her small white head cocked, her pink-rimmed hazel eyes watching us.

When River had conducted the mind-joining spell, it had taken us almost fifteen minutes to really connect, so that I could see her memories through her eyes. It was weirdly fast with me and Reyn, and it seemed that I'd barely started the form before I was startled by a flat, snow-covered landscape stretching endlessly out before me....

Horrifying images flashed in my mind, and I couldn't stop them: I saw my mother flaying Reyn's uncle, the bits of flesh tearing through the links of his chain mail—but it was different than I remembered it that night. It took me a second, and I blinked, confused, but then realized that I was seeing everything through Reyn's eyes, through his mind. His emotions. It was surreal to see these devastatingly familiar scenes overlaid with a different viewpoint.

I saw Reyn's father killing my siblings without a second thought. Reyn saw the gouts of blood arcing through the air, smelled the hot, coppery stink of it. He felt the cool stone hallways of the castle; the warm air in that room, rolling out through the doorway where he stood. My mother shouted harsh words he didn't understand, but no one else made a sound: not Reyn's father, even when Sigmundur had sliced deeply into his arm; not my sisters as their heads were lopped off. Reyn saw Tinna's head and thought with a pang that she'd been vividly pretty, even in death, even as her golden hair landed in a puddle of blood.

Reyn had been told to stay in the hall and keep watch.

He prayed for some of Úlfur's men to run toward him so he could chop them down like trees and prove his worth. Though he'd been going on his father's raids since he was fifteen, this was Erik's most ambitious and had required days of watching and waiting as he plotted out the timing and the steps of the attack.

The scene changed suddenly: Reyn was on a sturdy, rough-coated white horse, its breath coiling in plumes from its nostrils as it ran on a road dense with hard-packed snow. My father's castle, barely a mile away, was in flames that reached three times its height into the deeply black sky. Even before Erik's men had ridden away, its large blocks of stone had been splitting from the heat with enormous *cracks*, like thunder from lightning close enough to touch. Reyn wondered if he was imagining feeling tiny ashes floating through the night air, landing on his hair and cheeks. He thought he could smell burning flesh. They'd left his uncle and his brother Temur in that castle, dead. They would be among the ones burning.

Reyn's father and his men, Reyn's two remaining brothers, and Reyn himself had raced from the castle on their horses, thick-boned and heavy-coated—proper warhorses— thinking that their decimation of my father's castle was so complete that no one would dare to come after them.

Heavy leather bags full of loot swung against the side of Erik's horse. Minutes later he reined to a stop, slid to the ground, and tipped the bags bottom up, dumping their contents onto the snow. The night was so still and quiet that they could faintly hear the screams of my father's villagers as they watched their lord's castle splinter.

"Strike a torch, you," Reyn's father directed, and a man named Selke did, the flame showing his mail spattered with blood that also striped his face and hair. "We left Nori and Temur behind. But let's see what we brought away."

Reyn's brother Temur had been older than him by more than a hundred years. Reyn had been told that, but it was an idea he had trouble grasping. He'd heard people say that Nunc Nori was 520, but again that had seemed like ancient history. Reyn was twenty; his mother—his father's fourth wife—was thirty-six. All their talk of ages and centuries seemed like fairy stories.

"Eileif, watch the road," his father said, using Reyn's birth name, and Reyn did but cast quick glances at what Selke's torch illuminated.

"Books!" said his brother Gurban, so named because he was the third son. "Papi, you brought *books*?"

"Books can be more valuable than gold, nitwit," said Reyn's father. He set them aside in a pile and sifted through the rest. I almost gasped as Erik picked up my mother's small wooden chest, beautifully inlaid with ivory, that used to sit on a special shelf in her room. When he shook the chest, gold jewelry I recognized and loose gemstones tumbled out onto the leather bag. The men laughed when they saw it—the winter would be easier with this wealth. I felt the men's curiosity and then dismissal as Erik held up my father's celestial compass, entwined brass circles with animals and figures engraved on them: a bull, a man pouring water from a jug, a crab, a pair of twins. Reyn's father, not understanding its purpose or significance, threw it aside.

It was becoming harder and harder for Reyn to keep his eyes focused on that narrow road, its blue-white snow disappearing in the distance. His father held up our red goblets carved from crystal and overlaid with filigree gold. "I want to drink mead from this!" he said, and his men laughed as my eyes burned with memories of my parents drinking from those goblets.

One by one Erik the Bloodletter picked up the objects and put them aside, as if he were looking for one particular thing. And then he held up the broken half of my mother's amulet, a ring of gold hanging from a gold chain of thick, finely worked links. To Reyn it looked like another necklace, but his father was awestruck, tracing the patterns on the front with a thick, bloodstained finger. The back was smooth and plain and a brighter gold than the front.

"This is it," he breathed.

"Aye?" Selke said, sounding doubtful.

"Aye," Reyn's father said firmly.

I saw Reyn, his face tense, insist that it wasn't safe. But his father held a circle right there on the side of the road, where they would be visible as soon as anyone came around the southern bend. He put Selke's torch in the middle, and they joined hands around it, like for one of their festivals. Reyn's father put the golden chain around his neck and began to sing.

It was a bizarre sensation, feeling the bloodlust of battle begin to seep out of Reyn's bones, leaving him cold and weary. He was hungry and thirsty and didn't want to be on this road, so exposed, so vulnerable. His head started to ache as his father sang, and I felt the pressure increasing until it felt like someone had cut off the top of his skull, poured in liquid pain, and closed it up again. Risking his father's anger, he broke from Sven's hand and put his palm to his ear as if to keep his brains from spurting out. Through lightning-laced tunnel vision Reyn saw that every man there, including his father, also looked in torment. But the fierce mask of determination on his father's face was one Reyn knew well: Nothing would stop him except death.

Very dimly I was aware, as Reyn was, of the horses shrieking in panic. I heard them break free and run off into the woods. Reyn wavered on his feet, about to faint. Suddenly there was a horrible splitting sound, as if God himself had struck an axe into stone. A sudden burning punch to Reyn's chest knocked him breathless backward into the snow, and as he struggled to get up, a humming white tornado of flame roared up from Selke's torch and gathered every man in, like a mother cradling children to her breast. By the time Reyn had blinked twice, everyone was…gone. The flame died and sputtered out. There was nothing except a perfect circle of scorched earth, fifteen feet wide. Months ago Reyn had told me what happened, but seeing it right in front of me through his eyes, feeling his shock and fear, was so much more horrible than I'd ever imagined.

Reyn struggled to his feet, his chest numb with a searing pain. In shock he looked down and saw a hole right through his thick leather breastplate, the one hard enough to deflect almost anything except a spear or a broadsword.

There's a children's game where one turns in a circle, looking for hidden clues, and Reyn felt like that now, dumbly staring at the untouched trees, the melted snow running over the scorched ground. I felt his disbelief as he looked but couldn't find even lumps of melted chain mail. Not a trace of burned books. Not a splinter of rent crystal. No skin. No bones. No gold. As if none of it had existed.

Reyn sat back down in the snow, his mind reeling, ill with confusion and a burning agony he couldn't escape. His chest felt as if someone had rammed a red-hot spear through it. It took minutes to unbuckle the leather straps at his shoulders with trembling fingers, but at last he eased the armor off, dropping it in the snow. Beneath it he wore a fur jerkin. There was a hole in it, tinged by blood. Even though he was shaking with shock and cold, he took it off. Beneath it, his linen undershirt was soaked in blood, and through a hole in the cloth was a circle of raw, charred flesh that hurt more than anything he'd ever felt, hurt enough to make him feel sick and faint.

Reyn thought, I'm going to die here, tonight. He had no horse, no companions. He was numb and ill and close to passing out. Any minute now someone would come down the road, either from the next village to find out what the fire was, or one of my father's terrified villeins, what few there were left, fleeing the site of devastation and horror.

All he had to do was lie down. The cold and snow would do the rest. He'd heard it was a peaceful, relatively painless death, freezing. You just got sleepy, you quit shaking, and then you drifted off. He'd seen enough of our kind die to believe that he, too, could die, and maybe that easily.

At that moment, that sounded like what Reyn should do. His father was gone. His brothers. His father's men. Why should he be left alive?

Then he saw it.

Stuck to the inside of his leather armor was the gold ring his father had been so impressed by—the broken half of my mother's amulet. It was what had burned through the leather, the fur, the linen, and his skin. With a jerking hand he dumped snow on it and waited a minute, then swept off the snow and picked it up. It was unmarred, but its heavy chain was missing.

I felt Reyn wonder what it was and if it had truly caused this tragedy. Why was it the only thing that had survived? It...and him.

Holding on to a smooth, black-barked tree, he slowly got to his knees, then stood. He put his jerkin back on. Scooping up a handful of snow, he packed it against his raw skin through the hole in the fur. The freezing snow increased the pain, and he saw stars, acidic bile rising in the back of his throat, but soon it would numb everything.

He put his armor back on and started walking. Within three steps his boot chinked against the gold chain from the amulet. One ring was twisted open. He put it and the amulet into the small leather pouch tied at his waist, not sure why he was keeping it except that it was all he had.

They'd left their boats moored on the southern shore— Ìsland was an island. Reyn didn't know if he could sail the smallest boat alone. Probably not. But there was nothing else he could do.

The middle of my chest had started aching as if I had heart- burn, and then I was floating back to the here and now. Reyn and I were separate people again, sitting on my bed. I blinked, disoriented, and quickly looked at Reyn. His face was solemn, the blades of his cheekbones drawn with viv- idly remembered anguish and pain.

As for me, I'd witnessed the deaths of my family all over again. Then, joined with Eileif, had gone through his per- sonal horror as well.

Letting his breath out slowly, Reyn leaned back against the wall, his long legs stretched out. Dúfa had curled up in an angular lump at the end of my bed and was asleep, impervious to the shredded emotions in the air around her.

"How did you get off of Ìsland?" I asked.

He was silent for a minute, and I wondered if he'd refuse to answer me. Those aged golden eyes roamed my room, as if to reorient himself.

"I traded boats with a local." His voice was raspy, and he cleared his throat. "I'm taller than my father, and blond. I took after my mother—he'd captured her in the west. Far west. My father—you saw—was shorter, darker, looked more Asian."

I nodded. Yes, I'd seen.

"I told the local I was Norse and that my crew had mutinied. We traded boats, and I sailed his much smaller boat back to Noregr. Crossing the northern countries took three months. It was spring when I got home."

The amulet was warm in my hand. How shocking it had been to see its power misused—its effects. I crossed my legs under me. How shocking to see—feel—Reyn so young, not jaded, not cynical, not damaged.

"You went home and you were alone, with no father," I said. "What did people say?"

Again a long hesitation. "I was...a mess, still, after three months. That goddamn burn never healed, felt like acid eating a hole to my heart. My mother believed what happened, but she was...so uneducated. All she knew was how to wash clothes, make a bed." It was said without disrespect: a simple acknowledgment.

"All she knew was that she was free, a widow. Some people thought I'd killed everyone myself." A flush of anger and shame rose on his face. "Some felt strongly that I, as the youngest and most expendable son, should have died also, or never come back. It was... such a bad time. I was heartsick, shell-shocked, and in constant pain. I couldn't sleep, could barely eat. But all around me, the hunters were making plans."

Reyn and I had never, ever talked like this, so openly and without guile or defense. I sat very still, not wanting to break the spell. He spoke slowly with lots of pauses—was he translating the memory? He would have remembered it in his original language.

He went on: "Then, about a week after I got back, my uneducated mother came to me, angry. She said, 'You are the chief of this clan, but you lie here like a woman, moaning? Don't you see how the wolves circle around you?' I stared at her dumbly. 'Your father was awake when he was awake,' she said. 'And awake when he was asleep. An insect couldn't cross this land without him knowing it. And now your cousins plot to kill you in front of your face, and you do nothing!'"

Reyn smiled wryly. "I think she hit me with something, her slipper. Whacked me in the head. So I got up and tried not to look sick. I stepped out of my tent and almost immediately saw what my mother had meant. My father had been chieftain for a long, long time—and my mother was right: He knew everything that went on. My whole life I'd been living like—not an heir, because I was the fourth son. I knew I'd never inherit, and I hadn't paid attention to anything. But now I was a grown man and, unexpectedly, the heir. I strode around our camp, looking stern, and by the end of the day I knew that I had two choices: I either had to step up and become a real chief, with all that that implied, or I had to pack up, steal a horse, and get the hell out of there forever. If I did nothing, I would surely be killed, probably within a day or two."

You know, I'd always thought that my life hadn't been a picnic. I've been in some terrible situations, and a couple of them had involved the handsome work of art sitting next to me. I'd been poor, starving, at the mercy of a man to live, more than once. And of course losing my family. Losing my first husband. Losing my unborn baby, and then later losing my only child, my son, my sweet little Bear. I'd felt—hardened by all this, lacquered over with a brittle shell that almost nothing could get through. I'd also felt that I deserved a good time, after going through all of that. My money gave me freedom, and I wanted freedom from pain, from feeling anything. But pain is like lava—it wants out.

Hearing about Reyn's anguish made me realize that though I'd known parts of his story, it hadn't felt real to me, certainly not as real as my past. Having lived through it, through his eyes, it now felt terribly real. Right now I was ... truly empathizing with someone else.

"What did you do?" I asked.

"Oh, I wanted to banish myself forever. I didn't have it in me to be chief." Reyn wasn't looking at me—maybe he wanted to pretend he was talking to no one, sharing this with nobody. "As I understood what being a chief would entail, I—my heart sank. I'd never realized the constant guard my father had lived under, the constant manipulation and plotting he'd used. It was complicated and exhausting, and I'd never wanted to be chief anyway.

"But if I didn't become chieftain, one of my cousins, or maybe someone else, would. And would they do a good job? My father had worked for hundreds of years toward amassing the amount of land and power he had. Would it all get broken up? Still, escaping was very appealing. But…what would my father think if I did that?" Reyn gave a short laugh.

"He would have been furious, disgusted. He probably would have killed me for being weak. I…couldn't bear that thought." His face was still, his eyes trained on a spot on the wall. I didn't even breathe.

"The next day I walked up to my two cousins as they ate dinner with their families, and I slit their throats." His hands moved in the air, miming grabbing someone's hair from behind, and slicing a blade across a neck, left to right.

Oh God, how awful.

"Their blood sluiced through the air, and it was like writing the strength of my power, right there. And I took control of my clan, immortal and mortal alike. And I ruled with an iron hand, for a hundred years."

I didn't know what to say. I knew some of what that clan had done, to me, my neighbors, other villages. Anyone hearing my stories—including me—would feel that there was only one way to see it, one way to judge it.

But to even this, even this destruction and murder and ruthless control—there was another side. River had told me once that what has a front has a back. And the bigger the front, the bigger the back. I saw what she meant, finally.

The old Nastasya would have made a sardonic remark here, turned this story into a joke, because that would be so much better than feeling the anguish or admitting that bad things existed and affected us and hurt.

As the new, possibly improved, probably boring Nastasya, I had no idea what to say. Or maybe I did.

I put my hand on his knee and looked into the face that was so easy to lose myself in.

"I'm so sorry."

ou might think that after our mind-meld, Reyn and I would be skipping around, holding hands, radiating rainbows of shared joy. Sadly, neither of us was normal enough for that. We settled back into a cautious truce, some sword practice interspersed with the occasional hot kissy-face—getting out of the farm truck, against a wall, in the barn, weeding the garden. Cold, dirty, wearing gardening gloves, my nose running? Apparently irresistible to the Viking wonder.

Valentine's Day came and went, and Amy made a pretty heart-shaped cake, red velvet with poured ganache frosting.

Ottavio ate two pieces while she watched him, her gaze sharp as a knife. Something was going on there, but I didn't know what.

Once, in the twenties, a nice guy who was smitten with me had showed up with a lovely Valentine's Day card and a heart-shaped box of chocolates, which were hard to come by back then. In my caring, sensitive way, I believe I laughed, ate a chocolate, and tossed the card over the back of the couch because Katy was in the middle of a hilarious story that I don't even remember now, except that it had a duck in it. Later the guy was gone, and I hadn't noticed, hadn't missed him. I ate some more chocolate.

That pretty much excuses me from eligibility to ever receive a valentine from anyone ever again in my whole life, I think. So I didn't even hold my breath about whether Reyn would surprise me with anything. And he didn't. Which was fine. I still spent a lot of my waking hours picturing him with his shirt off.

To help take my mind off jumping him, I became busy-bee Nastasya: continuing to study spellcrafting with Asher and River and meditation with Anne. Daisuke was helping me get a tiny bit of a handle on herb magick, I actually had most of the star stuff under my belt, and Rachel was my homegirl for crystals and gems.

Ottavio, Daniel, and Joshua seemed to settle in for a nice, long family visit. How. Lovely.

Ottavio had decided his mission was to watch me like a

research scientist, and I soon got used to him scouring my lesson plans, looking at my books. I started tucking post-cards of the Kama Sutra into my texts, watching from a distance and snickering like a third grader at his tight jaw and looks of disapproval.

One day in late February, I staked out a spot in an unused classroom in the big barn and settled in to voluntarily med-itate, lighting a candle and putting four crystals at the four compass points to help me concentrate. Unbelievably, Otta-vio came and sat before me, coldly and silently daring me to protest.

I decided to meditate about being a woman, the power that we have to create life, the monthly cyclic event that ties us so primally to the earth, and took a fun-filled foray into a memory of how women have dealt with that monthly cyclic event through the ages. Reusable cloths that you have to wash and dry, anyone? Wads of dry moss?

He lasted five minutes.

His surveillance was irritating as hell, but I was deter-mined not to let him get to me, not to run to River com-plaining about her meanie-mo brother. I sucked it up and went about my business.

As for Daniel, I saw that he was beginning to grate on even River's nerves a bit. She and I were dusting in the front hall when he came out of River's office, her carefully kept ledger in his hands.

"What on earth are you doing with that?" River asked.

Daniel squinted down at the book. "What's this here?" he asked. "I can't quite make it out." River looked from him to the book, then said, "That was for a delivery of feed cake for the cows."

Daniel frowned. "Why is it so much? Feed cake is surely cheaper than that, isn't it?"

With an air of disbelief, River answered, "I order the organic feed from Peter Sorensen. It's better."

"Organic feed? For cows?"

River had practically smacked his hands away from the book, her face tight as only an older sister's face could be.

Later that same afternoon I heard him ask Asher whether they had gotten three estimates for the broken windows, as he'd suggested, and whether it would be better to get a new, more efficient farm truck instead of repairing the one we had.

When I saw Asher more than an hour later, his face still looked pained.

And Joshua. At least this brother mostly kept to himself and didn't talk much. He seemed to be there as an extra body in case of trouble, and besides giving me the occasional wary, suspicious eye, didn't bug me much. I saw him around, repairing things, trimming tree branches, patching holes in the chicken-coop roof. Making himself useful. I wished Ottavio would also find a more worthy occupation than stalking me.

Fortunately, after about a week, River started putting

them on cooking teams, barn chores, etc., so that was fun, seeing ol' Ott shoveling horse poop in inappropriate Italian sportswear. I wondered where the fourth brother was, and what was taking him so long to come here and be disapproving of me, but no one mentioned him and, God knows, I wasn't about to ask.

Regardless, I made progress, even successfully scrying to find where the devil-chicken had been hiding her eggs lately. (Rather brilliantly, in the small lean-to housing one of the water heaters.) Chicken and eggs were now ensconced in an empty stall in the barn.

In my "spare" time, I started work on my shops in town.

Hiring a bulldozer and turning them into a parking lot was, I admit, a temptation, once I realized how much work I'd gotten myself into. But that would look bad.

River suggested I try going to the local unemployment office, to see if I could find help. So on a Friday afternoon I pulled open the glass door and was confronted with men and women who all looked as if the rug had been pulled out from under them. And I guessed it had.

"Uh, hey," I said, and a few heads turned. "Um, anyone here know carpentry? Construction? Plumbing?" I thought for a second. "Probably roofing? Floors? Electrical stuff? Anyone know their way around a paintbrush?"

No one understood why my "dad" was letting me have a whole project for myself and why in the world he would give me a fat budget, but when it came down to having a paycheck or not, they were happy to be hired by a crazy teen-ager who was offering decent wages.

Toward the end of February, I was having the construction process explained to me by Bill, a weather-beaten man probably in his mid-fifties who looked a lot older. He'd come with his own hard hat, which I thought was so cool.

"First you have to have a plan," Bill said. "So you can tell people what they'll need to do."

"Plan, check," I said. I guessed he was implying more of a plan than *Fix this up*.

"Then you take care of the roof, the foundation, the windows, and the outside walls."

That made sense. "Okay."

"Then you demo—take out all the broken stuff." He squinted at me, looking a lot like the Marlboro Man in a hard hat. "Are you sure your dad knows what you're doing?"

"Yes," I said, nodding firmly. "This project will...teach me responsibility. And planning. Budgeting. And stuff."

"And he's in construction, but you don't know any of this?"

"I was at school. And church camp. But you know, Bill, you seem to have a good grip on this. You should be the main guy and organize the other guys. Make them do things in order."

Bill looked at me. "Like a general contractor?"

I seized this. "Yes. The general contractor."

"General contractors get paid more." He slapped his work gloves against his worn jeans, sending up a bit of dust.

"Okey-dokey."

So Bill became the go-to guy, and I became the one who brought in Subway for lunch and kept a supply of Snickers bars and walked around nodding seriously, saying "Looks good." I got into the pattern of doing study-type things in the morning and then showing up at the shops around noon. That day I had brownies. I figured, give them some sugar, they'll work harder, right?

A tall woman with straight, corn-yellow hair was talking to Bill. They shook hands, and then he pointed at me. She came over, looking like someone out of a Wyeth painting.

"I'm Mary," she said. "Subcontracting sheetrock and painting." Her denim shirtsleeves were rolled up to her elbows, revealing hard forearms. Her white cargo pants were speckled with many colors of paint.

"Hi, Mary," I said, shaking her hand.

Without smiling, she gestured with her head to another woman who was carrying in a four-by-eight-foot piece of drywall. "That's Josie. She works with me."

Josie turned around at the sound of her name, and I gave her a little wave, feeling like such a poser in my size-six work boots. She smiled at me, then headed back out for more supplies.

"Great. Thanks," I said, and scuttled off.

I was hoping the whole thing would glide into a video montage set to fun music, where I'd see little cuts of activity and then go immediately to the "after" picture. There could even be a short blooper reel, like when Harv put his elbow through a window and needed stitches. Of course he had no health insurance, so guess who got to pick up that tab?

But this, like every single other freaking thing in my life, had no fast-forward button. Instead it was day after day after day, and each day had a whoooole twenty-four hours in it.

There were some good things. I was seeing the shops slowly (I mean slowly) being restored, and that was kind of fun. Since I was downtown so much, I saw Meriwether, sometimes several times a week. That was really nice. She and Lowell were chugging along, and her dad was considering asking Mrs. Philpott to a movie, which made both of us squeal with disbelief and excitement.

I still hadn't seen any sign of Dray, but practically the whole rest of the town was popping in to eyeball what we were doing. Dexter's Ace Hardware, two blocks away, was injected with new life as Bill made me order tons of hardwarey stuff from them. I started getting most of our lunches from Pitson's deli counter, and Julie Pitson, the owner's daughter, began experimenting with recipes. She'd wanted to go to New York and be a chef but had fallen in love and gotten married at nineteen. So we guinea pigs were paying the price for her life choices.

"What is this?" I asked suspiciously, peeling back the white butcher paper. "Julie, I swear to God, if you put wasabi aioli on another tuna salad, the guys will riot, they really will."

"You tell them to eat it and shut up," she said. "That there is Brie, watercress, and Granny Smith apple, touched by a bit of champagne Dijon."

I looked at her.

"I'll throw in some chips," she muttered.

Then there was the mysteriously growing number of pay slips I found myself signing. I'd originally hired eight guys. Bill had subcontracted out the sheetrock and the plumbing, so that was five more people. Now, almost three weeks later, I had twenty-two people on the payroll.

"Bill!" I yelled. I had set up a card table and a folding chair for myself in one of the bay windows of the last shop on the right.

Bill came through from one of the back rooms.

"What is this?" I demanded, waving a pay slip. "Who the hell is Rusty?"

Bill looked around, then pointed to a short, red-haired teenager who was sweeping up drywall dust. Of which there was an abundance.

"I'm paying him to sweep?" I made my voice frosty. "You subcontracted the sweeping?"

"Well..." Bill took off his hard hat and brushed his sleeve against his forehead. Just then a heavyset woman with curly, fading auburn hair bustled through the street door.

Seeing Bill, she said, "Whew! Sorry to be a few minutes late. Got held up at church."

Bill mumbled something, looking at the ceiling, anywhere but at me.

"Mama!" Rusty had heard her, and I saw immediately that he was what Russians used to call "angel-touched." Down syndrome. Back in Dostoyevsky's day, people believed that these children had a special innocence and a direct line to God, and they were treated accordingly.

Rusty's mother beamed at me. "I can't thank you and your father enough for this, sweetie. When Bill said Rusty could work here two hours in the afternoons—well, I can't tell you what a difference it makes." She lowered her voice. "He loves this job—he feels so important."

"Hi, Mama," said Rusty, and she kissed him.

"Hey, angel," she said. "You ready to go?"

They headed out the door, and the woman turned around again and mouthed *Thank you* one more time.

I looked at Bill, who pulled his lips back from his teeth in an ingratiating grin, like a deerhound. Without saying anything else, I went back to my card table. After a moment, Bill headed off.

Dropping my head into my hands, I felt a wave of...discomfort sliding over me like a cloak. Discomfort tinged with anxiety. Formerly treated by an immediate and substantial influx of something mood-altering, preferably of the margarita persuasion. Four short months wasn't enough to completely wipe out old habits, old ways of coping, and everything in me right now was screaming to jump up and find the nearest bar. Which I happened to know was a run-down pub called Salty's, out on the service road by the highway.

And this was just me being emotionally incapable of dealing with life—I wasn't even a legitimate alcoholic. It made it seem extra pathetic, somehow.

Around me were the sounds of change—sawing, hammering, people talking loudly. Inside me everything was changing, too. Suddenly I felt unmoored, unsure of who I was, what I was doing. For a frantic second I longed to be back where I was six months ago, even though I now understood that to be my all-time low. But it was a low I knew, could do, was intensely comfortable with—until I wasn't comfortable with it anymore.

For the last four months, River and the other teachers had told me, over and over, to slow down and feel the feeling. Sit with the feeling until you know what it is. Thanks to their guidance, I could now accurately identify fear, panic, dismay, disgust, anxiety, anger, fury, and disdain. Figuring out why I felt any of those things was something else entirely.

My breathing was coming more shallowly. I wanted to tear out of there more than anything. I would kill for something that would make me not feel this. But why was I feeling it? What was going on?

"What's going on?"

My head jerked up at the voice, startled, as if God herself had reached out and put her hand on my shoulder.

God? Not so much. It was Dray.

She'd come in through the street door and was standing

in front of my card table. I hadn't seen her in months. She was wearing a short, inadequate jacket with tattered faux-fur hood fringe, and her hair was growing out its weird brown/green combo that made it look like she was trying to hide in a jungle.

"What?" I said.

She waved fingers with chipped black nail polish at all the activity. "What's going on? What are you doing here?"

"I bought these eyesores," I said. "Now they're fixing them up. Either that or I have to start charging the rats rent."

Neither of us smiled.

"What are you gonna do with them?"

Her eyes were still caked with heavy eyeliner, but she'd chewed off her lip gloss, and her bare mouth made her look younger than a really old seventeen.

"What have you been doing?" I asked. "I haven't seen you in ages."

A familiar look of bored patience. "My mom sent me to my aunt's for a little while, to help with the new baby."

"Whose baby?"

"My aunt's. Anyway, now I'm back. At my mom's."

"How was the baby?" I was surprised by an unconscious softening in Dray's eyes.

"He was cute," she said, sounding almost like a regular teenager. "Kind of a lump, you know? But then he started smiling. That was pretty cute."

"And now you're back."

"Duh. So what are you gonna do with this place again?"

"I'm praying people will rent these shops. And there are four apartments upstairs. I want to rent those out, too. They'll be all fixed up."

Speculation came into her eyes. "How much are you gonna gouge for the apartments?"

"Not that much. They're little. And on this street. In this town."

Dray looked at me, and I wondered if she would try to rent one of the apartments, get away from her mom again. I knew one thing: Her loser boyfriend was not going to be welcome.

As we'd been talking, two men had stopped and looked through the glass, going to the other bay window and cupping their hands around their eyes to see better. Now one pointed to me, and then they came through the street door.

"Hello," said one of the men. He was tall and slender with a pink-cheeked, well-groomed air. The Burberry coat didn't hurt.

"Hi," I said. Dray sidled away, meandering toward the back, maybe to see the apartments. They were all open right now, with people going in and out. With a twinge I prayed she wasn't going to nick anyone's tools.

"Is the owner around? We looked for an agent's number," the man said. "We're hoping to rent the shop on the end." He pointed down the street, meaning the shop at the opposite end of this one.

"That would be great," I said, not believing it could be this easy. "What would you do with it?"

The men gave each other a quick glance, like, *Do we talk to the kid or what?*

"We've always wanted to open a coffee shop," the other man said.

"Oh God, yes!" I said. "Yes, that would be perfect! Let's go look at the place right now!" I grabbed my coat off the back of my chair and then saw their hesitation. "Um, this is my project. My...dad is making me do this to teach me responsibility. And stuff. But I've been dying for a coffee shop in this town. I'm sure it will be okay with my dad."

"Coffee shop?" Josie, one of the drywallers, had been refilling her tray with drywall mud. "I've always wanted to bake things for a coffee shop. I make the best pound cake ever. And cookies. And coconut cake. And—"

"You guys need to exchange phone numbers," I said. "This sounds great!"

All of my dreams were coming true!

hope you didn't believe that last sentence. I'm of the "When life gives you lemons, make lemonade, then wonder why life didn't give you freaking sugar so you could drink the stuff" school of thought.

And despite my deep and sincere longing for a coffee shop in this cute-forsaken town, my current and most genuine dream was still basically: "I want to feel better." Plus all the stuff about my heritage and whatnot, father's heir, mother's daughter, *blah blah blah*.

But I had to admit, things were coming together nicely, for once.

At dinner that night, Anne asked, "How are the shops, Nastasya?"

I was in the middle of an internal rant about quiche and how unjustified I found its existence, so I was glad to put down my fork for a moment and quit seething. "Well, you saw them yesterday, right?"

Many of my fellow REers had come by, over the last couple of weeks. Not Reyn. Not the Brothers Three. Not the anti-Nastasya league, which these days was really mostly Solis by himself.

"Yes," Anne continued. "Did you decide about Luisa Grace?"

Luisa Grace was a bleached-blond local woman who wanted to rent one of the middle shops. I wasn't sure she was on the up-and-up—she didn't look that craft-conscious. But we would see. She'd said she was hoping to include other local artists also.

I took more bread to fill in the corners of my stomach that would be going quicheless. "I think it should be okay, but if her stuff doesn't sell, she'll be up a creek."

"Who else are you renting space to?" Ottavio's voice made me blink—he'd quit talking to me directly weeks ago. I was just happy that so far his surveillance hadn't extended to the shops.

Part of me, I freely admit, almost said, *The devil, Hitler, Voldemort, and the inventor of acid-wash jeans.* I had to shove more bread in my mouth to stop myself.

When I could speak, I said, "Ray and Tim, the coffee-shop

guys. Possibly Luisa Grace. Miss Gertrude Sully, who wants to open a consignment shop. Have you seen her? I always think the next words out of her mouth will be, *I'm ready for my close-up, Mr. DeMille.*"

"That should be interesting," said Rachel. "A consignment shop would be fun."

I'd never heard Rachel use the word *fun* before.

"The other shop in the middle is still open," I said. "I think a local girl, Dray Somebody, might rent one of the upstairs apartments. Another woman, Holly Mavins, is separating from her husband and renting an apartment. Two other girls, students at the tech school over in Wessonton, want the third. The fourth one is empty."

One more piece of bread for the road, unless there was dessert. "Is there any dessert?" I asked, my hand poised over the bread basket.

Fifteen pairs of eyes were looking at me. As always it was an effort to not get lost in the golden-lion ones.

"What?" I said. Did I have butter on my nose? Had I spilled something on myself?

River smiled gently. "You've changed."

My glance quickly went to Reyn's face, hoping his expression would help me read this situation. He looked thoughtful but was giving nothing else away.

I sat back. "You told me to get a big project."

"It's a wonderful project, my dear," said River. "Don't

misunderstand me. You're … blossoming, like a flower. I'm enjoying it."

I looked at her solemnly, my cheeks starting to burn. There it was again: that feeling of anxiousness, of discomfort. "Oh, good," I said casually, then got up. "That was a great dinner, thanks." I carried my plate into the kitchen, put it by the sink, and then ran out into the night.

I'm very big on, you know, running out into the night. It usually turns out badly for me. And yet I do it. What an unusual pattern. I should probably look at that sometime.

At least this time I didn't run far away to the fence by the road, where Innocencio had found me two months ago. This time I ran for the horse barn, because it was warm. Inside it was dimly lit and quiet. Molly, River's German pointer and Dúfa's mother, was still settled in one of the empty stalls with her puppies. Her six offspring were nuzzled up next to her in the straw—Dúfa, of course, stuck out like a potato in an apple barrel. Her white, angular form was such a contrast to the fat-bellied, snuggly puppies with soft, spotted gray fur and heads already liver-colored like Molly's. From here I could see the odd maroon splotch on Dúfa's side, as if someone had spilled wine on her. I had no idea what Reyn saw in her.

She might feel the same way about me. I'm not even fuzzy.

Next I slipped past the stall where the devil-chicken was, glancing over to see her wide-awake and staring at me with complete malevolence. I flipped her off, then walked past the horses, which were *whuff*ing quietly, dozing, or munching on hay from their racks. At the end of the aisle was the steep ladder leading up to the hayloft, and I went up it, having to wait a minute at the top to give my eyes a chance to get used to the dark.

Soon I made my way across bales of itchy, dusty hay into a small alcove under the eaves. Far off I heard a rumble of halfhearted thunder, and a moment later the ceiling above me was ringing with raindrops.

It was very cozy.

I lay on my back, looking up at the eaves, hoping they were waterproof.

When would I quit having these panic attacks? When would I be able to deal with whatever emotion came down the pike? I kept thinking I was making so much progress, but then someone would say something or something would happen and I would flip out again, unable to stand being here, being me, being in my skin. Would that ever change?

A tall, dark form suddenly materialized near my feet, and I shrieked, only to see the dim light outlining raggedy gold hair that needed a trim.

"*Shh.* You'll wake the whole barn," Reyn said, sitting on a bale of hay next to me. I sat up, brushing hay off my sweatshirt.

"I didn't hear you come up."

His smile was visible even in the darkness. "Yep, I've still got it."

I scowled. "Marauder stealthiness isn't necessarily something to brag about."

"I prefer to think of it as Boy Scout caution."

He wasn't a big joker, and I couldn't help grinning.

"I assume you're not in here to commune with the horses," he said.

Sighing, I shook my head. "Don't know why I'm here," I admitted.

"You just wanted to run."

I wrapped my arms around my knees and nodded, embarrassed. "Don't know why."

He slid off the bale of hay and sat on the floor facing me. "You're trying to feel your feelings? Is that why the chicken looks so pissed?"

"Yes, and probably." As dangerously compelling as he was when he was regular old taciturn Reyn, this slightly lighter, more approachable Reyn was devastating. As per usual, I wanted to climb onto his lap. But with an uncharacteristic self-awareness, I recognized that though the impulse was, God knew, legitimate—still, wanting to do it now was exactly like hungering for a margarita: something to distract me, make me feel different from whatever I was feeling.

Reyn nodded. "I hate sitting with my feelings. Really hate it. Never want to do it."

197

"Me too!" Could I jump him now? Now that he was clearly the only person in the world who truly understood me?

"But I understand why one needs to do it," he said slowly, twisting a piece of hay between long, strong fingers.

"Explain it to me again," I said unenthusiastically.

He hesitated, thinking. "The whole time I was chieftain of my clan, my main emotion was...anger. Whatever the situation, my response was almost always anger. When I was angry, I knew what to do: conquer something. Subdue something. Break something. Finally, after a hundred years of that, I just...melted down and left, left my people forever. It was another two hundred years before I realized that anger is my best weapon to mask fear or uncertainty." He gave a crooked grin. "Only two hundred years."

"Quit showing off."

"Even after I gave up being chieftain, I still...fought. In almost any war I could find. Because expending anger on a battlefield was such a release. And it helped me to not do it in regular life, to people who didn't deserve it. Here, I've come to see that the only true negative emotion is fear." His voice was quiet, almost masked by the sound of rain hitting the roof.

"Fear?" But Reyn never seemed afraid—only angry. Oh.

"Every negative or hurtful emotion comes from fear," Reyn said. "Fear that you'll get hurt, fear that you'll lose something, fear that someone won't love you the way you love them. When I fear something, it's unbearable. So I get angry instead."

"Oh—like when you yelled at me for doing badly in class," I said, a little string of Christmas lights going off in my head.

His face was grim. "I'm afraid that you'll get hurt if you don't get stronger, faster." He already seemed angry, a muscle twitching in his jaw.

I was afraid of a lot of things—River giving up on me, me liking Reyn more than he liked me, Brynne not wanting to be friends with me. I was afraid of Incy and whatever he was into—and that the so-called master was real, and truly interested in me. I was my father's only heir—what if I'm a complete screwup? What if that's all he got, one living screwup to inherit everything he'd worked for, everything he and my mother had been?

But something else was going on. Slowly I tried to follow the thread of anxiety.

"Yesterday, at the shop, I found out my general contractor has been hiring more people than I knew, kind of putting as many people on the payroll as possible—including a boy who's . . . simple, who's doing all the sweeping. I wasn't mad at Bill—he's trying to create jobs for people, and no one's sitting around on their ass and getting paid for it. But after the boy's mom came to get him, she was so thankful to me, said the job meant so much to him, and I felt terrible. I wanted to run, didn't want anything more to do with the shops, never wanted to see any of them again."

Reyn's hand reached out and took mine, and its strong warmth made me feel like I was connected to a...mountain or something.

"And then just now, everyone all—happy for me, I'm blooming, whatever—I never want to go through that. I don't want anyone to say anything ever again. I'm doing the stupid project, and they should just shut up about it, you know?" My free hand clenched a bunch of straw.

A small, white, triangular head nudged around Reyn's side, and I almost jumped.

"Jesus, did that dog climb the ladder?" That was just freakish.

"What are you doing, girl?" Reyn murmured, picking up Dúfa and setting her on his lap. She gave his chin a sleepy lick, sprawled, and zonked out immediately.

"The ladder is really steep," I pointed out. "And the rungs are far apart."

"She's really something," he said with amused pride.

"She's really a freaking *monkey*."

There was never anyone else who was as beautiful when he smiled, I thought, feeling a little dazed by the overwhelming force of longing.

"But back to you," he said, stroking the small head. I couldn't help feeling resentful of Dúfa—why did she get to sit on his lap and climb on him and lick him?

When I didn't say anything, he looked at me. "Have you figured any of it out?"

I shook my head, waved my hand around the hayloft. "This was as far as I got."

"Do you feel like...maybe you don't deserve to have anyone think good things about you?"

I blinked, and my mouth opened with a witty retort, but nothing came out. He waited patiently. "Well, I mean...I kind of don't," I muttered, not looking at him. "I'm...so awful. I mean, I know that."

"Nas...we're *all* awful. That's why we're here." There was wry amusement in his voice. "Remember when you were pissed at Charles and Jess and told them off because they were in no position to judge you?"

I nodded.

His voice was amazingly gentle. "You're judging yourself so much more harshly than anyone else here. You know everyone here is or has been a walking disaster—even River. With the stuff she's done, do you think she deserves to have anyone think well of her today?"

"I know what you're getting at, Dr. Phil," I said stiffly. "But all of River's bad stuff was, like, a thousand years ago. A *thousand*. A thousand *years*. My stuff was last *fall*."

"I'm not going to wait a thousand years for you to get over yourself," he said. He took off his barn jacket and spread it on the hay, then scooped Dúfa off his lap and snuggled her up in it. She didn't even wake up.

The man made a nest for a *puppy*. I'm sure this eliminates any doubt in your mind about what I was doing with him.

Reyn sat up on his heels and braced his hands on his thighs, his laser gaze focused on me. Please, please don't suggest sword practice.

"Come here." Very soft.

"What?" I bluffed.

He crawled toward me and pushed me down into the hay very slowly. With one arm he gathered me to him, so we were face-to-face on our sides. Some of my hair fell in my eyes, and he smoothed it away as if I were Dúfa.

"I'm not going to wait a thousand years," he said again, and a little shiver fluttered in my chest. "And you may not wait a thousand years for me. You, me, everyone here, everyone in the world, immortals, regular people—everyone is a work in progress. Some of us have farther to go. Some of us will only go backward. You're going forward. I'm going forward. And you can't stop me or anybody else from...thinking good things about you." His eyes roamed down my body with its shapeless sweatshirt and typically ratty jeans. Starting under my arm, he pressed my sweatshirt flat against me, learning my shape beneath it.

Several of my brain cells were still functioning, and I murmured, "I'm not a good person. I feel like I'm tricking them when they think I am." His hand slid under my sweatshirt and started to tug my undershirt out from my waistband. Reyn pressed his mouth against my temple, my brow, his lips moving sweetly against my skin.

"How about if we just think you're a person doing some good things?"

I couldn't focus. One of my hands was trapped, but the other one was already gliding over the smooth skin of his back, a sheet of heavy silk stretched over taut muscles.

"What?"

I felt him smile against my forehead, and he moved down a couple inches and kissed my mouth, causing my arm to curl around him and pull him closer to me.

"I'll tell you later." And then we were all wrapped up in each other, kissing and kissing so deeply, the way we did, as if we'd been starved of kisses for four hundred years and could now have our fill.

CHAPTER 15

kay, everyone all together now: What happens when things start going right?

The shit hits the fan. You are correct, sir.

Bad dreams I couldn't remember woke me in the deepest part of the night. I had no idea what they were about, but my heart was pounding and my breathing shallow with some unnamed dread. I lay awake until dawn.

Finally, a good hour before I had any hopes of breakfast being ready, I got up, pulled on some cords, a turtleneck, a thin scarf (of course), and a sweater, and went downstairs to check the chore chart. I was on eggs. But the devil-chicken was in the barn, so I wouldn't have to deal with her. I picked up the wire basket in the kitchen and practically skipped outside—

Only to stop in confusion: A big, charred line, maybe two feet wide, circled the house, as far as I could see. Some kind of circle of protection, maybe, that River and the other teachers had done last night? Okay, only two feet wide and easy to cross, but one second pre-hop, I hesitated. Just to be sure, I went inside to ask; with my luck, the first person to cross it would totally screw things up, and a big purple cloud would follow me all day so everyone would know. Like I needed that.

River was just starting to set things out to make breakfast and looked up in surprise when I came in. "You're up awfully early."

"Couldn't sleep. Hey, is that big circle okay to go over? Should I just jump?"

She blinked. "What big circle?"

"Uh...the one outside that goes all around the house? Seems jumpable, but I didn't want to mess it up." Responsible Nastasya.

River quickly wiped her hands on a dishcloth. "Show me."

Turns out, big charred circle all around your house? Not a good thing. Not someone writing *I heart you* on the front lawn with bleach. There was a big brouhaha; much consultation; some pained looks given to yours truly by very old Italian men; general consternation. River and Asher decided to have the four teachers disperse it, purify the ground beneath it, and then rake hay over the charred earth.

Between you and me, it made my knees quake. Despite the ongoing suspicion and disapproval from River's brothers, everything had been quiet for weeks; I'd pretty much allowed myself to believe that with Incy safely put away at Louisette's, maybe everything would just...be okay. But that would be too easy, wouldn't it?

Later I was trying to decide whether to go to town—would it be better to, say, crawl under my bed and hope everything would just blow over? What if I stayed there for several days?

"Are you wondering about going to town?" River asked, coming upon me in the front hallway.

I scowled. "No. Of course I'm going to town."

She didn't smile. "Maybe you should stick close to home today."

Naturally that made me grab my jacket and shove my arms into it. I'm nothing if not stubborn and impulsive.

"Nastasya—we don't know who did this or if they're still around or who their target is. It seems likely that the target is you. You, in town by yourself—"

"I'll be surrounded by a bunch of burly guys," I pointed out. "And burly gals."

Anne came up then, pulling a red beret over her shiny, dark pageboy. "I thought I would go with you today, Nas. Want to see all the action close-up."

I looked from her to River. "Like you couldn't be more subtle."

Anne grinned. "Nope. And I'm driving."

Once downtown, we were both impressed by the bustling activity at my shops. There was now a Dumpster in the empty lot next door, and it was filling with debris. Even as we drove up, a pickup truck was disgorging five guys in jeans and work shirts.

We had to gently push through a small crowd of locals who were standing around, watching everything.

"Wow—this project has really ballooned," Anne said as I opened the door of the shop on the end, the one that had my office in its front window.

"I'm paying more people every week," I said.

Anne looked around the big space, empty except for saw-horses to hold large pieces of plywood or drywall. "This looks wonderful, Nastasya! Wow, this really takes me back—this store used to have a wonderful lunch counter. Is this the shop you haven't rented yet?"

"Yeah."

Workers walked by, greeting me by name. I saw a battered Toyota stop at the curb; a guy got out and tipped his hard hat at Anne and me. Then the other car door opened, and a woman got out holding a tin lunch box.

"Alan!"

The guy stopped, took his lunch, and kissed her with a shy smile. Up close I saw that the two of them couldn't be more than twenty-two or twenty-three. The woman gazed after him, her eyes shining. Then she focused on me.

"Are you the girl that's doing this, like, for a school project?"

"Kind of," I said.

"Well, it is just so cool," the young woman said. "And man—I swear, the day I admitted we finally had to go on food stamps—that was the day Alan came home and said he had a job."

"Ah," I said, sensing my first twinges of alarm.

"It was like God's hand, reaching down to help us up."

Oh no. "Oh, good," I said weakly, aware of Anne's eyes on me.

"Well, bless you," she said, heading for the door. "I'm going to remember you in my prayers, you can be sure of that."

"Oh, okay. Thanks."

Then, mercifully, she was gone, and I let out a breath.

"It's so hard," Anne said, and I turned to her, grateful she knew how I felt. "Being Saint Nastasya."

"Oh, jeezum," I said, swatting her arm in disgust.

Laughing, she headed toward the back. "I'm going to check out the rest of the place."

"Yes, *please*," I said, irritated. "Please go and check things out."

I could still hear her chuckling as I sat down at my little desk in the window.

The day before I had decided to buy the empty lot next door, the one that the Dumpster now sat on. It wasn't very big, but it was a real eyesore, with patches of broken concrete, three cement steps that led nowhere, weeds growing up through the cracks, and a bunch of trash that people had dumped. If I bought it, I could have my enormous workforce clear it out, rip up the concrete. Then I could make it into a little garden, kind of how River described, and people would at least have one nice freaking place to sit and not have to stare at their dying Main Street.

I got on the phone and called the number on the ancient FOR SALE sign that lay half buried in mud.

It was almost lunch before I had tracked down the right person, and by the time I hung up, I felt like my last nerve had just been squeezed by a python. A python with an aggressive sales quota to make.

Leaning back in my chair, I closed my eyes and rubbed my temples for a few minutes. Anne hadn't returned, and I wondered where she'd gone.

When I finally sighed and opened my eyes, it was to see Joshua standing over me, holding a hammer.

My heart leaped into high gear, not in a fun way but in a "is this guy going to whack me in the head with a hammer?" way.

"Joshua," I said evenly, refusing to show fear. Except that my eyes were probably about to pop out of my head. "What's up?"

He raised his hammer slightly. "I'm here to work."

"So . . . you know carpentry? Or something?"

"Yes."

"My general contractor is a guy named Bill. He looks like the Marlboro Man in a hard hat. He can push you in the right direction."

Joshua gave one brief nod, and I watched him head toward the back, where a lot of rebuilding was happening. He was tall, wide, and rangy, just like Reyn. I wondered how many times they'd faced each other on the battlefield. I wondered what the rest of his story was. He'd been in the memories that River had shown me, but he had been so different then—I barely recognized him. Well, a lot can happen in a thousand years. It was funny that bright, vivacious Brynne, with her striking, teen-model beauty, would be attracted to him.

Lunch that day was curried-chicken wraps with lime-peanut-cilantro sauce, which of course César couldn't have because of the peanuts. That's all I needed, another hospital bill. Alan traded him his lunch.

"This is terrific," Anne said, taking another bite. She and I were eating at my "desk." "You got these from Pitson's?"

I nodded. "We're at the mercy of thwarted-chef Julie Pitson. Pass the sauce, willya?"

Something made me glance up, and I saw a man standing at the window, looking in. When he came in he seemed vaguely familiar, but I couldn't place him. You see a lot of faces in 450 years.

"Yes?" I said, knowing he was about to ask for work.

"Why, Roberto!" Anne said, standing up and giving him a hug. "Nastasya! This is River's brother Roberto!"

"Oh good," I said. "You can never have too many." I put my elbows on the table and held my forehead in my hands.

"We've been enjoying our visit with Ottavio, Daniel, and Joshua!" Anne said, perky as all get-out. I groaned quietly.

"Who's Joshua?" Roberto asked.

"The one right below River."

"Mi stai prendendo in giro!"

"She's not kidding," I said glumly. "And now we have the complete set. Excellent."

"Come, Bertino," said Anne. "I'll give you a ride to the house. Nastasya—you're doing something wonderful here. I'm proud of you."

I managed a tight smile. After they left I sat for a moment, wondering if Roberto was an actor or a model or something. Surely I'd seen his face before. Well, he had the family resemblance to the others, I guessed. His hair was lighter, longer, and curlier than his brothers', and his face looked younger and less troubled, but still, House of Genoa all the way.

Woo-hoo. Couldn't wait for dinnertime.

And at dinnertime, I got that Roberto seemed to be the family favorite: Even Joshua's and Ottavio's faces softened when they looked at him.

"I was in town, before," Joshua said. "You didn't come find me?"

"No one mentioned you were there," Roberto said, looking at Anne.

She blushed. "I was so surprised to see you, I forgot."

At the head of the table, River was beaming, looking around as if all her favorite people were here. Since no one had seen Joshua in at least fifteen years, it must have been the first time all of them had been together in ages.

"My brothers," she said, warmth in her voice, her face glowing. "We are together." She reached out and took Ottavio's hand on her right, Daniel's hand on her left.

Good thing you didn't kill them all, I thought as I helped myself to some pork tenderloin.

"And Joshua—you were downtown, helping at Nastasya's shops?"

Across the table, Reyn's head jerked up, the motion making Joshua turn sharply. Seeing it was just Reyn, he dismissed it and poured himself more wine. (Thank the goddess for Wine Wednesdays.)

"Yes."

"What were you doing at the shops?" Brynne looked avidly interested, and I wondered if she was reviewing her own carpentry skills so she could come help, too. Right. By. His. Side.

Joshua looked surprised at her question (meaning he blinked once) but answered. "Helped frame out some rooms in the apartments."

"It's good to be with my family," said Roberto, "but I'm afraid I'm not here just to visit."

No, *of course not.*

"I'm sure you've heard the news by now," he went on.

"What news?" River asked, pausing in the middle of dishing up some mashed potatoes.

Her youngest brother looked sober. "The house in Australia has been attacked. Three of the family are dead."

Everyone fell silent.

Okay, I had been *right here.* No one could pin this on me.

"Oh no," Rachel murmured.

"That's not all," said Roberto. "The house in Brazil has also been attacked. Fernanda barely escaped. Someone is targeting immortals—the immortals of the main houses."

Heads swiveled toward me as if pulled by one string.

This was awful news. I took a bite of pork, my mind trying to put pieces together. "Did they say that someone had tried to steal their power?"

Roberto shook his head. "It sounds like it was just an attack. Brett, in Australia, is sure that no one took his sisters' or his father's power when they died. He inherited it all."

"But we don't suspect Brett?" I asked. None of this was making sense.

"No, of course not," Ottavio said, but I didn't know why it was of course not.

This was all weird. Incy had known where I was; the assumption was that someone had told him. The so-called master? Or whoever Miss Edna was? It was all so convoluted, and I couldn't see the big picture.

When I looked up again, Roberto's gaze was fixed on me, his head tilted to one side as if he was pondering something. Then his eyes flared suddenly, his eyebrows rose slightly, and he looked away, suppressing a grin. He cleared his throat and drank from his wineglass, not looking at me again.

And then...the angle of his head, the way he was tilting his wineglass...oh my God. Oh, jeez. I realized why he looked familiar. Oh my God, how embarrassing. He'd obviously just remembered, too. Crap. Well, the sixties have a lot to answer for. Jeezum.

The rest of the meal was subdued except for the slight entertainment of watching Brynne watch Joshua and then looking up to see Reyn's eyes smoldering at me because, I guessed, I had broken the "don't let my sworn enemy frame rooms in your shop" clause. I blew it off—I didn't have time for weird alpha-wolf crap. As for Roberto, the less I looked at him, the better.

The dim ringing of a phone came to us—there was one landline in this place, and only one actual phone, which was connected to the wall in River's office.

Quizzical glances all around, and then River got up.

"These attacks are so strange," said Daisuke. "Why are they happening now?"

"It isn't the first time," said Asher. "Do you remember— let's see, it was...I think it was around eighteen hundred? The African house was attacked, and so was the one in Salem."

"Who was behind those?" Brynne asked.

Asher shook his head. "We still don't know."

We heard the door to River's office close. Her footsteps in the hallway were slow, and when she came into the dining room, her face was white and strained. Unseeing, she sat down slowly and then put her hands over her face. Her shoulders began to shake, and then we heard a sob. River was crying.

I'd never seen River cry like this, and I was appalled. I wanted to jump up and put my arms around her, stroking her fine silver hair, the way she'd stroked mine through numerous crying jags. Asher got up immediately and knelt by her chair.

"Cara, what is it?" Daniel asked softly, putting his hand on her arm. All of her brothers looked wide-eyed and solemn—she'd probably been the anchor of their family for a millennium.

Finally River took some gulping breaths, shaking her head as if to deny the reality of what she knew. "Louisette is dead. And Innocencio is gone." She turned to Asher, hiding her face in his shoulder while everyone exchanged horrified glances. River's sobs resumed as my stomach turned to ice-cold acid and the blood drained from my face.

Maybe all this really *was* about me.

CHAPTER 16

y mother didn't wear any particular robe when she made magick, just her regular clothes, which were beautiful, warm and heavy, often embroidered by her own hand. Actually, I hadn't seen her making magick that often—only a few times that I could remember. The most vivid time was the night she died, when she was trying to save us. I wonder if she knew that she had, in fact, saved me? One of her five children was still alive. But...I can't say that I think she would be very proud of me or happy I'd made it till now. Maybe someday. It was hard to think that far ahead.

Now, standing in front of the mirror on my wardrobe door, I looked at myself in my white linen robe, feeling vaguely sacrificial. "*Baaaa*," I said to my reflection, and retucked the scarf around my neck.

It was nine o'clock, and we were about to head out into the night to perform a rite of scrying and protection, a big circle with all of us. Today had been weird and jangled—I hadn't even gone to town to check on my investment. We stayed at home, moving and talking quietly, studying silently on our own, performing chores by rote. The only real inter-action I'd had with anyone was with Reyn, whacking the hell out of things with my girl sword, behind the barn. River had stayed in her room until dinnertime, and when she appeared she'd asked us to make a circle with her tonight.

Reyn, I thought, just as a tap sounded at my door. I opened it to see him standing there in his heavy topaz linen robe, his face solemn. Automatically I looked down, expect-ing to see the small white dog that followed him everywhere.

"She's in the barn," he said. "I didn't want her to get underfoot."

I sat on my bed. We hadn't talked about anything earlier—just, *Get your center of gravity lower! Use your arm muscles, you pansy! Boom! You just died!* That had been fun.

I was reluctant to go to tonight's circle, and not just for the usual reason that making magick almost always meant feeling like crap afterward. Because Innocencio had come here to get me, he had ended up at River's aunt's place. Now

River's aunt was dead, and my former friend was in the wind. I felt so incredibly guilty, and everyone who saw me tonight would know it.

Reyn sat next to me on the bed, and I thought longingly of all the more appealing things we could be doing instead of dreading a circle. "You didn't make Innocencio kill Louisette," he said.

"He only knew her because of me," I said.

"You just can't think like that. It doesn't do any good." He raked one hand through his tawny hair. "Plus, you know, this isn't all about you."

I looked up. "No, I thought it wasn't, and was so glad, but then this thing with Incy happened, and—"

"No, I mean—this situation is not about you and your guilt or whatever feelings you have," he said. "Your feelings aren't what's important here."

I felt my bottom lip get stiff.

Reyn groaned. "I'm putting this badly."

"Once again," I muttered.

He shot me a glance. "Yeah, I know how sensitive you are, Miss Tact. I don't know how you walk around with that mushy heart of yours."

I sighed. "So . . . you don't think I caused this?"

"No." His voice was certain and reassuring. "No more than Helen caused Troy to fall."

I made my eyes big. "Oh God, were you there?"

He patted my knee. "So funny. You know I'm only ten

years older than you. Now, are you ready, or do you need to sit here and lose yourself in your own importance some more?"

"Almost ready." I slid off the bed and squirmed underneath it. Reyn had already seen where I kept my amulet, and I hadn't had time to find a good new place for it. I pried off the floor molding, stuck my hand into the hole, and pulled out the handkerchief filled with the warm, heavy amulet; tarak-sin of the House of Úlfur the Wolf.

"I can't wait to rub this in Ottavio's face," I said, putting it around my neck.

"That's my girl," Reyn said.

The last time we'd had a big circle outside, there had been snow on the ground. What would it be like to make magick with River's brothers, most of whom I didn't like at all? Would our personal feelings get in the way, or would it not matter?

Guess what color Ottavio's robe was. Yes. Black. Like Jess's, but of a more beautiful fabric—a rich, heavy jacquard, black on black. And for the first time I saw the House of Genoa's tarak-sin: a thick ring, solidly made of old gold and set with a ruby the size of a finch's egg and the color of congealed blood. It looked big and heavy on Ottavio's long, tapered finger, but he seemed comfortable with it—he'd been wielding it ever since he and his siblings killed their parents to get it.

The bright flash of Brynne's red robe caught my eye, and I held out my hand to her. Smiling, she came and stood on my other side, somehow managing, perhaps through sheer force of will, to maneuver to be next to Joshua. His robe was a deep, dark green, with symbols embroidered on it in a dark red thread. Stars, moons, comets, and other heavenly objects scattered across their field of green, shining in the firelight.

A hand on my shoulder made me turn, and I saw River's face, her grief cast into sharp relief. She took in my amulet, hanging below my breastbone, leaving a warm spot.

"Has Ottavio seen it yet?" she whispered.

I shook my head, and for just a moment her face showed a trace of a smile.

"Welcome, my friends and family," she said, looking at everyone. "As you know, it seems wise to create a more powerful circle of protection around us. Asher, my brothers, and I have crafted a multilayered spell that will confer the strongest protection we know. We should be able to go about our business, our daily lives, even travel, confident of the spell's protective powers."

Excitement started to flicker inside me like tiny fireflies— I felt alert and braced for anything.

"The form of this spell will be different," River went on. "I will start it, Asher and my brothers will add their parts, and then you may all join in, one by one, until at last we've woven an unbreakable circle of power and intent. Does anyone have any questions?"

"How will we know when to join in?" Rachel asked.

"People may join as they feel ready," River explained. "I think you'll be able to recognize it. Don't worry if time passes and you haven't felt the push—I know it will come to each of you."

"Okay," said Rachel. She'd been here off and on for years but had apparently never seen anything like this. I told myself to pay attention, because this was big and significant and I had to learn it, be part of it.

Shoulders back, eyes on the fire, I breathed in slowly, trying to let go of every thought in my head, which was like trying to clear a handful of wiggling eels out of a closet. Breathe in; breathe out. Breathe in strength; breathe out fear, hesitation, worry, impatience.

River began to chant slowly, barely loud enough for me to hear. I kept breathing deeply, my eyes locked on her, my arms feeling the slight heat coming from Brynne and Reyn on either side.

Soon River started drawing sigils in the air, tracing ancient, invisible symbols whose very shapes imbued magick and power. Most of them I didn't recognize, but some I knew. The runes eolh, for protection, and thorn, for overcoming adversity, were repeated several times. Ur was for strength; peorth was for hidden things revealed. My father's library had had books written entirely in runes; when I was little, my sister Eydís and I had scratched our names into a foundation stone, spelling them out in the runic alphabet.

ᛘᛁᛦᛋᚺ

River began to walk clockwise around the fire. Seamlessly Asher blended his voice with hers and also drew sigils in the air, tracing out our purpose for the universe to see and hear. The chant was now more songlike, the words lengthening, rising and falling like a cantor's prayer in a synagogue.

Roberto joined them, his voice surprisingly smooth and deep. For an instant I flashed on how he'd looked in the sixties—the long, curly hair, scraggly beard, hippie clothes. Blinking, I put it firmly out of my mind. When Joshua fell into line, his rough tones underlay theirs like rain held heavily in a cloud.

Daniel was next, and interestingly his voice was less distinctive, less strong.

As Ottavio joined them, his tarak-sin glowed in the firelight as if the large red stone contained a fire of its own. How old was that tarak-sin?

My hand rose and brushed across my amulet, which was warm and heavy against my chest. This was its first taste of major magick in 450 years. Was it eager? Did it know? A more unsettling thought came to me: What if I truly couldn't channel Tähti magick? Could I accidentally undo everything they were creating here? River trusted me; she trusted my amulet with me. I would have to trust in her trust.

Gradually the six of them came to a gentle stop, their feet landing lightly like leaves settling onto the surface of a pond. Their song was beautiful and eerie to listen to, their faces transported as they sang. Eyes unfocused, they each faced the flickering fire.

The first person to step forward and join their song was Daisuke. His clear, light tenor seemed to sidle up to their chords, winding around it. There's no other way to describe it except as threads or roots interweaving, the way a rope is made strong by twisting many strands together.

Anxiously I waited for "the push," for something to say, *Okay, Nas, jump in!* Rachel joined, then Charles, Amy, Solis, Anne, Jess. Reyn stepped forward, and Lorenz followed him right after. River had seemed certain it would come to each of us, but what if it didn't? What if this circle of protection was rejecting me because I was inherently dark? I clutched my amulet tightly and frantically wondered what to do.

Brynne left my side and joined the others. She had a beautiful singing voice, a little deep, a tiny bit rough around the edges, but warm and lovely. Then I was alone, on the outside of the circle.

It was my worst fear coming true. I wasn't getting the call to join. I was dark. I was being rejected. My amulet made me dangerous and Other. Not Tähti. Terävä.

I couldn't bear it. I couldn't be the only one left behind. With my breath lodged in my throat, every muscle wound tight enough to snap, my amulet making a circle of heat on my chest, I stepped forward. I was joining by force, probably at a place in the spell that wasn't right. The first sound out of my mouth was a dry croak, my throat threatening to close entirely with fear and uncertainty. But I pulled in a thin, squeaking breath, closed my eyes, and tried to set free my mother's song of power.

My voice did not glide into place. I could feel it now, their powers and their voices. Ottavio's voice, the magick he was making, was like his robe: dark, even black, but a lustrous black, smooth and supple, layered with meaning and learning and intent. It was unexpectedly beautiful. River's thread shone like liquid silver, like her hair, a fine, strong line of clarity and purpose. Joshua's magick was rough and ragged, frayed at the edges. Reyn's was similar but deeply amber and layered with pain and regret. Daniel's was a bit weaker. Anne's was lovely, blue and direct. Not everyone felt like they were there 100 percent. Mostly, yes. But there were a few tiny gaps that I couldn't put my finger on—gaps that shifted, appearing and disappearing like a cloud before a wind.

My own voice was sticking out like Dúfa among her siblings. *Please let me join*, I whispered to the universe. *I want to be like them, I want these to be my people. I want this to be my home.*

Hot tears started in the back of my eyes, so I kept them clamped shut and drew in another wavering breath. I had never understood the words or sounds I was able to replicate. Had my mother created them, or were they passed down to her? I let my song of power nudge its way into the others, praying that nothing would explode, no one would stop and stare, that I wouldn't get knocked back twenty feet. That a huge white tornado of flame wouldn't consume me and everyone around me.

My magick was gray.

It was the first time I'd experienced it as a color—usually it was an emotion, a sound, a physical feeling, an intellectual acknowledgment of its existence. Here, now, my ribbon of song was gray. Not silver, like River's. It wasn't beautiful, like Ottavio's, wasn't seductive, like Reyn's, nor bright, like Brynne's. It was gray, and it was growing stronger.

River's voice shone above all as she revealed layer after layer of the spell, magick and more magick and then deeper magick still. I opened my eyes and focused on her, aligning my song with hers. Though we were singing different words from languages that far predated either of us, our songs *felt* the same.

I've described magick as being a chrysanthemum of joy and light blooming in my chest. This wasn't like that. This was power being channeled through me, coming from deep within the earth and flowing out of my mouth as words, now somewhat harsh-sounding to my ears. I didn't feel joy as much as awe and tension, almost trepidation. My cord of gray gathered power to itself, rapidly strengthening, twisting on itself, becoming the gray of iron, the gray of steel.

This spell was...I can't describe it in any way that would do it justice. It was an almost crystalline structure, as if River were building a city around us, made of points of light and cords of power. Each layer was another layer of protection: for this house, all our land, our vehicles, our livestock, our crops, each one of us individually. River named each animal, each person, using not our common names but magickal names that were seminal, bred into our bones and blood, names that perfectly and uniquely defined each of us and no other.

My amulet was like a furnace, taking my gray magick and firing it, drawing it through incandescent heat and light. Like iron, it went in raw and unformed and came out tempered, frighteningly strong like a sword's blade, vibrating with each blow of the smith's hammer.

I didn't know how to control it.

My hard magick was laced tightly throughout the spell, informing each part of it, underlining everything River had designed. I saw it more clearly than the others', perhaps simply because it was mine. River's silver cord was the only one that shone as brightly, that was everywhere, touching everything.

Then it hit me: the heart-stopping perfection of it, the wonder, my shocked amazement and comprehension of what we were doing, the art we had joined together to create. It was glorious and magnificent, frightening in its strength and glory. I was filled with awe and fear and a trembling, wild exhilaration that I was part of this and this was part of me.

Finally it felt complete. A cloak of protection flowed over us like heavy fog over a valley. Dreamily I felt it settle weightlessly on my shoulders, felt it kiss each leaf on each tree, felt it soothe the animals in the barn and the chickens in the coop. It covered Molly and her puppies, Dúfa wiggling in her sleep. It covered Jasper, the other farm dog, where he slept in the corner of Titus's stall. It touched the wind, the grass, the dirt beneath our feet, each board of the house, each pane of glass, each pebble in the driveway.

I breathed in, testing my perceptions. My magick still poured strongly through me even as River began the rite of dispelling. Then, with startling rapidity, my magick diminished, edging itself out of the spell, its furious torrent dwindling to a trickle.

When my magick ended abruptly, I dropped to the ground like a beanbag. I didn't feel sick so much as completely drained, a vase emptied of water and flowers and now containing only air. Brynne knelt next to me.

"You okay?" She sounded limp herself.

I nodded and made myself get up onto my hands and knees. While I waited a few moments to see if nausea was going to hit me, I looked around. River was a bit unsteady on her feet; Ottavio and Joshua stood on either side, holding her up. She was looking up at Ottavio, and they wore identical expressions of... uncertainty?

I got to my feet and felt Reyn's hand under my elbow, steadying me.

"How are you, my dear?" River asked, searching my face.

I could barely talk, but I nodded. "Okay." Had she noticed that I joined by force?

"How was your amulet?"

My hand closed around it protectively. "It was good. I worried that it wouldn't know what to do, but I think it was okay. Could you feel it? Did it seem... fine?"

"I did," she said thoughtfully. "I felt your magick very strongly and felt how your amulet focused it, honed it to be harder somehow."

I let out a breath. "That's how it seemed to me, too."

She gave me a gentle smile and then we all started gathering our shoes and walking back to the house. It had been the most amazing, most beautiful, and most awe-filled experience I'd ever had. My joining in had been accepted, hadn't it? I hadn't done anything to mess it up, had I?

The next morning, Ottavio left us, heading for Boston to get some answers.

CHAPTER 17

t breakfast the next day everyone was solemn, as if we'd witnessed the birth of a planet. I was glad I hadn't barfed afterward, but later in my room my senses had felt raw, scraped hollow, empty, shocked. This morning I'd practically crawled downstairs, lured only by the smells of bacon and coffee, two of nature's perfect foods.

"Who is Ottavio seeing in Boston?" Anne asked.

"Our friend Tallis," River said. She folded her fingers around the warmth of her coffee cup and inhaled its aroma. "Plus I think he'll poke around. Try to get any sort of information."

"That will go well," Daniel murmured, and River glanced at him.

I took another piece of bacon and chewed, reveling in the heavenly explosion of salt and fat and baconness on my taste buds.

Finally I could put it off no longer and stood up, creaky and sore like an old woman. Ha ha ha! I just realized what I said.

River met me out in the hall as I was fumbling with my jacket. She gave me a faint smile, brushed her hand across my cheek, and headed toward her office.

Reyn came downstairs just as Joshua joined me in the hallway. I quickly made plans to duck and run, should stupidity overwhelm them as I stood there.

"Thought I'd go with you to town," Reyn said, not looking at Joshua. Joshua's hazel eyes narrowed even as I said brightly, "That would be great! A worker I don't have to pay!"

"Oh, you have to pay me," Reyn corrected me.

The next two weeks went by in choppy stops and starts, and I started to count the days until spring officially began.

Despite the spell of protection, there was an undercurrent of tension throughout River's Edge. Everyone carried on— the spring gardens were being tilled, now that the ground was no longer frozen. The cold frames were set with new seedlings to be planted in the ground eight weeks from now. Molly's puppies were weaning themselves off but scampered after her wherever she went, five little furry bundles of chunky legs and oversize paws getting under everyone's feet.

Dúfa became a construction dog downtown, starting each day by following Reyn purposefully as he worked but then petering out by nine o'clock and collapsing on someone's jacket or under my feet at my card table.

My project was visibly nearing completion. The four downstairs shops were finished, with each store having a main showroom and, in back, a small room for storage, another small room for an employee lounge, and a bathroom. All the sinks and lights worked; everything felt fresh and clean. Ray and Tim, the couple who had wanted to open a coffee shop, were in the last building getting it ready. They'd painted the walls a deep eggplant and were installing refrigerated cases, a counter, and adding another sink to the front room. I planned to be first in line for a latte.

The outside was completed; seeing the freshly painted building was still a bit of a surprise when I first turned the corner down the block, but I thought it perked things up.

As the guys finished up their jobs inside, some of them moved to work on the empty lot next door. The workers had broken up the concrete and were using it to make raised flowerbeds along the sides of the two buildings that bordered the lot. The trash was gone, the old concrete steps had been set against a wall to serve as seating, and in general, it was much less heinous.

I felt protected. I did. But I also felt—like something was about to happen. The first day I was back downtown, I was in one of the upstairs apartments, looking over what the builders had been doing. I was all by myself, things were quiet, and something made me quickly write the rune eolh in the air and do a little ward-evil spell, right there. Which was like swinging a flyswatter around after we'd already chewed up the landscape with the huge guns of the circle. But I did it anyway.

River was continuing to search for any trace of Innocencio. It was hard to believe that someone so flamboyant could disappear into the wind. I prayed over and over that he wouldn't come find me again.

Ottavio called River nightly from Boston. The news he had was unsettling: He could find no sign of the building where Miss Edna's club had been. I'd told him everything I could remember about its physical location, but despite going practically door to door for a couple square miles, he'd found nothing.

River had told him where to find the warehouse where Incy had taken me, Katy, and Stratton; and he had. But he reported that it looked completely unused—a thick layer of dust covered everything as if it hadn't been disturbed in years. Upstairs in the loft, he saw no trace that anyone had been there—no footprints in the dust, no signs of a struggle, no wide stain of Katy's blood. River, Asher, and Reyn had all seen it; I didn't have to worry about not being believed. But it was bizarre and scary that such a scene should be able to be so completely erased.

Anyway. The apartments were almost finished. I'd wondered if Dray would come back, try to rent one, but days went by without her return. Reyn and Joshua worked at opposite ends of the building, like third graders separated by a teacher, but they didn't cause trouble and I didn't have to kick either of their asses.

Brynne did indeed come to see "how things were."

"Good lord, what are you eating?"

I tried to swallow the too-big bite I'd taken. "Mpf," I said, waving my hand. When I could speak: "A quesadilla with shrimp, polenta, peas, and shallots. I'm praying that Julie Pitson gets pregnant again so she won't have so much time on her hands."

Brynne sat on the other folding chair and held out her hand. I put a quarter of the quesadilla in it, and she took a bite. She rolled her eyes happily, making ecstatic sounds, while I watched her and grinned because Joshua had come up silently behind her and could hear everything.

"Oh my God, that was orgasmic!" Brynne said, waving her hand in front of her mouth.

"Better than Anne's mocha layer cake?" I asked innocently.

"Oh, well, that—that, I just want to rub all over my body. But this was damn good."

I looked above her. "Yes, Joshua?"

Brynne froze, her eyes completely round.

"José's guys want to know if you can get a ghost out of apartment C," Joshua said, his face expressionless.

With very small movements, Brynne mimed strangling me.

"Ghost?" This was different.

Joshua nodded, and I got up. "Come on, Brynne. If you get scared you can hold—ow!" I took a couple hops, rubbing my shin where Brynne had kicked me. That girl had an anger-management problem.

The apartments' entrances were all in the back of the building, accessed by a single staircase and a balcony that ran the length of the rear wall. Upstairs I found José and his crew. Several of them quickly finished up their quesadillas and stood.

"What's up?" I asked José in Spanish.

"*Hay un fantasma,*" José said, and several of his workers nodded solemnly.

I looked at Joshua. He shrugged: Maybe there was, maybe there wasn't.

"*Qué tipo de fantasma?*" I asked. What kind of ghost?

"*Una mujer, señorita.*" A woman, miss.

"*Y qué dijo?*" What did she say?

José and the men exchanged glances.

"*Ella dijo que quería a la mujer con el pelo de nieve.*" She said she wants the woman with the hair of snow.

"Whoa," said Brynne as I felt a cold breeze brush my face.

"Tell me more," I said faintly.

. . .

"I thought the shops were covered," I said to River that night.

"They are," she assured me. "They absolutely are. This is very strange."

"You think?" I snorted and poured myself some Wednesday wine.

Do immortals believe in ghosts? Of course we do. We're not stupid.

"What else did she say?" River asked.

"José said that was all," Joshua said, dipping a hunk of bread in his pea soup.

"How do *you* know about it?" Well, *that* was a mean voice, coming from Reyn.

Slowly Joshua turned until he and Reyn were facing each other. I can speak only for myself, of course, but I think I can safely say that all of us at the table were expecting Joshua to tell Reyn to go screw himself. I held my breath, easily imagining either or both of them leaping up with a roar and going for the other's throat.

"I was in the next room, painting," Joshua said. His voice was even, but his fists were white-knuckled. "José asked me to tell Nastasya. He didn't think she'd believe him."

"And she would believe you?" Reyn sneered. River put her hand on his arm, and he almost jumped. The look he gave her was instantly aware, instantly embarrassed.

"Those buildings aren't that old," Anne said in the awkward silence. "I wonder who it is?"

"I wonder if it's a ghost," said Solis. "Or if it's someone trying to get at Nastasya by pretending to be a ghost. Or not even pretending—but the workers could only experience her as a ghost."

"But you felt nothing?" Asher asked me.

"I felt a cool breeze on my face," I said. "But that might have just been, you know, feeling creepy. I stayed awhile and walked through each room, and I didn't see or feel anything else."

"Hmm," River said, looking thoughtful.

The next day, she, Asher, and Anne all came down to my shops and examined every inch of every building. They even scried a bit behind closed doors. But they too found nothing, felt nothing.

The rest of the week was quiet, ghostwise, and I went back to dealing with business at my card table in the bay window. One day, late, most of the workers had left, but I was catching up on writing checks, which seemed to be a full-time job. José came up and stood by me, holding his baseball cap in one hand.

"Uh-oh," I said, examining his face for clues. It was dark outside, and most of the lights were off inside as well. The streetlamp shone in through my window, casting an amber glow on the floor. "More trouble?"

"No, senorita. I want to thank you for hiring my crew."

His English was so heavily accented that I wished he would switch into Spanish. But I got that he had rehearsed this and wanted to show respect by speaking in what he didn't know was not my first language. Or even my third or fourth.

"Well, Bill hired you," I pointed out. At least I hoped Bill had hired them. Were people now just showing up and working? The thought made my head ache.

"But you pay us."

I was apparently paying the larger part of the West Lowing population, but whatever.

"You guys do good work," I said.

José stood there, shifting his cap from hand to hand. I was starting to get uncomfortable: Okay, he had thanked me, now move on.

"Is there . . . something else?"

"Your money made—I sent my pay home to my wife, and she came here," José said in a rush. "She had my son here last week."

Oh. It all became clear. The baby was an American, born on American soil.

Because I'd given José a job.

"Congratulations," I said, trying to inject warmth into my voice. "But Bill is the one who hired you." *Go thank Bill. I didn't know about you, I didn't hire you on purpose, it was a fluke, I didn't mean to help you or your wife.*

But no good deed goes unpunished, as they say, and José wasn't letting go of this.

"You allow him to hire us," José persisted. "Many people would tell him no, no foreigners. Bill is my neighbor. He told me to come work here. He say there is a girl who will pay you for hard work. She pay everybody."

So I had a reputation as a sap, a soft touch. Excellent. Hundreds of years of hard-boiled toughness stripped away with one stupid project that River had made me do. Goddamnit.

"I pay everybody who *works*," I said limply, my hands balling up at my sides. I felt like such a fraud. Didn't he get it? I wanted to scream, *I'm not trying to help people here! I'm trying to help* myself!

"I work hard for you, miss," José said proudly. "And I thank you."

"You're welcome, José," I said with clenched teeth. I tried to stretch my lips into a smile, and finally, nodding, José gathered his tool belt and left.

I was near tears. I just wanted people to get on with their business and let me get on with mine. My chin trembled, and I gritted my teeth harder, furious. I wanted to torch the building, to run through and break everything, so I'd never have to endure someone's thanks again.

I sank down at my card table and covered my face with my hands. A slight sound made my head jerk up—was it the ghost?

It was Reyn. He walked over, silent as a leaf in his work boots, and held out one hand.

"What?" I snapped.

He bowed, like an old-fashioned courtier.

"I'm not in the mood for this," I spat out. "What do you want?"

With a look of exasperation, he grabbed one of my hands and pulled me to my feet. Then he half led, half pulled me to the middle of the shop. I dragged my feet, seething. He started humming something and then, holding me at his side, began to move. Being stiff and unresisting got me nowhere. After several moments I recognized archaic dance steps.

My eyebrows rose. "What the hell are you doing?"

"How about," he said softly, "if I just think of you as a person who does good things?" He forced me to move with him, two small steps forward, two small steps backward, a step to the left, a turn. He hummed, matching his steps to music I'd heard recently only in BBC costume dramas.

His hand on my back was warm, his steps light, soundless, and of course, incredibly graceful. This marauder, this Butcher of Winter, was being kind. And thoughtful. And romantic.

My shoulders relaxed a bit as my feet struggled to remember the steps.

Back then—the late seventeenth century—couples didn't dance alone. Everything was done in groups, all sorts of weaving in and out and tangling your skirts and forgetting who your partner was or where you were in the dance. Plus it was always muggy, even in winter, the ballrooms brightly lit with a thousand candles, all of them putting off smoke and heat.

But here it was cool and dimly lit by the streetlight. There was no one else, and only we could hear the music.

"This is a lot easier with just one other person," I said, revolving slowly in a circle around him, our hands raised, my left palm to his. "I could never keep it all straight."

He smiled, and as I held pretend skirts out of the way, he revolved around me, first facing me, then with his back to me, as we rose on our toes, up and down.

I let out a deep breath. "You might as well know. I'm the worst dancer. They used to call me 'the pretty one, who dances like a bear.'"

He laughed then, forgetting to hum. "That was you?"

My mouth opened. "Oh, come on! I wasn't that famous. Infamous."

This new Reyn teased, "You'll never know."

My feet felt lighter, along with my mood. We held hands and took rhythmic steps in a line, one two, one two.

A motion out of the corner of my eye revealed Joshua standing silently in the doorway, holding his leather tool belt, watching us.

Reyn's muscles instantly tightened in a line from his fingertips up his arm, making his whole body rigid.

Though self-conscious, I wanted to keep moving; I was finally starting to enjoy something that had always been a trial for me.

Wordlessly Joshua walked toward us. Reyn's tension was like a newly strung bow. To my shock and then delight, Joshua stopped on my other side and after a moment matched his steps with ours. He held out his fist, and I lightly draped my hand on it the way I used to, so long ago, and with men not one-hundredth as attractive or interesting as these two.

There—on the linoleum floor of the darkened, empty shop—the three of us moved in patterns we'd learned hundreds of years ago in different countries. We'd been different people with different names and different lives. Now we were, today, humming an old minuet and dancing, two steps forward, two steps back, a step to the left, and a turn.

It was really quite delightful.

CHAPTER 18

s the days passed, River was still subdued, smiling less easily, looking pensive as she moved about the farm. I continued to study most mornings, but also escaped out to my shops every day. The mood there was brisk and purposeful, and it was gratifying to see rooms finished and freshly painted, seeming full of potential.

No one heard or saw any ghost. Reyn and Joshua both came to work, but the momentary truce of our shared dance faded rapidly. Once again it was like having two angry lions circling each other, leaving me wondering which one would rip out whose throat first.

In between the exhausting and cramp-inducing chore of signing away gobs of money, I had some downtime to read and brush up on all the spells that I had been ignoring for the past, oh, four hundred years or so.

One day I was nodding off over a thick tome with the alluring title of *Various Worts of the Americas* when I blinked and there stood a little group of raggedy people, right in front of my desk. Another couple blinks and my eyes focused enough to see that it was Dray; with her was a hard-looking woman with bleached-blond hair and a face that looked like she had started smoking too young and hadn't quit yet: Luisa Grace, an oddly pretty name that didn't seem to fit her. The guy was tall, pale, skinny, and unhealthy or unfortunate enough to have awful acne.

I'd talked to Luisa Grace before, something about crafts?— but what was her connection with these two? If these motley three wanted to rent an apartment together, I was going to be in an awkward position.

"Hey," said Dray.

"Hey," I said cautiously.

"You know Luisa," said Dray, pointing at the woman. "And Skunk." The guy.

"Um, hi," I said. Skunk? Really? I realized that all of them were holding bags or boxes, and my heart sank. I mean, no way was I—

"Show 'er," Dray directed, and Luisa Grace opened her white garbage bag...and pulled out a stuffed patchwork teddy bear.

"Like I tol' you before, I make these bears," said Luisa, sitting it on my card table. "Out of old bedspreads. Like this." She pulled out three more; one made out of white cotton chenille, one out of blue seersucker, and another patchwork one, this one in pastels.

They were so cute. I picked one up, saw the neat, precise stitching; the pert, round ears.

"This is awesome," I said.

"I sell 'em at craft fairs," said Luisa. "And like at the farmers' market. They go for anywhere between sixty-five dollars and like two-twenty or so, depending on what they're made of."

"Whoa," I said, touching its button nose.

"I sold over a hundred and fifty of them in the last six months."

"Wow," I said.

"I make 'em, and my kids stuff 'em for me," said Luisa.

"Cool."

"Skunk," said Dray, and nudged the guy. He set his beat-up cardboard box on my desk and started pulling out T-shirts.

"I make screens," he muttered, dropping a pile of shirts on the table.

"He means he silk-screens T-shirts and stuff," Dray said.

I picked up the T-shirts one by one. They were covered with skulls, bomber planes, angry slogans, pictures of brass knuckles, etc.

"I like this one," I said, holding up one with red bomber planes dropping green bombs onto some dinosaurs.

Skunk nodded. "That one's Christmassy."

Dray was holding a small box that had once contained twenty-four cans of cat food. She opened it up and pulled out handmade jewelry: bracelets of telephone wire woven in complicated patterns, a necklace with links that were strips of an aluminum can rolled up like beads, another necklace with a pendant that was a hunk of frosted glass surrounded by copper wire.

"Did you make this stuff?" I asked her, and she nodded diffidently.

"It keeps me off the streets." She sounded bored.

"Like I said, I want to rent the shop with the blue front," Luisa confirmed. "To sell my bears in. And for other people who want to sell their stuff. Handmade crafts. These guys, and I got a friend who makes little jackets for wine bottles. So cute."

We "negotiated" the lease for a while, which means Luisa tried to bleed me dry, but finally she and I agreed on rent and signed the papers, and I had my second shop tenant. I didn't know how long Dray would continue to make jewelry, but I actually really liked her stuff and told her to save one of the bracelets for me to buy when they opened.

The consignment-shop lady had fallen through, but the third shop got rented the next day by a woman whose husband repaired guitars and violins—she wanted all his crap out of the house. But she also did simple tailoring, like cuffs and hems, and she was going to set up her sewing machine in one corner, and they would be there together.

Three new businesses on Main Street in this dinky town. Already more people were walking by, coming over to check it out after shopping at Pitson's or Early's. Ray and Tim were almost ready to open their coffee shop—You're Grounded—and the city health inspector was due this week to certify them.

Brynne now came to the shops every day, in her oldest overalls, with a bright cloth around her bouncing corkscrew curls. She'd joined a painting crew. If she didn't manage to actually be in the same room or apartment as Joshua, she was at least nearby.

One day she, Meriwether, and I were eating lunch together, laughing at something, and it hit me: We probably looked like three normal teenage girls, sharing lunch. Like regular friends. It was an interesting feeling. So weirdly everyday.

Of course, two of us were immortals who were trying to work through dark pasts. But other than that, we could just be three teenagers bonding.

And yet through all of it, I was eternally aware that Innocencio was still nowhere to be found.

But March went on without any more weird or upsetting things happening. Spring was definitely trying to get its act together; the woods were even more dotted with the bright yellow blooms of forsythia, fuzzy paws of pussy willows, and the deeper reddish yellow of witch hazel—bright pockets of color that made me ache for warmer days and long hours of sunlight.

Ottavio finally came back, unfortunately. Without him around, the tension in the house had been visibly lessened— or at least much of the tension: We still had Reyn and Joshua snarling at each other, and Daniel irritating all of us by offering savvy business tips and telling stories about the various fortunes he'd made. If I were River, I'd tell him to shut the hell up, but who knows? Maybe she still felt guilty for plotting to kill him a thousand years ago.

When I came downstairs one morning to find Ottavio setting the dining table, my stomach clenched. He looked up, his black shark eyes seeming to pierce right through me. I gave him a big, sunny smile and sat down on a bench.

"Ottavio!" Roberto kissed his older brother on both cheeks as Rachel set a tureen of oatmeal on the sideboard.

With a sinking heart I realized that breakfast would be a recap of everything he'd found out, which would sound like, *The world is imploding, and it's Nastasya's fault.*

With seventeen of us, the table was crowded and we were all squished in together. Showing admirable tenacity, Brynne had situated herself next to Joshua, casually brushing against him every time she reached for something. She leaned forward, and Joshua's gaze focused on her streaky caramel-colored hair, three inches from his face. He blinked a couple times, and it was right then that I felt he finally got stung by the Brynne seductive charm.

"Though the place called Miss Edna's seems to no longer exist," Ottavio intoned, "I did find one or two people who had heard of it. They were reluctant to discuss any of it. They seemed nervous, even scared, and refused to say much."

I'm sure it had nothing to do with his forbidding demeanor. Glumly I speared a breakfast sausage and put it on my plate.

"I know you talked to Tallis. Did you find Tante Marie?" River said, asking after some of their old immortal friends.

"I spoke to her—she's been hearing disturbing rumors about Terävä magick being made, big magick, dangerous. She was in England to check on her family." Ottavio angrily sprinkled salt on his oatmeal the old-fashioned way.

"What kind of big, dangerous magick?" Daisuke asked.

Ottavio looked frustrated. "No one seems to know. The closest analogy I can draw is that it's like someone stockpiling weapons. Someone, or a group of someones, seems to be gathering power through dark means. But I can't get any information about who or why. And you heard about Simon?" This was directed at River.

She nodded. "Simon is a friend of ours in Canada," she explained to us. "He's not from one of the houses, but he's very old and quite powerful. He was attacked but managed to fight off his attackers."

"Did he know them?" Rachel asked.

River shook her head, looking concerned. "He said he couldn't even tell that they were human."

"Wait—couldn't tell that they were human?" I asked. "I mean, what are our options? They had to be immortals—

humans. It's not like he was attacked by yetis or aliens. Right?" Or ghosts.

A glance passed between River and Ottavio, and I thought, Oh my God, there are *aliens*, and no one's ever told me. Maybe *we're* aliens. Maybe all *immortals* are—

"Not necessarily human," Ottavio said reluctantly.

"What?" Brynne looked startled.

"There are things worse than human," Joshua said, looking at his plate.

"Okay, you are freaking me out," said Brynne, putting down her fork and crossing her arms.

"Not everyone believes in them," River said a bit impatiently.

"Evil spirits," Roberto said, not sounding worried. He glopped more oatmeal into his bowl and reached for the butter and salt. "Things neither dead nor alive. There have always been fairy stories about evil people hooking up with them, getting them to do their bidding. Or the evil spirits overwhelming their human partners."

"Those things?" Brynne said. "Are you saying they're *real?*"

River made an impatient gesture with her hand, as if she wished Ottavio hadn't said anything. She was probably used to feeling that way.

"They're not real," said Solis firmly. "No one's ever said they were real."

River looked at him. "I've never known anyone who's thought they were real."

We all recognized that this was not a strict denial of their existence.

"Our danger comes from real people," said Daniel.

"I agree," said Asher. "We don't have to attribute these dark works to unknown beings. This is a person, or people, who are human enough to be greedy and power hungry."

Just then the door to the kitchen swung inward. We all looked up in surprise to see Anne standing there, pale and upset. I hadn't even realized she wasn't at breakfast.

"Every plant we set out is dead," she said simply. "Not from frost. Everything in the greenhouse, all my seedlings. All of the early peas and cabbages in the cold frames. Even the seeds I'd started in peat trays in the big barn."

"Why? What happened?" Lorenz asked.

"That's not all," said Anne, not answering his question. "In the root cellar—we have bushels of carrots, turnips, potatoes. All the things we store down there all winter. We're down to the last of them, fortunately—because what's left down there is rotten, full of worms."

"I got potatoes last night," Jess said in his scratchy voice. "They were fine."

"And I got butternut squash from there a few days ago," said Anne. "It was all fine then. This has happened in the last day."

"But our protection spell," I said. "That really powerful protection spell. How could anything get through?" Oh. Because maybe I had flawed it, weakened it.

"I don't think it could," said Asher. "Maybe this was set in motion a while ago. Before the spell."

"The spell wouldn't wipe it out?" Amy asked.

"It might not," River admitted, looking horrified. "The spell as we crafted it was about warding off evil, protecting each and every thing from spells, starting the second after we finished it. Somehow, unbelievably, I didn't think to put in anything retroactive. So if our seeds and seedlings had been spelled, our circle probably wouldn't have counteracted it."

Well, now I felt like going back to bed and staying there. For weeks.

As it turned out, even bed was not the haven of solace and warmth that one would hope. That night we were awakened by flashing lights, sirens, and a bullhorn telling us to all come outside, slowly and with our hands up. (Yes, they really say that.)

I was sitting in bed, groggily wondering what the hell was going on, when Reyn crashed through my door, his eyes wild.

"What's wrong?" I said, suddenly extremely awake. I scrambled for my jeans, pulling them up over the long johns I slept in.

"You're okay," he muttered, pushing a hand through hair that was already sticking up.

Outside the sirens screamed, and I wondered if all the poor farm animals were freaking out.

"What's going on?" I repeated. I pushed my feet into my clogs as fellow Riverites streamed past my door toward the stairs. Then we were out in the hall, hurrying downstairs as someone on a bullhorn kept ordering us to come out. It was like being in World War II again, and I could feel how tense and anxious we all were.

"Is it a fire?" Anne asked, sniffing the air.

River opened the front door slowly. Looking past her, I saw six or seven squad cars had driven up onto the grass, close to the house. Each had an armed policeman pointing a rifle at us.

Shading her eyes against the spotlight, River walked out onto the porch. We all followed her, starting to go down the stairs until one cop shouted at us to stop right there.

"Who runs this place?" A man not in uniform stepped forward. He was wearing a bulletproof vest under his open jacket.

"I do," said River calmly. "My name is River Bennington."

The man consulted a clipboard and spoke to a woman who had gotten out of an unmarked car.

"Who else lives here?" the man asked.

"My fellow teachers and students," said River.

Several cops opened car doors, and we heard excited barking. The K-9 unit. This seemed surreal, unbelievable. I still had no idea what was happening.

"How many people are here now?" The man consulted his clipboard again.

"Twelve of us live here," said River. "And we have five guests."

"Is everyone here outside?" The man looked at us, as if counting.

River turned around and also counted us. "Yes," she said. "Everyone's here. Can you tell me what's going on, officer?"

"We received a phone call that you were holding people here against their will," the man said brusquely. "Keeping hostages. The person reported at least one murder. Said the body was buried on the property."

River looked positively stunned—she almost swayed, and Asher stepped close and took her arm. "What? Who reported that? That's ridiculous!"

"I'm sorry, but we have to search the place," the man said, not sounding sorry.

River sat down on the bottom step of the porch, almost as if she could no longer stand up. Three different K-9 units set off; one inside the house, one into the side yard, and one headed toward the back, where the barns were.

The rest of us sat down, too, and a judge would have been hard-pressed to award the "most shocked expression" trophy.

"This is ridiculous," I said, echoing River's words. "Who would say something that absurd?"

"I don't know." River had grabbed a shawl, and now she wrapped it more tightly around her shoulders. "But I guess if the police get any kind of tip like that, they're duty bound to check it out. They couldn't risk it being true and not following up on it."

"If this is some local causing mischief, I want to know who," Ottavio snapped.

"You and me both," Reyn murmured. He sat close to me, solid and warm, and I remembered how strong he was, how capable he was to deal with anything, even crazy cops.

Asher remembered about Molly and Jasper in the barn and got permission to go put leashes on them so they wouldn't interfere with the K-9s.

"Where's Dúfa?" I asked Reyn.

Reyn pointed at his feet, and I saw the familiar white head, the pink-rimmed eyes. She was peering through his legs, growling softly at the cops.

"This is so weird," said Brynne, huddling for warmth. She'd drawn her long, bare legs up close and tried to wrap her coat around them.

Several bad thoughts crossed my mind at that point—like, What if Incy had killed someone and buried the body somewhere around here? Stuff like that.

It took almost two hours for them to go over every inch of the property. Finally, after conferring with the woman, the man came over to River, much more conciliatory. "I'm very sorry, ma'am," he said. "Obviously this was a nuisance call."

"Can you find out who it was?" River sounded calm and dignified.

"Believe me, we'll be looking into it," he said. "We know it came from a cell phone in the area. We'll be triangulating its position."

"So someone called up and said we were killing people out here?" I still couldn't believe it.

"Yes," the man said. "Not only us—they called the FBI, too." He nodded to the woman, who was talking into a cell phone. "Can you think of anyone who would want to cause you harm? Someone who would set you up for something like this?"

Slowly River shook her head. "I actually can't think of anyone. We're just a school—an organic farm. Nothing controversial. We've always gotten along with everyone in West Lowing."

The man nodded. "I'll ask around. We will investigate this—these were serious accusations. You could sue someone for defamation. And we could prosecute him or her for filing a false claim."

River nodded. "Can we go inside now?"

"Yes, ma'am. I'm really very sorry, but you understand that we had to investigate such a serious claim."

"Yes, of course," River said, standing up.

I thought, after all that excitement, I wouldn't be able to go back to sleep, but in fact as soon as my head touched my pillow I was out heavily, dreaming weird, dark dreams that I couldn't remember when I woke up.

ith Ottavio back, he and River amped up their quest for answers, and we often saw them poring over old books, maps, and charts of various kinds. I was curious about what they were looking for, but at the same time reluctant to get sucked into it. I was committed to facing hard things now, but that didn't mean I had to face every hard thing all the time.

My adjunct project was coming along. Of course there wasn't a plant nursery in West Lowing. I had to go twenty miles away to Wintonville to get some kind of shrubbery situation that would survive these heinous winters. I started to direct Harv and crew about where to put what, but he was itching to create an urban oasis with, like, rhododendrons. So I left him to it and went back inside, where it was warm.

But on the surface I was pleased with my shops, now almost complete. This had been a good project for me. And it would be good for this benighted town, too. I had made all this possible. It had been my idea. And though I loathed in-person displays of gratitude, this had been a good thing. I had done it for myself, but it wasn't bad that it had helped out a bunch of people.

And what was stopping me from doing this somewhere else? There were other abandoned buildings around here—and in the neighboring towns, too. And even in big cities—I could gentrify the heck out of any number of places.

A worker standing in front of me, his thumb running blood, broke into my happy reverie.

"Yuck. What happened?"

"Caught my thumbnail on the table saw. Pulled it off. First-aid kit is out of Band-Aids."

"Ew. Okay…"

"Pavel."

"Okay, Pavel. You go wash it off—with soap—and I'll run across the street. Hang on. Have you had a tetanus shot lately?"

Pavel, already on his way to the sink, nodded.

"And don't drip blood on my floors."

"Yes, ma'am."

I trotted across the street to MacIntyre's. A glance at my watch showed it was only two thirty—Meriwether would still be in school. In the first-aid aisle I got an assortment of Band-Aids, the good kind that really stay on, and went to the back. There was no avoiding it—Old Mac would have to ring me up.

And there was Mrs. Philpott, standing at the back counter, talking to him. As I approached I heard Mrs. Philpott murmur something, laughter in her voice, and then... Old Mac smiled. Smiled sincerely, his eyes crinkling at the corners. I stopped where I stood, staring. He looked so normal when he smiled. It was amazing. He himself was like an eyesore of an empty lot that Mrs. Philpott was renovating.

He didn't look thrilled to see me, but he didn't scowl quite as hard as he'd used to. Mrs. Philpott said, "Hello, dear," and I said hello back. Then he checked me out, and I skibbled back across the street, where I helped Pavel stick his thumbnail into place and then carefully put several Band-Aids over the whole thing.

The next morning I was on egg duty. When I blearily ducked under the low doorway of the chicken coop, I almost stepped on a chicken, still and cold. Quickly I looked—several other chickens were dead on the ground, and some were dead in their boxes. There were no signs of struggle, like from a fox or a snake. Just dead birds. I went to get River.

"I've called the vet," she said quietly as we surveyed the

coop. I'd put on rubber gloves and was picking up the dead birds and putting them in a cardboard box. The vet would check them for disease or parasites, but I didn't think she'd find anything. I thought they'd been killed by magick, and I was pretty sure River thought so, too.

"I can't believe the spell didn't work," I said in frustration. "It seemed so powerful—"

And it came back to me, how it was probably my fault that it hadn't worked because I had joined without receiving a real signal. I stopped, my hand holding the fourteenth chicken over the box. It was one thing to think it might be so; it was another to see the effects of it, all these birds, needlessly dead. Slowly I put the bird in, stacked on the others, while I tried to keep my face as blank as possible. I turned around as if to look for more chickens and walked to the back of the coop, peering at the ground as my cheeks burned.

"I'll go wait for Sharon in the driveway," River said, and went out. I leaned against the old wooden wall, my mind racing, my chest tight. I wanted to get back out into the fresh air and away from chicken poop, chicken feathers, and chicken death, but I had to face it: *I* was the reason the spell of protection hadn't worked. We'd all been floating around, confident that the amazing, powerful, beautiful spell that River had created was keeping us wrapped in a cozy cocoon of safety.

Except. Except I had been there that night. I'd stepped

forward, adding my voice to the others, forcibly melding my magick to theirs.

My magick. That I had channeled through my amulet.

I slid to the ground, my heart pounding. My magick hadn't felt dark to me, but I'd made so little in my life—would I be able to tell? River was sure my family's tarak-sin could be used for good or bad. It seemed so much more likely that it was designed to be dark, destined by a Terävä craftsman to create Terävä magick, always.

I hadn't gotten a sign, I'd forced my way in, and I had ruined the whole spell of protection, all of River's work, all of everyone's effort. Until this moment it had just been an idea, a nebulous fear. Now, in this chicken coop, it seemed horribly real. That beautiful, ambitious, awe-filled experience had been for nothing.

I felt sick.

Breathing fast and shallow, I picked up the box of dead chickens and left the coop. Sharon the vet's car was coming down the driveway, her truck tires crunching on frost-heaved pebbles. My fear and dismay made my hands shake as I stood there.

Still, River was mostly concerned with the chickens. If she saw or felt anything odd about me, she probably thought I was also upset about them. She took the box from me, and I escaped.

I was hugely relieved to hear that none of the other animals seemed affected—the horses, cows, goats, and few sheep that River kept all seemed fine. The vet would check them out, just in case.

I saw Molly, her remaining pups scampering about her, and Jasper, the corgi mix that helped herd the smaller animals, but my heart stayed in my throat until I caught sight of Reyn's tall, rangy figure and the gawky, long-legged white puppy getting underfoot.

Thank God my darkness hadn't killed Dúfa.

Several of the farm vehicles wouldn't start. Solis blamed it on the last cold snap we'd had. This late in the year, maybe the antifreeze had quit working. Yeah, it sounded lame to me, too.

I couldn't face anyone and didn't want to hear all the possible theories. I needed to figure out what to do, how to tell River. Finally I got the little beat-up car started and I drove to town—everyone else was staying at River's Edge to try to figure out what was happening.

When I saw Bill waiting for me at the curb, his face grim, I thought wildly, What now?

"What is it?" I asked, bracing for, like, half his crew to have fallen and broken their necks, or someone to have accidentally sawed off an arm or something.

"Upstairs," he said.

One of the four apartment doors had been jimmied open, the shiny new brass lock and doorjamb broken. With my heart about to beat out of my chest, I pushed the door open and stifled a gasp when I saw a body lying on the floor.

Then the body groaned and shifted slightly. That's when I noticed the beer bottles, the empty cans, the cigarettes that had been stubbed out on a floor that had just been sanded and refinished.

Filled with fury, I strode forward, finding two more people sleeping it off in the empty dining alcove. Bill followed me down the short hallway to the bedroom, where a couple of fully dressed girls had passed out on sleeping bags.

One of the girls was Dray.

I turned around and stalked out, wanting to shout and kick them and yell in their hungover faces. I closed the apartment door behind me and leaned against the railing, trying to control my anger.

"Stupid-ass punks," said Bill, his voice filled with disgust.

I thought about how Dray had been making that cool jewelry that she was going to sell at Luisa's shop. How dare she bust into one of my new apartments—one of the shiny, fresh, totally cute and fixed-up apartments! With her loser friends! Feelings of betrayal and hurt made my stomach burn.

And I recalled with piercing shame how I had done the exact same thing more times than I could remember, just for fun. My friends and I had had money, we could stay in any hotel, but sometimes it had seemed funny to break into some place, a friend's place, and party there. It had felt naughty and daring and humorous. They had seemed like stuck-up, materialistic assholes for caring and getting angry.

I had just joined that club. Karma was such a bitch.

I put my shoulders back and headed down the balcony to the stairs. "Where's a bucket?"

Yes, karma was a bitch. In my day I had experienced the distinct horribleness of being woken by a bucket of cold water in my face, and that morning I shared the lesson with Dray and her party pals. It was pretty damn satisfying. I don't even remember the stuff I yelled at her, the angry words she yelled back. She knew she'd screwed up, so that put her a step ahead of where I had been the last time I'd done this. I hadn't recognized my own culpability until... um, perhaps this morning.

She was embarrassed and furious, I was furious and furious, and I actually planted my boot on one of her friends' backsides as he clumsily headed down the stairs, cold and sopping wet. The five of them might have been even more hostile, but having to exit in front of a pissed-off construction crew whose work they'd just damaged took a lot of wind out of their sails.

I was glad the next day was Saturday.

day when we woke up and found no animals dead and no charred circle around the house was a good day. I didn't even mind being put on horse duty—my dread at having to deal with horses didn't compare to my dread of finding them dead.

Once Sorrel was clipped to the crossties in the barn aisle, I got the hoof pick and stood by her near shoulder. Gently I ran my hand down her leg and tapped the back of it, and she obediently lifted her foot. I'd done this countless times, so I barely had to think as I skimmed my hand over the sensitive part of her hoof, then began cleaning dirt and debris out from under her horseshoe.

Yesterday the knowledge about the spell of protection had really hit me in the gut.

Today, doing this mindless, repetitive work, my brain again bloomed with the regret of knowing that I had put everyone and everything here in danger. It was awful.

Here's the thing: I hadn't done it on purpose. I mean, I had joined the spell on purpose, knowing that I'd had no signal to do so. But I hadn't set out to *ruin* it. I pictured myself telling River, pictured the dismay that would come into her clear brown eyes. Then I pictured the understanding, the forgiveness. After all these months, I now *knew* that I would be forgiven. I *knew* she wouldn't kick me out.

But she would be disappointed in me.

I was embarrassed—more than embarrassed. I hated proving her brothers right. I was scared of being proven right myself, about how my tarak-sin could create only dark magick.

A small wet nose poked up through my knees, followed by a white head.

"Dúfa, you silly," I murmured, unable to let go of Sorrel's hoof to pat her. "Get away from these horse feet."

"Dúfa," Reyn called, and gave a short whistle. Immediately she ditched me and raced to her beloved. She'd gotten a lot bigger all of a sudden but was still gawky and awkward on those long, straight legs.

Looking up, I saw Reyn holding a pitchfork to muck out the stalls. He was wearing beat-up gray cords tucked into wellies and one of his plaid flannel shirts. I saw a bit of blue T-shirt beneath the shirt collar. I realized his skin was a light tan—obviously I knew that. But it just occurred to me that it was the end of winter and he was light tan. So that must be his regular skin color. All over.

I bent over my task, but this hoof was done and I was forced to let Sorrel have her leg back.

Reyn leaned the pitchfork against a stall partition, then bent down and stroked Dúfa between her ears. Her eyes melted with adoration.

My own heart swelled in a frightening way. The sight of the gorgeous man, the homely puppy, the love between them—I felt like I'd been punched in the chest. Swallowing, I tapped on Sorrel's rear leg and she lifted it. I was grateful to have this excuse to hide my face.

I was really falling for him. What a frightening realization. A montage of Reyn-filled scenes popped into my head—our old-fashioned dance in the empty shop, making out in his truck, making out in the hayloft, sword practice, eating Mexican food...Reyn angry, cold, playful, light, graceful, demanding. I gave a little cough to smother the moan building up inside me.

"Watch." He'd managed to sneak up on me as I writhed around in my reverie.

I let Sorrel's hoof down. "What?"

He pointed at Dúfa, standing alertly in the barn aisle. Her floppy ears were cocked, mouth open in what can only be described as a smile.

"Yes," I said. "The cuteness, it hurts."

"No, *watch*." Without saying a word, Reyn made a fist with his right hand, holding it horizontal to the floor. Dúfa sat, her eyes intently on him.

Reyn opened his fist and held out his hand, palm down. The puppy dropped to the ground, belly to floor. When he made a little motion she flattened herself further, laying her head on her front paws, eyebrows raised so she could keep her gaze on him.

When Reyn turned to me and grinned with pride, the barn seemed a bit brighter.

"Very nice," I said. "I can't believe she's learned all that— she's so young."

Reyn beckoned Dúfa to him, curling his hand upward. She leaped up as if on springs and ran to him, wagging her long tail. "She's a smart girl," he said, rubbing her head.

I waited for the inevitable comparison to me, where I came in second, but I didn't get it this time. The wonderfully familiar scent of his shirt drifted to me, and as usual I fell under its sway. Dark gold eyes met mine, and I tried to keep at least some of my hunger out of my face.

"I like to see you with horses," Reyn said.

I made a face. He knew how I felt about horses.

"You learned to ride when you were little." A statement, not a question.

I looked away, not wanting to talk about it.

"Saddle or no saddle?" Reyn? Annoyingly persistent? Why, yes.

"No saddle." Then, of course, I was thrown into memories of me and my sister Eydís, standing up, balancing on the bare backs of our running horses, seeing who could stay up the longest. (Me.) We'd had races across the flattish place close to the steam geysers, holding on to our horses' manes, clutching their sides with our legs. I was a better rider than Eydís, and when she turned twelve, right before she died, she'd decided she was too old to ride like a boy, with her long skirts hiked up.

But I'd loved it. Always loved horses. Wished I could have had an immortal one.

Reyn reached out and drew his hand softly along my back as I tried to keep my lip from trembling. I drew in a deep, tightly controlled breath, not looking at him.

"We share the same history," he said very quietly. "I understand you, who you are. And you understand me."

I kept my lips pressed together. To my right, one of the barn kittens was sneaking up on Dúfa's softly swishing tail. This should be good.

Then Reyn was holding my chin lightly, and I helplessly closed my eyes as his lips met mine. We were standing in the middle of the barn aisle—anyone could see us if they came in. But I was drawn into his warmth and comfort, all disquieting thoughts fleeing.

A sudden, high-pitched yelp and then a small, snarling hiss made us break apart. Dúfa had leaped after the kitten, who was rapidly and expertly scaling a stable wall in front of the interested eyes of Geoffrey, Reyn's favorite horse.

"Dúfa," Reyn said. The small dog was torn—surely the cat deserved justice—but her beloved was calling her. . . . In the end, she reluctantly left the kitten, coming to plonk herself dejectedly in front of Reyn. "Good girl," he murmured.

He turned back to me, the warmth of his chest still comforting me. "A closet, the pantry, the hayloft, the woods, the barn. Why can't we do this somewhere normal?"

"Normal?"

"Like my room," he said, his voice low. A delicious shiver raced down my spine. "Or your room. Or a hotel room."

I looked at him then. Somehow, the fact that we always met up in goofy places made it seem less important, less premeditated. The idea of actually *planning* to be together seemed so much more serious. My feelings for him were growing more serious, too. I tried to dampen the panic rising in me—I knew that I was really bad at relationships, still.

Beside me, Sorrel shifted her weight, pulling a bit at a crosstie.

"I should finish this," I said breathlessly. You are the biggest coward ever.

Reyn gave me a look that echoed my private internal assessment and told me my days of being such a wuss were numbered. I finished up Sorrel's hooves, then curried her until her coat was soft and perfectly clean. When the weather got warmer she would lose a lot of this thick winter fur, and then her summer coat would be smooth enough to shine.

The horses my father had had were big warhorses, even more heavily built than Titus, and not as gentle. My father had also kept a couple of "lady horses" for women or children to ride. One time I'd tried to climb up onto Djöfullinn, my father's own horse. His name meant "devil," so you won't be surprised to hear that I'd barely reached his broad back before I found myself stunned on the ground with the breath knocked out of me. I remember trying to suck in air, unable to move as Djöfullinn's huge hooves stomped nervously around my head. My father's steward caught me, yanking me by one arm out of the way of the horse's slashing feet. And then he'd told my father, and I'd gotten whipped with a birch switch. Between the bruises from falling, the arm almost pulled from its socket, and my whipped butt, I'd eaten standing up for a week.

But my father had loved that horse, and only my father could ride him, to battle, for festivals, for the village races, for hunting with his men. Faðir had ridden him the day his brother had come, my uncle Geir. They'd ridden off together, but only my father and his men came back. Only recently had I realized that my father must have killed his brother, in the old-fashioned way of immortals, so he could keep his power.

I stopped, brush in hand, as thoughts scrolled through my brain. What had Faðir said? That they'd gone hunting, that Geir had insisted on a race, that he hadn't known the woods stopped abruptly at a cliff...so had Faðir hounded him off a cliff? Or had he killed him and then thrown the body off the cliff? My heart squeezed painfully, remembering, and I realized that my father must have killed the horses, too. God.

Uncle Geir.

My uncle...the standard of five black bears...

Jess came into the barn, carrying pails of oats. I jumped up. "Jess—do me a favor, put Sorrel back in her stall? Thanks!"

River was in the front parlor, having tea with the Fun Four. I hesitated in the doorway, my brain humming.

"Yes, Nastasya," River said. "What is it? Will you join us for tea?"

Yeah, that's gonna happen. "Um, I just had a thought," I said. "I was wondering if I could talk to you? Alone?"

Ottavio put down his cup, offended. "There are no secrets among us."

I looked at him with pity. "You don't really believe that, do you?"

River was already standing up. "Let's go upstairs."

"Whatever you have to say to her can be said in front of all of us," Ottavio insisted.

River rolled her eyes at him and took my arm.

When we were sitting on my bed, I told her the story of Uncle Geir, how he'd been the only uncle I'd ever heard of or known about. But I vaguely remembered hearing my father say something about the five black bears on our family standard—how they represented five brothers. Maybe he meant five brothers from long before his time, or maybe he himself had once had four brothers. What had Geir said? That he was the only one left? The memory was foggy. It was a whole bunch of lifetimes ago. Obviously. And I'd been, what, maybe seven years old?

"Just now when I was currying Sorrel, it made me think of my father's horses and how he'd ridden off with Uncle Geir and his men. He came home without him, saying Geir had gone off a cliff."

River listened intently, the way she did, her eyes never leaving my face.

"I've always believed that Uncle Geir was killed, four hundred and fifty years ago. And that he was the last uncle. And he probably was. Almost certainly was. But... what if he hadn't quite been killed enough? Like, if Faðir slit his throat but didn't cut his head off completely, and then they went over the cliff..." Yes. This is the family I came from. "And he wasn't quite dead, do you see?"

River nodded slowly.

"It would have taken time to heal, maybe even years, and before he could come back for revenge, we'd all been killed anyway," I said. "Or—what if he wasn't the last uncle? I have no idea if there were others, when or if they'd been killed."

"But wouldn't Geir or some other brother come forward sometime in the last four hundred years to claim the Iceland throne?" River asked. "The whole world believed the entire house in Iceland had been killed. No one knew that there had been one survivor. Surely Geir would have come to claim his power?"

"Hmm. Yeah," I admitted. "Obviously he would have. I can't come up with any reason why he wouldn't. I don't know—it was just a weird thought I had, and then I remembered my vision about the procession, from my meditation. I don't know. But you're right—if anyone else was left, they would have taken over long before now."

I sighed and leaned against the wall. "I just want to know who's behind all this," I said, completely inadequately. "Like, *could* it be someone we all thought was dead? Someone from the Russian house? Or the house in Libya? But why would they be attacking everyone now? I don't understand." I picked at the hem of my blanket in frustration.

"I know," River said. "It's almost all I think about—trying to solve this, trying to figure it out. I've done everything I know to reveal who's behind this—"

And again the glaring, unwelcome thought that my

magick had ruined the spell of protection. And maybe even other spells, too. Maybe my presence alone, or the existence of my amulet, was making magick wonky in this whole area.

"What is it?" River asked.

I shook my head. "Nothing. Just thinking through all the possibilities."

If she grilled me, I would last about thirty seconds. I hated lying to her—my life had become so much simpler now that I didn't have to remember and keep up a long list of lies. In fact, I was opening my mouth to blurt out everything when we heard the doorbell ring downstairs. Hardly anyone ever rang the doorbell—we didn't get many visitors, and the mailbox was at the end of the driveway, a long way from the house.

Lorenz called, "Nastasya! Package for you!"

River and I made surprised faces at each other. "Been ordering shoes lately?" she asked.

"I wish."

Downstairs I found a white, medium-size square box on the narrow entry table. Lorenz's scribbled signature showed where he'd accepted it from the delivery guy.

"It's heavy," I said, lifting it. "I can't see who it's from— the return address is all smudged."

"Wait—" River said. Quickly she stepped forward and brushed her fingers over the box, her eyes closed.

"Do you feel anything?" I asked softly.

Opening her eyes, she frowned. "I don't know. I don't

think so. I—" She shook her head. "All the same, would you mind opening it here, in front of me? In case it isn't . . . benign?"

"No, of course," I said. "I hope it's chocolate. Several months' worth of Snickers bars."

The smell hit us as soon as I cut the tape. Puzzled, I pushed aside some crumpled newspapers, and then—

It took several seconds for my brain to process what I was seeing. It was Incy? Incy in a box? *What?*

"Holy Mother," River said, her voice cracking.

Then it clicked, and I realized I was looking at Innocencio's *head* in a *box* that had been mailed to me. Someone had mailed me his *head.*

My hands flew from the box as if on fire, and I staggered backward. The truth struck me like gunfire: This is Incy's head this is Incy's head so he must be dead Incy is dead and someone *mailed* his *head* to me—

It was too much. Reason shorted out. I stared at River as her face grew dimmer at the end of a long, black tunnel. I don't even remember falling.

Someone was holding my hand. No, someone was patting my hand firmly. Someone was holding my head, smoothing my hair. I was on a hard surface. My head hurt as if I'd hit it on something.

"Sweetie." River's voice. "Poor honey."

I swallowed. "What?" By concentrating I was able to open my eyes, and I looked up to see a circle of faces over me, solemn concern on all of them. Rachel and Lorenz were there, still wearing kitchen aprons. "What happened?" My voice was a croak.

It came back like a freight train, barreling through my consciousness, a fresh horror that made my eyes snap open and lock on to River's face. "Oh my God. Oh no."

"Yes, dear," she said, her face sad. "I'm so sorry."

"Oh God." I tried to sit up. Roberto was kneeling next to me, and he put his arm around my back. I tried to scramble to my feet, only to find that my knees were wobbly.

I breathed in and out as I crouched there, my hand over my mouth. I searched the crowd for Reyn or Brynne, but they'd missed this terrible scene. "Oh God."

"I'm so sorry, sweetie," River repeated.

"Where is it?" My voice cracked.

"On the table," said River.

I swallowed. "Is it . . . real?"

"Yes, dear. I'm afraid Innocencio is dead."

That just made no sense. My brain threatened to shut down again. I was shaky, my senses lit with nauseating adrenaline, my ears full of a high-pitched, anguished keening that only I could hear.

I moved toward the box.

"Dear, do you—" River said, her hand on my arm.

"I have to see." Maybe it was fake. Maybe we had all been fooled.

Sheer nerves kept bile from rising in my throat as one

trembling hand reached out to the box. And there he was again. Innocencio's beautiful, unearthly, appealing face. I'd seen it almost every day for a hundred years. He looked like he was sleeping.

But there was dried and crusted blood on the plastic lining the box, and the smell made me feel sick. I'd seen severed heads before, of course. I mean, my own family. Later I'd been in town for the French Revolution. The last time I'd seen Incy, in fact, my friend Katy's head had rolled toward me on a dirty warehouse floor. Because Incy had cut it off.

"Maybe Innocencio didn't kill Louisette," Asher murmured, and River looked at him. "Maybe someone killed Louisette and kidnapped Innocencio and then killed him as well."

Another layer of sadness darkened her eyes. "Yes. It's possible. This gives us new questions to ask, anyway." She came to me again, putting her arm around my shoulders. "I'm so sorry, my dear. Perhaps you should go lie down? We can bring you up some tea."

A hysterical bubble of laughter threatened to erupt as I remembered Anne's sister Amy joking about how they thought tea solved everything here. Including a severed head, apparently.

Being in my room would feel claustrophobic. "I think...I want to be outside."

River's eyes searched mine. "You won't leave the property?"

She meant, *You won't run away, try to run away from this pain? Like you always do?*

My throat tightened. I shook my head. As I went out through the dining room, Solis said, "We have to find out where this box came from, who mailed it."

"We should call the police." That was Charles.

In the kitchen I saw a meal half prepared and hastily abandoned. The kitchen door led outside. As if sleepwalking, I plodded out toward . . . anywhere.

he world looked surreal, colors a bit off. The sun was warmer today. It felt weird on my skin, as if I shouldn't be able to feel warmth or anything normal. I was chilled through, down to my bones, as if I'd never be warm again, didn't even know what warmth was. Warmth—sunshine...

ß ß ß ß ß ß ß ß ß ß ß ß ß ß

"*Sea—there you are.*" Innocencio jumped off the boulder onto the sand. I was bent over the low tide, scouring the seabed for shells, bits of driftwood, pieces of sea glass. My usual outfit of a sarong was wrapped around me and knotted on top of the thin cloth covering my neck; one hand held up two corners of the hem and I was putting my finds into this pouch.

We'd been in the French Polynesian islands for a couple years. I had gone totally native—living in a hut on the beach, wearing lengths of local cotton as clothing.

I looked up. "Sky—you're back!" We kissed each other's cheeks three times, left, right, left, and I patted his shoulder with my free hand. "And how was..."

"London," he supplied, frowning that I hadn't remembered.

"That was a short trip!" I said, and then spied a beautiful, tiny conical shell half buried in the sand. I pounced on it and swished it in the water to get the sand off.

"I was gone more than two months." Innocencio-Sky leaned against the huge rock and crossed his arms over his pale blue linen suit. The tone of his voice made me look up, and I saw irritation on his beautiful face, which was paler after two months in London. In...I thought—March?

"So this is what you've been doing?" He gestured to my damp dress. "This is why you wouldn't come for spring in London?" He shook his head. "Everything was in bloom. You know April is the best month."

Oh. April. I started some brain gears whirring, trying to get up the speed required to have a conversation with Incy.

"I was planning to come out," I said vaguely. "Time just got away from me."

Several years earlier, Incy and I had stopped off in New York City before catching a cruise ship to Greece. New York had always been one of my favorite cities, and it was where we'd first met, back in the 1880s. But in the early 1970s, New York City was a pit. America was in a recession, and NYC had been hard-hit. The city was dirty, run-down, with lots of crime. Hundreds of thousands of people had moved to the suburbs or to other cities with slightly healthier economies. Whole blocks of the Upper West Side were abandoned, with brownstone after brownstone boarded up, graffitied, used as squats by homeless people or drug dealers.

It was awful seeing it like that, and to help take our minds off it, we drank a bottle of champagne and then went to the Metropolitan Museum, on Fifth Avenue. Even the Met seemed lackluster, stuffy. Of course we went to see the Old Masters, many of whom I'd seen when they were current: the New Masters. Or even: the Shocking Upstarts.

I sat for a while in front of a couple of Vermeers—the light in his paintings always brought me back to the north with a nostalgic recognition. I'd lived in all of the Scandinavian countries over many lifetimes. There's a unique quality of light there, and Vermeer caught it as if by magick and imbued his luminous paintings with it. It made my heart feel heavy and leaden.

We decided to quickly dash through the Impressionists

and then get an early dinner before seeing some Broadway play or something. Impressionism sometimes seems the most accessible of all the art periods, the most cheerful. Maybe it's all the colors. I don't know. But compared to, say, the German Expressionists, the Impressionists are a bright, humming skip through the park.

But I digress.

The whole point is, that day we'd seen several paintings by Gauguin. Who was, you know, very into Tahiti. The way he painted it made it seem lush, wild, and primitive; bursting with life and juice and sunshine.

So we went to Polynesia instead of Greece, and we stayed there for years.

Leaning against the rock, bits of seaweed strewn close to his handmade Italian sandals, Incy sighed. "I sent you how many wires? You should have come out. I met some great people. Boz was there for a while—we stayed in his fabulous townhouse in Whitehead Crescent. You said you would."

"I meant to." I gave up on the day's hunting—Incy needed appeasement. "I can't believe you're back already. I was going to come out in a week or two." We scrambled up the rocks to the narrow path that led down to this secluded beach. I was one-handed, but Incy, watching me climb up after him, didn't offer help.

"I'm sorry," I said as we headed toward the road. "I really did mean to. You know I love being in London with you, April or no. I guess island living has made me fuzzy-headed."

Incy didn't say anything. "But man, I'm so glad you're back!" I put extra enthusiasm into my voice. He glanced at me. "I missed you so much," I said, feeling a twinge of guilt, because I guessed I hadn't missed him quite as much as he'd missed me.

In Tahiti my name was Sea Caraway. After we'd first come and bopped around the islands for a while—Bora Bora, Tahiti, the Marquesas—we'd settled on Moorea, the island closest to the big island of Tahiti. To Incy's amusement and then concern, I had fallen in love with a little hut on a beach. Pineapple fields came up practically to the back of my house, and for ten months of the year the air was heavy with the sweet fragrance of pineapples ripening under an untamed sun.

Incy thought I was nuts, living there—he had the biggest room at the hotel right down the beach, where he could order room service and get drinks at his reserved lounge chair.

But I loved my hut. Living there was like a fantasy, like a dream.

Incy had already had enough. He'd only stayed this long because I wouldn't leave. After the fifties and sixties, where I'd lived kind of big lives in the middle of society, I'd needed a break. I hadn't even aged and killed off my Hope Rinaldi self of the sixties—just had her disappear.

"Miss me? I doubt it," said Incy, pulling a big yellow hibiscus off a tree by the side of the road. He started shredding it with his fingers, leaving bright yellow shards of flower behind him like songbird feathers.

"Incy, of course I missed you." I linked my free arm through his. "I just got lazy and preoccupied, that's all. But now you're back! What say we celebrate at the Blue Dolphin?" Which was a semifancy restaurant at one of the diving resorts. "Just let me dump this stuff and change. I want to hear all about London, everything you did, everyone you saw, every bit of gossip." In truth, I would have loved to go back to my hut, sort my finds, light a lantern when it got dark, and maybe eat some fish and rice when I got hungry. But this was Incy, and I'd hurt his feelings, and it would be good for me to get out and mingle.

"Are you sure you're not too busy?" A bit snidely.

"How could I be too busy for someone in a gorgeous suit like this?" I gestured to his blue linen. "You got that on Savile Row. I'm thinking... Josiah Underwood?" I named a bespoke tailor whom I remembered Incy liking.

Incy grinned at me, and I relaxed. "Good eye," he said. "How long will it take you to get ready?"

"Two minutes," I promised. And so we went to dinner at the Blue Dolphin, and Incy told me everything he had done, and how much he had missed me, and how I needed to come next time, and so on. It was just—the rest of the world seemed so bleak right then. Vietnam, and the recession, and petrol prices. After the joyous, shocking creativity and bursting life of the sixties, the seventies seemed like a cheap movie, grinding down. I wanted to be away from it.

On Moorea the only constraint I had was Incy, but he

was also my only friend, the only person who really knew me, and for the most part he was fun and funny and my main source of excitement. While he occasionally needed extra tending, there was no suggestion, back then, that he would ever become the monster who had killed two people in front of me just months ago. Or that I would, on an otherwise ordinary day, open a box to find his head inside.

🌀

I came out of my reverie to find myself shivering on a bench in the barn. Moorea seemed so, so long ago. Sea Caraway had been calm and content, and tan—basically the opposite of me now. I breathed out heavily, wishing I could inhale wild salt air instead of this warm, horse- and hay-scented stillness.

Oh, Innocencio. He'd been so full of life. That's such a cliché, but it was true. Somehow Incy had managed to pack lots of extra living into this one life. My chest ached. I got up, feeling every one of my 459 years, and mindlessly climbed the ladder into the hayloft.

It was dark up there and warmer than below. Bales of Timothy hay were stacked up neatly. The piles were getting low—soon the horses and cows would be eating regular grass, outside. In the meantime, there was enough loose hay to mound into a nest and flop down into.

Innocencio was dead. Every nerve I had was raw, and I

cursed myself for not snagging a bottle of wine on my way out of the house. Something stronger would have been even better. Maybe I should go to town and—

I didn't want to go to town. But I didn't want to *feel* this, to *know* this. I wanted to be able to pretend that Incy was fine, not formerly a homicidal maniac and then dead. Actually *dead*. My brain kept shoving that information away, as if it was too big to get through the info ports.

We had gone through a lot together. And even after Boston, that horror, I'd still been able to look back and remember good times with him. Or at least better times.

When we were in Tahiti, he'd made me tie him to a big palm tree on the beach so he could experience a hurricane to the utmost. The wind and rain had lashed him for hours. He'd been scratched, bruised, and exhausted afterward. And exhilarated. Thrilled.

During Prohibition we'd been in a speakeasy in Chicago. I was wearing a gorgeous bias-cut gown by Vionnet. The place got raided, not by cops, but by gangsters stealing the already stolen liquor. There was shooting, bullets piercing wooden benches, making plaster chips fly. Incy and I had to duck under a table and crawl beneath an acre of benches and tables to reach the hidden trapdoor that not many people knew about. I'd been so furious about ruining my dress, but Innocencio had been laughing, excited. "This will be such a good story!" he whispered. I cut my knee on broken glass and swore.

We'd had lovely meals together, been in jail together, and went through the worst storm ever on a cruise ship off the coast of Australia. I was with him on safari when he accidentally shot himself in the foot. He'd been on crutches for a month. I teased him about it for twenty years.

He'd been with me in India when the train we were on crashed. Almost everyone in the first three cars had died. And yes, I took rings off fingers, wallets from jackets. I don't know what I was thinking—that person, Britta, seems foreign to me now. But at the time it was like, Oh, I can have *more*. More jewels, more gold, more whatever. Incy had made fun of me, poor little rich girl. But he hadn't stopped me. He accepted just about everything I did.

The hay tickled my neck as I blinked away tears. I didn't want to cry about this. I'd cried so much here in the last five months. When would I be cried out?

But it was, like, poor Incy. He'd laughed, partied, done more than anyone I knew. Grabbed every situation and wrung the life out of it. Had he ever been happy? Had anything ever been enough?

Since I got back from Boston, I'd been looking over my shoulder. I'd been saying ward-evil spells all day long. I was scared of him. Especially after he'd disappeared from Louisette's and we thought he'd killed her. Which maybe he had, still. I'd been so afraid that he was going to come for me again, that he would truly never let me go. Now he was dead, and I never had to fear him again. He existed nowhere, not on another continent, in another country, town. He existed no more, forever.

The tears began running then, leaking out of my eyes and trailing down the sides of my face. I turned onto my side and curled up, wishing I had brought a pillow.

Incy was dead, and I would never, ever see him again, see him smile, laugh. I would never feel his arms around me, smell the distinctive Italian cologne he always wore. I cried, feeling disloyal because I was relieved—not only because I no longer had to fear Evil Incy, but also because I would never again have to endure the weight of Lovely Incy, always there, always in my life, always by my side. It had been exhausting and stifling at the same time as fun and exciting. My whole life felt lighter with the sure knowledge that he would never be back, never need me again. That felt terrible; despite the unforgivable crimes he'd committed in Boston, my relief still felt like a betrayal.

This wasn't one of those gasping, almost barfing, wretched sobbings that feels like it's being ripped up from your stomach. This was quieter, a deep sadness that colored my soul blue. And unlike other crying jags, when it feels like time has stopped, I was aware of each passing minute, and every minute took me further away from him. Both good and bad.

Something cold and wet touched my forehead, and I gasped, my eyes flying open. A white face, broader now across the cheekbones, lacking the snub nose of a very young puppy, leaned over me.

"You've got to quit climbing ladders, girl," I told Dúfa brokenly. "It's just so weird."

She bent down and licked the tears off my cheeks. My first thought was, Ew, and then I realized her soft tongue felt comforting, and then I thought, Ew that I'd even thought that.

Reyn's tall figure blocked the faint light from the bare bulb at the end of the barn.

"I just heard," Reyn said. "Figured you'd be here." He nudged Dúfa closer. She licked my face one last time, then settled down next to me, her narrow spine pressing against my stomach. It felt comforting, like a furry hot-water bottle. I patted her tummy, and she squirmed closer to me. Then Reyn lay down in back of me, draping one arm over me. We were like a nautilus, with larger curves moving down to smallest.

It felt so good. My eyes were wide open—this felt so good, which meant it would feel so bad when I didn't have it. Which meant I should ditch it now, before I get used to it, so I can avoid the whole pain thing.

I lay there stiffly, imagining a future with no Reyn. I knew the day would come when we no longer had Dúfa, and that thought alone was awful. But no Reyn? Would there ever really not be a Reyn? Like there was no Incy now?

I swallowed, feeling how stuffed up my nose was. "At least now I don't have to worry about my sword skills."

"There will always be someone else," Reyn said quietly against my hair. "You will continue your sword lessons."

Yes, my life would continue even with no Incy anywhere in the world. It was bizarre.

"I'm so glad he's dead, that son of a bitch, after what he did," I said, tears leaking down onto Dúfa's white fur. "Bastard!"

"I know." Reyn's hand rubbed my stomach the way I had rubbed Dúfa's.

"I'm going to miss him so much." My voice broke, and I started crying in earnest. "I loved him so much."

"I know, sweetie. I know." He held me while I cried, rubbing my arm, my side, smoothing my hair. His gentle fingers picked hay off my sweater and then trailed lightly along my cheekbone. Every once in a while he reached farther and petted Dúfa, too, who sighed in her sleep, her little side moving up and down. Reyn was so solid, so warm, his arms protecting the two of us.

Eventually I was achy all over from crying. Reyn hadn't said anything in a long time. Carefully I sat up and looked over at him. He was dozing, still and silent even in sleep, the way raiders were. I'd never seen him asleep before, and I could take my time examining him without feeling the laser-sharp gaze of those golden eyes looking back at me.

God, he was beautiful. In a completely different way than Innocencio. He was colored like wheat and sun and mead, his skin a light tan like smooth deer hide. With his eyes shut, his cheekbones were more obvious, the symmetry of their planes ending at his strong nose. It had been broken enough times to have a bit of a bump on one side. His hair, thick and sun-shot, with the slightest wave to it, had fallen over his forehead.

The hand I held was wide and big, with calluses arcing across his palm right below his fingers. I wished I knew so much more about him. I would have liked to have seen him in other eras, other clothes, other occupations.

Or maybe I wouldn't. Maybe he'd been awful. I had been.

I sighed and raked my fingers through my hair, combing out bits of hay. This man had seen me at my worst, looks-wise, clotheswise. Did he care? Would he like it if I got all spiffed up? He probably wouldn't care.

I nudged off my clogs and lay down again, draping his arm over me as I faced him. Resting my head on his shoulder, I felt drained. Again and again I had a quick flash of Incy's face, and I flinched every time. I was so tired. I closed my eyes.

When I woke up it was raining, a brisk spring rain hitting the roof directly over my head.

Reyn was looking down at me; we were tangled together warmly, snuggled into the hay. Dúfa had moved and was now sleeping right where the roof met the loft a few feet away.

Incy. It all came back to me. Oh my God. I put my hand over my mouth, feeling an aching throb in my chest: the knowledge that Incy was dead.

Reyn looked at me solemnly. "You sure do like haylofts."

"I do seem to be strongly drawn to haylofts." My chest was

still tight with pain, but I was distracted by Reyn pushing one knee between mine. "Maybe because I lived on so many farms? Did you have a house like that, the barn animals downstairs and the people upstairs?"

"I was never a farmer." He started kissing my hair, my forehead. "I lived in tents, like yurts. I never stayed in one place long enough to have a house."

Wiggling closer to him, I pushed one hand under his sweater, feeling the smooth softness of the worn flannel shirt against his back.

"I'm practicing staying in one place." His voice was a murmur against my cheek, a vibration against my chest. When he finally kissed my mouth, it was a relief and a refuge from the terrible images burned into my mind.

Our kisses ignited, as always, like lightning striking a tree: suddenly explosive and white-hot and charged with electricity. His fingers ran over me, creating trails of heat and skimming the scarf around my neck. Without a word he started to unwind it, and reflexively I grabbed it with both hands.

"I've seen the scar." His voice was very quiet. "I have one just like it."

Slowly I brought my hands down. Keeping his eyes on mine, he took my scarf off and set it close by.

I unbuttoned his shirt, spreading it open and sliding it off his shoulders. When I saw the scar burned into his chest, I kissed it as if I could make it disappear. A little sound from deep in his throat sent a shiver through me, and I smiled. I felt powerful, strong, able to make Reyn tremble and breathe fast. Those high cheekbones were flushed and his amber eyes glittered with intent as he pushed my shirt up, and my plain men's wifebeater beneath it. Then we were skin on skin, burning hot, holding each other and kissing. The rain drummed on the roof over our heads, and it felt private and safe.

Oh, yes. Yes, at last, after so long.

I reached for him, my fingers clutching his arms as if he could save me from a flood. He grabbed my jeans at the waist and pulled, and I felt the warm, scratchy hay against my legs.

Impatiently he shrugged his shirt off, and I sat up and pulled him down on top of me, my hands sliding over his smooth skin as if he were polished stone heated from the sun. Our mouths were so hungry—I'd never wanted to kiss anyone like this, never wanted to be as close as possible, never held anyone so tightly.

When he moved down to kiss my stomach, my breasts, the skin at the edge of my boring underwear—that was when I felt the first icicle of alarm forming in my chest. Had I really thought this through?

What was I doing? What would he expect of me after this? Would he think he owned me? Expect me to be all lovey-dovey, all wrapped up in him? I had no idea. I mean, I wanted him. But for good? I didn't know, and right now didn't much care—it felt too wonderful.

It took only a few seconds for him to realize something had changed, to stop what he was doing and look up at my face.

"What's wrong?" His voice was raspy; he was breathing hard.

"What? Nothing. Come here." I closed my eyes and reached for him, trying to shut down all thought. When he resisted, I looked up at him.

"Lilja, what's wrong?" His voice was a bit sharper.

"Nothing! Come on, it was just getting interesting." I gave a flirty smile, one from an arsenal I hadn't opened in a century.

He moved back, sitting on his heels in the hay, looking at me. Awkwardly I pulled my shirt down with a couple of hard yanks.

"What's your problem?" I was starting to feel embarrassed.

He shook his head slowly, thinking. "I thought we were on the same page. But . . . Lilja—" He pushed his hair off his forehead with an abrupt gesture. He was still breathing hard. Still looked magnificent. "Do you want me?"

My head came up. "Yes," I said with complete sincerity.

"Do you love me?"

My mouth dropped open. We had never, ever talked

about love. He was changing the rules on me, right here. "What are you talking about?"

"I love you." He looked very calm, considering the terrifying words he was recklessly flinging around.

I gasped. With no warning, Incy's voice was in my head: *No one will ever love you the way I do.*

"What?" I asked Reyn, appalled.

His face shut down, and he reached for his shirt, thrown over a bale of hay. He pulled it on with quick, efficient movements, and it was painful to not be able to see his chest anymore.

"What do you want from me?" I demanded, winding my scarf around my neck. "I mean, I'm offering to go to bed with you here! Not to brag, but a lot of guys would be happy with that and not ask for more."

Anger lit his eyes as he did up his pants. "I'm not a lot of guys." The words were ground out between clenched teeth.

"Look," I said, getting to my feet and pulling on my pants. "Why do you have to bring love into it? You know I . . . trust you. I want you. Why do you have to push the other thing?"

He sneered at me. "Because two out of three ain't bad?"

My hand raked more hay out of my hair. "Look—I'm just not good at the girlfriend thing. I'm sorry, but I'm not. I wish I was. Wish I could give you what you want. But I know me. I will betray you. I will leave you. I will screw you over. I always do."

"Well, now I feel special." His voice had a particular bleakness, a coldness that made me want to cry again.

It hurt to glance at him, just for a split second. "You *are* special. You've gotten this far, which is a lot further than anyone else has gotten in more than a hundred years. And I do care about you."

When Reyn stood, he seemed to loom over me. His face was tight, his fists clenched, but I would never be afraid of him again. I knew he would never hurt me.

"You are so full of shit." He was trying to control his voice. "You are such a fucking coward."

"How am I a coward? I'm willing to go to bed with a northern raider!"

He gave me a furious look.

"Why can't we just have sex and be done with it?" I demanded. "Why does it have to be anything more? You *know* how much it hurts to lose something! You *know* how devastating it is to lose someone you lo—"

Gold eyes flared, but I'd stopped myself in time. A white shape moved in the hay; Dúfa was looking concerned, her head tilted.

I was done with this stupid conversation. I jabbed Reyn in the chest, almost breaking my finger. "And make your dog quit climbing ladders," I hissed. "It's weird!" I stomped past him and climbed down the ladder so fast, I almost slipped and fell, which would have been unbearable. I hated myself for wondering if he would come after me, but I heard nothing as I raced to the barn door.

Running back to the house by myself in the dark, in the cold rain, was the highlight of one of the worst days of my life.

CHAPTER 22

ne does not quickly get over receiving the head of one's former best friend in the mail. In fact, this was going to haunt me for the foreseeable future. Remember we've talked about how long my forever is?

One does not quickly get over Reyn. Why was he being so difficult? Why couldn't we have something simple? A very small part of me wanted to sidle up next to the word *love* and poke it with a stick, but my brain shut down fast every time I thought about it.

The next morning everything at River's Edge was overwhelming and heavy. I had shivering, heart-stabbing flash-backs of Incy every time I walked through the front hall, and the burden of knowing that I had corrupted River's big spell of protection was becoming heavier by the minute. I knew I had to tell her about it. But how? Would she confirm my most dreaded fear, that I was inherently dark? I just couldn't face it.

Reyn's words, calling me a coward, telling me I was full of shit, flung themselves at me approximately ninety times an hour.

It was Sunday; no one would be working at the shops downtown. I remembered how Dray and her loser friends had trashed an apartment—yet another bad thing—and decided to go clean it up, get out of here for a while.

"It's not safe," Asher told me, seeing me put on my jacket.

"I'll be okay." Famous last words. How many bodies had been found in ditches after someone confidently uttered that phrase? I'm guessing a lot. I grabbed the car keys.

"Take Reyn with you."

Ha ha ha! Yes, why don't I ask him for a favor *right now*?

"I'll be back by lunchtime." Assuming I didn't just face the car west and keep driving until I hit the Pacific. Perhaps kept going *into* the Pacific.

As I drove to town on autopilot, my brain was bombarded with questions: Could my uncle be alive? Had I truly ruined things forever with Reyn? How did I feel about that? When would I tell River about her spell?

Focus on the positive. Everyone was always saying that to me.

I parked on the street right in front of MacIntyre's and rested my head on my hands on the steering wheel for a minute. Think positive, positive.

Well, I was still here. That was something. Things here were pretty rough, pretty uncomfortable, and yet I was still showing up for breakfast, still sleeping in my bed each night. I hadn't run away. At least, not yet. I gave myself props for that. And let's set the bar really low, right?

My shoes rang on the metal steps that led to the apartments, and I stopped on the landing by the second door. Seeing the apartment that Dray had broken into made me angry all over again. Someone had replaced the door's lock and the frame, but the inside was still a mess. Someone had brought up cleaning supplies, so I picked up a garbage bag and started to throw things into it with more force than necessary.

There was nothing wrong with what I had done with Reyn. It was his fault that he was choosing to be weird and difficult. For a second I stopped, remembering his face, the way his voice had sounded when he said *I love you*. A stupid, very tiny part of me had felt joy and exhilaration at those words. But I just wasn't up for a whole, full-fledged relationship. It takes all my energy and my *extremely* limited emotional balance just to deal with being *me* twenty-four hours a day.

I stomped a beer can under my foot and threw it in the trash.

Why had he even pursued me? He knew what a mess I was. He shouldn't have even tried!

I'd started sweeping the floor when the sound of a car door shutting made me glance out the front window. In the next moment, I sucked in a quick breath and stepped back.

It was the creepy couple from last fall.

I'd been working in MacIntyre's. This couple had come in and bought allergy medicine and left. That was it. But their presence had turned my bones to jelly, and I never knew why.

Here they were again, and they were having the same effect on me. With no warning, I was terrified, panicky, my heart pounding. Very slowly I took another step back, trying not to cause a sudden movement that would catch their eyes. When I thought I was out of sight from the street, I dropped to my hands and knees and scrambled over to the apartment's front door, which I locked with its deadbolt, pocketing the key.

Then I crawled back to the window and very cautiously peeped above it.

It was the same car as before, an expensive black Mercedes. The woman's straw-colored hair was longer, pulled back from her face. The man was still beautifully dressed in a dark business suit, and still looked cruel.

Fear made my stomach seize. My heart pounded in my throat. I wished I had worn my amulet today—I'd taken to often wearing it under my clothes. But would it have drawn them to me? Would they have been able to feel its power?

Without making a sound, I repeated every ward-evil spell I knew, all the ones I'd been saying since Incy had disappeared. I'd quit saying them yesterday, after—

I peeped again; I couldn't see them. Oh God, if I heard their footsteps on the metal stairs outside I didn't know what I would do—jump out the window? Scream for help? You'll appreciate this irony: The person I most wanted to see was Reyn. If he were here, I'd be okay.

You *are* a coward, my hateful inner voice whispered. And a hypocrite. And a user.

If I had my way, my inner voice would never work here again.

The couple came out of MacIntyre's. Shading her eyes, the blond woman looked up and down the street, glancing at the row of shops. I sank lower, unable to swallow. Were they looking at the farm car? Could they feel my energy still attached to it?

My next cautious look showed them standing there, talking to each other. After several minutes of me not being able to breathe, they finally got back in their fancy car and drove away. I lay down on the floor, feeling as if I'd just run ten miles.

For another half hour I lay there silently, to make sure they weren't coming back. Before I left the apartment, I looked out every window, searching each shadow, each parked car to make sure they were really gone. At last I peered around the front door, then slunk down the metal steps as fast as I could. Rushing across the street, I leaped into the farm car and set a new speed record going home. All the while my brain was frantically trying to convince itself that it had been a weird coincidence, that they hadn't done anything to me then, and they hadn't done anything today. It didn't matter. My fear wasn't rational, but it was real, and profound, and only an idiot would ignore it. I was becoming slightly less of an idiot these days. *Slightly*.

Having actual faces to be scared of spooked me more than anything else.

When I got back, I went looking for River and found her in the kitchen garden with Reyn, Joshua, Amy, and Brynne. They were pulling up plants and throwing them onto a fire that was surrounded with white stones, with four large gray stones at the four compass points. The spring cabbage, Brussels sprouts, peas, turnips—all of those had died, withering and turning black.

Since the awful scene in the hayloft, I'd seen Reyn only at breakfast. I'd expected him to be cold and reserved, obviously angry, but he seemed to be making an effort to look normal. He should be glad that I had been honest, at least.

As usual, River's clear brown eyes looked intently into mine, as if she could see down into my soul. I tucked the end of my fleecy scarf a little tighter around my neck.

"You went to town?"

"Yes." I couldn't talk to her here. Reyn spared me not a glance as he pulled up turnips and threw them on the fire. Brynne and Joshua were working side by side, their heads close. When she heard my voice she straightened, looking adorable in a red sweater, brown corduroys, and paisley-print cowboy wellies. Making sure that Joshua couldn't see, she gave me a wide, goofy grin and clasped her dirt-covered hands together: true love. Swoon.

Joshua looked up, so I couldn't react. Why was she so attracted to him? He was distant, taciturn, a loner, a fighter—

Okay, never mind. You don't have to rub my nose in it.

"You get those." Amy's low direction to Reyn made him look at her. She gave him a little smile and pointed to the carrot beds. "I'll get these over here." He nodded, just as I remembered once again that before Ottavio had come, Amy had had a crush on Reyn. Maybe had it still. I didn't know.

Reyn could act on it now, if he wanted to. He was probably done with me forever.

"You okay?" River patted my shoulder, careful not to get dirt on me.

I nodded and decided to go back to the house. Maybe I would voluntarily meditate or have some tea or something.

"Lunch!" Roberto was heading toward us, his brown, too-long hair flopping stylishly over the collar of his plaid shirt and suede vest. The ensemble would look goofy on anyone else, but River's youngest brother could pull it off. Had he really remembered where we'd met? Because I needed that embarrassing complication right now.

"Okay, let's take a break, guys," said River, peeling off her gloves. She looked around the ruined garden and sighed. "I guess we'll try to replant here, after we dispel any bad energy?"

"Definitely," said Amy. I wondered how long she was going to be around. She was just visiting, which implied an end to the visit. Oh God, I'm such a loser.

"What's for lunch?" Joshua asked his brother.

"I don't know. Pasta or something. I didn't cook."

"I want mac 'n' cheese," Brynne said, dropping her gloves into a basket.

"Yes," said Roberto. "That would be groovy." His espresso-colored eyes met mine for a split second, then he turned and headed back to the house. But not before I'd seen a hint of a grin. I rubbed my temple. Yeah, he remembered.

To my surprise, Reyn was the last to go. He took his gloves and dropped them in the basket, then rolled down his shirtsleeves, buttoning the cuffs. A navy blue hoodie was draped over a raspberry stake, and he picked it up.

I looked at him—he seemed bleak rather than angry.

"So, when can you free up some time for a sword lesson?" Of the two of us, I was the more shocked that those brash words had come out of my mouth.

"I saw some creepy people in town," I said quickly while he was still looking for some no doubt scathing response.

Straightening slightly, he actually met my eyes. "What do you mean?"

As we walked to the house, I told him about the weird couple and the unexplainable effect they had on me. Despite everything, I was driven to share my fears with him. As though he might still care.

Why yes, I confuse the hell out of myself. Why do you ask?

He was silent after I finished my tale of muscle-freezing fear. Would he just walk ahead, ignoring me? Would he use this moment of uncharacteristic vulnerability to throw my rejection back in my face?

"Maybe sometime around four," he muttered, then left me behind while he took the kitchen steps two at a time.

I lingered outside for a moment, enjoying the unexpected and unearned warm glow of happiness inside.

've had so many different names. As I've said, all immortals must change their names and identities every so often; if you live in one place for forty years and never look older, well, people talk. Or come after you with pitchforks and torches. That kind of thing. I'm one of the lazy ones—never loving any place so much that I would go through the pain in the ass of pretending to age or die. I always just moved on after ten or twelve years, started over some place with new forged documents.

In my life, I've been Icelandic, Norwegian, Swedish (okay, somewhat unimaginative at first), Italian, German, Bohemian (from Bohemia), Swiss, Austrian (Austria is so pretty), Dutch, French, French, French, French again, French one more time (I was having a good run), American, English, American, German, Finnish (owned a small vodka distillery), French again (it was the 1930s, and I loved the clothes), Swedish again, Norwegian again, American again, English again, and now, as Nastasya, English. Mostly. I have several different current passports, driver's licenses, etc.

Have you noticed the distinct lack of Hispanicness? No South American, Brazilian, nothing farther south than France in Europe and Texas in America. No Australian. Maybe it's just where I'm from, what my original cultural heritage is, but I'm not an emotionally open or demonstrative person, and those cultures seem to embody that. You may be thinking, Oh, Nastasya, you're a cuddly, little, affectionate open book! In which case I would think that you were crazy, or perhaps had come into this story late.

Because I'm not. The only person I *ever* kissed and hugged of my own volition, many times a day, was my son, Bear. I'd kissed him constantly on his sweet, bright face; his smooth, round arms; his chunky legs. He was the being, the soul, that I've loved the most in my entire life. It didn't end well. I've never been inclined to go overboard since then.

Somehow, hundreds of years of increasing insularity, ever-thickening walls of protection, and a growing dislike of being touched physically or emotionally, had culminated in Los Angeles in 1982, when Nastasya Crowe was born.

♪ ♪ ♪ ♪ ♪ ♪ ♪ ♪ ♪ ♪ ♪ ♪ ♪ ♪

Innocencio had finally put his foot down about Tahiti and Sea Caraway. I think I could have stayed for several more decades, working on the best tan I'd ever had—we Icelanders are not a supertan bunch. But I left my hut behind, and we met up with Cicely, Stratton, Boz, and Katy in London. Then Incy and I went to New York to see if it was fun enough for everyone to come over.

"Who are you going to be?" Incy asked. He had already ditched the name Sky and reverted to his favorite one, Innocencio. We were lying on opposite couches in the living area of a suite in the Four Seasons, because our apartment wasn't ready.

"It's cold here," I said, and took a deep sip of my whiskey sour. Room service had brought up a large pitcher, to save time.

"It's New York. It's November. Of course it's cold." Incy's voice was a little bored, a little impatient. I hadn't wanted to leave Tahiti, but no one could withstand months of Incy's cajoling sprinkled with alternate bits of whining and insistence. I'd finally caved after he promised me a gorgeous high-rise apartment, interesting people he wanted me to meet, and an exciting art scene.

The apartment was being turned into a condo, so there was a ton of legal stuff to work out. The interesting people became interesting only after snorting coke in the bathrooms at Studio 54, and then it only lasted about half an hour. The art scene *was* exciting, but it was also angry and often political.

"I thought we decided we hated New York." I pushed my feet under a couch pillow to warm them.

I could hear his let-out breath from eight feet away.

"That was in the seventies, at the height of the recession," he reminded me in a too-patient tone. "This is the eighties, business is booming, and New York has new life pumping through it."

To think I could be in a cloth hammock between two palm trees right now—I unclenched my teeth to swig more whiskey. Usually I was much more agreeable, but I just didn't want to be here. There was no way he'd let me go back to live in Tahiti by myself. Bread 'n' butter, that's what we were. He was my best friend, the person I was closest to in the world. Why was I so pissed?

I shrugged, which was lost since I was lying on my back. "It seems dirty here. There're homeless people everywhere. I had to step over one to get to a taxi yesterday."

Innocencio sat up. His naturally curly hair had been gelled straight on the sides and poufed into a small pompadour on top. Sharp, angled sideburns struck a slightly sinister beauty to his face. "Fine! Where do you want to go?" he demanded, and stood up to point a finger at me. "And don't you dare say Moorea!"

"Paris."

"No. Paris is horrible in winter; you know that."

"And yet here we are in *New York*."

His mouth twisted angrily, and one hand smoothed his hair with controlled force. I lay on the couch, watching him with a mulish, petulant expression, wondering how far I could push him.

It was amazing, how he could will himself to change his mood, his face, change what he wanted or was willing to do. When he let out another breath, most of the tension left his body. He came to sit on my couch, nudging me over with his leg.

How well I knew that charming, rueful expression. It was the one he wore right before he got what he wanted by making it look like I was getting what I wanted. This ought to be good.

"As it so happens, just this morning I heard from my friend Lee, in Los Angeles. You know Lee—you met him in Boston. Maybe Milan."

"Can't place him."

"His name was…Amerigo back then. It must have been Milan."

"Oh. Him."

"He's in Los Angeles, and get this—he's a regular on a soap opera."

"Is that a TV show?"

Incy looked pained at my ignorance. "Yes. They come on every day. My *point* is, he's mingling with all these Los Angeles movie and TV stars. We should go *there*."

I used two fingers to fish around in my drink for the maraschino cherry and ate it.

Incy jumped up, happy again. "It's sunny there all the time, remember? Sunny and warm, the way you like it. We'll go, we'll mingle with stars, we'll crash parties—it's perfect. I'm calling a car to take us to the airport."

Somewhere on the way to the airport, I became Nastasya. Doors slammed shut inside me. The poor, broken-down neighborhoods we drove through seemed to reflect exactly how I felt inside. Incy was bouncing, glad to be doing something new, excited about the idea of mingling with stars and knowing he could now claim that he had done all this just for me so I would be happy. I was so tired of fighting with him—the last year in Tahiti had been fight and make up, fight and make up. It was exhausting.

And really, it took so little to make him happy, as he'd pointed out a hundred times. What did it cost me to go to Los Angeles for a while, for the winter? Nothing. But look how much joy it brought him. My life would be so much easier now. In fact, my life was so immeasurably better when Incy was happy that it was almost as good as being happy myself.

On the outside I let myself be jollied into a better mood,

listened to him chatter on the six-hour flight, and dutifully stretched in the sun when we landed at LAX.

The air smelled like smog and jet fuel. As far as I could see, the land was covered with buildings and roads and lights, stretching on into the desert, crawling up the mountains like beetles, swallowing the land with a concrete mouth. I liked cities, always preferred cities, except in Moorea. But this city seemed too sprawling, too...uncontained for me.

Our hotel had a pool that was a joke compared to the South Pacific. The scent of coconut oil and cigarette smoke clung to my skin. Most days I napped on a lounger, waking up to order frothy drinks with fruit speared on plastic swords. The pineapples had no taste.

One night we went to a party, given an invite by a friend of a friend. We'd gone shopping for some proper clothes, and I was in a white Halston with a halter top. I'd tied a pale silk scarf around my neck and fastened the halter strap on top of it. My skin was naturally burnished and tan; my hair was long and I'd dyed it dark blond—my natural color shone through as highlights. When I saw myself in the mirror, I saw a beautiful, striking woman with eyes as black and cold as outer space. Incy hadn't been so happy in ten years.

As gorgeous as I was, I blended into the woodwork at this party. More stunning women than I'd ever seen in my life were there, all of them taller than me. A couple of immortals were there—Incy's friend Lee and some of the models.

Innocencio was in his element, people magnetically drawn to him, his charisma almost as palpable as his beauty. He left with someone or a couple of someones, and I fended off bloated egos and crushing insecurity for another hour before I felt like surely death would be better than this.

The next day I cut off my long blond hair in the hotel bathroom with a pair of sewing-kit scissors. Every time I saw it, it reminded me of Moorea, where I'd been at least within spitting distance of peace. So what if I'd been running away from the world? So what if I never had to challenge myself? So what if I wasn't learning or growing or bettering myself? So what if I never talked to anyone from our crowd again?

The long golden chunks had fallen to the bathroom floor, leaving me with a ragged, choppy do above my shoulders. When Incy saw it, he hit the ceiling—he liked it when I was beautiful because it made him look even more beautiful. Horrified, he'd made phone calls until he located a stylist to the stars who could see me this minute.

The exclusive, snobby stylist did nothing but *tsk* during the salvage operation, sending Incy sympathetic glances, like maybe he thought I was some strung-out starlet who'd finally snapped.

When he was done, I looked in the mirror, and—I didn't know what I was looking at. Didn't know what I was doing, why I was there, what in the world I would do with myself.

I remembered that I didn't have to know. Incy knew. He would take care of all that.

The hollowed-out person in the mirror gazed back at me with dull eyes. "Dye it black," she said.

These days River's Edge seemed chock-full of tension with a heaping side of grim. Okay, we'd had a lot happen: the windows blowing out, the seemingly useless spell of protection (ugh), the burned circle around the house, the dead chickens, the destroyed garden. And yes, the box with Incy. Each time I remembered that, which was many, many times a day, I was jolted again by shock and horror.

Plus quite a few of us were having bad dreams, disturbing visions during meditation, good ol' fashioned feelings of dread and uncertainty.

Reyn and I were still having sword lessons. During which I sometimes "forgot" how to hold my épée, so that he had to touch me, moving my hands into position. Because, yes, I am exactly that pathetic.

One night in late March, after dinner, River asked us all to stay for a meeting.

"My friends," she said, her face solemn and lined by worry, "as you know, as we've seen, something's happening in the world of immortals. It's quite widespread and feels unquestionably evil. I feel certain that it will touch our lives here, and probably soon."

"Have there been more attacks?" Charles asked, the candlelight on the table deepening his bright red hair and diminishing the freckles on his cheeks.

"Things are happening almost every day," Asher said. He, too, looked weary and concerned. "We've heard from many friends and colleagues around the world. At first it was mostly immortals from the remaining major houses who were being targeted. Now it seems the attacks have broadened."

"An immortal learning center in Africa, a place much like this one, has disappeared," Ottavio said in his deep voice. "*Disappeared.* Thirteen people lived there; they're gone, and there's no clue what happened to them."

Brynne and I looked at each other, equally somber. When I reflexively searched Reyn's face, he was still, his gaze focused off into the distance.

"We've been approached, obviously," River went on. "The incidents here have been sad and destructive but not deadly— at least not yet, not for us." Just for chickens and plants. "We four teachers and my brothers are all certain that it's only a matter of time before a much darker and stronger force tries to wrest away our power."

"But we don't know who is this darker and stronger force?" Lorenz asked, his Italian accent sharpening. "We have no ideas?"

River shook her head. "It could be one incredibly dark

person with a sweeping agenda of death and ruin, or it could be a family or a group—something as unfocused as some Teräväs seeking to kill as many Tähti immortals as they can."

"We've scried many times," Anne said. Her dark, shiny hair curved perfectly under her jawbone and brushed her collar in back. "But the images we've received have made no sense—like gibberish."

"Our scrying could be affected by whoever's behind all this, anyway," said Asher.

"None of this seems aimed at one particular person or family?" Solis didn't look at me. Way to be subtle.

River shook her head firmly. "There are few major families or learning centers that have been untouched. Some have been only threatened, like us. Others have been utterly destroyed, their members killed."

"I can't believe this person hasn't left clues!" Jess said, his voice gravelly. "We should go to some of these places and hunt until we find something that will lead us to the bastard!"

"That would be one approach," said Daniel. "It does sound better than sitting here with 'victim' spray-painted on the house."

"That's an option," River said calmly. "But no matter what course of action we take, one fact remains clear: We must prepare for the worst. I believe we're facing a battle. I don't think any of us has ever faced anything like this in our lives."

Since her life began in 718, she pretty much meant that no one had ever heard of anything like this.

"We've talked, and we'd like to urge any of you, anyone who wishes to stay out of this, to leave River's Edge."

My eyebrows rose, and there was shifting and looks of surprise around the table.

"You can leave now, tonight," River continued. "I know of some places that I'm sure would still be safe—hidden places that are well cloaked. Any of you are welcome to head for them and stay in safety until this is all resolved somehow."

"None of us want to leave!" Brynne said. Obviously she hadn't seen the look of hope on Charles's face. Or, for that matter, on Solis's or Rachel's. Who could blame them? Anyone in their right mind would want to be out of this.

River gave Brynne a gentle look. "Each of us must decide for herself. Or himself."

"If there's going to be a battle, then there will be a battle." Daisuke hadn't spoken before now, and Joshua and Reyn both turned to listen to him. Daisuke had been a samurai once; had they recognized it? "We should prepare for the worst." There was no fear on Daisuke's face, but no excitement, either—only a calm certainty.

"Should we . . . go to Genoa?" I barely recognized my voice as my own. "Should at least some of us go to protect your house, your family's birthplace?"

A tiny smile softened River's face for a moment. "No, my dear. Everything that is important to me is right here."

Okay, got it—the four brothers. But what about books or jewelry or magical tools? Maybe fabulous tapestries? Wouldn't they be worth saving? I would give a lot to have even one book, one thing that had belonged to my parents. Was their family's legacy so protected?

Slowly River looked from face to face, crowded as we were around the long table. Candlelight had shadowed cheeks, made eyes look brighter and more intent. "I urge all of you, please—if you want to leave now, there will be no feelings except love and good wishes."

For the first time Joshua spoke: "Look, don't stay if you're going to be a liability. If you're not committed, body and soul, if you're not able to hold your own in a fight, physically or magickally, do us all a favor and leave."

"Joshua," River said, distressed.

"He's right." It seemed to gall Reyn to have to admit that. "Someone who isn't willing or able to fight, who doesn't want to save his life by any means necessary, is nothing but a chink in our armor."

River looked like she wanted to refute that but couldn't.

"I admire the self-knowledge that tells a person he or she is more useful somewhere else," Daisuke said more tactfully. "This situation is not for everyone. If a battle comes to us, it will be very bad, as battles always are. There is no shame in not wanting to be a soldier."

Well, since he put it that way...

"You don't have to decide this minute," River said more

briskly. She stood up and started gathering plates to take them to the kitchen. "I'll be in my office for the next hour. Please come see me, if you want to go to a safe haven, with my love." Taking the plates, she pushed through the kitchen door with one shoulder. Three of us made stacks and brought them to the kitchen. River gave me a strained smile, then left.

"Kitchen duty seems of lesser import, after talk of battle," Daisuke said, trying to lighten the mood.

Anne tied an apron around her waist. "Kitchen duty is never of lesser import." She snapped a towel at him, and he grinned and reached for another apron. I headed upstairs to my room to think.

CHAPTER 24

t breakfast the next day, we discovered that Charles, Lorenz, and Rachel had left. Despite her look of hope last night, I was surprised about Rachel at first. She was so strong, so advanced in her studies, and I knew she loved River and River's Edge dearly. But maybe she believed that she would be a weakness in a fight, and she left so as not to be a liability, as Joshua had said.

And yet, after that tense meeting, after the departure of three of us, nothing happened during the next week. I didn't go to town, though the project was finishing up and I was dying to see it. I told Bill that I had the flu, and that he was in charge but to not go crazy with my charge accounts.

Here at home we were all on edge, looking around warily as we walked from house to barn to field. The vegetable beds that we'd replanted showed their first, tentative shoots of pale green; the horses and dogs all seemed calm. Dúfa and one other puppy were the only ones left; Asher planned to keep the other one, a perfect, classic specimen of a German pointer, whom he had named Henrik. The remaining chickens were fine and annoying as ever. The one I had defeathered was now covered with spindly, unimpressive tufts that Anne thought would develop into real feathers. So that was good.

But no matter where we were or what we were doing, we kept a sharp eye on everything around us. We listened to the birds in the woods for any cries of alarm. We watched the horses and especially the dogs for signs of nervousness or aggression. Each night before bed, River, Ottavio, and Asher walked around the house, checking it for dark marks or evidence of unknown magick. We were paired up and assigned watches.

Every day, the weight of what I had done to River's spell got heavier, and the more certain I became that I myself was the biggest and perhaps only chink in their armor.

Six months ago, four months ago, two months ago, the answer would have seemed clear: Fly out of there as fast as possible. Go somewhere else, where I wouldn't have to think about it, could convince myself it had never happened. But I knew what I had to do. It totally sucked. And I'd put it off as long as I could. If I didn't admit it now, I might cause everyone here to die. But no pressure.

River was in one of the classrooms. She and Anne had spread an array of crystals out on the worktable, from tiny, gemlike ones to chunks as big as my fist.

"Hello, my dear." River's smile was strained.

"Hi. Um...as usual, I need to talk to you." I mumbled the words, dreading the conversation that would take place. I knew I'd be forgiven, but my inescapable family darkness, the darkness that had ruined her spell of protection, would probably dictate that I should go take a holiday somewhere hidden. Which I didn't want to do. But would if she asked me to. Even though I would hate it.

River hesitated a moment, and I said quickly, "You look busy. I'll come back later."

I'd already turned to flee when her gentle hand on my shoulder stopped me.

"Let's go to my room," she said.

We didn't talk on our way back to the main house. We went through the kitchen door, through the dining room, and up the main staircase like we had hundreds of times before. As we passed my door I was overcome with longing to leap inside, shut the door, and curl up on my bed. It was hard to force my feet to keep going, to turn right and follow River to the end.

I'd never been in River's room, though of course I knew where it was. At her doorway she brushed her fingers down the doorframe, whispering. A door-lock spell.

Inside, her room was not much bigger than mine, and just as simple except instead of a narrow single bed she and Asher had a double-size four-poster bed made of black wood. It stood so high that I'd have to climb up and jump down, if it were mine. Immediately I pictured Reyn sprawled across the white down comforter, looking at me with glittering eyes, and I shivered.

"Shall I ask for tea? I should have thought of that before we came upstairs."

"No, I'm good," I said. Some days I felt I would float away on tea.

There were two scaled-down armchairs, old-fashioned and tufted, the kind you'd see in England in the 1890s, set before a window. A small, round Shaker table stood between them, and River's knitting basket was beneath it. "Let's sit here," she said, gesturing to the chairs.

I sat. Now that I was there, my stomach hurt. Nervously I retucked my scarf deeper into my dark turtleneck sweater.

Patiently River waited, obviously wanting me to start.

Maybe I should just say something like *I'm worried about the remaining chickens, and maybe we should move them into the barn, and maybe someone*—"I ruined your spell of protection."

River straightened and looked at me more alertly. "The big spell?"

"Yeah. The big spell." My throat was so tight, I couldn't swallow.

"Why do you say that?"

"I didn't mean to." Possibly the lamest words in any language. *Je n'ai pas l'intention. Ich habe nicht zu bedeuten. Ik was niet mijn bedoeling. Io non volevo.* "I didn't mean to. But we were all there, and you said that each of us would get a signal—feel a push—about when to join."

"Yes?"

My voice was barely audible. "I never got a signal." Okay, it was out. It had been an anvil on my chest for weeks. Now it was out.

"What do you mean?"

Did I have to spell it out? What part of "I ruined your spell" did she not understand? "Everyone got a signal," I said. "Everyone joined, one at a time, as the spell went on. I was there, and I wanted to be in it, but I never got my signal."

"Then why did you join the spell?" River sat back in her chair, and panic flared in my gut. She would forgive me. But would she still like me? Care about me? Because, finally, I believed that she did. She did sincerely care about me. But here I was, disappointing her in a huge, important way. Like I always did.

I swallowed, wishing I had asked for tea. "I couldn't stand not being part of it," I muttered. "Everyone had joined. The spell was huge and complex and masterfully designed, like architecture, like a skeleton. I waited and waited for the push so I could join in. But I never got one. Because of who I am. What I am. I hated that. I didn't *want* to be *that* me—I wanted to be the me that was part of it." Out loud, this sounded even more selfish and uncaring than it had in my head. I fixed my eyes on a tiny split in a floorboard—it was like I'd forgotten how to look bored, how to sound casual about important things. Crap. "Anyway. I wanted to be part of that beautiful, amazing spell. I couldn't be the one left out. So I just stepped in."

"And then what?"

"At first my voice didn't blend as smoothly as the others. But I closed my eyes and sang, seeing it all come together in my head. And soon my voice seemed like all the others—part of it, seamless. It was like art."

River nodded without smiling. "Did you think the spell was perfect?"

I started to say yes, then I thought back. "No," I said slowly, and River's gaze sharpened. "I mean—the form was perfect. The design. The layers, the limitations, the powers invoked. That was all . . . the most perfect thing I could ever imagine. But there was something wrong."

"What do you mean? What was wrong?"

With surprise I saw River's hands in her lap, folded together as if she was trying to keep them still. Her knuckles were turning white.

"What was wrong?" Her voice was almost a whisper.

"There were—" I didn't know how to describe it and

didn't want to criticize something she'd worked so hard on. "Like, chunks missing. Like it was a tapestry, and the design of the tapestry was perfect, and the finished weave was almost perfect, but here and there, there were little patches of wool missing, tiny little bare patches. Or places where something was patched over. I was surprised—I didn't mean to do that, but maybe I did. Everything in me—all of me wanted to be part of the beauty. But since I wasn't supposed to be there, maybe adding my voice damaged the structure somehow."

River let out a breath and sat back in her chair quickly, as if I had slapped her.

Alarmed, I scrambled for something to say. "I'm so sorry, I was wrong, I didn't—"

"*Shh!*" River said, waving a hand at me, and my jaw snapped closed like a marionette. She almost leaped from her chair, hurried to the door, and opened it. "Asher! Asher!"

Oh God, she was going to get Asher to physically throw me out! This was so much worse—I should have realized how bad this was—I should have admitted it right away. I'd been lying to myself, trying to convince myself that it wasn't so bad, that she could forgive me, that she would never ask me to leave.

Hot, embarrassed tears sprang to my eyes as I stood up. "You don't have to get him—I'll go!" I choked out. "I'll just go, right now!"

That got River's attention, and she turned to look at me. "What are you talking about? Sit down!"

Shakily I sat and wiped my sleeve across my eyes. Okay, first there would be a yelling at. Accusations and censure and whatnot. Well, I deserved it. I'd done wrong, and I would sit there and take whatever they threw at me. It was the least I could do. Then I would get out of there or do whatever she wanted me to do. I could only imagine how tired she must have been of trying to fix me.

In just a minute Asher came, looking concerned as River closed the door behind him. He took her hand, then saw me sitting miserably in the chair at the window, trying not to cry.

"What's wrong, love?"

River pulled him over to the window and grabbed a low stool for him to sit on. "Nastasya, tell Asher everything you just told me. Don't leave anything out."

So I had to humiliate myself again. Sniffling, I nodded, and then in a low voice that kept cracking, I went through my whole stupid tale of how I had ruined everything.

"Tell him about the missing parts," River said.

"I guess—it was my fault," I said. It must be, if River was making me tell Asher about it. Not meeting their eyes, I repeated my tapestry metaphor. When I was done they sat back and looked at each other, not saying anything. This whole scene was starting to seem kind of bizarre.

"Huh," said Asher at last.

"No one else felt it," said River breathlessly.

"Except you and me," said Asher. "And Nastasya."

"Should I go now?" I asked in a tiny voice. "I just need to get some stuff."

"Go where?" Asher asked, confused.

"Uh . . . leaving? River's Edge? Because I ruined the spell?"

"*Tsk*—I forgot to clear that up," River said. "You didn't ruin the spell."

I repeated her words in my head, but they still didn't make sense. "I never got a signal to join in," I reminded her. Had she missed that part?

For the first time River gave me a slight smile. "You did, sweetie."

Whoops, there I went, right through the looking glass again! "Wha-huh?"

"Your overwhelming feeling of wanting to be part of us," she said gently. "Your refusal to be left out. The desire to join so strongly that you took a chance and stepped in. That was your push."

Okay, speechless here.

"Were you expecting a voice in your head?" Asher asked. The corners of his eyes crinkled, though he still wore an air of weariness and worry.

"Yes?" I mean, yes, *obviously* that would have been good.

"Everyone's push is different," River explained. "It can be

quite striking or more subtle. The signal you got was actually quite strong—you described it as being overwhelming, didn't you?"

Still had no clue what was going on. "Uh-huh."

"So you got an overwhelming feeling, and you joined," said Asher. "What part of that seems unclear to you?"

"Besides all of it? It was just a feeling! Feelings can be wrong! It was just what I *wanted*."

They looked at me, and I felt even more clueless and dense than usual. Which, as you know, is really saying something.

"No, my dear," River said at last. "When you're honest with yourself, in touch with who you are, and you know what your goals are—then, no, feelings can't be wrong. And what you want will make sense."

I felt like they'd hung me upside down by my ankles and shook me. I'd been feeling awful for *weeks*, every time I remembered what I'd done. They were saying it wasn't me.

"Then—what made the spell not work?" I blurted. "It was so strong! But things are still happening. It doesn't feel safer here than it ever did!"

Asher and River met eyes again, speaking without words. I remembered how Asher had said they'd been together for more than sixty years.

"We don't know," said Asher. "Clearly it should have worked. Except that during it, River and I both felt the missing pieces of the pattern, as you did. It wasn't you—but we haven't been able to pin down who it was."

"Like, someone working on it from a distance, like the other stuff?"

"It was someone here, Nastasya," River said. "Someone here deliberately ruined the spell, and so skillfully that almost no one would ever notice."

Oh my God. My brain started firing on all cylinders as I processed this information and its implications. *Someone here?* "Ottavio?" I tried to keep the hope out of my voice.

River gave me a weak smile and shook her head.

"Someone who knew what they were doing," I said, thinking.

"Yes." River nodded sadly.

"Someone very strong."

"Yes," she said again.

"I'm not strong enough and don't have any idea of how to do it." Let's just rule me out right now. Quickly I ran through the people here, determining whether they were strong or knowledgeable enough. Of course I didn't know them as well as River and Asher did—no doubt they'd already gone through this painful exercise.

"Not Lorenz or Charles," I said, and they nodded. "Not Jess. Not Brynne. Daisuke could, but he didn't." Somehow I was sure of that.

"Right," said Asher, looking depressed again.

"I'm guessing Rachel could, but I'm pretty sure she didn't." How weird—to be summing up who I thought they were and how well I knew them. Having gotten rid of the easy ones, the people who were left required more thought. "I don't think Reyn is strong enough. I'm sure he wouldn't do it." A northern raider has standards, after all.

River and Asher looked at each other.

Uncomfortably I realized I didn't want to narrow it down any more. The thought that someone here, someone I'd eaten with, done chores with, studied with—it suddenly hit me much more strongly.

"Oh my God," I said slowly. "It really was one of us. I, like, *just* got that."

River nodded. "It's a hard concept to accept."

"I need two things from you," said Asher. "I want you to think back and carefully examine your memory to see if you picked up on any clues of who it might have been. And two, I'm asking you to keep this to yourself. River and I haven't mentioned our suspicions to anyone except each other."

So if word got out, they would know where to look.

"Okay," I said. "Okay."

And that was it. My big confession. Their big revelation. And the sure knowledge that someone among us was dangerous.

CHAPTER 25

n the late 1570s I had saved up enough money to buy a one-way boat trip from Iceland to Norway. When I was little, my father had shown me on a large, beautiful map where Iceland was and Greenland and where Norway and Sweden were. He talked of other countries as if they were incredibly compelling and yet to be avoided at all costs. I asked him if he had ever been to any of those places, and he'd said yes. When I asked if he would go back to them someday, he'd said no, he never would, by God's will.

After my husband died in 1569, I'd made my way to

Reykjavík and became a house servant. My mistress, Helgar, had been the one to tell me the shocking news that I was immortal (immortal!) and offer up some of what she knew about our powers, habits, history. Which wasn't much. Her unquestioning, untroubled belief of the inherent darkness of all immortals had followed me for the last four hundred plus years.

When their stable groom had started to pursue me too strongly, I panicked and left—gathering up my things in a cloth bundle, sneaking out in the middle of the night like a mouse. The stable groom wasn't a bad man—he was offering marriage, and he wasn't unkind. No one could figure out why I would refuse him—they literally couldn't understand, like being married would save me from something. But I never wanted to be married again.

Reykjavík was a port, and it was easy to secure a place on the next trade ship headed for the mysterious, exotic, foreign... Norway. That trip was indescribably awful. There's no way to truly get across just how bad—I mean, to put it into perspective: Once, Incy and I were on a cruise ship off the coast of Australia. A huge storm came up that the ship couldn't avoid. It was actually really bad—this huge, heavy, luxury liner being tossed around on much huger and more powerful waves. The ridiculous power of the ocean.

People gathered in the chapel, crying and praying loudly, sure that we were going to go down. They held hands and stumbled from wall to wall, over and over.

Incy and I were pissed; we wouldn't drown, but if the ship sank, we were going to be frozen and miserable for who knew how long until another boat came along to sweep up the survivors and/or bodies. Besides being pissed, I was incredibly seasick, barfing a record twenty-seven times, long after I had nothing whatsoever in my system. It was, I promise you, an incredibly awful situation. The fact that the boat didn't sink and pulled into harbor only one day late didn't cheer up the passengers and crew nearly as much as you would think. People were still crying as they practically crawled down the gangway; more than a dozen collapsed on the concrete and kissed the ground; and I myself, finally standing still on hard pavement, got sick all over again at the lack of motion.

But it had not been that bad, compared to the crossing from Iceland to Norway. For one thing, as sick as I was on the cruise ship, I was inside, warm and dry. I had fresh drinking water at the ready, once I could lever myself up to the sink. If I had been able to eat anything and if I could have somehow made my way to the kitchen, I could have had food that was still good. And the storm part of that cruise lasted only a day and a half.

The trip to Norway was made right before trade stopped for the winter. And this was Iceland and Norway, so the weather already sucked. Add in the Little Ice Age effect of the Middle Ages (look it up), and we're talking beastly, bone-cracking cold; searing, razorlike wind; dim, halfhearted days that began at ten in the morning and ended at two in the afternoon.

It had been a narrow boat, maybe thirty feet or so in length, and a bit more than ten feet wide? Completely open to the elements: wind, ice, freezing rain, regular rain, salt water kicked up from waves, etc. There was no covered place anywhere, even for the captain. Dried and salted herring was the basic menu staple, but occasionally they served more herring, and sometimes for breakfast or dessert they dished up herring. I remember some people cheering when they finally broke into the rubbery, pickled shark meat. My own meager supply of half a loaf of bread and some dried apples had been drenched immediately and disintegrated into salty paste.

My bed was a double layer of sacking on the deck, and my pillow was the soaked cloth bag of my one extra overdress, my one extra apron, my one extra hair cloth. Instead of a day and a half of being tossed about and sick, this trip was almost three weeks of constant physical misery. All made worse by the fact that I knew no one in Norway, had no idea where to go, had almost no money, no real plan, except to try to get hired somewhere.

It had probably been the bravest thing I've ever done—leaving behind everything, everyone I knew, leaving behind my country, my past, and the person I had been. I took a Norwegian name, Ragnhild, the first name I had that wasn't Icelandic.

The second-bravest thing I've done was to come here to River's Edge, to try to save whatever Nastasya was left inside. Because anyone could have bet that it was going to be hard and I was going to hate what I saw. And I had.

The third-bravest thing was now, today, for me to stay. I was staying despite a frightening battle coming. Staying despite my lack of confidence in my own powers and skills. I'd known these people a bit less than six months, and none of them was related to me. One of them had been my family's sworn enemy. A couple of them couldn't stand me.

But here I was, and here I intended to stay. My first brave act had been to leave people; my third brave act was to stay with people. It seemed both brave and incredibly stupid, as so many brave things do.

Gosh, good thing I'm not paranoid, seeing danger everywhere, or this whole "traitor among us" thing would really get me down!

"Honey, you look so down," said Brynne, putting a sack of dried beans on the kitchen worktable. "What's going on?"

On a scale of one to ten, the desire to blurt out everything to Brynne was about a thirteen. Besides Reyn and River, she was the person I was closest to here. I trusted her.

"Besides the huge battle they think is imminent?" I filled a big pot with water, added some salt and pepper, and dumped a bunch of beans in to cook slowly all afternoon. Voilà—dinner. "Isn't that enough?"

Brynne nodded while I grabbed my jacket, then the two of us headed out to the big barn. Since I wasn't going to town anymore, it freed up a lot of time for me to work on my magickal skills. Maybe I was imagining it, but I thought I was improving, strengthening, magickwise.

"Oh, Nastasya—Brynne." Solis was just coming out of the herb workroom. Like the other teachers, his face looked tired and worried. "I'm glad to run into you, Nastasya. I would like to offer to teach you again." His blue surfer-boy eyes were sincere. "I'm very sorry I had trouble trusting you before. So much has happened—it's been a hard path to navigate. But if River has complete faith in you, then obviously I do, too. To make it up to you, I thought I could show you some interesting properties about stinging nettles. Or work with you on scrying with crystals."

Hmm. I had been so mad—and hurt—when Solis had sided with River's butthead brothers. Now he was coming back and admitting his mistake. The polite and trusting thing would be to accept his offer in the generous spirit with which it was intended.

Unfortunately I trust only a couple of people, and I'd stopped being polite back in the eighteen hundreds.

So I was comfortable with shutting him down.

"No, thank you," I said.

He looked surprised. "Uh...I can see I hurt you more deeply with my thoughtless actions than I realized. I assure you, Nastasya, that I truly regret anything I've done that upset you."

I started to get pissed. He was a teacher here, and he'd done practically everything except wear a sandwich board that said NO NASTASYAS ALLOWED.

"I guess we'll both get over it," I said.

Solis glanced at Brynne, but she shrugged. A door opened down the barn aisle, and Anne and River came out, talking quietly with their heads bowed. Then the outside door opened and Jess, Amy, Daniel, and Reyn came in. Reyn was the last and the tallest, and just as he walked in, his head blocked a shaft of sunlight so that it made a glowing halo all around him. Stuff like that is so unfair.

Anne looked up and smiled. "This is well met," she said. "I was just wondering if we should have a group meditation, and this would be a great group."

Yay.

"I think not, dear," said River, and Anne blinked. "No?"

River looked uncomfortable. "Group meditations might be too emotionally charged right now. Perhaps just you and I and one or two other people? But nothing over four or five people, and I'd like to be present. Just in case. If someone needs me."

This was weird, and I looked around quickly. River didn't know who to trust. She didn't want to take a chance that one of us might be working against her. I don't know if everyone picked up on that, but I saw speculation enter Reyn's eyes.

After several awkward moments, Brynne said, "I'll just go along to the workroom…" and left. Amy, Jess, and Daniel followed her.

River smiled at Solis and took his arm in hers. "Walk with us," she said, moving toward the door.

He smiled easily as they went outside. "Delighted."

Reyn and I stood there and looked at each other. Despite a couple of sword lessons, we really hadn't talked about… what didn't happen. I'd rejected his offer of love, and he'd rejected my offer of the rest of me. He'd been distant but not furious, quiet but full of thought. I kept waiting for him to throw it in my face or get mad all over again. It still stung, what he'd said to me about being a coward and so on. It stung, but instead of getting pissed and writing him off, I'd actually thought about what he'd said.

We just didn't see it the same way.

"Are you going to one of the workrooms?" I'm known for my scintillating conversation. Not really. But you knew that.

He raked one hand through his hair, making it stand up a bit. I tried not to think about his hair brushing my chin as he moved down…I gave a little cough, hoping my face wasn't red. Since it felt like I was standing next to a fire, that hope was slim.

"I guess I'll go to where you aren't," he said finally.

He wasn't trying to be mean, I was pretty sure. He was being straight-up, and I shouldn't blame him for feeling that way.

But of course I did blame him. In an ideal world, I should get to say or do anything I want, and everyone else around me should understand it and agree with it and there would be no repercussions. I'd had 450 years of being disappointed on that score, and grimly I realized that I probably had another century, *at least*, of continuing to be disappointed.

"Well, okay then," I said, wishing I had a snappier comeback. I raised my chin. "I think I'll go to the barn!" Ha! His own domain!

Golden eyes narrowed and his lips flattened, but when he spoke his voice was even. "Okay. Then I'll go to a workroom."

I kept my chin up and my expression cool. "Maybe we could have a sword lesson later."

Slowly he shook his head. "I just don't think...I can today." He looked so pained that it was clear he wasn't just trying to thwart me. It looked like being around me at all was hard on him, and getting harder.

I mean, so many people feel that way about me, but for other reasons.

Not feeling victorious at all, I headed out into the spring sunshine and went to the barn.

Here's something that will crack you up: I decided once again to meditate. I hoped this time I wouldn't have Ottavio's beady eyes staring at me as I did. But where could I go?

Six horses in a ten-horse barn meant four empty stalls. The devil-chicken was in one—every day we peeked over to see if her hell-spawn had hatched yet, but so far nothing. River was starting to think that the eggs had died when the other chickens had.

Molly, Dúfa, Henrik, and Jasper the corgi had staked out another stall and were asleep on the hay-covered floor. One stall held the barn tools, like pitchforks, wheelbarrows, and wide push brooms.

Which left one stall free. I didn't want to go up to the hayloft; besides all the emotional short-outs my brain had even thinking about it, part of me was afraid that meditation could still turn out to be like a bad drug trip. I didn't want to be twelve feet off the ground if I became convinced I could fly.

Lit candle + hay-filled barn = fire hazard, so I'd brought a hunk of amethyst to focus on. My mother's—my amulet was warm under my sweater. Inside the stall, I pulled the sliding door mostly closed, then sat down in a corner where I would be out of sight of any casual passerby. I bunched up a small mound of hay, glad that my butt wouldn't be on a freezing floor for once. I sat down, wiggled to get comfortable, and set the amethyst on the ground in a patch of sunlight. It glowed with a sparkling, inner purple light. I kept my eyes locked on it, reminding myself over and over again to pay attention, to not get distracted by the dusty air, the prickly hay under my legs. I breathed in and out slowly, batting stray thoughts from my head like flies. At one point a barn cat came in and sniffed me, actually standing on one of my legs and getting so close to my face that its whiskers almost made me sneeze. But I breathed in and out, and soon the cat wandered off.

Minutes passed, and the more I stared owl-eyed at the chunk of amethyst, the more it began to seem like I was looking at a photograph of the cosmos—a vast, deeply purple plain pricked with twinkling lights that had existed millions of years ago.

Show me what I need to see, I thought. In the skyscape, I myself was an infinitesimally small mote. My unnaturally extended life on this earth meant I was a star that twinkled for a hundredth of a second instead of a thousandth of a second, like other people.

And there it was: Sirius, the Dog Star. The brightest star in the sky, the main star of Canis Major. It was interesting but unexplainable why the eight major houses of immortals in the world were placed as closely as possible in the same formation as the stars in Canis Major.

I was lost in the sky, floating among the pointy lights, and yet dimly aware of myself sitting there, my legs crossed, every muscle relaxed. As I looked at the cold, distant stars, it seemed the sky slowly changed. Now I was looking down on the world from a great distance. A chill wind blew my hair about my face. I was floating, but moving closer to Earth with every second. The star constellation became a rounded, 3-D model on Earth's surface, with the world spinning to show the placement of the eight houses.

What did that mean?

I was plummeting to the ground but felt no fear, only a kind of wondering curiosity. Below me the world turned on its axis so that now North America was below me, then Europe, then Russia. The eight houses had become rivers, each one branching out. Not actual rivers with water and currents, but lines, with more dark lines spiking out from them in all directions. Some lines ended abruptly; others forked. Some had been forked but came back together. Some lines became a lighter blue, and some doubled back on themselves to meet up with their star-center.

The lines were now a fine web covering the land surface of the world. It looked like a coral reef, dense and complex in some places, sparse in others. Deeply colored sometimes but with splotches bleached white in irregular clumps. The web was dotted with glowing, twinkling lights, making it look alive and vibrant, pulsing with energy.

I was over Iceland, seeing the ragged edges, the deep inlets where the frigid sea had bitten into the brittle land. It still amazed me how relatively accurate early mapmakers had been, measuring distances from mountaintop to mountaintop, putting spits of land into perspective.

And there was our land, my father's kingdom: the narrow bay, the larger inlet, the patch of ground between sea and mountain that had been my entire world for my first ten years. Was I going to drop down, right onto the scorched and deadened ground where my father's hrókur had been destroyed?

No. The land below me was flattening, paling. I no longer saw ocean and mountains; I no longer saw the Dog Star and its rivers of long lives. It was a . . . drawing, on a table, in the library here at River's Edge. A drawing on old, old parchment, fragile and darkened with age. It showed a tree whose gnarled black roots seemed to clench the ground they were in. The tree's trunk was covered with deeply carven bark, shaded from peach to dark brown and looking almost exactly like a landscape itself.

The branches were twisted and few. Many had been lopped off—some quite short, others longer. The tree had been so severely pruned that it looked deformed—unbalanced and leggy.

Oh, and there I was. On one side of the tree, a single branch hung dejectedly alone, its end sprouted like a broccoli stalk. Names began to bleed through from the underside of the parchment, and I saw my name, Lilja, etched beneath one curling vine. My vine had six leaves growing from it, though one leaf had fallen, and a line joining mine with a name I couldn't read.

To either side of my vine appeared the names of my brothers and sisters; these had been bluntly snipped. To the left were my mother's name, Valdis, and my father's name, Úlfur, and to the left of those were other branches of different lengths. One or two had been hewn short, but there was a great waterstain blurring the image, melting ink into clamshell hems and obscuring the whole top right quarter. The water spread rapidly, soaking the parchment, blending bark and root and branch into one big, gray swirl. I tried to snatch it up out of the water, but my hands grasped nothing—

—and that was the movement that brought me quickly out of my meditation. I sat on itchy hay in a barn stall and was breathing heavily, my eyes wide. What had I seen? What had all that meant? I needed to go lie down and think about all this before I forgot.

My heart was pounding; I have to get up, I thought. But as I was trying to coordinate my muscles into synchronized movement, Dúfa pushed her way through the gap of the sliding door and dropped a dead rat at my feet.

With a startled gasp I made sure it really wasn't moving, then stared at the puppy. She sat in front of me panting cheerfully, looking incredibly pleased with herself.

"Dúfa?"

She turned at Reyn's voice and gave a small yip. When Reyn pushed open the stall door, he saw me sitting on some hay in the corner with a dead rat in front of me.

There is no etiquette school in the world that could prepare one to have just the right words at a time like this.

Reyn scanned the stall in a split second as though to get more context clues to help him figure out what the hell was going on. Finally he looked at me.

"Nice rat."

"Dúfa just dropped it in front of me," I said, my voice sounding odd to my ears.

Hearing her name, she bent down and picked up the rat again, shaking it fiercely as though to rekill it.

"Ew," I said, and finally managed to get to my feet. If she let go of it and it sailed into my legs, I was pretty sure I would jump and scream like a little girl. "Maybe—take it away from her?"

Reyn shook his head. "No—it's her kill. She'll probably eat it."

"Ah." Yuck. But okay, full disclosure—I myself have eaten rats. Present me with enough of a famine, have me living on peeled bark and grass, and I would eat rats again and be glad of it. But would I play with it first? No.

"You okay? Why are you in here?"

I picked up the amethyst, careful to stay out of shook-rat range. "I was meditating."

He showed no surprise. "Oh. It's dinnertime."

"Already? It's still light out."

Nodding, Reyn stood aside so I could leave the stall. "Well, spring," he said.

Yes, I thought. Spring, blessed spring after a winter a hundred years long.

We walked back to the house.

CHAPTER 26

fter dinner I stood at the sink, automatically swishing a soapy sponge over the plates, stacking them to be rinsed. My mind was still full of everything I'd seen during my meditation. I hadn't gotten anything anywhere about who among us might possibly be working against us, but maybe it had been there and I just hadn't figured it out yet. Or maybe there was just no way to tell.

At dinner Asher, Solis, and Ottavio had discussed ways to make this place physically safer—planning escape routes in case of fire, setting whatever spells they could think of to ward off whatever they could imagine. Daisuke, Joshua, and Reyn had asked if we should work on battle skills, fighting techniques, and determine who might be the front line and who would be the water boy and gun loader in the back. Not exactly—but kind of like that.

I had been the one to suggest that we all pack up and head to some beach somewhere, soak up some sun, have drinks with umbrellas in them. Just avoid this whole shebang.

Anyway. Here I was on kitchen duty. I mean, if we were really in imminent danger, would we still have to do dishes? No, right? Shouldn't I be stockpiling toad wort or bloodstones or something? Still, the quiet rhythm of washing dishes was kind of soothing. My mind was running through a smorgasbord of thoughts, but my hands were doing something useful.

Swish, wipe, stack. When I'd first come here, there had been only thirteen of us. After all the additions and subtractions, we were now fourteen. Fourteen plates.

"Hello?"

Startled, I looked up to see Amy smiling at me.

"Huh?"

"You must be deep in thought," she said. "I asked if you wanted me to take over, since you've already done most of them." She pointed at the sink.

My immediate reaction was, God, yes! Then I realized that it had been peaceful, standing here swishing, and that it seemed to help me think. Like having something to do freed up my brain power, such as it is.

"Oh, thanks," I said, stacking another plate. "But I guess I'll just finish up. Maybe you could start putting stuff away?" I nodded at the clean and dry serving bowls from dinner.

"You betcha," said Amy, and picked up a heavy, cast-iron casserole.

She was still dogging Ottavio, forcing him to speak to her whenever she could. From being completely oblivious, he'd moved into irritation, then prickly caution, and nowadays he seemed mostly on guard but not angry. This is what we do here instead of watch TV.

My hands in their yellow rubber gloves felt the heat of the water; I could smell the water itself, its traces of minerals coming from our well, and the lavender scent of the dish-washing soap. The kitchen window, newly installed and double-paned, didn't radiate cold the way the old one had. It was black and chilly outside.

I was busily scrubbing an enameled pot when it hit me: Today I had meditated *on purpose* by myself for the second time, and now I had chosen to finish washing dishes instead of escaping at the first chance. My hands stilled; the thought was so shocking that I had to approach it a little at a time. When I'd first come here, I'd hated everything River made me (and everyone else) do. The plan was always just to do it till she would relax and let me weasel out of it, maybe a couple of weeks. She'd told me the value of it, experiencing every moment, paying attention to whatever you were doing. Though I'd nodded to humor her, I'd known it was a bunch of touchy-feely crap that I would dispense with as soon as possible.

But here I was. I had drunk the Kool-Aid. She'd gotten to me after all.

Huh. This realization was rocking my world. It might seem small to the innocent outsider, but to me this was a tidal wave of change that I'd never, ever thought would be possible. Or desirable. Or tolerable.

Suddenly I felt like I were back on that Norwegian trade boat, but without the nausea and the herring. Just—at sea, leaving behind everything I had known, facing an unwritten future that might be wonderful, a whole new life, or might be a hard, painful, horrible disappointment.

As awful as I had been when I got here, as deeply necessary as I knew change was, still, now that real, bedrock change was here, it was shocking and scary. I knew the awful Nastasya—knew how to be her. This was a Nastasya that I didn't recognize. If this was good, part of being healthy, then it was positive. But I didn't know how to be this person. I didn't know how to be good every day, all day long. I didn't think I even wanted to try.

"Nastasya, what's wrong?" Daisuke leaned over and put some glasses gently in the sink. "You look like you've seen a ghost."

"Uh..." I was freaking out, full of terrifying self-knowledge, and it was taking every sinew in my body to not:

1. Run away.
2. Run away.
3. Or run away.

Daisuke's question solidified into concern. I was frozen at the sink, hands still in the suds, feet cemented to the ground. My eyes were wide and panicked, but I couldn't put two words together. A man of action, Daisuke took my hands, ditched the gloves, and then propelled me forcibly out of the kitchen. Amy and Jess watched with surprise, but no one interfered.

My skin was cold, and I was breathing fast and shallowly, as if I were about to faint. Out in the hall, he called for River, and she came out of the front parlor immediately. Not even asking what was wrong or what had happened, she took one look at my face, then got on my other side and together she and Daisuke steered me upstairs and into my room. It was ridiculous; I felt horribly conspicuous and self-conscious, and yet everything inside me was locked up, jammed, and I couldn't do a damn thing.

Quietly Daisuke backed out and closed the door behind him. River pushed on my shoulders till I sat heavily on my bed. Shaking, I leaned sideways as River pressed me down onto the mattress and pulled my covers up over me. She turned my radiator up; the comforting hiss of steam told me my room would soon be a cozy haven. Then she sat on my bed, put one hand on the lump of me under the covers, and she waited.

Staying here, being in my own bed, my mind screaming, I realized that panic (I mean panic without an outside physical cause, like a marauder) doesn't last as long as I thought it did. My panic, which I assumed would consume my life and thoughts for the foreseeable future, lasted about half an hour. I'd never sat with it long enough to know that.

Gradually I quit shaking, the room's warmth and River's presence getting through to my animal brain. As I calmed down, my synapses started firing more in unison, and soon actual words were scrolling through my consciousness.

Finally I looked at River. She looked back at me.

"Two things," I said, with a dry throat. She went to my little sink and got me a glass of water. I drank it, feeling like a lettuce leaf being revived.

"First." I took her through the whole meditation: purple sparkly, falling to Earth, landscape, tree, missing names, etc.

"I don't see how all that could be any clearer," she said, when I was finished. "That is, I don't know *why* you saw the eight houses, but it's significant, and I'm going to think about it. The tree is obvious, especially your family tree with your parents and siblings cut off too soon."

"What were the leaves on my vine? Am I supposed to start six more houses? Was the one fallen leaf my father's house? Or was it, like, what I should have been doing with my power but failed at?"

Her face grew gentle. "No, my dear. The one fallen leaf was your son, who died."

The usual stone arrowhead of sadness wedged itself in my heart.

"No," I said after a minute. "I don't think that's it. Remember the five other leaves?"

River just looked at me.

"No," I said again. "Because there were *five* of them, remember? So it's not children. Obviously."

River bit her lip and looked at the wall.

"River, there were *five* of them," I said stubbornly. "I'm not ever going to have any more children. *Ever.*"

"Well, it was your vision, not mine," she said. "It's a shame so much of it was ruined by water. It's like you either didn't know or didn't want to know what the rest of the tree looked like."

"Yeah," I said, pushing the painful, ridiculous notion of more children out of my mind.

Her look was irritatingly understanding. "What was the second thing? You said there were two."

"Oh." I let out a deep breath, feeling my muscles tighten again. "Well, I meditated today, as I just said. Voluntarily. By myself. For the second time."

"Uh-huh."

"Then I was washing up after dinner. Amy came up and

said she could take over because I was almost finished, and I said…I said, 'No, thanks, I'll just finish up.'"

Delicate eyebrows arched. "Really? You turned her down?"

"Yeah. So…I'm freaking out." *Clearly.* I huddled under my blanket again and retucked my scarf tighter around my neck. Because I didn't think I could truly change, deep down. I mean, yeah, Noble Nastasya had been doing the project in town and giving people work and whatnot, but no matter what benefit it had had for anyone else, it had all been to help me, myself—not them. And true, Good Nastasya hadn't gotten in real trouble for a while, but we all knew it was coming, right? It was just a matter of time. It was just that nothing had presented itself to me. But something would, eventually. Something always did. Life always offered me possibilities to screw up in big, unfixable ways. Always.

For a couple minutes River looked thoughtful, gazing off at nothing, sitting very still. My heart began to pound again, and I closed my eyes.

"You don't recognize yourself," she said at last.

Everyone should have a River. Think of how much therapy you could avoid by not having to explain your feelings.

"No." Muffled from under the blanket.

"You're worried you can't keep it up."

"I *know* I can't keep it up! I mean, *forever*? No. Probably not more than a couple hours. Maybe a day." My voice was rising in hysteria and I curled into a tighter ball. All of her work and teaching, all of her patience—coming to get me from Incy—all of that was so I could *sort of* do the right thing for a *day*. An *afternoon*.

"Honey?" River leaned over me. "You don't have to keep it up forever."

"What are you talking about? Of course I do." Or was it, like, maybe I do one century on, one century off, so in 21-something I could just let rip and be horrible again?

"No, sweetie. No one could commit to that or believe they could make good choices all the time, forever. I don't believe that about myself. If I had to promise someone I would, I think I'd go crazy."

Color me suspicious, but wasn't that *exactly* what her whole life was about? I sat up.

"How can you say that? You're the most good person I know! But I'm...*me*! I don't know how to do this!"

"Nastasya, you know I wasn't always like this. I had to learn how to change—we all did. Everyone here did. And it takes time, sometimes a lot of time, to change. Sometimes decades or a hundred years. Or three hundred years." I wondered if she was talking about Reyn. "All of us wondered—and sometimes still wonder—if we can keep it up. But you don't have to keep it up forever. Do you think you can stay out of darkness for an hour?"

I narrowed my eyes. Was this a trick question? "Yeah. Probably. I guess so."

"That's all you have to do," she said. "That's all any of us can do. And sometimes it's minute by minute, believe me."

"I don't understand."

"Try to be Tähti for the next hour. If you do that successfully, then try for the hour after that. When you get that hour under your belt, sign up for one more hour. And if you feel shaky, then go for ten minutes. You don't have to promise to be Tähti for the rest of your life. But try to be, just for one hour at a time."

It took a while for that to sink in.

River brightened. "The good news? It gets harder the more powerful you are."

My horror showed on my face, and she laughed.

"When you can't do too much, or aren't that focused, it's a bit easier to leave something alone," she explained. "Leave someone alone. When you're very strong and you know you could crush them like a meringue—that's when your self-will and control really get tested. That's when the minute-by-minute stuff comes in."

"Oh, *great*!" I needed to stop learning stuff *right now*.

River laughed again, and reached over to push my hair off my face. "You were really freaking out before."

"Yeah."

"How do you feel now?"

I did a self-check for fear and panic. "Better." Oddly enough.

"And you know what I noticed?"

"What a weenie I am?"

"No. That you didn't run away." Her cool fingers left a trail on my cheek. "Good job," she said quietly. "Well done."

The next day when River looked in at the devil-chicken, she found seven little puffballs running around, cheeping their annoying fluffy heads off. New life had come to River's Edge.

CHAPTER 27

'd been practicing using my sword on my own, doing constrained, quiet katas in my room, getting used to the feel of my downsized épée, its weight and balance. I'd tried hacking at winter-dried vines growing on trees that were now budding and covered with thousands of baby leaves, light green and as delicate as rice paper.

But when Reyn asked if I wanted to spar, of course I said yes. As usual, we went out into the open yard behind the work barn, which was good because no one could see me being all Mighty Mouse with my swordlet. I had to admit, I was enjoying learning sword craft. I would never be as good as someone who had grown up doing it, but I embarrassed myself less and less. It was true, what Reyn had said: I did like whacking the hell out of things.

When we sparred, Reyn used probably about 5 percent of his actual strength, but to me it still felt like a challenge, and my scarf got damp with sweat.

I lunged at him, keeping my center of gravity low.

"And...you're dead," Reyn said for the hundredth time, easily flicking my sword out of my blistered hand and touching me in my ribs with the tip of his blade.

"Goddamnit!" I said, rubbing my burning palm.

"This isn't fencing class," he said, waiting for me to retrieve my épée. His breathing hadn't even changed, while I was panting like a dog on a hot road. "You don't have to stay in a straight line with perfect posture, and you don't get extra points for following the rules. This is about stopping someone who's trying to cut off your head."

"I *know*." I took a bandanna out of my pocket and wrapped it around my hand. A blister had torn open and stung. A lot.

"Maybe you don't have the right teacher." The quiet voice from the edge of the clearing made us both spin around. Joshua stepped forward. He was holding a sword.

"It's hard enough for *him*," I said, gesturing at Reyn, "and he *likes* me. You have no hope of getting through a whole class of Nastasya."

"Maybe he just wants to show off his skills." Reyn's voice was flat.

"Maybe you don't want me to," said Joshua.

And just like that, the hills were alive with an overabundance of testosterone. I thought they'd called a truce several weeks ago—our triangle dance had been so lovely. But here they were, rabid badgers, already circling each other slowly. Reyn tossed his heavy Viking sword from hand to hand, not taking his eyes off Joshua. Joshua was rolling his shoulders, directly facing Reyn, his face hard.

Like, who had time for this?

"Maybe you guys should get a room," I suggested.

"I need you to move out of the way," Reyn said quietly, not looking at me.

Sighing, I headed toward the edge of a clearing and stood beside a large tree. I could jump behind it if I needed to. I remembered that Reyn and Joshua had faced each other in several wars over several lifetimes. For the past month, they'd kept a tight leash on their animosity, but it looked like those halcyon days were over. I wondered if I should trot back to the house and warn Anne to get a bunch of tea going, because these jackasses were probably going to sever at least one arm. But I decided it would be better to stay.

Actually, it wasn't funny. I grew increasingly uncomfortable as they circled each other, their eyes sharp and cold. Reyn always moved with controlled grace, whether he was milking a cow, riding a horse, or frying an egg. But this was different—the difference between the precise, economic movement of a ballet dancer and, say, a tiger with furious, hungry energy coiling in its muscles, its eyes mesmerizing the thing it wants to kill.

I'd seen Reyn like that before, and I'd never wanted to see it again. I'd been afraid of seeing it again.

And homeboy Joshua complemented him perfectly. River's brother had always seemed damaged and remote, his innate danger lying in wait beneath an imperfectly sealed mask. The mask was gone now. This wasn't Reyn descending on a village; it was two matched, elemental creatures following a script only they knew.

What buttheads.

The tension was unbearable as their silent feet described their circle of combat. I crossed my arms, my hands clenched into fists. At some unseen signal, they suddenly came together with a heart-stopping rush of power, their swords making a distinctive, surprisingly loud clanking sound that I hadn't heard in centuries. Sparks flew as their blades swung and met over and over, first high above their heads, then low to one side, then to the other side.

Leaves crackled behind me, and I turned to see Brynne, her eyes glued on the battle, her face solemn. "I've never seen anything like that," she murmured.

"I have. It gets worse." Surely they wouldn't really cut

each other's heads off, would they? My heart couldn't approach facing that, so I concentrated on just watching, as if I had paid to see this performance.

The week before, Reyn and I had been sparring a bit. I'd really let loose and was going at him in every way I could think of, blade swinging forward, backhanded, everything. After what felt like three hours, I'd been bent double, chest heaving, feeling like I was going to barf from exertion. It had been six minutes. That was how long I lasted, and I still got killed four times. If I were ever in a life-or-death battle with someone wielding a sword, it needed to be over in less than six minutes. And they needed to be mortal.

"Not exactly the two musketeers, is it?" Daisuke murmured next to me. The telltale sound of tempered steel crashing against tempered steel had prompted several people to come see what was happening—Asher had run up holding what I assumed was his own sword. When I glanced down, I saw that Daisuke had one tucked into his belt—long, thin, and slightly curved like a saber.

"No," I agreed. This was no duel of honor, with one hand flung artistically into the air and the opponents taking turns with thrusting and parrying. His angular face distorted with loathing, Reyn slashed savagely at Joshua, both hands on his leather-wrapped hilt, the force of his blows shaking his arms to his shoulders. The bloodlust on Joshua's face reminded me that long ago, River had planned to kill him before his power eclipsed her own.

"Oh, goddess, I knew this was coming." River's voice was quiet as Asher reached for her hand and held it.

"This didn't have to happen," I said tightly. My stomach muscles were knotted with tension—I dreaded seeing someone get devastatingly hurt, but I couldn't look away.

River sighed. "Yeah, it probably did. Those idiots."

"And what happens afterward?" Brynne asked. "The winner will dance around, saying 'Pwned!'?"

"Nothing that innocent, I'm afraid," said River.

Nowadays when people think of war, they picture soldiers hunkered down somewhere with a bazooka and huge shells exploding in the distance. The sounds are explosive booms and sharp, crackling automatic rifles. But for most of my life, war had sounded like clanging metal; men shouting; horses screaming; the twang of arrows; the stretching, popping sound of a trebuchet; the whistling *thunk* of a spear. The smell of fire.

This scene reminded me of what war had once been: man on man, hand-to-hand combat. And actually, that's one thing that I do think was better in the old days—war. It was brutal, bloody, savage, and devastating—on a much smaller scale. Men had to be close enough to see one another to attack—none of this long-range missile crap or planes dropping bombs on people or places they'd never see. You can tell I'm still pissed about World War II.

Brynne's hissing intake of breath snapped my attention back to Reyn and Joshua.

First blood had been drawn.

An arcing spray of red spattered Joshua's face, but I couldn't tell whose blood it was. With an ungodly roar, he spun around and slammed his sword against Reyn's. It would have knocked me into the middle of next week, but Reyn absorbed it without flinching, did a half turn himself, and struck out with his blade—

—which went right into Joshua's side. Like, zip! And then was pulled out again quickly.

Everyone except Daisuke gasped.

For a fraction of a second Reyn looked shocked—it would have felled a regular person—but then Joshua snarled and raised his blade, and the fight went on, though their clothes were now being stained with Joshua's flowing blood.

"Can you make them stop?" Brynne whispered to River.

River looked at her sympathetically. "What do you think, sweetie?"

Reluctantly Brynne turned back to the show. I couldn't imagine what she was thinking—she'd been jonesing for Joshua for a while, but now she was seeing a side to him that she had probably never imagined.

And look at me, with Reyn: that's who loved me, who wanted me to love him—the guy who had just run a sword through my friend's brother.

I mean, okay, the brother had shown up uninvited, clearly wanting a fight. But still.

Then it happened: After what felt like an hour of slashing

and clanging and grunting and roaring and hissing, Reyn and Joshua simultaneously reached the defining moment. Somehow, with perfect timing and exactly the right series of movements, they each swung with all their might and… suddenly stopped, their positions mirrored, each with a bloodstained blade less than an inch from the other's neck.

Brynne and I grabbed each other's hands; I felt Asher holding River in place. Seconds ticked by agonizingly slowly. The two of them were as still as startled deer, though their chests were heaving like bellows. But no hand trembled, no foot moved, no muscle coiled in preparation of attack.

It was over. It just took them a while to accept it.

Very cautiously they moved their swords away from each other's necks, one fraction of an inch at a time. Then again in unrehearsed unison they swung their swords down, stepping back quickly and silently out of the other's reach.

"This was great. Let's do this again soon," I said, but with zero bravado.

"I might be sick," Brynne murmured, looking pale and upset. Daisuke put his arm around her and started to lead her back to the house. He sure was doing a lot of stunned-female wrangling lately.

As soon as it looked like the berserker factor was waning, River hurried to her brother and put her hand on his side, which was bleeding freely.

Frowning, Joshua looked down at it, then pressed his

hand on it more firmly to stem the bleeding. "That was a lucky hit," he said dismissively.

I tensed, waiting for Reyn to leap forward at the insult—but to my surprise, after a moment he laughed, his teeth very white against his blood-spattered face.

"Yeah," he said, "it was."

Slowly Joshua grinned. Reyn grinned back. Then both of them were laughing, Reyn leaning on his sword to keep from doubling over. The dirt beneath their feet was laced with blood; the leaves had been kicked away. Their clothes were nicked and sliced from knee to shoulder, and they each had at least three other smaller wounds that were blooming roses of blood into the fabric.

Then Joshua grimaced, and River said, "Let's get you to the house, you ridiculous imbecile."

"Yeah, okay." He submitted to his older sister's will and started to walk, limping slightly, toward the house. Pausing, he turned to look back at Reyn. "God's teeth, that was great!"

Reyn nodded. "A long time coming, and well worth the wait."

From then on Reyn and Joshua were, if not best buds, at least no longer seething enemies.

Joshua got eighteen stitches. Reyn wore butterfly bandages for a few days to hold his cheek together. Anne made him drink some tea as well.

I will never understand men. I mean, a thousand years

from now, I will still have my head cocked sideways like a dog, going "Huh?"

I was woken at one AM by my cell phone playing "Copaca-bana," which meant that someone—probably Brynne—had pranked me by changing my ringtone.

"Hello?"

"Yeah. I get one phone call, so I decided to treat you to it." The voice was young, brash, and scared.

"Dray?"

"Yeah. Who were you expecting, the Easter Bunny?"

"I wasn't *expect*—" There was some fumbling, and then a woman's voice came on and said, "Is this Ms. Nastasya Crowe?"

"Yes."

"Your pal here was caught breaking into one of the apart-ments on Main Street. She says you gave her permission. Like, permission but no key, right?"

"Oh." Again? Dray was screwing me over *again*? Okay, where was my sword?

"Are you going to come get her? It's you or her parents."

The dead silence I heard after that told me Dray would do anything to avoid calling her alcoholic mother. Calling her dad wasn't an option—she had no idea where he was.

"Yeah. I'll come get her." And boy, will she be sorry.

It was weird setting off into the night in the farm car—I hadn't left River's Edge in more than a week. It occurred to me that it probably wasn't smart to go out by myself, especially at night, but since when has "not smart" stopped me from doing anything?

It wasn't hard to find the West Lowing Police Station, though I'd never been there. It was the only one in town, in a small, unassuming building that looked like it used to be an auto-repair garage. Anger and cold had woken me right up, and as I parked in front of the station, I was rehearsing all the furious things I would say.

If I were a cop, I wouldn't release a minor to a nonrelative, but maybe the police knew Dray's mom and were taking pity on Dray. At any rate, they allowed me to sign for her and gave her a manila envelope with her worldly possessions in it.

We pushed through the glass door and went out into the brisk night air.

"Okay, later, dude," said Dray, and started to saunter off.

I grabbed the sleeve of her jacket like a snake striking. "I don't think so. You got me up in the middle of the night, made me go to a police station, and this is all because you were breaking into my property *again*? You're not going anywhere." I pushed her toward the car, made her get in, then drove us a bit away from police eyes and stopped.

Dray yawned, looking out the car window. Since I had often performed that exact same *I don't care* move, she didn't fool me.

"Really, this *on top of* you and your lowlife friends crashing in my building?" I said. "What the hell were you thinking?"

"I was thinking I wanted a place to sleep!" she snapped,

then looked out the window as if she hadn't meant to say that much.

So, not at her mom's, and she must still be broken up with her jerk boyfriend.

"We just got the lock replaced! It took me a day to clean up your crap!" I remembered that day, when I'd seen the creepy couple again, and I became aware that I was parked on a dark street, out in the open. I needed to get back to River's Edge, but right then inspiration struck. "And you're gonna work it off."

That got her attention. "What?"

"You're going to show up at the work site tomorrow and report to Bill," I said, liking this idea. "And you will do whatever he tells you to do until you work off what you owe me for damage. Like two hundred dollars." I pulled that number out of the air.

"That's bullshit. I'm not going to do that!"

I started the car. "Let's go back to the cops."

She tried to open the car door, but I kept punching the locks on my side. It was ridiculous, and I felt like a Keystone Kop. Finally she gave up.

"I can't do that," she said sullenly. "I've got to make my jewelry and stuff."

"I'm going to throw your *jewelry and stuff* out into the gutter," I said callously.

"You can't do that! Luisa rents the shop. If she wants me there—"

"I am the *owner*, Dray. How about I tell Luisa she's no longer welcome?" Which I couldn't do, legally—she had a lease. But Dray probably didn't know that.

Dray was silent.

"Because of *you*." I was being a hard-ass, but I was also wondering what would have happened if someone had done this to me, say, decades ago. Just really had me in their clutches but used it to make me do a good thing instead of some bad, blackmaily thing. Probably nothing, right?

"Do what for Bill?" Still oh so sullen.

"Whatever he needs. Sweeping. Carrying out trash." Dray's face hardened. "Fixing windows. Putting up sheetrock. Painting." She looked a tiny bit interested. "Laying stone in the new little park. Planting plants. Helping to make a fountain." She looked at me speculatively.

"That might not be so bad. But what happens after I earn the two hundred dollars, which, by the way, is way overpriced?"

"If you're a good worker and don't piss Bill off, you'll be on his crew, working with them. Being a carpenter or something. His sheetrock foreman is a woman, and so is her number one. You can do anything those guys can do."

Months ago I'd told her to leave town, which of course had seemed like a cinch to me and totally impossible and intimidating to her. But here was an option to stay in town and earn money. Without being a waitress, which she would suck at, with her nonexistent people skills. Since she'd probably shoplifted from most of the stores in town, I doubted any of them would hire her.

"I need a place to stay." She said it so quietly, I barely heard it.

"No way am I letting you into one of my apartments. You can put that thought out of your head."

Mulish expression. Ugh. It was like watching a home movie.

"I think you have two options," I said. "One is the women's shelter, and one is asking Luisa if she's a big enough sap to let you sleep on a cot in the back room of her shop. I wouldn't, if I were her."

"I'm not a battered woman."

"You don't have to be battered. Just a female in need of a safe place to stay."

I could practically see thoughts and arguments scrolling across her face.

"Okay."

I whipped the car into gear and raced to the women's shelter before Dray could change her mind. She got out, and I made sure she went inside the building before I drove away. I didn't know if she would immediately sneak back out or show up to see Bill tomorrow. Some things a person has to do for herself, and people can only change when they're ready.

'Cause I'm an expert, right? I'm so together myself? Who was I kidding?

Getting back to River's Edge seemed to take a long

time—I was nervous and checked my mirrors obsessively. If I could just get back without getting kidnapped/spelled/attacked...

With relief I turned into the long driveway, trying not to look at the dense trees lining the drive. Trees where anything could be hiding. Bigfoot. Werewolves. Evil immortals. I was so busy looking that I didn't notice that the car's engine-temperature light had come on, and the needle was at the top of the uh-oh red area.

Right as I was getting out, I noticed it. Crap—someone had forgotten to put water in the radiator or something. Then I saw the flames darting playfully out from beneath the hood. Oh no—I'd ruined River's car! What had happened? There was a fire extinguisher right in the front hallway—I turned to run to get it...and the car exploded, knocking me off my feet, making me sail exhilaratingly through the air about ten feet, and then dropping me into a much less exhilarating crash landing. A fireball sixteen feet across curled up into the night sky as I blinked stupidly at the gravel that had so suddenly appeared under my face. By the time I had blinked a couple more times, lights had started popping on inside the house, and then River, Ottavio, Reyn, and a couple others were racing outside in their nightwear.

"Nastasya!" River said, sinking to her knees next to me. "Are you all right?"

I nodded, or at least it felt like I was nodding. My ears

were still ringing, and her words were a bit fuzzy, as if my head were wrapped in cotton wool. Now my cheeks stung, and so did the palms of my hands and my knees. Slowly I pushed myself up, getting new pain signals from all over.

"What happened?" That was Ottavio.

"You sure are hard on cars." Asher, on the other side of me.

Reyn had the extinguisher from the front hall, and he put out the engine fire.

That's when we saw them: the farm truck, the other car, the four-wheel-drive SUV that River kept for heavy snow. Their hoods were up, engines ripped apart, windows broken. Not a single one was functional. Which meant we had no way out of there except on foot.

or millennia, people traveled on foot. On foot and on horseback and by boat. A fast horse was worth much more than a serf or a slave. A fast horse was worth more than many landholdings, farms, cows, wagons. A fast horse could be life or death.

Everything, the world over, had been geared to the speed of a man walking, a horse running. Nowadays, of course, people run for sport or for fun. People decide to walk across a country for charity or as a strange but admirable life adventure. They allow themselves as much time as they need. It's a choice, an anachronism.

Here, tonight, in western Massachusetts, having no vehicles, no option but to go anyplace on foot or on horseback, it seemed shocking and scary. Not fun, not picturesque, not charming.

"Could this have been done by locals?" Amy was wrapped in a fleece robe, her long, dark hair tousled around her shoulders.

Asher was examining the truck, its ruined engine. "What's the point of this!" His loud exclamation startled us all. "Why are they toying with us? What do they want? Why not just attack?" He rubbed his eyes with one fist. "I'm just so... fed up. I want this to be over."

River went to him and put her arm around his waist, murmuring softly to him. He nodded brusquely a couple times, saying, "I know, I know."

"How long ago did you leave?" Reyn asked.

"Yes, Nastasya—where did you go at this hour?" That was Ottavio. "Why would you leave the safety of the farm to go out by yourself in the middle of the night?" He looked down his nose at me, and I wondered if he really thought that I would suddenly break down and confess everything, prove him right on every point. I mean, come on.

My palms were scraped and bleeding; I assumed my knees were, too, and possibly my cheeks.

"I left a little after one," I said. "My friend Dray, from town, got arrested trying to break into my apartments. Again. I went down and read her the riot act, then dropped her at the women's shelter, then came straight back."

"It's barely two," said Amy, nodding.

"My point is that this happened between one and two," said Reyn. "They wouldn't have spared one car—they had no idea someone would take it. They would have done all of them. So it must have happened between the time Nastasya left and the time she returned."

"If she even went anywhere," said Ottavio.

"Ott," I said tiredly, "you can check with the cops, check with the women's shelter."

"Good grief, Ottavio," said Amy. "Don't be stupid."

Dark eyes flared, but he pressed his lips shut and didn't respond.

"So someone was physically here, wrecking the engines, just a while ago," said Joshua, and Reyn nodded.

"And if they hadn't done the little car, but then saw it coming back and quickly did something to it to make it explode, then that person was right here," said Reyn. "And could be here still."

"Everyone get inside," said Daisuke.

Every moment of that endless night will be stamped on my memory for a long, long time. Basically we all went back into the house and got ready for a battle. Reyn, Joshua, and Daisuke scoured the area for any signs of who might have destroyed all the vehicles. They reported seeing not a foot-print, not a handprint—and they were all experienced trackers. The rest of us got what weapons we had and camped in the front hallway, where there were no windows to break except on the front door. A group of four stayed in the kitchen, where the other outside door was.

River, Daniel, and Jess got Molly and the other dogs and brought them into the house as well. The dogs remained calm, though alert, with no raised fur, no growling, no tense listening for anything.

It was incredibly nerve-wracking and incredibly weird, sitting there with my sword and my amulet—there was no way to not feel like a poser with either one. But I'd much rather be a poser than a helpless victim. For the first hundred years of my life, I'd felt like a victim a lot—until Eva Henstrom, the woman I'd met in the tailor's shop, had opened my eyes and facilitated a sea change in me. Since then, I'd constantly worked toward being in control of my own life; keeping what was mine, getting out of anyone's influence. There had been big ups and downs, of course. But until now, I'd never stayed for a fight or battle of any kind.

And now here I was, committed to staying there, willing to fight. It wasn't like Brynne was Tinna, and I'd kill any-thing that threatened her. Jess wasn't Háakon, innocent and deserving of protection at any cost. River wasn't my mother, beautiful and terrible and the person I'd loved most until I'd had Bear.

But I stayed. I kept awake with the others and knew that, sooner or later, we would be fighting side by side. And during that fight, one person would reveal him- or herself as a traitor.

We were not attacked during the night. We were not attacked the next morning, when tow trucks hauled the ruined vehicles away. We were not attacked when Amy and Roberto left with the tow trucks and bought a large, four-wheel-drive SUV and a large van that could seat eight people. I recognized them for what they were: emergency escape vehicles. How were we going to keep them safe?

The day was quiet, subdued. There were things that had to be done, animals that needed tending, apocalypse or not. Our work was hurried, almost silent, and very tense.

Many of us were too anxious to eat, but River insisted, going on about blood sugar and energy levels and whatnot. I picked at my sandwich, trying to get a few swallows down.

"We think our enemy is trying to wear us down, scare us—put us off-balance so that when they attack we'll be considerably weakened," said Joshua. His appetite hadn't been dimmed—he was on his second sandwich.

"So far it seems like a good plan," Jess said drily.

"Yes," River agreed. "It does, doesn't it? Joshua, Reyn, and

Daisuke, as our three most experienced fighters, have developed some countermeasures."

"Oh good," Brynne murmured. I wondered if she was still interested in Joshua or if the little swordsvaganza had upset her too much. After this life-or-death thing, we would have to chat.

"We will take turns keeping two people on watch in the cupola on the main building," said Joshua.

"I didn't know you could get up there," Amy said.

"You can," said River. "The glass has a film on it so that we can see out, but no one can see in. There's a telescope up there, and someone will be on lookout at all times, with a partner to relieve him or her. I wish this had started before the trees began to leaf out—it would have been easier to see."

"You need a Gatling gun up there," I said, poking at a piece of bread.

"I wish," said Reyn, and we met eyes for a second.

"We will also be doing some focusing exercises," said Anne. "We need to be calm and alert—we can't let fear fog our abilities."

Too late, I thought glumly.

"We will be practicing spells of war," Asher said simply. "Disarmament, subterfuge, illusion, and weapons."

"In addition to these, we'll keep as normal a schedule as possible," said Solis. "We need to eat. The animals need care. We need to look as if we think the cars were just one more sally, but not like we're actually prepared for war."

You know, in addition to never caring enough about anything to want to fight for it, I also just don't *like* war. Sometimes it brings people together, makes people rise to their finest hour, blah blah blah—but mostly it's just really scary, incredibly destructive, and humanity at its worst. I hate it, don't want to be around it, don't want to experience it in any way. This totally justified my lifelong pattern of flight: It was so much easier and less painful. I mean, I was hating being part of this. Part of River's troop.

But if I didn't stay, I knew that there would be no more hope for me ever, and my life would be a grim, bleak, endless wasteland of despair and loneli—

Okay, okay, you're right, that's pushing it. Basically, staying *was* better, though it was harder and more painful. I hate life contradictions like that.

Reyn had written up a list of who would do what when—people were assigned to watch or lessons or practice, and then I noticed my name hadn't been called yet. It was a little like being the last one chosen in school, though I don't know what that's like.

"Nastasya? Can you come with me for a minute, please?" River stood up.

"Sure."

In the hallway River headed toward her office, and I saw that Ottavio was already inside. Jeezum, what now? Like my nerves weren't rattled enough. Swallowing a sigh, I followed her. Her office was quite small, and with Ott taking up much more than his fair share of space, I felt a little hemmed in.

Weirdly, River locked the door after us, turning the key slowly and silently.

Uh...what was going on?

Then River ran her fingers lightly along the underside of her desk. She said a few words, and the wooden side of her desk rose, like a hatch. I stared. I'd been in her office lots of times—I'd *seen* her pull those file drawers out. Silently she pointed, and I bent and looked. There were stairs going down into the darkness. This was a trapdoor to a hidden passage.

River reached in and flicked a switch. A dim string of lights illuminated at least twenty stairs. Ottavio motioned for me to go down.

"You first," I whispered.

Dark gull-wing eyebrows slanted severely over his long, straight nose. But he went, swinging himself through the small opening and then standing up once he was on the stairs.

River gave me a nudge.

Okay, I've gone through underground tunnels before, like in France during World War II, and that speakeasy in Chicago. In general, they get my vote. They're good things. But my very first experience with a hidden tunnel had been the night my family died. I'd been standing there in a burning room, my feet soaked with my mother's blood, and I'd seen a door open—a door I'd never seen or known about. My father's steward and his wife had saved me. I'd snatched my mother's broken amulet from the edge of the fire, wrapped it in a cloth, and tied the cloth around my neck so I would have my hands free. It had burned through the cloth and seared its image onto my neck, and that was my scar that will never heal.

This tunnel was really quite like my first tunnel.

"Go," River urged.

This was *River* talking to me. Though I had no idea what this was about or what would happen now, I crouched down, went through the hatch, and stood up on the stairs. Ott was already twenty steps below.

Large eye hooks were screwed into the stone wall, and a thick length of rope swooped from hook to hook. I held on to the rope as I made my way carefully down the stone steps—they're always stone, aren't they?—feeling River right behind me.

Guess what. At the bottom of the steps there was a small room-size space, and from that space three tunnels branched. Each one darker than hell. I mean, kill me now.

"This is a Stephen King movie," I said.

River patted my back. "No, my dear. This is your complicated, exciting, real life."

Actually, doing dishes and milking cows was starting to sound pretty good about now.

"Who knows about these tunnels? Where did they come from? What do you use them for?"

"Just a few of us, so of course don't tell anyone," said River, answering my first question. "I started work on these when I first bought the property almost ninety years ago. I got them to where I wanted by the late sixties. I like having options."

"Huh," I said, trying to wrap my mind around this new development. "Ott? Aren't you afraid of me knowing about this?"

His lips pressed together. I bet his jaws ache by the end of the day. Every day. "Yes, of course."

"We made a bet," said River. "So don't let me down. I *will* share the pain."

Well, now I was intrigued.

"They're a maze," said Ottavio. "So pay attention: Take the right tunnel. When it forks, you take the right tunnel again. In that tunnel you'll see..."

My jaw dropped open as my brain scrambled to keep up, but River put a hand on Ottavio's arm. "There's an easier way, dear."

Thus it was that Ottavio, king of the House of Genoa, and *moi*, heir to the Iceland house, and River had a group mind-meld.

We moved into the left tunnel, which was unlit. I felt a cool breeze wafting over my face and hair, so I knew this wasn't a dead end—there was circulation coming from somewhere. Quickly River drew a large, perfect chalk circle on the stone floor. Ott and I stepped into it, and River closed it behind her. It was much darker here, and Ottavio made a quick gesture with his hand at chest height. A small, crackly blue light ignited and hung there, in the middle of the three of us. I couldn't see anything burning—the light existed by itself.

River smiled at my disbelief. "They call it witch fire," she said. "You can even throw it at people."

"That is *awesome*," I said, staring at it. See? *This* is the stuff I wanted to be learning—not another freaking ointment you can make from mint.

Ott looked pleased with himself.

We held hands. River's was cool and familiar, fitting into mine. Ott's was large and steely. River murmured words to help us focus on the light and clear our minds. I wasn't at all sure I wanted my brain synapses to be intermingling with Ottavio's—but I had to trust River. I mean, I *had* to, right? Because if she wasn't exactly what I believed she was, then my life truly would be over. I truly wouldn't have anything to believe in, and I would have to call it a day.

I was getting to be definitely intermediate, if not advanced, at falling into a meditative state as fast as a sneeze. It felt like I'd taken only about five deep breaths when the dark walls receded into the distance. I felt warmer and more comfortable, and I saw River and Ottavio as if we were standing outdoors somewhere in muted light. All of the weight and dread of the upcoming battle slipped off our shoulders like a heavy jacket.

I was anxious about Ottavio and reflexively shut down when I felt his consciousness edge mine. He shut down, too. River put on her patient face and slowly sang us both back into relaxing and trusting.

It was like being on a roller coaster, a slow roller coaster— I was both driving and being driven, watching myself take this journey even as I was experiencing it. Ottavio poked around in my memories a bit. I felt his solemnity at the deaths of my family, felt him accept who I was and acknowledge that if I ever learned anything and wasn't a total screwup, I would be very strong indeed. He wondered if I had taken my family's powers when they died, and of course I hadn't—hadn't thought about it, hadn't known that it could be done.

I saw River's and Ottavio's shared memories—some joyous, like celebrating the festival of Saint George, patron saint of Genoa; some dark and evil, as River and Ottavio plotted against business associates and other people who had thwarted them. I saw Ottavio marry and his mortal wife dying of the plague. One of the plagues.

Roberto had once been spoiled, conniving, and jealous— I saw how he changed and became the family favorite. He had an inner sweetness as well as a deep appreciation for beauty. Ahem.

Joshua had been scarred and incensed when he learned of River and Ottavio's plan to kill their siblings. Even then he'd been tall and lean, with an almost feral, hungry look and no softness or tenderness in him. River grew to love him fiercely, protectively. He would come back from some war, and she would take him in. His physical wounds healed quickly—it was his psyche that became more and more scarred. I felt her despair and concern.

Ottavio was the oldest, then River, then Joshua, Daniel, and Roberto. Daniel was the one somewhat lost in the middle. He lacked Ottavio's stern attention to responsibility and didn't share River's generous strength. He disliked war and couldn't fathom Joshua's dogged need for battle. Daniel did like money, though, and proved a savvy investor and manager of the family fortune.

They were fascinating insights into the family, this ancient, powerful family that had come from all over the world to be together, to stand together through whatever happened.

Ottavio saw me losing my son, saw me poor and desperate, then beautiful and rich, then poor and desperate again; being hateful, being careless and selfish. He saw Sea Caraway and the original Nastasya, with a junkie's pallid, bony face and harsh, black-lined eyes. He saw how I tried to drown all feelings, wall myself off. How I shied away from emotion like a cat from a fire. And he saw where I was now: how I was trying, wasn't sure I would make it, didn't want to let River down.

I saw River, Ottavio, and their brothers make a blood pact to be loyal to one another always.

I saw a younger, dark-haired River picking up a girl from a gutter—a horse and wagon had knocked her into the muck. She was in a servant's worn clothes, and when River pulled out a handkerchief to wipe the girl's face, the girl flinched. And then was astonished by River's kindness.

My eyes went wide, and I drew in a quick breath as the girl's face appeared: She was Eva Henstrom, long before I knew her. My mind flew back—she'd said a woman had helped her. Had she mentioned the woman's name? I didn't think so. But it had been River—six hundred years ago.

Ottavio turned to business: He went over the layout of the tunnels, again and again, until I could walk through them blindfolded and find my way out. Along the way he showed me sigils of concealment, illusion, fear—if someone was following me, they would feel an unexplained dread and become confused and panicky.

River also imparted what she could: spells of protection and also of attack. It started to feel like too much—I couldn't take it all in; it would soon leak out of my ears. Would I remember any of it? I didn't know.

Slowly we surfaced from our meditation. In some ways a mind-meld is like seeing people in their underwear—afterward you know them better, are embarrassed, and yet feel warmer about the vulnerability they shared. Plus it was exhausting, and I was starving.

I tried not to sway on my feet, feeling overwhelmed and perhaps exhilarated. River looked at Ottavio.

"Do you see?" she asked softly.

He nodded, looking at me. For the first time his eyes weren't shooting black ice; he still didn't like me, but he believed who I was and why I was here. He believed I wasn't the traitor.

I swallowed. "I wonder if there are any gingersnaps left."

River smiled and rubbed my arm. "Let's go see."

CHAPTER 29

iver had a friend come pick up all the horses. She arranged with the farmer next door to let our two cows, the sheep, and the goats go through a gate onto his property, so they were off our land and pretty far away. Though our enemy had already targeted the chickens once, River hoped that in a big fight, they would seem too insignificant to bother with.

I was glad the animals were gone. The idea of something awful happening to them—of me having to know that something awful had happened to them—had only increased my fear, especially after Daisuke's story of the hex barn.

This is what war is like: You pare down, try to keep your valuables safe, and brace for the worst. It was like that wagon train to California—in the beginning people took everything they thought they'd absolutely need and regretfully left behind the things they didn't have room for. As the trail went on, they found they could live without many things that had seemed essential when they set out. Farther on, after fording rivers, enduring drought, after some of them died and some went crazy, they found they could do without even more.

By the end of the trail, their needs had been reduced to: water. They discovered that the only thing they really, really needed was their lives. Everything else was replaceable, everything else was worthless, compared to the value of simply still being alive at the end of the day.

So now all we worried about was staying alive, because someone out there wanted us dead. After the many, many times when I'd cared so little whether I lived or died, when I did stupid, risky, self-hating things because my life had no value—it now felt strange to be focusing on survival. And not just to be polite, either. I was not ready to die. Or give up my power, the power I'd never bothered with. I wanted more time to come to grips with my relationship with Reyn. And to learn more. And be friends with Brynne, and be a success story for River. And to be really toasty warm one more freaking time.

"Are you quite sure we can't just pack up and head someplace sunny?" I asked at dinner that night. It felt weird, knowing about the escape tunnels. Other people had to know about them, but I had no idea who.

River shook her head. "Thank you for asking. Again. But this needs to be dealt with now. Going somewhere would only delay things. I, for one, need to know who's behind this and what they want."

"They want power," said Joshua, not looking up. "As much as they can get."

"Have any of the attacks been simultaneous?" Reyn asked. "Like, in two cities on the same day? In different parts of the world at the same time?"

"No," said River. "We plotted the attacks on a world map and dated them. While some of them are quite close together, it still looks sequential."

"Why?" Daniel asked.

"Wondering if it's just one person or group, or whether they have cells all over the place, making a joint attack," Reyn said.

"Right now we're assuming it's one person or group," said Joshua. "After dinner I want to go over our plans again. Remember, no matter who comes, how many there are, or how they engage us, this is a battle. This person or people have killed our friends all over the world, and now they're coming for us."

"Don't worry about right or wrong," said Reyn flatly. "Don't follow gentlemen's rules of engagement. This isn't a historical reenactment—this is life or death. If you stab someone in the chest, it will *annoy* him. If you shoot someone in the heart, it will only slow him down. Go for the throat, push in, then swing sideways as hard as you can, like we showed you."

It was all so chillingly real.

"Don't fight fair; don't worry what you look like," Joshua continued. "Do whatever you have to do to stop our enemy, no holds barred."

"Like at a sale at Loehmann's," Brynne said.

Joshua and Reyn blinked identically.

"Yes, like that," said River.

Joshua shook his head as if to clear it of such a fluffy notion. "Expect to get hurt. Expect to feel pain. Don't let it make you panic. You know that as long as your head is still on your body, you're okay. Keep going."

There were solemn nods around the table. My knees were shaking, and I pressed my feet hard into the ground to make them stop. I cared if we won or lost. I cared if my friends got hurt or killed. I cared if someone destroyed River's Edge. God, this sucked so bad. What had I been thinking?

Once more we went through the plans of attack and escape, marking exits and routes on a diagram as if we were on a plane preparing for some emergency that would never really happen. Reyn and Joshua did most of the talking, but Daisuke would jump in sometimes to clarify something or add another viewpoint. The other two listened respectfully. I wondered what Daisuke was feeling underneath. Was he regretting being called into battle again? He could have left if he'd wanted to. Did he feel that fighting would set him back on his path?

In the end, there was no time for moral uncertainties or wavering conviction. In the end, everything about it was a surprise.

"Nastasya? Could you please do me a favor?" River asked. I got up from the kitchen table and stuck my sword into the scabbard on my belt.

"Sure," I said.

She was apologetic. "I know it's almost dark—I should have thought of this earlier. I need some things out of one of the work cupboards." She handed me a list and a basket. "They should all be in the cupboard in Anne's classroom— take as much of each thing as you can."

"Okay," I said. Sure, I love being in the dark. Outside. By myself.

"I can go with you," Daniel said, picking up his sword.

"Good idea," River agreed. "We don't want anyone outside on their own."

There was maybe a two-and-a-half-minute window where there would be a bit of fading light. I felt that River was perhaps being a bit lackadaisical about my health and well-being and then realized with a sinking feeling that I was probably one of the more expendable people there.

Head up, eyes alert as we crossed the yard, I kept one hand lightly on the hilt of my sword, the way Reyn had showed me. I thought longingly of the days when I was a horrible waste of a person but was relatively safe.

"So," said Daniel, "who do you think is behind these attacks?"

He was the brother I knew the least; my only dealing with him had been when he'd tried to bribe me to leave River's Edge. Since then he'd seemed the most opaque of the brothers. I remembered my shared vision with River and Ottavio, about how Daniel in some ways had been the forgotten middle child.

I glanced at him. He was not, strictly speaking, quite as handsome as either Ottavio or Roberto. His features were a little softer, less finely cut. How funny that Brynne had passed over this well-groomed, civilized individual in favor of Joshua, who had much less to offer. At least on the surface.

"No thoughts? Opinions?"

"I don't know," I said. For some reason I didn't want to talk about my possible uncle, or possible old friends, who could be behind this, like Cicely. Not that she could get an attack together—she couldn't even plan a dinner party.

"Do you feel like being here has made you stronger?" he asked, pulling open the barn door. "Like, have you learned a lot of powerful magick?"

My eyes narrowed. River had the nosiest, most buttinsky brothers. But maybe he wanted to make sure I'd be an asset in this situation.

"How about you?" I countered, heading to the workroom.

"Oh, I'm strong enough," he said mildly. He waited in the doorway while I quickly pawed through the shelves, checking River's list, making sure I'd gotten all of it.

"Okay," I said, going over the list one last time. "I guess that's it." I picked up the basket and headed for the doorway, but Daniel didn't move.

"Let's go," I said bluntly.

He shrugged. "I haven't had a chance to talk to you. I was wondering what you thought about River, and the whole setup here."

I guess a polite person would have answered, made congenial conversation with the brother of her mentor. But we know where I stand on politeness. "Why?"

Daniel looked taken aback. "I think River's worried about you."

"In what way? Let me out."

Reluctantly Daniel moved aside—I practically had to elbow him out of the way to get by.

"She thinks you're a liability."

His quiet words made me pause in the barn aisle, and I turned to look at him.

"Did she say that?" I asked tightly.

He shrugged again. "She's not sure she can trust you," he

went on, seeing he had my attention. "She doesn't think you know enough to help. She and Ottavio are still convinced the attacks are somehow related to you."

It was all I could do to not hyperventilate. Hurt, panicky thoughts ripped through my brain like barbed wire, shredding my confidence and making me question everything.

Daniel came a few steps closer, a sympathetic look on his face. "It's just—the bad stuff started happening once *you* came. And then you went off with Innocencio—she's told me how horrific the scene in Boston was."

My cheeks burned at the picture of River telling Daniel this.

"You haven't been here long enough for her to really know you." He gave a short laugh. "Believe me, she can take some convincing. You have to prove yourself over and over."

Sickening, too-familiar feelings of embarrassment and shame spread their icy tendrils through me, making my heart pound and my jaw clench. And then—

—and then some much savvier part of me said, Hang on. Are you going to believe this guy you hardly know, or are you going to trust what River said herself and what your own eyes and ears and heart tell you?

Not long ago, I would have trusted what Daniel was saying immediately—I had no reference against which to weigh trust and honesty, no compass point to determine what was real and what was illusion.

But—my head was so much clearer now. I now knew

when I was being honest with myself, and that crucial change allowed me to see honesty in others.

Daniel was bullshitting me. Why?

"I know it's hard to take in," he said kindly, moving closer. "She's always been skilled at presenting a face that hides what's really going on. It's difficult to tell what her real motivations are, what uses she has for people."

"Daniel. What the hell are you doing?" I wasn't angry yet, though well on the way. Mostly I was just confused. Was this some kind of test?

"Nastasya, it's okay. It's not your fault. But River has told me that it would be so much easier for everyone if you left."

Hello, anger. *It's not true it's not true it's not true—*

"Really?" I said calmly. "Because she's told me that if I leave, she'll hunt me down like a dog in the street, then duct-tape me to my bed to keep me here. Force-feeding me tea and lessons and food with fiber."

Quickly his eyes widened, then he frowned. "No. She didn't say that."

My mind was clear as a freaking crystal ball right now. "Yes, Daniel. She did say that."

He tried again. "She doesn't always say what she means."

I was breathing through my nose, trying to keep a rein on my emotions. But right now I could have cheerfully stood over him and dropped an anvil on his head.

"Actually, Daniel, I've found she says exactly what she means. Even when it's not what you want to hear." I thought about the times she had called me on things, just nailed me. "At all."

Now he looked irritated. "Listen—" he said, and then brought up his hand so fast, I didn't have time to react. He snapped his fingers open at me and an invisible cannonball slammed into my chest, knocking me to my knees. In an instant I was reminded of Incy and the London cabbie, how he'd flattened the guy just with gestures in the air.

As Daniel did to me, now, tilting his fist sideways to smack me to the floor.

Oh my God, not again, I thought, my head ringing. Then I let my anger rip. Lying sideways on the floor, I pictured my palm filling with that so-awesome witchfire, and I made a hurling motion with one hand.

To our mutual shock, it worked, and a spinning, crackling ball of witchfire as big as an orange streaked through the air and hit him in the throat. He staggered backward, gagging, and then a dark figure ran up silently behind him... and brought a shovel down hard on his head.

His eyes rolled back, and he collapsed. I was instantly free.

"What a prick," Brynne said, breathing hard, looking down at him. "Hey, how'd you do the fire thing? That was awesome."

"Ottavio taught me. Oh my God—Daniel is the traitor!" I said. "We have to get to the house and tell River!"

Brynne nodded quickly, and I reached down to grab my basket, scooping the spilled bottles back into it.

"How can we make sure he stays out?" I asked, then was stopped by an awful thought. "Brynne—why were you out here alone?" I straightened slowly and looked at her. Please, not Brynne, anyone but Brynne.

"I'm not alone. I came to help *him* get axes and stuff. Shovels." She inclined her head, pointing to the back of the barn.

Looking past her, I saw...Joshua, striding toward us. "Found some rope," he said tersely, and knelt to tie Daniel's hands together and then his feet with practiced, efficient movements, as if Daniel were a wayward sheep.

And I guess he was.

Daniel's eyes popped open. "Dominicus—you must help m—" Joshua stuffed a handkerchief in Daniel's mouth and jerked him to his feet by the rope.

"Okay, grab what you can," Joshua ordered us. "Look sharp as we cross the yard. Don't run. Head straight for the kitchen door." Keeping hold of an increasingly furious Daniel, he pulled out his sword, a long, two-handed affair, heavy and ornate. Brynne and I grabbed the axes and two shovels and followed him out into the dark.

I was never so relieved to get into the kitchen. We burst through the door, surprising Anne and River, who leaped up, on guard.

"Here's your stuff," I said, dropping the basket on the kitchen worktable. "And here's your worthless, pox-ridden, asshole brother."

River's mouth dropped open as Joshua half dragged Daniel into the kitchen, roped and gagged.

"What in the world?" Anne exclaimed.

"He's our traitor," Joshua said simply, and at that moment I realized what an incredible blessing it had been that I'd had witnesses in the barn. I had backup. I was so grateful, I almost wept.

"What?" River cried as Daniel angrily shook his head, mumbling around the handkerchief.

"He told Nastasya a bunch of crap," Brynne said, looking at him with loathing. "How you didn't trust her, wanted her gone."

Anne's intake of breath was audible.

River was silent, looking from one brother to another. After a minute, she nodded slowly. "Oh, Daniel," she said. "Who are you working with? Why would you do this?"

Wild-eyed, Daniel shook his head violently.

"His head is bleeding," Anne said.

"I hit him with a shovel," said Brynne. "He'd knocked Nastasya down and was going for her. So I whacked him."

Daniel stilled, the idea sinking in that they had really seen and heard what he'd done to me. His eyes narrowed, and he gave a massive burst of strength against his ropes.

Joshua jerked the rope, keeping Daniel off-balance.

"Daniel!" River said more strongly. "How could you do this? Who put you up to this?" Her face was stern, her voice angry. Underneath everything, I felt her deep sadness and disappointment that betrayal would come from one of her own brothers.

Defiant brown eyes glared at her. Joshua reached over and yanked the handkerchief out of Daniel's mouth.

"*Talk*, brother." Joshua's voice was as quiet and sharp as a blade scraping ice. If it were aimed at me, I'd be about to faint with fear. Daniel said nothing, and Joshua yanked harder on the rope. I saw the livid welts on Daniel's wrists where the rope was already rasping his skin.

"You never should have aligned yourself with her," Daniel said, motioning at me.

"Why is that, Ugolinus?" River's voice was calm, but a calm that hid a roiling, growing anger underneath it. Daniel had called Joshua Dominicus; River called Daniel Ugolinus. I was assuming these were their original names and so had extra weight, the way Lilja had extra weight for me, snapping me back to my childhood.

"Sometimes people inherit who shouldn't." His cold gaze seemed to harden River's face.

"Really?" Her mild tone was deceptive. "Like who?"

"If your choice is between a worthless piece of trash or someone of great learning and power—" Daniel began, then grunted, wincing in pain as Joshua twisted the rope so that it tightened more around Daniel's wrists. The top layer of skin peeled away beneath the rough, dirt-stiffened rope.

My face burned—we knew who the worthless piece of trash was in this scenario.

I'd seen River irritated, angry, and disappointed, but I'd never seen her look like this, and I was glad of it. The warm, forgiving, generous person I knew, the beacon of salvation in my life, was becoming a marble statue before my eyes. She was becoming Diavola, as I had seen her in a vision when she was barely three hundred years old. The Diavola who had killed her own parents, who had plotted to kill her brothers for their power. It had been more than a thousand years since Daniel had seen Diavola, and it was dawning on him, making him blink and look a bit less certain.

Slowly River leaned closer to Daniel, and if this were some teen vampire book, it would be right now that she would lunge and rip his throat out. There was no point in hoping that could still happen, I reflected.

"What person of great learning and power are we talking about, Ugolinus?" Her voice was a whisper, a caress. The faintest breeze a serpent created right before its strike.

Daniel pressed his lips together.

Joshua put his hand on Daniel's neck and tightened his fingers, pinching a nerve that made sweat break out on Daniel's face, made him draw in a shaky breath.

"Answer her, brother."

I prayed I never heard that voice directed at me. Brynne's hand touched mine, and I gripped it anxiously.

Daniel said nothing.

"I'll take care of him," said Joshua, and yanked the rope, leading Daniel out of the kitchen.

"You'll regret this!" Daniel started, then gagged as Joshua stuffed the handkerchief into his mouth again. Joshua pulled his brother through the swinging door, and the rest of us stood there, shaken.

Letting out a deep breath, River seemed more herself, though she looked drained as she turned to me. "Tell me what Daniel said and did."

I told her, and she looked more and more upset as I went on.

Clear brown eyes looked into mine. "Did you believe him?"

Of course I wanted to show how steadfast and faithful I was, unshakeable, etc. Then I remembered that River knew me.

"At first," I admitted. "Just for a minute. Then I thought maybe this was some test or something. Then I thought he was being sketchy."

"So you didn't believe what he said?" She seemed very intent on my answer.

"I...you know, wouldn't be surprised if you didn't trust me." My voice was barely a whisper, and she inclined her head to hear me. "Wouldn't be surprised if you'd given up on me." I raised my eyes to hers. "But—I think you would have told me, if you did. You've never told me that. Yet. And I believe you more than I believed him."

With a small, sad smile, River put one hand on my cheek.

"Thank you for trusting me," she said softly. "Daniel was lying. Thank you for believing in me."

She was thanking *me* for believing in her? Trusting *her*?

The kitchen door suddenly crashed open, and we all jumped. Reyn stood there, his face hard. "Something's coming," he said tersely.

or a moment we all stood there, looking at one another as if someone knew what the hell was going on.

"What's coming?" River asked.

"Don't know," said Reyn. "Get out of the kitchen."

In an instant River had shot the bolts home on the kitchen door and we all hurried into the dining room. Reyn started to shift the enormous sideboard to block the swinging door. Ottavio came in to help him, and the rest of us put our backs against it.

Footsteps pounded down the stairs; Amy and Asher rushed to meet us in the dining room.

"The woods!" Amy said. "There's people—dark shapes—moving toward us!"

"How many?" Reyn snapped. "From what direction?"

"At least forty," Asher said. "Maybe more. Coming from all directions."

My mouth dropped open. Forty! Oh my God! We were thinking maybe one or two, maybe a dedicated group of five! Forty? *Forty* evil immortals coming for us? Erik the Bloodletter and his team of eleven had taken my father's entire castle! And we'd had guards!

"Oh, holy mother," River breathed, her hand to her mouth.

Then it began.

The first stunning crash made me snatch up my sword, my heart pounding. We'd closed all the wooden shutters on the windows, but what we really needed was a house encased in solid steel. That had been spelled to repel magick.

"River! Quickly!" said Anne, upending a box of salt, drawing a circle on the floor of the entrance hall. River and Ottavio stepped into it, and Anne trailed a line of salt to close it. Holding hands, the four of them began raising their power, building on the layers of spells they'd been crafting for days.

Something burst against another window's shutters; the

sounds of breaking glass and an explosion barely preceded the fireball that lit the parlor as if it were daytime.

"Get into position, everyone," Reyn commanded. Very briefly we met eyes; I was surprised by the level of pain in his. Was he surprised by the fear in mine? Probably not.

"There are more on this side of the house than the other," Daisuke reported as he strode in from the dining room. "I added a spell to the sideboard in front of the kitchen door."

As soon as it had flared, the fire outside winked out. River's eyes were closed with concentration, but her shoulders were relaxed: With supreme focus, she'd managed to shut out everything but her spell.

An unearthly wailing and ululating from outside hit me like a fork scraping across ice. Almost immediately my head seemed foggy, and I absently looked down at my sword, wondering what I was doing.

"Block it!" Joshua shouted, appearing from River's office. "They're sending out spells! Block them! Close your minds!"

His words woke me, blowing away the clouds, and I shut my mind to outside forces, as Anne had taught me so many times.

I heard footsteps on the front steps and felt almost immobile with fear. I just couldn't face them—I wished someone could get to them from behind, just mow them down from in—

"Reyn!"

"What?" He was poised for battle, not taking his eyes off the door they would surely break through at any second.

"We should go through the tunnels!" I said. "River! *River!*"

Slowly River opened her eyes—she had heard me.

"Work your magick from the tunnels," I said urgently. "We'll go down and come out in back of them, in the woods! When they break in, the house will be empty!"

"Yes, of course!" said Roberto.

"Come on!" I said, motioning Reyn toward River's office. He stared at me. "What tunnels?"

"They'll torch the house," said Asher, hooking a long, snub-nosed arrow into position on his crossbow. He cranked it a few times, tightening the cable.

"An arrow? Won't that just piss them off?" I asked.

"It's going to be on fire," Asher said simply. "It will surprise them. You guys all head out through the tunnels. Circle back and come at them from behind. Jess, Solis, and I will stay here, working on distraction and disruption."

"It doesn't matter if they torch the house," River said as Anne dismantled the circle as fast as possible. "The only thing that matters is that we win."

"I'll open them up," said Joshua, pushing past me.

"Tunnels?" Brynne asked as we hurried into River's office. "We have tunnels?"

Reyn was nonplussed when Joshua opened the side of River's desk, looking from Joshua, to me, to the desk. Joshua ducked through first, keeping his weapons close to his sides, then I crawled through and stood up on the steps, an old pro at this hidden-tunnel thing. Daisuke, Amy, Brynne, Roberto, and Reyn all followed. I was at the bottom when I heard Solis say, "Go! Go! I'll spell it closed after you!"

I didn't see Daniel (if he was down there) as we ran through the dimly lit tunnels. I thought about how angry and disgusted Joshua and River had been and shuddered at what Joshua may have done to him.

"You knew about these tunnels," Reyn said, not even breathing hard as I panted beside him, feeling like my lungs were on fire.

"Uh-huh," I got out.

"Where do they come out?"

"Five places," I said, recalling the mental images River had ingrained in me. "Two hundred yards behind the big barn. A hundred and fifty yards to the east of the chicken coop. A hundred and seventy yards to the southeast of the parking area. In the horse barn, beneath Titus's stall. Beneath one of the cold frames in the kitchen garden. And there are dead ends, too."

Just then Joshua stopped at one of the main intersections. "Reyn—take Brynne," he said, and Reyn nodded. "Nastasya, you go with Daisuke, and you, Bertino. Amy will come with me. All right?" Three teams, each led by a seasoned warrior, each with a mewling liability in tow. Actually I guess I was the only one mewling. Silently. In my head.

I wanted to go with Reyn, but when he grimly nodded, I understood: He didn't want to be distracted by me, worrying about me. If he had to, he could sacrifice Brynne. As Joshua could sacrifice Amy, and Daisuke could sacrifice me. War just simples things right up.

Joshua knelt and drew a small square in the dirt, then some other squares around it. "This is the house," he said, pointing, "and the outbuildings. Here's where the tunnels come out. Reyn, you come out here, in back of the barn. Daisuke, you go east and come up in the woods beyond the chicken coop. You'll probably be able to see the enemy right away. I'll take Amy and come out behind the car park." He looked up, his face hardened and sure. Reyn and Daisuke both nodded briefly.

"And we'll all move toward the house," said Daisuke tensely. I'd seen him glancing at his sword in dislike, even revulsion. But like me he was committed to defending River's Edge, a place where so many had turned their lives around, and River, the person who had saved us. "Cut them down, one by one. Our best bet would be to pick off the periphery, then rush in and clean up the rest."

"Like, actually kill them?" Amy sounded doubtful.

Daisuke gave her a pained smile. "I'm afraid so. This is a war—they're not here because they want our gold. They mean to kill us, every last one of us. And they will, absolutely, unless we kill them first."

"Easier in the old days, eh?" said Joshua without humor.

"Yes," said Reyn.

I really, really didn't want to leave Reyn. As Daisuke, Roberto, and I turned to go, Reyn grabbed my arm, spinning me to face him. There, in front of everyone, in the *middle* of a *battle*, he bent and kissed me hard.

Holding the back of my head with his sword-free hand, he hissed into my ear: "Do not die. You hear me?"

I nodded and whispered back: "Before I even get in your pants? I don't think so."

"You ready to fight, or you need to canoodle your lady some more?" Joshua's snarl made Reyn jerk back, his eyes narrowed.

"Ready," he said coldly. "And I'll see you on the other side, if you manage not to get your pansy-ass killed."

I saw Joshua grin before he and Amy ran off into the darkness.

Then Daisuke tugged on my hand, and I ran after him, putting all thoughts out of my mind except: Fight. Victory. Survive.

The three of us reached the end of the tunnel too quickly. I would have been happy to run for another hour or so, if it meant I could avoid what was waiting for us aboveground. But Daisuke slowed and then stopped, his hand out to us, motioning us to wait.

"Remember—they're immortals up there." Daisuke's voice was pitched so low that a chipmunk five feet away couldn't have heard it. "Obviously it would be easier if they were mortal—easier to kill and able to be killed at a distance."

"We need that bowler-hat thingy from that James Bond movie," I whispered. "We could just throw it from far away and cut off someone's head."

Both men looked at me silently, then Daisuke went on as if I hadn't spoken. Fine. A girl tries to help.

"We'll come up behind them, so stealth is imperative."

Roberto nodded. I was like, Duh.

Nodding at my sword, Daisuke said, "Aim for the throat. Stick it in. Swing sideways as hard as you can. Have you ever cut off someone's head?"

I shook my head, feeling a little sick. "I've seen it done."

"It's harder than you expect," Roberto said softly. "Hitting bone is a shock. The trick is to slam all your power behind it."

Okay, I was going to throw up. Grotesque memories of poor Katy peppered my brain like birdshot. I nodded, trying to breathe.

"I was glad to see that they look human and not like wraiths or evil spirits," Roberto said in a low voice.

I stared at him. "Evil spirits was a possibility? I thought people were kidding!"

Again they looked at me. I gazed at my feet and tried not to burst into hysterical tears.

"Let's go," Daisuke said, and started to climb metal rungs set into the earth.

I followed Daisuke, and Roberto followed me. There was

a trapdoor at the top. Daisuke turned a metal latch and then very, very slowly pushed up on it. For a few moments it didn't budge, but then a small shower of dirt sprinkled down on us, interspersed with bits of leaves and twigs. Silently Daisuke slithered out through a narrow opening while I held the trapdoor open for him.

After thirty seconds of silence, his quiet voice floated down to us. "Okay. Come up."

My heart in my throat, I held my sword to one side and climbed out. I was clammy with fear, my grip on my sword hilt tense and aching. Was it too late to run away?

Then I remembered that Reyn already thought I was a big coward.

Crap. Crappity crap crap.

As silently as possible, I climbed out and got to my feet fast. Out there it was as dark as the inside of a barrel—some distance away, past the chicken coop, I saw the house. It was already on fire. The flames made it easier to see the dark forms ringing it—some were on the porch, still trying to hack in the spelled front door; others were shouting harshly.

"Hey." Roberto touched my shoulder, and I startled. "You okay?"

I blinked and whispered back, "Yeah. Just—four hundred years later, my village is still under attack."

He nodded wryly. "Ever will men go to war, for all reasons or none." It sounded like a quote.

Daisuke pointed to the right. I looked but didn't see anything. Next to me, Roberto nodded, so I squinted again and peered through the trees. Still nothing. Then—a hint of a shadow moved from one tree to another. As I stared, it happened again.

Reyn. Coming toward the house from behind the big barn. Over by where we parked the cars, Joshua would be coming out with Amy.

Daisuke raised his eyebrows at us, and Roberto nodded somberly.

"These people corrupted your friend so that he would kill you." Daisuke's words were like feathers in the night air. "They have killed at least twenty immortals around the world, that we know about. They're promoting dark magick, causing evil and destruction where they go. Now they're here to destroy River's Edge. If they can, they will kill you, and all of us besides." His almond-shaped eyes looked into mine. "Nastasya—these people mailed you Incy's head in a box."

My blood turned to liquid nitrogen, and my breath stopped short. All I could see was the darkness of Daisuke's eyes.

I breathed out and nodded. "Let's go cut off their heads."

CHAPTER 31

wish I could tell you that I became a Valkyrie, striding soundlessly through the woods, blending with the shadows of night. That I fearlessly ran forward, sword held high, to smite evil and defend the good and the righteous.

And really—I should tell you that. You'd never know the difference. How would you check up? It's not like "Weird Battle Takes Place in Small Massachusetts Town" was ever going to appear in the *Herald*, with interviews from locals and eyewitnesses.

But it wasn't like that. It wasn't glorious; I didn't feel

righteous. It was horrible and terrifying, and I would have happily weaseled out of it at any moment if I could have gotten away with it.

Daisuke did move like a shadow, like a wraith, through the darkness of night. I followed him, matching my strides to his longer ones, stepping only where his feet had been because he could cross the woods without making a sound.

I couldn't hear Roberto behind me, but when I glanced back, he was right there, his handsome face still and cold, barely outlined by a sliver of moon. I must have looked pinch-faced and petrified, because he suddenly smiled and breathed, "How about when this is over, you and me get a bottle of champagne, put on Jefferson Airplane, and see what kind of far-out vibes we make?"

My eyes narrowed, and I suddenly felt ready to kill things. Roberto laughed soundlessly. Daisuke touched my arm, and I followed him.

"Burn it all!"

The guttural voice went right through me. Right in front of us, the mob of attackers suddenly split off, some grabbing branches and lighting their ends from the house fire. Two of them ran toward the chicken coop, not six feet from where we stood. This close, their faces lit by fire, I didn't recognize them. They weren't from my past, and I felt relief.

Without speaking, Daisuke stepped out quickly and grabbed one. Before the man could scream, Daisuke pulled his saber and swung down with ferocious strength. The man's head dropped to the ground like a bowling ball, spurting blood all over the tender, new spring grass under our feet. I pressed my hand to my mouth, trying not to shriek, jumping out of the way of the pulsing blood coming from his neck. The blood smelled hot and coppery in the chilly evening air, foul and disturbing among the fresh scents of the woods.

Oh God I can't do this I can't do this I really can't. . . .

Roberto had efficiently and silently taken care of the other one, and he was now kicking dirt over his torch to smother the flames. Like a zombie I did the same to the other torch while Daisuke wiped the blood off his sword. The men looked at each other.

"Two down," said Daisuke, sounding very sad.

Roberto nodded.

Just get through, Nas. Get through, don't get killed. It will all be over soon.

But not soon enough.

Daisuke took a deep breath, nodded at us, then tore out from behind the coop. His saber raised, he screamed a horrible, unintelligible war cry that sounded like an animal being gutted. As if pulled by a string, I followed him, my own sword raised. The only thing I could think of to yell was what my siblings and I had shouted at each other when we played war with wooden swords that my father's captain had made for us. It was in Icelandic, and as my voice got carried forward, several men snapped their heads around to look.

They were taken unaware, and Daisuke beheaded two of them before some of the others even reacted. All around us were the soul-chilling sounds of battle: the unexpectedly loud clashing of blade upon blade; fighters grunting and hissing with effort; shouted swears and curses. The sudden indrawn breath of someone getting run through with a sword. Hate-filled invectives spewing from a mouth that went slack when its head left its body. The stomach-churning, heavy thud of a head hitting the ground, and the weighty, sack-of-potatoes slump of its body following it.

Someone ran at me, screeching, a sword swinging up. The hours of practice with Reyn took over, and I moved as if this were just another exercise, ducking and backing up so that the whistle of the blade missed my ear by inches. Spinning on one heel, I used both hands to swing my sword up as Reyn's voice mocked me in my head. *Use all your strength, you sissy! You're not trying to tickle someone!*

I slashed sideways as hard as I could and connected solidly with my attacker's shoulder—my angle had been completely off. But it was enough to slice deeply into his shoulder, almost severing his arm, and that hand dropped his weapon. Rage filled me—that they were here to ruin our peaceful life, that they thought they had the right to destroy things and take what wasn't theirs. With a roar I didn't even recognize, I wedged my sword up out of his body, changed my angle, and slashed sideways with all my strength.

And cut off my first head.

Hot, bitter bile rose in the back of my throat, making me gag. But someone else was almost upon me. I raised my sword automatically, crying out as it connected so heavily with his blade that it stunned my arm up to my shoulder. My hand felt numb and tingly, but I ignored it and swung backward.

"You won't have the height or strength to best your opponent," Reyn had said. "Unless you're attacked by a child, or a gnome." I'd made a face at him. "You'll have to rely on speed, accuracy, and surprise. So move around, try to be unpredictable. Never present a face-on target."

In a ridiculous attempt to be unpredictable, I spun so my back was to him and raised my sword fast over my head. It connected again, and when I quickly turned, I saw blood streaming from my attacker's skull. Rage filled his eyes, and he grabbed my arm because I'd made the mistake of getting too close. In an instant I'd kicked back and high with my left foot and got him hard in his package, which, immortal or no, was enough to make any man pause. Before I could even raise my sword, Roberto leaped over, chopped off his head, then returned to his own battle.

"You are nothing!" The woman's hiss made me whirl in surprise. A tall, blond figure was rushing at me, and in a split second I recognized the creepy woman I had seen in town, at the drugstore and out on the street. Adrenaline reignited in my veins as she came at me with her short sword, barely more than a dagger, pointed right at my stomach. Without thinking I swung viciously out and to the left, hitting her neck and almost severing her head—right as she buried her dagger in my gut almost up to the hilt.

Her head lolled grotesquely to one side, held on by a sliver of skin, and her knees buckled. I looked down at my stomach in surprise, wondering why the hilt was sticking to me like that. Then a shocking wave of pain swept me from head to boot, making me gasp, turning my blood to ice water, making sweat pop out on my forehead.

The woman had slumped sideways on the ground, but she was blinking up at me and smiling even as blood began to run out of her mouth. "*Þú ert ekkert,*" she said in Icelandic. "You are nothing." Her words were wheezy, barely comprehensible, her cut airways making blood bubble around her lips.

Daisuke was there immediately and finished the job by slicing neatly, almost delicately, through her remaining nerves and skin and edging her head away with his foot. It took many seconds for the light in her eyes to die, for her sardonic smile to go slack.

"Nastasya!" he said, one hand on my shoulder.

I blinked and slid my eyes sideways to his face, afraid that even that motion would hurt.

"The battle continues. You must fight," he said. His face was traced with ribbons of spewed blood. His voice made little puffs of vapor in the air.

I looked at him, my ears full of a rushing sound.

"Nastasya! Listen: This will not kill you." He motioned to the dagger sticking out of me. "I know it hurts, but pain is just a feeling, and feelings cannot hurt you. Do you understand?"

I was drawing in shallow breaths over teeth locked a quarter inch apart.

"Do you understand?"

I couldn't nod.

"This will hurt," he said, and with one smooth motion he pulled the dagger out and stuck it through his belt, my blood dripping off it.

A sickening tremble went through my body; my knees almost buckled, and I was shivering, colder than I had ever felt.

"Daisuke!"

Roberto's loud cry made Daisuke turn, his sword already coming up. It met the person lunging at him, plunging right through his throat. With only one hand, Daisuke swung his sword to the left, then the right, and that was another immortal taken care of.

"Nastasya!" Daisuke almost shouted. "We need you! You must ignore your wound and fight! Or stand here and die." His last words were quieter, and got through to the keening animal inside me. I managed to nod.

An enormous blast surprised us; the front door had been blown open. Several attackers flew through the air, off the porch, to land heavily on the ground. Somehow, Joshua and Amy were there, blades flashing with reflected fire. Amy looked ruthless and determined as she held someone down with her foot and slashed at his neck.

I didn't die. I kept going. I followed Daisuke as he ran to the back of the house. Every step almost made me faint with searing pain and fear. I couldn't help glancing down to see blood running down my front, soaking my sweatshirt and jeans.

The only time Daisuke paused was when we had to run past Solis's body.

Attackers charged forward to meet us. Daisuke hacked at a smaller figure as she raced up, and when she faltered, I swung my sword. The pain of the movement made me retch, but I was scared to lean down and make myself an easier target. A tall, dark man surged past me, toward Roberto, screeching like a wounded jackal. It was the Indian man, the creepy blond woman's companion.

My angle was off and I was a half step too far away, but I took a big stride forward and swung at him sideways, chopping into his side. It slowed him enough for Daisuke to turn and finish the job.

My face felt cold and wet. I hadn't realized I was crying. All I wanted was to see Reyn and River okay, not hurt, not dead.

Fast footsteps seemed to come out of the night air. We turned but not quickly enough. Someone hacked at Roberto, giving a bellow of rage. Daisuke was already on the attacker and kicked him to the ground, then furiously sliced off his head. I heard the blade hit bone and winced, then turned to make sure Roberto was okay. He wasn't there. He'd disappeared. Numbly I looked around, but it wasn't until I saw Daisuke's dismayed face that I thought to look down.

Roberto's body lay at my feet, his head a few feet away. His handsome face was slack with death, expressionless. River's youngest brother was dead.

I leaned over and threw up.

"We must help the others," Daisuke said almost kindly. Taking my arm, he set off, towing me like a millstone behind him. With one arm I wiped my chin, but I kept on my feet. I pushed myself far beyond any limit I'd imagined, light-headed, in shock, and in such pain that I couldn't get two thoughts together.

There was no one alive on the far side of the house, so we continued to the front. It was so tempting to just fall face-first into the dirt and lie there crying, but if I did that, no doubt someone would come along and cut off my pathetic head.

The front of the house was quiet except for the hissing and creaking of the weatherboards as the house burned. Asher was on the porch heading toward the front door, but he turned to see us.

I was relieved to see Amy there, though she looked shocked and bloody, and one arm was hanging limply at her side. Brynne was swaying on her feet, her beautiful face laid bare along one cheekbone, blood coloring her shoulder and side. She saw me, my blood-soaked front, and her ruined face crumpled. She held out one hand, and I gripped it weakly, so glad to see her alive.

But where was Reyn? Where was River?

Asher saw Daisuke and looked behind him for Roberto. Daisuke shook his head. Asher paled, his skin white beneath the blood and dirt. Then he saw my stomach, my green face, my eyes like black wells.

"Where's Anne?" Daisuke said.

"I don't know," Asher replied, his face grim. "Jess didn't make it."

"We saw Solis." It took a few seconds to recognize the thin, reedy voice as mine.

"Oh no," said Amy.

Of our number, Jess, Solis, and Roberto were dead. I was afraid to ask about the people dearest to my heart, the people I didn't want to live without, in the literal sense of the words.

Where was Reyn? Oh my God, if I saw his body lying somewhere—the thought that he might be dead made me panic more than the horror I'd confronted so far. The question came to my lips, but I held it back—as long as I didn't know, there was a chance he was alive. If someone confirmed he was dead, I didn't know what I would do. Better not to know.

The front door was ablaze, the old wood burning easily. Paint curled off in strips, browning and then blackening from the flames. I started up the steps, determined to go inside with them.

A force welled from the fiery door, holding me in place and making Asher and Daisuke stagger. Then a tall, heavy-set figure strode right through the fire, pulling a smaller person by one arm: River. Her face was bruised, blood trickled from her nose, and she seemed dazed. Asher lunged toward her, but the big man held out one hand and invisibly knocked him sideways. He scrambled to stay on his feet.

Behind them, a tall, thin woman came through the flames as if they were Halloween decorations. Anne followed her, seeming barely conscious, head down, stumbling as she crossed the threshold. Anne's and River's faces looked singed, but the others were untouched.

My hand gripped my sword hilt. Tension rose all around me: Joshua, Asher, Daisuke—their muscles were tightening and coiling.

When the man stepped forward, the slight spring moon shone on his face. I frowned. He was big and burly, like a warhorse, with close-cropped red gold hair and a fashionably short goatee. Some mote of thought struggled in my consciousness, like a firefly in a jar that was running out of oxygen.

That red gold hair . . .

Almost immediately his eyes lit on me, locked on me like lasers.

"Lilja af Úlfur." The deep, bearlike voice went with his size.

The firefly in my brain flickered. I became aware of a growing warmth under my sweatshirt. I'd been icy and clammy since I'd gotten stabbed, but this warmth emanating from the center of my chest seemed to thaw the worst of the cold. The unbearable, shredding pain in my gut dimmed a tiny bit.

It was my amulet. I'd been vaguely aware of it throughout the night, but I hadn't had a moment to think about it or dream of using it.

Now it was waking, coming to life.

"Lilja," the man said again. "*Dóttur bróður míns.* How glad I am to meet you at last."

Daughter of my brother.

Now everyone was looking at me.

"Who—" My voice broke, and I coughed. "Who are you?"

"My lovely niece, I am the true heir to the Iceland throne. Your uncle Egthor."

aising my chin, I tried to strengthen my voice. "I've never heard of you."

"Of course you haven't," said the man. His hair, the exact shade as Eydís's, glowed like the fire. "Why would your father mention me? I was his deep secret—the one brother he didn't kill outright."

"Where have you been? Why didn't you show up sooner?" A very, very slight sound came to me, drifting on the air like the single plume of smoke from a spent match.

"I've been where your father left me," Egthor said. "In the tunnels beneath his hrókur."

The only tunnel I knew about was the one that led from Father's library out to the woods. The one I escaped from.

"You were beneath the castle when it burned?" I asked. The translucent ribbon of sound curled under my chin and drifted toward my ears.

His face hardened. "Yes. Unfortunately. But now I'm free. And here to take the power that should have been mine four and a half centuries ago."

I felt warm now. The flow of blood from my stab wound had slowed to a slight seeping. I was less swoony, and the pain had diminished considerably. Against my skin, the amulet was becoming uncomfortably hot. It came to me, what I was hearing: It was the memory of my mother's voice, singing her power into being. It was the song she sang the night she died.

"Why would you be the true heir?" I asked. I kept my voice faint and broken, and I looked whipped, bloody, and beaten.

"I was the better student, and my father's favorite. It should have been mine." Anger entered his voice. His hand tightened on River's arm, and she swayed.

The song was rising clearly in me now, and for the first time I understood it, like a child first learning to read, the jumble of shapes settling themselves into letters, then words with meaning. It called upon the powers of the earth, the wind, the water. It called to all the powers to flock to me like birds coming to roost in a tree. The feeling was dazzling, painfully joyful and exquisite, and yet I was aware that this power could be used to work great evil and to cause great harm.

"But my father was the oldest." I assumed.

"He was the black sheep!" Egthor shouted. "A bitter disappointment to our father! He studied not, spending his days wenching and drinking!"

Behind me, Amy murmured tiredly, "Wenching? Really?"

"I studied! I worked! I learned our family's magick side by side with my father. He was proud of *me*. Your father was a disgrace." Egthor was getting worked up, and his tight grip on River's arm meant she was getting shaken.

My mother's voice was strong inside my head. Next to Egthor, River raised her chin slightly and looked at me, and I tried not to react: Her eyes were lucid and focused, sending me a message. *You can do this.*

"But my father was still the oldest."

Anger colored Egthor's cheeks. I quickly went on: "But why have you waited so long? Why not take over when I was a child?"

"He has only recently been freed." For the first time the woman next to Anne spoke. Her cheekbones were prominent beneath dark, hooded eyes. Her hair was fine and silver-colored, like River's. Uh-oh. "I was curious about the Iceland house and went exploring there."

I'd explored there, too, very briefly. I'd gotten such bad feelings from the scorched, deadened earth that I'd never gone back again, ever.

"I found your uncle. He'd been chained in the tunnels, held in place by bolts going through his wrists and ankles," said the woman, painting a sickening picture that filled me with revulsion. "The whole place was spelled to deaden his power. No magick could be worked there."

"Holy mother," Asher said.

My uncle held up one arm. The skin was healing, but there was a deep impression in his wrist where a spelled bolt had held him in place for four centuries. The shocking knowledge that my father had kept his brother prisoner like that was unutterably horrible. I didn't want to know it.

"Why didn't he just kill you?" I asked, my voice small and ashamed.

"He needed my learning." Egthor sneered. "The lessons he'd mocked were suddenly useful to him. He said he would keep me alive as long as I could teach him something. I was there for a year and a half before the northern raiders, those savages, came."

Oh my God, he killed Reyn. And where was Ottavio?

"And then for four and a half centuries after that. Fortunately, for the last three hundred years or so, my brain wasn't worth much, so I wasn't too aware of my situation."

There you have it: one of the huge downsides to being

immortal. You can't starve to death. You stay alive, your body wasting away, your brain sputtering into nothing without fuel. In my uncle's case, someone cutting off his head would have been a mercy. My father put him there; he had done that to his brother. Would I ever be able to think of my father without horror and disgust?

"I found him eight months ago," said the woman. "I released him and nursed him back to health."

"Why?" My body was humming with power, strong and light.

"I understood him," she said. "I, too, have been cheated out of my family's power. When my cousins killed their parents, they were greedy. Now I'm here to collect my share."

"Agata," River murmured, and Egthor shook her again.

"Yes. Your cousin Agata," he said. "We make a good team. Immortals around the world have gotten a taste of justice. For too long has the balance of power been unequal." His archaic phrasing interspersed with modern language added a further air of unreality to this situation.

"Well, you're not equalizing it," I said. "You're just taking it and keeping it. Do you see the difference?"

Nastasya. It was River's voice inside my head, audible as a bird's song. *We must end this.*

I didn't know how to do the thought-transfer thing, so I just thought, *Yeah*, and hoped it somehow got to her.

Egthor acted as if he hadn't heard me. "After Agata freed

me, I searched for Valdis's amulet. I should have felt traces of it, should have been able to find it. It was only a few weeks ago that it came to me in a dream, that it was whole again. That it had been found."

"Hmm," I said, stalling for time. Inside I was trying to focus, joining my mother's power with mine. It was so clear to me—how much easier it would have been for me to just wrest power out of everything around me, the way Teräväs do. Instead I was taking the time, using my waning energy to craft a channel for the magick to move through me.

I remembered how Incy had held me in a fog, encased in layers of magick so that I couldn't move. I put those memories into my spell.

I couldn't kill Egthor or Agata—unless they ran at me, yelling, a sword raised. But with them just standing there, all I could stomach was a binding spell.

"So give me the amulet, Lilja," my uncle said. "I'm your only living relative. I know more magick than you could possibly imagine—and I could teach it to you. I can show you how to use the amulet, how to increase your power ten-fold. You will be *my* heir."

"Really?" I said, making my voice wearier.

"Yes. Not only that, but I can share with you the history of our family."

That did make my head jerk up, my eyes lock on him sharply. I'd longed for that my whole life. I'd been so young when my family died—I knew almost nothing about them or our lineage. I would give anything to know it, to understand my family, my parents better. To understand where we came from and how our magick had arisen.

Egthor saw my interest and pressed: "My father taught me the history of our family for thirty-five generations back. I'm the only source of that knowledge in the whole world."

Oh, now *that* hurt.

"So give me the amulet," he said cajolingly. "You and I—and Agata—can become impossibly powerful."

"We don't need her," Agata said sharply. "You and I together are enough! You always wanted her dead—Edna—that silly boy—"

"Oh my God," Daisuke murmured. "Innocencio."

"She has the amulet," Egthor said.

"Kill her and take it," said Agata.

It was then, when Egthor looked at me, considering, as if thinking *Well, I guess I could just kill her and take it*, that it all became quite apparent to me. Whatever evil my father had perpetrated on Egthor, however violent the past had been, still, these two people had gone all over the world, killing immortals and taking their power. They had worked on Incy to try to kill me. They had seduced Daniel and made him turn against River.

They had mailed me Incy's head.

He had most likely killed Reyn.

Taking a deep breath, I opened my mouth and my mother's power, my power, poured out of me. The song came out imperious and terrible, full of menace and strength, as strong as a hurricane, solid as the earth, fierce as fire, and unstoppable as the ocean. I let the magick move through me out into the night, let myself be a conduit only. It was harder, it took more thought, but it was how I chose to wield my power.

Egthor and Agata froze, aghast, as the binding spell hit them with full force. I felt the wound in my gut open again with searing pain, felt the startling, warm flow of blood returning. But I sang on, watching as Egthor unwillingly dropped River's arm and Agata released Anne.

Egthor's face shone with effort as he struggled to resist my spell. I felt Agata working against me—I could feel my song weakening, being subdued by their greater knowledge. A cruel smile raised the corners of Agata's lips. She wanted to crush me like a flower under her heel. She wanted me dead, didn't want to share Egthor with anyone. My throat began to close as if a fist were squeezing my windpipe. Oh God, oh no.

Two voices joined mine, bolstering my magick with theirs. Supporting each other, River and Anne were calling magick out of the earth, out of the night air. They laid their song over mine, and the pressure on my throat eased. The smile left Agata's face.

One by one, my friends added their voices, blending and

weaving around my central, strengthening core. Egthor dropped to his knees, snapping his hand out, screaming words of his own that I deflected. I pulled my amulet from beneath my shirt, held it up as it glowed with ancient power. When Egthor saw it, his eyes widened and his screams became more desperate. Agata was shrieking, her words dark and spiky, sharp as needles and acrid as bitter melon.

But she was no match for me, for us.

My words drove Egthor and Agata to their knees, to curl up on the ground with the enormous weight of my binding on them. Carefully I began to wrap it up, to slowly knot and finish off the spell, much like knitting. And then a pack of dogs, baying and snarling, burst through the door of fire: Molly and Jasper, young Henrik and Dúfa. They were furious, teeth bared, fur rising in lines down their backs.

"Molly!" River said, and Asher whistled fiercely. The dogs looked at him, and he sternly ordered them down the steps. Reluctantly they passed Egthor and Agata, growls rumbling deep in their throats, their fangs more frightening than I would have imagined.

And then a tall figure strode through the door of fire. My heart stopped beating for a moment, my voice faltered, and I forgot to breathe.

His face was burned and blistered, his shirt smoldering and charred. In his hands was a long, two-handed claymore, and he raised it swiftly and sharply above Egthor's head.

"Wait!" I shouted at Reyn. For Reyn it was, alive, in pain, and full of berserker rage.

"Wait," River echoed.

"He dies *now*!" Reyn said, the raider fury on his face making him both distant and familiar.

"Wait!" I pleaded, walking forward and wincing with a renewed, searing pain. Reyn saw the front of my clothes soaked in blood and his eyes flared, new anger lighting them from within. "Reyn—he knows my family history! He knows all the stuff I don't!"

Slowly River turned—she looked older, her face thin and drawn, her hair seeming a lighter silver. "Reyn—please."

"You want to rehabilitate them?" Reyn practically spat. "Like Innocencio? They deserve to die!"

"And I don't?" River asked, sounding pained and exhausted. "You don't? Are they so much worse than we were?"

Reyn's jaws clamped together, and he stared at River. "You want to give them three hundred years to turn good?"

The faintest shadow of a smile crossed River's face. "No, my dear. I just want to give them one day. And then a day after that. Maybe a day after that."

I didn't realize Asher had left until he came back, holding clinking lengths of silver chain. When Egthor saw the chain, he started weeping silently, tears rolling down his face.

"You won't be in a dungeon," Asher murmured, taking Egthor's hands and snapping spelled wrist cuffs on him.

Lying on the porch next to him, Agata was incensed, her eyes popping, lips pressed together so hard, they had turned white. Wearily, River bent down and tried to pry open Agata's fingers, which seemed locked unnaturally tightly, muscle and bone constricted as though in death.

The effort made sweat bead on River's bruised forehead, but determinedly she got several fingers open and took something from Agata's palm. I drew in a sharp breath as River put on the tarak-sin of the Genoa house, the large ring hanging heavily on her narrow finger.

Agata had had the tarak-sin. With shock I realized Ottavio must be dead.

Asher knelt down and pulled Agata's hands behind her back.

"I'm sorry, Agata," he said, locking cuffs on her thin, bony wrists. "But you know we can't let you do this."

It looked like she was trying to spit at him but couldn't.

Asher rose, his face soot-smeared and tired, and searched our meager crowd. "Daisuke. Joshua. Anne. Can you come with me? I'll take them to Benoit's, in Minnesota."

Egthor moaned. He did look like my father—his face had sharper angles, and my father's hair and beard had been longer and often braided and tied with leather cord. But he was the most familylike of anyone I'd seen in 450 years, and I couldn't take my eyes off him. I walked toward the porch, the pain in my stomach becoming the center of my being, the enormous thing all of me revolved around. Just lifting one foot onto a step felt like someone had buried an axe in my stomach.

"You will tell me everything," I told Egthor, raising my voice.

He snarled at me, his cheeks wet with tears. Reyn kicked him, and Egthor winced. I gave Reyn a look.

I was Lilja af Úlfur. I refused to share in my father's shame, the memory of his cruel and ruthless acts. But his power ran through me, and it always would. Narrowing my eyes, I made my face cold, bringing all my anger to the surface.

"You will tell me everything," I said more harshly. "I am the heir to the House of Úlfur! I have my family's power!" I held my amulet higher, the moonstone shining whitely. The hunger that showed on Egthor's face as he stared at it was uncomfortable to see. Gritting my teeth against the pain, praying I wouldn't faint and keel over backward, I forced myself up the steps.

"You will tell me everything," I hissed. "You will teach me what you know. Or I'll strip your skin from you with a word, cut off your head, and feed you to the dogs!"

River's face was expressionless; Reyn's was watchful. At the bottom of the steps, Dúfa's whiplike tail thumped once, as if politely accepting the offer of Egthor's head.

Egthor's eyes widened, but he didn't respond. Then Asher tugged on the chain, Daisuke and Joshua came up to help him, and Anne started murmuring spells under her breath.

Egthor and Agata were led away. River awkwardly sat down on the steps and buried her face in her hands.

The world started to dim around the edges of my vision, and the rushing sound came back to roar in my ears. "Uh-oh," I said, and everything went black.

nd that, oh best beloved, is the story of how my life began, when I was 459 years old. Looking at me now, a leader in the immortal community, someone respected for knowledge and wisdom—

"You are so full of it," Reyn said over my shoulder. "No one's going to believe that."

I glared at him, trying to cover the screen with my hands. "Go away! No one asked you!"

"Leader in the immortal community?" He scoffed. "You missed the last meeting because you stayed up late to watch *Dancing with the Stars*!"

"Shut up! Again, no one asked you!"

"Plus, I'm taller than you said I am."

"Oh my God! How much did you read?"

"I'm really closer to six-one."

My mouth dropped open. "Oh. My. God. I can't believe you read this."

He grinned unrepentantly, and as usual it made a little butterfly of excitement flutter in my chest. I ruthlessly crushed the butterfly: There were serious issues at stake.

Standing up, I put my hands on my hips. Over on the couch, adolescent Dúfa opened her eyes, stood up, and stretched.

"You mad? You want to come get me?" Reyn raised his eyebrows suggestively.

I knew that look, and so did all the cells in my traitorous body, which started squealing and jumping up and down in anticipation.

"You need to leave," I said firmly, crossing my arms.

"You can't kick me out. I live here. Plus, I have custody of the child." He nodded at Dúfa, who jumped down and did the "downward-facing dog" stretch. She was growing into her long stick legs, and in general was a smidgen less awkward and funny looking.

"I own the building!" It was amazing how many times I had to keep pointing that out to everybody.

"My name is on the lease."

Why did I keep walking into that one?

Reyn moved toward me with big-cat grace. I frowned really hard at him. He put his arms around me and leaned down to kiss my forehead, my ear, my neck. My stomach gave a little flip.

"Come to bed," he whispered, and I ruthlessly suppressed a whimper. His large, strong hands stroked my back as he kissed his way across my cheek. It took way too long for his lips to move onto mine, but at last they did. My arms uncoiled and wrapped around his neck, and I couldn't help smiling against his mouth.

He started to walk me backward toward our small bedroom, past the little dining alcove with its Formica table and four unmatched chairs, down the hallway, and past the bathroom. Our bedroom looked out over Main Street, and Reyn yanked the shades down as he walked me toward the bed.

By the time I fell backward onto the mattress I was laughing, happier and more full of joy than I had ever imagined I could be. Dúfa jumped on the bed and licked my eyelid. "Stop," I told her. "That's so icky." She grinned at me, showing her big-girl fangs that had finally come in.

Reyn came down beside me, and I reached for him. We clung to each other, kissing as if it were the first time, or maybe the last time, as if we would never get enough of each other. Over and over I drank him in, loving his scent, the feel of his hair on my forehead, the weight of his hard body on mine.

Pulling back, Reyn looked into my eyes as if still memorizing my face and everything about me. My hands moved restlessly on his back, all smooth muscle and lean strength, and I tried to rise up to kiss him again.

"Let me look at you," he whispered. "I love you so much, my Lilja."

I swallowed, hoping I didn't get all weepy. "I love *you* so much, Eileif."

It seemed we said that to each other a hundred times a day. Maybe because neither of us had expected to ever love someone again.

"I never want to be with anyone but you." His voice was so quiet, his face so solemn.

"I hope you never are," I said, my voice breaking, feeling the sweeping wave of emotion taking me over. "Because I'd have to kill you."

I loved his smile, loved how his eyes closed as he kissed me again. One hand pushed under my shirt and then under the waistband of my jeans. He unsnapped them and ran gentle fingers along the top of my underwear.

"I can hardly feel the scar," he murmured. "It'll be gone soon."

I nodded, turning my head to kiss the smooth skin of his throat, feeling his pulse beating so strongly and steadily. "It's been two months. Should be okay by swimsuit season."

At that Reyn pulled back again, his eyes full of laughter.

I popped open the buttons on his shirt one by one,

delighting in the beautiful, golden chest that was revealed inch by inch. I was never able to help tracing my fingers across the scar there, pressing my lips to it as if I could maybe someday kiss it enough to heal.

It didn't matter if it didn't heal, if mine never did, either. So many other things had.

"That color sucks. What is that, like pond-scum beige?" Dray looked critically at the section of wall I'd put a first coat on. She crunched through more potato chips and shook the bag to get all the crumbs in one place.

"It's Toasted Marshmallow," I said, irritated.

"It's not that bad," Meriwether said loyally, looking up from her magazine.

"This is your *bedroom*," said Dray. "And your guy is the hottest, hottest thing I've ever, ever seen in my entire li—" She stopped when I glared at her. "What I'm saying is, you should paint it like blood red, something passionate and sexy."

"Actually, it's amazing how unsexy blood is."

"Peach is a nice color," said Meriwether. She took another one of my sour apple Now and Laters and unwrapped it.

"I like this color!" I said.

"Whatever."

"You know, you're my neighbor. Not my mother," I said to Dray, and she grinned.

"Knock-knock!" Brynne's voice came down the hall. "Girl!

You coming? Hey, Dray, Meriwether. School out yet? Um, is that the primer?"

"Four more days," said Meriwether, brightening. "I'll be able to see Lowell all the time—Dad gave him a job at the store."

"Oh, that's great," I said, pleased.

"Yeah," said Meriwether, blushing.

"Yeah, I'll go in there, and you guys will be making out in the bathroom or something," Dray said darkly.

"We will not," said Meriwether, but I could see she thought the idea had merit.

"Are you going like that?" Brynne gestured to my paint-spattered clothes. The long scar across one cheek was fading and shrinking every day, and it was now a very thin line. Soon it would disappear. As is our way.

"Crap, is it five o'clock already?" I put down the roller and threw the cover back on the paint. "One sec. Reyn's going to meet us out there."

"What color are you going to put over this?" Brynne asked pointedly.

"You know what?" I said, disappearing into the bathroom. "To hell with all of you."

The laughter of my friends filled the room. And my heart.

I know. So sappy. So, so sappy. Revoltingly sappy. But true.

River's Edge had changed a lot in some ways, and not at all in others. Large sections of it had been completely rebuilt after the fire, and most of the furniture in the parlor was new. The fire had been explained as faulty wiring, and had been put out by the time a neighbor noticed the smoke and called the fire department.

My uncle had killed Ottavio inside the house. Jess and Solis had died fighting the nameless minions that Egthor and Agata had collected from all over. I'd found out later that the creepy blond woman was in fact Miss Edna, who had run that grotesque bar that Incy had taken me to. I was glad she was dead.

I'd had bad dreams about Roberto's death for weeks afterward.

Out of four brothers, River had lost two. Daniel had been bound and taken to an immortal prison/rehab place in California, run by someone Solis had known. So far, neither Daniel, Egthor, nor Agata seemed to be catching the remorse bug, but River held out hope.

The attacks around the world had stopped, but most of us thought it was just a matter of time before some other ambitious Terävä decided to speed up his or her magickal progress.

Are you wondering about the bodies? Of course you are, because you're macabre and nosy and bloodthirsty. And who could blame you?

As you may have suspected, there was a grisly amount of slain immortals afterward, and there isn't a person in the world who could have explained them adequately to any modern authority. In the end, we'd taken them down into the tunnels and put them in one of the dead ends. A group of us had worked magick that essentially reduced them to dust. It was really gross and really, really depressing. Then that tunnel had been sealed up as if it had never been there, and spells were put on it that would last for at least a century, to keep anyone from knowing anything was there. I'd dreaded looking at the faces—scared of seeing Stratton or Cicely or even Nell—anyone I knew. But except for the creepy couple, they were strangers to me, though River, Asher, and Anne had gasped or murmured several times in recognition.

Then the dark days were over.

Now Brynne parked the latest little farm car in the gravel area, and we got out. Reyn and I had decided not to buy a humongous fancy house somewhere and instead had been living in town in one of *my* apartments for almost three weeks. But I came back almost every day for classes or just to hang out.

The crops in the fields and kitchen garden were growing— it had been a warm, wet spring, and the whole world seemed to be bursting with life. Every once in a while, just to keep my hand in, I groomed a horse or milked a cow. The chicken I'd defeathered was now indistinguishable from the others, and the devil-chicken's little chicks were full grown.

Henrik, Molly's last puppy, was growing into a show-stopper, with a finely molded head, beautiful, perfect conformation, and an elegant gait. Dúfa was Dúfa, but she was bigger.

As Brynne and I walked toward the house, I nudged her with my elbow. "Soooo?"

To my surprise she blushed and put her head down, her bouncy corkscrew curls making a halo around her head. "He succumbed," she muttered, and I stopped short on the first porch step, my mouth open.

"Reeaaally?" I said. "And are we overcome with joy? Did we hear angels sing?"

Brynne nodded, still blushing, and I made a mental note to say something embarrassing to Joshua later. He'd decided to stick around River's Edge for a while, first to help repair the house and get things back together, then because he'd realized just how much he'd missed connecting with family, and now, apparently, to make kissy-face with the Brynnster.

"You go, girl," I said, and we slapped high fives.

"Well," she said self-consciously, "I figured if he and Reyn could have a bromance, there was no reason why he should hold out on *me*."

"Very true," I agreed, and we went inside.

Yes. Joshua and Reyn, sworn enemies for *several hundred years*, were now likethis. Every couple of weeks they had horrible, scary, loud swordfights in the yard at River's Edge. Anne kept begging them to stop because they did occasionally make contact with each other, requiring stitches, tea, and healing spells. But it seemed to satisfy something in them.

Inside, River was just coming out of her office. She had changed, since March. After thirteen hundred years of dealing with whatever came her way, this last battle had taken something out of her. She had lost weight and looked like she had aged ten (human) years in the last two months. I was worried about her, but she kept insisting she was fine.

"Hello, my dear," she said, and we did the double-cheek-kiss thing. "How's your real-estate empire doing? I forgot to ask you yesterday."

"Going well," I said, rubbing my hands together mogul-style. "I was talking to that guy who gives away T-shirts if you buy a T-shirt, you know? I think I may have lured him into my old factory, out on Devan Road. I think the crew can fix it up in about ten weeks, and then he could open an arm of his T-shirt conglomerate there. Maybe Skunk could be one of his designers."

"That sounds awesome," said Brynne.

"Mwa ha ha ha," I said. "Soon I will own this whole town!"

River laughed and hugged me. I loved my real-estate empire.

In the dining room, Rachel was putting out a platter of salmon on the sideboard, and Charles was behind her with the last of the season's spinach. I was glad they had come back—Lorenz hadn't. But that's how rehab is—you come and go as often as you need to, for as long as you need to. I thought he'd be back eventually.

Amy had left several weeks after that night—Ottavio had died, and she seemed a bit lost. Everyone asked her to stay longer, but she'd taken off. I knew what that was like—in a new place, she wouldn't be reminded of everything every time she turned around. She could be someone different, someone who hadn't just gone through what she'd gone through. She'd be back, too, someday.

Reyn arrived just as we were sitting down. Okay, we hadn't been together very long, but I was still taken aback by how happy I was to see him, over and over. He kissed my cheek as he sat next to me, and then we all held hands and gave thanks for the food.

Asher stood up and tapped on his wineglass. "Everyone? Can I have your attention, please?"

I quickly took a chunk of salmon—who knew how much would be left the next time the platter came around?

"I'd like to announce that my friend Petrov will be joining us later this summer," Asher said. "I don't know of anyone with a greater knowledge of the history of immortals, and he's also very gifted in spellcraft. His addition will benefit our community greatly."

"Yay!" said Anne, raising her glass. "I've met Petrov, and he's lovely. I know you'll all like him."

River smiled and raised her glass with the rest of us.

"And another thing," Asher continued, and turned to face River. She raised a quizzical eyebrow. "The last seven decades with you have been the best of my life," he said, and we all went very still and quiet. Under the table, Reyn took my hand. "I mean, it's been really hard, also."

We all chuckled, including River.

"But they have been the best, because I've shared them with you."

River's face softened, and her eyes shone as she gazed at him.

"And I'm asking you, before family and friends, to marry me."

No one was expecting this, and there were many quick, wide-eyed looks around the table.

As for River, she seemed stunned, staring at Asher with her mouth open.

Looking unsure but hopeful, Asher took a small box out of his pocket and opened it. Inside was a gorgeous, old-fashioned ring, with a huge emerald in the center flanked by two rose-cut diamonds. Even from where I sat, I could see that the yellow-gold band was engraved with flowers.

Reyn held my hand more tightly.

River was still silent and staring.

"Wow—it's hard to surprise River, but you did it, Ash," Anne said, to break the tense silence. We laughed nervously, hoping this didn't turn into a train wreck right in front of us.

Still Asher stood there, warmth rising on his cheeks as he waited.

"Marry!" River said, her voice thin.

"Yes." Asher raised his chin.

"Marry!"

"You heard me."

"I... I've never been married." River actually looked frightened at the prospect.

"Whoa—never?" said Rachel.

"I love weddings," said Charles. "Like, a September wedding."

"No... never," said River, still looking stunned.

Asher just waited.

"Why... well, yes," said River bemusedly. "Yes. I'll marry you."

I was such a soft, little, gushy, emotional clam these days that I actually teared up and had to sniffle. Reyn put his arm around my shoulder and kissed my hair.

Anne started clapping, and of course we all joined in. River was both laughing and crying as Asher slid the ring on her finger, and then they kissed and hugged, standing there holding each other while we all cheered.

Reyn leaned over and whispered in my ear. "So... even River fell."

I quit laughing and looked at him quickly. He had his "I will be victorious" face on, and I felt a prickle of alarm. "Oh no," I said, uncomfortably remembering the *five* other leaves on the vine in my vision. "River's different. Sure, she should try it once. But *no one* wants to *keep* doing it."

Reyn just gave a slow smile.

Hmm.

Where stories bloom.

poppy

Visit us online at
www.pickapoppy.com